# RUNNING SCARED

# RUNNING SCARED

## Ann Granger

Thorndike Press
Thorndike, Maine USA

This Large Print edition is published by Thorndike Press, USA.

Published in 1999 in the U.S. by arrangement with Blake Friedmann Literary Agency, Ltd.

U.S. Softcover  ISBN 0–7862-2174–7  (General Series Edition)

The text of this Large Print edition is unabridged.
Other aspects of the book may vary from the original edition.

Set in 16 pt. New Times Roman.

Printed in Great Britain on acid-free paper.

**Library of Congress Cataloging-in-Publication Data**

Granger, Ann.
      Running scared / Ann Granger.
          p.    cm.
      ISBN 0–7862–2174–7 (lg. print : sc : alk. paper)
      1. Large type books.    I. Title.
      [PR6057.R259R86      1999]
      823'.914—dc21                                     99–37944

To my son, Tim, who gave up his free time
to help me in my research, with thanks

# CHAPTER ONE

I'm not the sort of person who goes out of her way to find trouble. It's just that trouble always seems to find me. Generally, I just try to make it from one day to the next and avoid hassle. I don't know why it never works out like that. It's so unfair, and especially as Christmas approaches and everyone's looking forward to the holiday. But my luck being what it is, that's when I ran into my latest set of problems. Because if you can be certain of anything in this world, it's that you never know what life's going to hit you with next.

It was a cold, rainy morning and I was helping out my friend Ganesh in his uncle's newsagent's shop when disaster struck. Ganesh not only works for his Uncle Hari, he also lodges with him over the shop. I don't know whether Hari really is an uncle or some other kind of relative, but uncle's what everyone calls him, even me. Hari is a nice man but nervous and fidgety and that gets Ganesh down. So when Hari announced he was going on an extended family visit to India, and in his absence Ganesh was to be left in sole charge of the shop in Camden, Gan just about danced round the place for joy.

I was pleased for Ganesh too, because it was high time he had a chance to run something

1

without interference from his family. All his life he's helped out in shops run by relatives. He'd helped his parents in their Rotherhithe greengrocery until they'd been dispossessed by the council, who were redeveloping. Now they run a fruit and veg place out of town at High Wycombe. It's very small and they don't need Ganesh, nor is there any accommodation for him, so that's why he's currently with Hari. I sometimes ask Ganesh why he puts up with being passed round the family like this, filling in where needed, but he always says I don't understand. Too right, I tell him, I don't. Explain it to me. Then he says, what's the point?

He's really capable and if he could just get his own place, he'd be fine. I wish he'd give up the dream of being in charge of a dry-cleaner's, though. He has a crazy idea he and I could run something like that together. Not a chance, I tell him. I don't want to spend my life handling other people's dirty clothes and I hate the chemical smell of those places, and the steam.

However, I didn't mind giving Ganesh a hand in the newsagent's while Hari was away, especially in the mornings, which is always the busiest time, though with Christmas coming up things would start getting really hectic pretty soon. Hari had given Ganesh authority to hire me as a part-timer and I needed the money. But I want to make it clear that one day I'm

2

going to be an actress—I nearly finished a course on the Dramatic Arts and everything once—but in the meantime I take any legitimate work going, including being an informal enquiry agent.

So, off went Hari, leaving Ganesh three pages of minutely detailed instructions in a curly alphabet and I turned up on my first day bright and early at eight o'clock. Ganesh had been there since six, but I have my limits. Everything went swimmingly for a bit and I was enjoying being a genuinely employed person. It was quite interesting in the shop and at the end of the first week I got my pay packet and felt I was a regular member of the public at last. Only 'last' was what it wasn't going to do. I should've known.

It was on the following Tuesday that things started to go wrong. The week had begun all right. Gan and I had spent Sunday putting up Christmas decorations in the shop. Ganesh's idea of a decorative colour scheme is red, lots of it, and gold, even more of that, enlivened by an occasional flash of hot pink or vibrant turquoise. When we'd finished with the shop it looked fantastic—perhaps rather more Diwali than Christmas, but Gan and I were really chuffed with it.

All Monday we gloried in the compliments from customers. Then, on Tuesday, a postcard of the Taj Mahal arrived from Uncle Hari and the atmosphere changed. Ganesh stopped

3

buzzing cheerfully and skulked around beneath the crepe paper chains. He'd propped the card on the gold tinsel-trimmed shelves behind the counter along with the cigarettes, and kept giving it hunted glances.

I'd already guessed that Ganesh was up to something because he'd been making furtive phone calls over the previous week and looking pleased with himself. I knew it wasn't just the approach of festivities and seasonal sales. I could see he was dying to tell me, especially during Sunday when we'd been pinning up the decorations, but I wasn't going to encourage him although I was longing to know. With the arrival of the postcard, he stopped looking smug and became clearly worried. Eventually, he came clean.

We were having our coffee-break. The early morning rush had thinned, there was no one in the shop for the moment, and the emptiness of the rainswept pavement outside suggested things might stay quiet all day until the usual early evening flurry of trade. We didn't have to go upstairs to the flat to make the coffee because we had an electric kettle downstairs which I filled with water in the washroom.

The building's old and long ago converted from what must once have been quite a nice house. There are two ways up to the flat, one from the shop, using the former back stairs, and a separate one from the street. The downstairs washroom was at that time a

4

museum of antiquated plumbing and fixtures, tacked on to the back of the building in what must have seemed at the time the height of modernity. It was all as clean as it could be kept given its general state, but that was terminal. The washbasin was hanging off the wall. The tap dripped. Any wall tiles were loose and cracked and the floor tiles had gaps between them. The vent for the extractor fan was clogged with dust and dead flies. The lavatory cistern was operated by a chain which had lost its handle. It clanked furiously whenever it was flushed and the cistern lid was loose so if you didn't watch out, there was always a chance it would fall down and brain you. The loo itself was the *pièce de résistance*. An original, no kidding, patterned all over with blue forget-me-nots. It had a wooden seat with a crack in it which pinched your bum. I tell you, anyone ventured into that washroom at his peril. I called it the Chamber of Horrors.

Ganesh, to be fair, had been grumbling to Hari about the state of the washroom ever since he'd moved there. But whenever Hari was tackled, he always replied that he wasn't a rich man who could afford to replace everything just like that. 'Besides,' he'd declare, 'look at such a beautiful lavatory pan. Where would I again get such a wonderful object?' He usually ended up by promising to get a new tapwasher, but even that got put off indefinitely.

On this particular morning, I steered my way to the counter carrying a mug of coffee in either hand and said crossly, 'The least you can do, Gan, while Hari's away, is fix that dripping tap.'

At that, Ganesh, who since the postcard's arrival had been brooding darkly in a corner like Mr Rochester on a bad day, brightened up. He chortled, rapped out a rhythm on the counter with his palms and, just as I was deciding he'd gone bonkers, let me into his secret.

'I can do better than that, Fran. I'm going to get the whole thing done out, ripped out, fixed up, everything brand-new, while the old bloke's away.'

He beamed at me. I stood there, slopping coffee and gawping. I'd only set my sights on the new washer. Ganesh must have got *Homes and Gardens* down from the shelf and let it go to his head.

'Hari won't agree,' I said.

'Hari won't know, not until he gets back and by then it'll be a whatsit, *fait accompli*, that's what they call it.'

'They call it a screaming hysterics,' I said. 'That's what Hari will have when he sees the bill.'

Ganesh took his coffee from me, stopped looking smug, and started to look obstinate. 'He left me in charge, right? I'm empowered to sign cheques on the business and everything, right? So I'm going to get it done and he can make as much fuss as he likes. What's he going to do, sack me? I'm family. He can't. Anyway, I know the stingy old blighter. He always carps at spending money, but once it's gone, he shrugs it off. When he sees how good it looks and how reasonable the cost was, he'll get over it. It's improving the property. That has to be good. And if he still argues, I'll tell him Health and Safety at Work rules didn't allow the old one. They probably don't.'

'It'll cost a bomb,' I said, playing devil's advocate. Someone had to. He was too full of it.

'No, it won't. I've got a really reasonable quote. Dead cheap. Bloke can start work on Friday and he'll be done, finished, gone in days, by the end of next week, certain.'

I perched on the stool behind the counter and sipped my coffee. It all sounded a bit too easy to me. 'How come it's going to be so cheap?' I asked. 'All the existing fittings will have to go, new ones put in. The extractor fan has never worked to my knowledge so that's got to be replaced. The plumbing's knackered. The walls will have to be painted, the floor retiled . . .'

'It's all taken care of,' said Ganesh airily. 'And he'll take away the old fittings and rubbish for me and everything.'

'Who will?' I asked suspiciously.

7

Ganesh's air of confidence slipped just a tad. 'Hitch,' he said.

I spilled my coffee. 'Hitch? Are you mad?'

'Hitch does a good job,' Ganesh said obstinately. 'And he's cheap.'

'He's cheap,' I said, 'because all the stuff he uses has been knocked off from a builder's yard somewhere.'

'No, it hasn't—or this won't be. I checked that with him first. Think I'm daft? It's all on the level. He's given me the name of his supplier and everything. I can ring them up—and I will, before he starts. I'm not daft, Fran.'

I could have argued, and perhaps I should have done, but in the end, it wasn't any of my business. I didn't doubt Hitch had given Ganesh the phone number of a 'supplier'. But I'd be willing to bet that, if Gan rang up, on the other end of the line would be some mate of Hitch's, sitting in a lock-up garage filled with dodgy goods. Ganesh is stubborn and always wants to know best. He wouldn't listen to anything I had to say. So why not let him get on with it? A new washroom would be nice. But that Ganesh, of all people, should behave like this took me aback. He was usually so sensible, never did anything without examining it from all sides first, never acted rashly, never gambled and never did anything which would upset his family (other than befriend me, an act which had them dead worried).

I let it go and concentrated on my coffee.

Ganesh obviously thought he'd won the argument so that put him in a good mood. An air of truce hung over the shop.

That's when the door opened. At first the only thing I was aware of was a cold draught which ruffled all the magazines on their shelves and sent the crepe chains threshing. A red one and a turquoise, twisted together, fell down. A squall of rain spattered the tiled floor. More tinsel fell off the shelves. We both looked up. Silhouetted in the open door was the figure of a man. He stood there briefly, steadying himself with one hand on the doorjamb, then staggered towards the counter and grabbed at it for support. Ganesh stretched out a hand towards the jemmy he keeps under the counter for opening boxes and fending off drunks. I stood there rooted to the spot, horrified and fascinated.

I faced a Halloween mask—gaping mouth, bulging eyes, streaked scarlet with gore which poured from a cut above one eyebrow, filling the eye-socket beneath. More blood dribbled from both nostrils. I knew I should do something, but I couldn't move. The clutching fingers scrabbled at the wooden surface, inarticulate sounds issued from the mouth and, with a last throaty gurgle, the intruder slid beneath the counter and disappeared from sight. A strand of silvery fronds floated after him, undulating gracefully in the disturbed air currents.

9

His disappearance jolted both of us into action and we raced round the other side. He was sitting on the floor, back to the counter, legs splayed, bloodied head grotesquely crowned with the tinsel strand.

'Cripes,' said Ganesh. 'Get a cloth, Fran.' He ran to the door, looked up and down the street, twisted the notice on the glass to 'Closed' and locked us in. Whoever had done that to the man on the floor, we didn't want them joining us.

We divested our visitor of his tinsel crown, got him to his feet and propelled him into the storeroom. He stumbled along between us, gasping, but, apart from the obvious, apparently not otherwise injured. We propped him on a chair and I ripped open a box of Kleenex to mop up the blood.

'Haven't you got something else?' hissed Ganesh, who even in a time of stress realised he had to write off that box of tissues as no-sale. 'Couldn't you have used loo paper?'

'Make him some tea!' I snapped.

Our patient gurgled and seemed to be regaining his wits. His nose wouldn't stop trickling blood so I wedged wads of tissue in both nostrils and told him he had to breathe through his mouth.

Ganesh came back with a mug of tea.

'Thag you,' mumbled whoever-he-was.

'What happened, mate?' asked Ganesh. 'Was it a mugging? You want me to call the

10

cops?'

'Doh!' cried the other in great alarm, sloshing tea around.

'Keep still!' I ordered. 'You'll start bleeding again. Perhaps he ought to go to casualty, Gan. He could have broken his nose.'

'Doh, doh! I dode want dat!' The stranger decided he couldn't communicate with both nostrils bunged up, so removed the blood-sodden wads and threw them in the waste-paper basket. I waited for a fresh scarlet waterfall, but it didn't come. My first aid had worked.

'No police,' he said firmly. 'No hospital. I'm all right now.'

'Please yourself,' said Gan in some relief. He didn't want the law in his shop. That sort of thing puts customers off. Nor did he want to take time to drive the guy to the nearest casualty unit. 'So long as you're OK, right? You were unlucky. It's safe enough round here in daylight, usually.'

The victim mumbled agreement. 'Yeah, I had a bit of bad luck.'

I wondered if he was going to give us any details, but apparently not. He was patting the inside pocket of his coat and progressed from there to the side pockets. Eventually he pulled out a handkerchief and passed it gingerly over his bashed features. When he took it away, it was freely smeared red. He studied it with interest.

11

Ganesh was getting restive. 'Look, mate, I've got to reopen the shop. I can't stay closed much longer. I'm losing trade. You can sit here as long as you need. Take your time, right?'

'I'm really sorry about this.' Our visitor looked stricken. He thrust away the handkerchief and began to fumble again at the inner pocket of his overcoat. 'I realise this is costing you money. Let me make it up.'

Now up to that moment, neither Gan nor I had doubted our friend had been mugged. So we were a tad surprised when out of the pocket came a wallet and out of that came a tenner. It wasn't alone in the wallet. It had some company, as I could see—a couple of fivers and a twenty at least.

I met Ganesh's eye. He was thinking what I was thinking. This wasn't a mugging. If muggers had had time to dish out that amount of facial decoration, they'd have got the guy's wallet for sure. Come to that, he still had his wristwatch and a gold signet ring. I couldn't make out the initials on the ring, which was a pity. They were sort of swirly and tangled up but one might have been C.

Our visitor was looking anxiously from one to the other of us. He'd misunderstood our exchange of glances. 'Not enough?' he asked and made to add another note.

'No, I mean yes, that's fine!' Ganesh took the tenner. We had shut up shop, after all.

I took a more critical look at our guest,

12

who'd suddenly become very interesting. He was in his thirties, a biggish chap, wearing a dark suit under that charcoal-coloured overcoat. His white shirt was blood-spattered and his tie askew. The damaged eye was swelling shut. He wasn't looking his best, but even so, he wasn't bad-looking. Still, there was something about him I couldn't quite fit together. He was dressed like a business type but didn't look like a man who spent his life in an office. There was a faint odour of nicotine about him which suggested he was a heavy smoker and offices tend to be smoke-free zones these days. You see the exiles, lurking unhappily in the doorways at street level, puffing furtively as they try to keep out of the rain.

On the other hand, he wasn't particularly an outdoor type, though he sported a recently acquired tan. Perhaps he'd been on holiday. It wasn't fair to judge in the circumstances, but to my eye his suit and coat weren't quite right. They were too well worn and unfashionable, the sort of clothes someone might keep in the wardrobe for the odd occasion when he needed to impress, but didn't wear day to day. His trousers weren't kept up with the snazzy braces they hand out to high-fliers with their business diplomas, but by a tooled leather belt with a fancy brass buckle which was definitely leisure-wear.

You see why I consider myself to be quite a

13

good detective. I notice these things. *You know my methods, Watson.* Here, I deduced, was a youngish, fit man who normally dressed casually but left home today tricked out to look prosperous and businesslike. Why? To impress someone. Not a woman. Not in that coat. No, a bloke, the sort who'd be wearing a snappy suit and wouldn't be impressed by chinos and a leather jacket. He'd set off to do a bit of serious business, but whoever he'd met had duffed him up. It suggested more than one person, because our new friend here looked well able to handle one assailant. For my money, he had set up a meeting with someone dodgy, perhaps even someone who'd had a minder with him, and it hadn't turned out as he'd wished. He shouldn't have gone alone. Unless, of course, he had good reason for keeping his business private.

Eat your heart out, my old violin-scraper.

'I don't want trouble,' Ganesh was saying. 'So, whoever's after you, do you think they're still out there, looking around? Will they come in here?' Before the other could speak, he added, 'Look, I'm not prying, but it wasn't a mugging, was it?'

I chimed in with, 'One mugger would've thumped you while the other grabbed your jewellery and dosh. Ganesh and I mean, if you've got a private fight that's your affair. But we don't want the shop damaged.'

'Don't suppose the insurance would cover

14

it,' Ganesh added, 'seeing as we didn't call the police.'

The stranger took his time thinking about his answer to all that and I didn't blame him. 'Take your point,' he said at last. 'Truth is, I don't know who's out there, if anyone. I'm pretty sure they don't know I came in here. They might be still scouting around for me, I suppose.'

He began to struggle up out of his chair. 'Don't worry about me,' he said. 'I'll take my chances.'

He sounded brave and doomed, like that chap who went with Scott to the Antarctic and walked out into the snow when the rations ran low. It seemed to call for some responding gesture on our part. Not for the first time I spoke up when I should've kept quiet.

'I tell you what,' I said, 'I'll slip out the back way, stroll round to the front as if I was coming here to buy something, and see if anyone's hanging around.'

'Take care,' Ganesh said, worried.

I had a question for the man. 'Who should I be looking for?' (Yes, I know it should be 'whom'—I went to a good school where they fussed about that kind of thing—but I was under pressure.)

'They're in a car,' he said. 'A silver-grey Mercedes. They stopped at the traffic lights down the block. I got the door open and rolled out into the road.'

15

'They', were careless, I thought, and they'd lost their man. Whoever was paying them wouldn't be pleased. They'd be moving heaven and earth to get him back.

'Nearly got run over by a bloody bus,' said our visitor, aggrieved.

'Is that when you smashed your nose?' Ganesh asked sharply.

'Do me a favour. Look, if you can see the car, two guys in it, one small, one big with a ponytail, that'll be them. But I reckon they don't know I came in here. My bet is, once they saw I'd got away, they burned rubber getting out of here.' He was quite perking up. I had a suspicion this wasn't the first tight corner he'd been in and squeezed out of. Curiouser and curiouser.

I had to ask. 'Why'd they do it?'

'Misunderstanding,' he said, and that was as much as I was going to get. I hadn't really expected more.

'You watch yourself,' muttered Ganesh to me.

'It'll be all right,' said our guest, not altogether gallantly. 'They won't be expecting a girl.'

\*       \*       \*

I hoped they weren't as I let myself out of the back door. I pulled up the collar of my fleece-lined denim jacket to keep out the rain and

16

hide my face, made my way along the alley at the back of the shop, into the side street and back to the main road again.

There was a bus stop there, so I lingered by it, scrutinising the traffic as if waiting for my bus. The street was fairly busy—taxis, vans, cars, one or two motorcyclists. No Mercedes. Double yellow lines precluded legal parking for most of its length and the only stationary vehicle was a red Post Office van.

I turned round and leaned nonchalantly on the metal post. The people passing along the pavement were the usual mob, mostly women at this time of day, some with kids. One or two of the men who passed looked scruffy but none of them like a minder. No ponytails. This was an open bus stop without a shelter and I was getting wet. I put up a hand to wipe water from my hair. A split second later, there was a growl of tyres behind me. Intent on the pavement, I'd failed to observe the arrival of a double-decker. A woman got off. The bus throbbed expectantly and I realised I was meant to board it.

'You getting on or what?' the driver shouted at me. I waved a negative at him. 'You hailed me!' he bellowed.

'No, I didn't!' I shouted back.

'You bloody did. You put your hand out.'

'No, I didn't. I was rubbing my head.'

'I gotta schedule to keep, you know!' he informed me.

17

'Well, go on and keep it, then!' I'd had enough of this.

He gave me a dirty look as he accelerated away. There was a man who lacked the Christmas spirit.

If anyone had been watching, that would have blown my cover, so I might as well go back and report all clear as far as I could see.

I strolled up to the shop. Ganesh, framed in gold, was standing on the other side of the glass door, peering between a sticker advertising Mars bars and one advertising Rizla cigarette papers. At my nod, he flipped the closed sign to open, and unlocked the door.

'Can't see anyone,' I said, wiping trickling raindrops from my face. 'All I got was into a barney with a bus driver. Where's our friend?'

'Cleaning himself up in the washroom.'

'Hope he doesn't leave it smeared all over with blood. Just think, when Hitch has done it all up for you, you'll be more fussy who you let go in there.' (Yes, 'whom', same excuse.) 'Did you warn him about the loose top on the cistern? It'd be a pity if he came out more injured than he went in. He might sue. He'd want his tenner back.'

'I told him!' said Ganesh testily.

There was a clanking from distant plumbing and the stranger reappeared. He'd got rid of all the blood, brushed his coat, and, swelling apart, no one would have noticed at a casual glance that he'd been in very recent trouble. I told him I'd been unable to see any Mercedes or ponytailed heavy.

'That's all right, then,' he said. 'I thought they'd have cleared off. They wouldn't have seen me come in here. I shouldn't worry.'

He'd now completely regained composure and was well up to dealing with his problems. I still wished I knew what they were.

'Thank you very much,' he said to me, nice and polite. 'I appreciate everything.'

With that, he opened the door and slipped out. He looked quickly in either direction and then set off rapidly.

Another crepe paper chain fell down.

'So much for that,' said Ganesh. 'Breaks up the morning, I suppose.'

'I wish I knew what it was all about,' I said wistfully. I gave Ganesh a quick rundown of my ideas about the visitor, adding, 'It's all very well deducing things, but you like to know if you got it right.'

'*You* would. Leave me out of it. I'm sure it's better we don't know anything.' Ganesh opened the till, extricated two fives, put in the tenner and closed the till. He handed one of the fives to me and tucked the other in his pocket.

'We earned it,' he said.

We? As I recalled, I was the one who went outside in the rain and made myself a possible target for aggro. Ganesh stayed inside and made the tea. But never argue with the man who's holding the money.

'I don't suppose we'll ever know,' I said, pocketing my fiver.

But I was wrong and Ganesh, as usual, was right. I mean, we *were* to find out what it was all about—and it would have been better if we hadn't.


## CHAPTER TWO

I walked out of the shop at just gone one o'clock. Things had stayed quiet after our visitor left, the rain either keeping people indoors or sending them scurrying past, anxious to reach dry destinations. As we pinned our now somewhat battered decorations back into place, Ganesh and I had rehashed the morning's main event. It remained a riddle and we went on to talk about Hari, whose postcard seemed to watch us accusingly from behind the counter. We wrangled about the washroom and Hitch's imminent arrival on the premises and half a dozen other things. Just as I was leaving for home, Ganesh presented me with a Mars bar. Perhaps he thought I was owed a bonus for going out in the rain to spy out the land, or possibly he felt guilty for letting me do it. I put the chocolate in my pocket.

There was a supermarket on my way. I called in there and used some of my fiver to buy a packet of tea and some pasta and a jar of pesto. Memories of the morning's events were beginning to fade. It had been just one of those spurts of activity which occur from time to time. Like a pebble thrown into a pond, they disturb the surface, create a few ripples, and then everything settles down again.

'Have you got any change?'

I heard the voice, though the question wasn't addressed to me. The voice came from a doorway just ahead of me and the request was made of a prosperous-looking elderly gent.

'Have you got any change, sir?' She emphasised the last word. She sounded pathetic. The old guy wavered, wanting to stick to his principles and walk on. But he couldn't do it, not with that childish desperate voice echoing in his ears, a young girl's voice. If that had been a man begging, he'd have told him to go and get a job. What he did now, as I knew he was going to do, was give too much. A small blue note changed hands.

The old gent huffed a bit and said, 'You know, my dear, you really oughtn't—' But he couldn't finish the sentence because he hadn't a clue what to say. He hurried away, distressed and angry, already regretting parting with the five-pound note.

I approached the doorway carefully. There

had been something about that voice which rang a bell. I peered in.

She looked wet, cold and miserable, and was stick-insect thin. No wonder the old fellow had coughed up. Talk about Little Nell. Rain had plastered her straight fair hair to her head. Her eyes were huge and tragic in a face which had the matt, pale complexion of the heroin user.

I said, 'Hullo, Tig.' Truth was, I'd hardly have known her if I hadn't heard her voice first, she was so changed from our last meeting.

She jumped and her eyes blazed in her waif's features. I thought she was going to take a swing at me.

'Take it easy,' I said hastily. Those frail-looking ones can catch you a nasty swipe. 'It's Fran, remember me?'

I hadn't seen her for the best part of a year. She'd passed through the Jubilee Street squat when I'd been living there. I'd got to know her as well as you get to know anyone in that sort of setup, which is always as well as they'll let you. She hadn't stayed long, a week or two, and had been no trouble. A cheerful, plump, happy-go-lucky fifteen-year-old who hadn't long been in London, she'd hailed from somewhere in the Midlands. She'd left home, she said, as a result of some family dispute, the old story. We'd rather missed her when she'd moved on, but I hadn't expected her to stay long. The feeling I'd had then was that she was trying to give her parents a scare, get back at them for some real or imagined injustice. When she reckoned she'd done that, she'd go home. If asked, I'd have guessed she'd have returned there long before now, when cold, hunger and street violence ceased to sound adventurous and just got real and frightening.

But I was clearly wrong. The change in her shocked me deeply, even though I'd seen kids like Tig before. They arrived from out of town, full of optimism, although I couldn't think why. What did they think they were going to find in London? Other than a whole community of people like themselves with nowhere to go and a host of sharks ready to prey on them? They learned quickly if they were lucky. The unlucky ones came to grief before they'd time to learn.

The thing that really stuck in my mind about her from Jubilee Street days was that she'd brushed her teeth after every meal, even if she didn't have toothpaste. There are a lot of people who think that being homeless means being dirty. That isn't true. Whatever the practical difficulties, homeless people try to keep themselves clean. Cleanliness means there's still fight in you, circumstances haven't ground you down. You still care about yourself, even if others appear to have written you off. When a cat ceases to groom itself, you know it's sick. People are no different. With them it's also a sign of a sickness, either in body or in spirit. The sickness in spirit is the more difficult to deal with. Looking at Tig now, I wondered which kind of sickness afflicted her.

We'd had a no-drugs rule in the squat and if she'd had the habit then, she'd concealed it very cleverly. But I didn't think that was the case. She couldn't have been that smart. I guessed the habit was recent. Actually, she wasn't that smart. Belatedly, I remembered that, too. Naïve, perhaps, but a bit dim also.

'Yeah, Fran,' she said eventually. Her eyes slid sideways, past me. I remembered her gaze as it had been, bright, full of good nature. Now it was dull and hard. 'Got any spare change, madam?' she wheedled of a motherly woman with a bulging plastic carrier. The woman looked concerned and parted with twenty pence. Tig put it in her pocket.

'How are things?' She seemed to be doing well begging, but there was a quiet desperation about her which made me wary because when they reach that stage, they can really freak out.

'All right,' she said. Her gaze shifted past me again, this time nervously.

I still had two pounds left from my fiver and I gave her one of them. She looked surprised and then suspicious.

'It's OK,' I said. 'I had a bit of luck.'

At those words, misery welled up in her face, and was immediately wiped away. Luck

24

had been avoiding her. She no longer expected any. But on the streets you hide your feelings. They make you vulnerable and God knows, you're vulnerable enough without the enemy within.

'Good for you,' she said bitchily and shoved the pound coin away in her pocket with the rest.

I persevered nevertheless—the memory of the old Tig made me do it. 'You heard what happened to the Jubilee Street house? They knocked it down.'

'Yeah, I heard. It was going to fall down anyway.'

That hurt. I'd been fond of that house and it had sheltered her, as well as me, for a time. She owed it better than that.

'It was a good place!' I said crossly.

'Look,' Tig said, 'you're really in my way here, you know? How'm I supposed to ask people for bloody change with you standing there nattering about sod all?' Her voice was aggressive but her eyes were flickering nervously past me again. She hissed, 'For Chrissake, get lost, Fran!'

I got the message. 'Here,' I said, and handed her my Mars bar. She needed it more than me.

She snatched it away and I walked on without looking back. I was too busy looking elsewhere and sure enough, I spotted him almost at once. He was a big bearded bloke, in

25

his twenties, wearing a plaid wool jacket, jeans and a woolly hat. He was loafing in the angle formed by a building which jutted out on to the pavement and under the shelter of an overhanging first-floor balcony. It kept him nice and dry and out of the draught. That dark little corner would be a mugger's haven in the evening and I wouldn't have seen him if I hadn't been looking for him. He wasn't a mugger, of course. He was Tig's protection, amongst other things.

I'd come across these street partnerships before and as far as I was concerned, the woman was scarcely better off in them than out of them. Don't get me wrong. I've known some really good partnerships which have started out there on the street, but it's rare for them to last, even the good ones. The fact is, you can't let yourself become dependent on anyone out there. You've got to stand alone, be able to take care of yourself, sort out your own problems. The street's a family of sorts, but it's a family of loners. Once you can't hack it any more on your own, you're lost.

Still, couples form, split, make new partners, just as they do in the world of the nine-to-fivers. There's the old man/woman thing, of course. But there's also a practical side to it. Tig's man might be an idle lout who hung around in warm corners while she stood out in the cold wind. But he was on hand if things got rough, either while she was begging, or at any other time. Mind you, he probably also took most of the money, if not all. He'd see she had enough to keep the drug habit going because as long as she was on that, she'd have to beg, steal, sell her body, do whatever was necessary to get the money to feed it. He might even have got her on to it in the first place. He'd look on it as a business investment. People were far less likely to give him money had he been standing in that doorway with his hand out. From the brief glimpse I'd had of him, he didn't look as if he'd been going hungry lately. Unlike Tig, who looked as if she hadn't had a square meal in days. But the worse she looked, the more she earned. He couldn't lose, really.

I felt a spurt of hatred for him, whoever he was. I'd never let myself be used like that, but then perhaps Tig's situation had got so bad that whoever he was he'd seemed like a good idea at the time.

I was feeling pretty angry by now. One morning can only hold so much hassle. I stomped on homewards, ready to take on the next person to cross my path. Fortunately, no one did, at least not until I got there and then the encounter made me more inclined to laugh than spit fire.

At that time I was living in a basement flat in a house owned by a retired lady librarian called Daphne Knowles. I'd come by the flat through the intervention of an old gent called Alastair Monkton, whom I'd helped once. The flat had given me more security than I'd had in years. I've been on my own since I was sixteen and I'm twenty-one now. The trouble with security, when you're not used to having it, is that you don't really believe in it. I somehow knew that flat wasn't going to be permanent, but I meant to make it last as long as possible. I was never going to get so lucky again, that was for sure.

It had stopped drizzling by the time I got to the street where I lived, and a feeble sun had crept out. The pavements looked clean and washed. As I passed the basement railings of the house next door, I saw coming towards me a sight which made me grin.

There were two of them, alike as peas in a pod, walking side by side, in step. Both were short, tubby, middle-aged and smug-looking. The one on the left wore a green tweed jacket and the one on the right a brown tweed jacket. Both had pale fawn trousers and polished brogue shoes. The green jacket carried a bunch of flowers and the brown jacket a bottle wrapped in paper. Tweedledee and Tweedledum, I thought, and wondered who they were, where they were going and what on earth they were going to do when they got there. They looked, with their gifts, as if they were going courting according to some out-dated ritual. I hadn't seen them around before.

Perhaps they were wondering the same thing about me, because they inclined their heads together, keeping their eyes on me, and whispered. We reached the steps to Daphne's front door at the same time and stopped by mutual consent.

'Well, well,' said Green Jacket. 'What have we here, eh?' He gave me a jovial smile which was so fake I could have ripped it off his face like a piece of Elastoplast.

I could have made a number of pithy replies but instinct told me to avoid this encounter.

'Excuse me!' I said, and made to pass them and run down the steps to my basement door.

I wasn't to get away so easily. Brown Jacket chimed in with his pennyworth. 'Now, let's see, eh? I believe you must be the young woman who lives in Aunt Daphne's basement flat.' He shook a podgy forefinger at me and looked pleased with himself.

Aunt Daphne? Were these two fat creeps Daphne's family? I felt sorry for her and glad, not for the first time, I didn't have anyone. I suppose my mother might be alive somewhere, probably is, but since she walked out on Dad and me when I was seven, I'd long since cut her out of the picture. I was brought up perfectly well by Dad and my Hungarian Grandma Varady but they're both dead now. No one could replace them.

'Yes,' I said bleakly, eyeing the pair. I'd never seen them call on Daphne but that didn't mean they hadn't been to the house. The basement flat was totally independent.

29

There was no reason why Daphne should know who visited me, nor I who visited her, unless—as now—we met on the pavement.

'Our young friend is a trifle *farouche*, Bertie,' said Brown Jacket. 'A product of our unsettled society.'

That was asking for a punch on the nose and he might have got one if there hadn't been an interruption.

Daphne must have been watching out for their arrival from a window, because now the front door opened and she stood at the top of the steps, peering down at our small group. She wore, as usual, jogging trousers and hand-knitted Fair Isle socks with leather soles attached. But she sported a new sweater and had been to the hairdresser. Her grey hair was waved and primped, and from beneath two sausage curls over her ears dangled long earrings. Daphne had dressed up.

My landlady is in her seventies but is twice as alert as many younger people. I'd got to know her quite well and felt rather protective towards her. Not that she normally needed protecting. She could look after herself. But she appeared anything but sure of herself just now, unhappy and perplexed, as if she didn't know what to do about the situation.

'Oh, Bertie—Charlie . . .' she said unenthusiastically. 'How nice. Oh, hullo, Fran dear.' She brightened when she saw me.

Bertie and Charlie climbed the steps as if

they were joined at the hip, and threw out their free (outer edge) arms in a sort of token joint embrace, Bertie (the green jacket) his left, Charlie his right. At the same time they clasped their gifts to their chests with their other hands. 'Aunt Daphne!' they cried. Bertie thrust out his flowers and Charlie, at the exact same moment, his bottle of wine. You'd have thought they'd rehearsed it.

'How kind,' said Daphne without enthusiasm. 'Do come in, boys.'

Boys? But perhaps it wasn't so unsuitable a term. There was something about them which suggested a bad double case of arrested development. I suppose it's cute to dress twin babies alike. It's just about permissible to dress toddlers so. But middle-aged men ought to have outgrown the desire to look exactly like someone else. If you couldn't help it—i.e. you were identical twins—you could at least develop an individual clothes style. But there's no accounting for the way people behave. I went downstairs and let myself into the flat.

I still hadn't got used to coming home and knowing that this was my place and it was private, I hadn't to share it with anyone and I hadn't to defend it against intruders who wanted to take it from me or the council who wanted to throw everyone out. It was early afternoon and I hadn't had any lunch. I put on a pan of water for the pasta and when it boiled, and before I put the salt in, poured off enough to make coffee.

I took my coffee into the living area and sat down on my old blue rep sofa. I started thinking again about the man who'd come into the shop. I don't like puzzles I can't solve and this time I had a strange feeling we hadn't seen the last of him. The pasta was ready. I strained it, stirred in the jar of pesto, and sat eating it before my aged, flickering TV set. The ghosted picture, as wasn't unusual, gave the viewer a sense of double vision and I couldn't help being reminded of Daphne's 'boys'.

There wasn't much to watch, no old film this afternoon, always my favourite viewing. I must have dozed off. I was awoken suddenly by the sound of voices and the clatter of feet on the front steps above my head. It was already dark on this wintry evening and the blue light from the screen was the only thing illuminating the room.

I ran to the window and peered out and upwards. I was just in time. A taxi had parked outside and the footsteps which had awoken me had been those of the driver, running up to the front door. Now he came back and in his wake came two pairs of pale trousers and some very thin female legs beneath a drooping skirt, all lit by the yellow lamplight. I'd never seen Daphne in anything but jogging pants, but obviously, wherever they were going, it was the sort of place you dressed up for. I wished I could have felt pleased for Daphne, having a night out. But I didn't. Wherever it was to be, I was sure she didn't want to go—at least not in that company.

I returned to my sofa and wished I knew where they'd taken her. I recalled the unhappy look on her face as she'd greeted them earlier. It made me feel uneasy and fuelled my misgivings about the tweeded pair. No decent restaurant would admit me nor could I have afforded its prices, but I could've lurked outside and kept an eye on things. I looked out of the window and saw that rain pattered down again on the pavement up there. I'd done enough hanging around in bad weather today. Daphne was with her family and if you can't trust your family ... Let's face it, I thought. You can't. You can't trust anyone, it's a fact.

*     *     *

The taxi came back at about nine thirty. The headlights strafed the front of the house; there was a slam of a car door. I was still watching TV in the dark. It was the film version of *Death on the Nile* with Peter Ustinov. I liked the scenes of hot sands and sun-baked temples, a contrast to the cold dank outdoors. I hoped Daphne had taken her coat. Voices called out 'Good night!' One set of lightweight footsteps began to climb the front steps, hesitated, turned and came back down again. They began to make a tentative descent of my basement steps. I hurried to switch on the light and open my door, letting the glow flood out into the basement well. I didn't want Daphne crashing head first down the rain-wet steps.

But she'd already negotiated her way safely to the bottom and was standing outside, clutching her coat lapels together against the chill air and peering at me.

'Oh, Fran,' she said, 'I'm sorry to bother you, but I thought there was a chance you might be in. I thought I could see the TV screen flickering. I wondered, if you're not doing anything, whether you'd like to come upstairs and join me in a glass of wine?'

*     *     *

'My nephews brought this,' she said a little later in her kitchen. She was wrestling with the corkscrew and eventually surrendered the task to me. The cork came out with a satisfying pop.

'The one good thing you can say for Charlie,' said Daphne, 'is that he brings a decent bottle when he comes. He fancies himself as a bit of a wine buff, you know.'

Wine bore, more likely. 'I haven't seen them before,' I said, pouring us out a glass.

Daphne rooted about in a cupboard and produced some savoury biscuits which she shook out on to a dish on the table. 'Help yourself.' She raised her glass. 'Cheers!' She was beginning to look much happier than she had when her visitors had arrived. A couple of curls in the brand-new hairdo had come adrift and her lipstick was smudged. She'd kicked off her smart shoes and donned her Fair Isle sock-slippers and looked much more the old Daphne.

'I don't encourage them,' she said, sounding rather as though she was talking of stray cats. 'They mean well, you know. I don't want to be unkind. But I don't like being bothered by people who know better than I do what I want. They think I need looking after.' An indignant note entered her voice and her long purple glass earrings bobbed in sympathy. 'Me! Do I look as if I need looking after?'

'You're fine,' I said robustly. 'And if you need anything, I'm here.'

'Yes, dear, I know. But Bertie and Charlie don't see it like that. They're my brother, Arnold's, sons. Arnold was older than me and he's been dead twenty years. He was a solicitor. The boys joined the firm as soon as they were able and took over when Arnold retired. Neither of them is married.'

That didn't surprise me. 'Are they retired now?' I asked.

'Oh no, dear. They're only fifty-one. I think they look older and they've always been quaint. I mustn't be nasty about them. They took me out for a slap-up dinner. Of course,' she sighed, 'they really wanted to talk business.

35

They always do.'

She took off the purple earrings and laid them neatly side by side on the table, next to her wine glass. 'My mother's,' she said. 'Amethyst.'

I should have known they wouldn't be purple glass. But then, Daphne was probably fairly well off and it sparked an unpleasant notion.

I asked, rather alarmed, whether Bertie and Charlie handled her business, i.e. financial affairs, because I wouldn't have liked that idea at all. But fortunately it seemed not.

'Oh no, because they're my principal heirs, you see. It wouldn't be proper. But naturally, they have an interest. They're worried about death duties.'

It was unlikely I'd ever have anything to leave but the clothes on my back and who'd want those? However, the thought that the duo stood to gain by her death made me, if possible, even more uneasy than the idea they might handle her money during her life. I knew I wasn't being fanciful because Sergeant Parry, my old CID foe, once told me that a person's still most likely to be murdered by a relative or close acquaintance. 'And it's pretty always sex or money,' he'd added. I didn't want to pry into Daphne's affairs but perhaps some outsider without an axe to grind ought to know more about what was going on. Besides, she obviously wanted to talk to someone.

She leaned forward. 'It makes sense, you see, for me to give money or even things away now. To avoid the tax when I drop off the twig. I mean, the house is left to the boys already. But if I, well, made it over to them now . . .'

'They want you to give them this house?' I cried tactlessly.

'I'd go on living here,' she assured me. 'It'd be a formality, that's all, to avoid the tax.'

She might trust them, I certainly didn't. They might or might not let her go on living there. It was more likely they'd try and bundle her into some sort of home. As for me, they'd certainly have me off the premises p.d.q. Really, there was no difference between those two and Tig's boyfriend. Both were after the woman's hard-earned cash.

'You aren't going to do it, Daphne?' I couldn't but sound appalled.

She took a long deep swig of Charlie's wine. 'I don't want to, but when I'm with them, they do seem to make such good sense.'

'You ought to talk to your own solicitor,' I said firmly.

'Yes, I shall do so. I won't be pushed, don't worry.'

'Look,' I said, leaning over the table. 'You know how you value your independence. That's what they want you to give up. You'll be their tenant, Daphne! I mean, even if you're not paying, you'll be living here on sufferance. You don't know how the future will pan out.

37

You might change your mind.'

She was nodding but sighing. 'It's so difficult when it's family. One ought to *like* one's relations.'

Not if they were like Bertie and Charlie Knowles, I thought, but managed by biting my tongue not to say it. I was fast forming the idea that the Knowles twins were very bad news.

Daphne was looking downhearted so, to divert her, I told her about the man who'd burst into the shop that morning.

'Dear me,' she said, and brightened up. Daphne likes a mystery. I'd seen plenty of them on her bookshelves and she sometimes lent me one, usually an Agatha Christie or a Ngaio Marsh. I liked best the Ngaio Marsh books about the theatre. Ever since I'd first met her, Daphne had been tapping away at a great lumbering old manual typewriter, piling up sheets and sheets of densely typed manuscript. I'd never plucked up the courage to ask her what it represented, but it wouldn't have surprised me if it had been a great novel, something on the model of *The Woman in White*. That's a book she likes very much, she told me.

'Perhaps he owes someone money,' she suggested.

But I said, not quite knowing why, 'Or perhaps he's got something to sell.'

'Ah . . .' said Daphne, reaching for the wine. 'But what could it be?'

'Something he ought to get rid of quick,' I said. Not knowing, of course, that he'd done just that.

## CHAPTER THREE

Hitch's Transit van rattled to a stop outside the shop three days later, at eight in the morning, minutes after I'd arrived for work. Along the side of the van was printed in tipsy capitals 'PROPERTY MAINTENANCE COMPANY'. The van itself was no great advert for the firm's skills, being distinctly unmaintained and showing evidence of rust and minor collisions. The rear doors were tied together with string.

Ganesh and I stood in the doorway of the shop like a reception committee for royals as Hitch, with a bit of trouble, extricated himself from the front seat. There seemed to be something wrong with the door catch and several bits of pipe, tools, paintbrushes, etc. fell out with him.

'Morning!' he greeted us cheerily, adding for my benefit, 'All right, darling?' He picked up the things which had fallen out, slung them back inside and slammed the van door. Something in the interior fell down with a clatter.

Hitch addresses all women as 'darling' and

39

it doesn't signify any affection or even recognition. It's no use turning PC on him and asking him not to do it. He doesn't even realise he has done it. Still, I tried.

'I'm fine,' I said. 'But I'm not your darling.'

'Right you are, darling,' he replied, walking past me into the shop. 'Where's this boghole you want tarting up, then?'

'Oy!' I called as he and Gan disappeared towards the back of the building. 'You can't leave the van there! You'll get a ticket. Double yellow lines.'

'That's all right, darling!' floated back to me. 'You stay by it and tell anyone who asks I'm just dropping off some gear. I'll be back in a tick.'

I stood there in drizzling rain for one minute and decided that that was enough. It wasn't my problem. I hoped they clamped the thing. I retreated inside and almost at once a customer came in, so I had an excuse.

I listened as Ganesh and Hitch, unseen, shouted at one another in the washroom, their voices echoing off the walls. Hitch only has one voice pitch—loud. It's infectious. After a few moments you find yourself yelling back.

The thing about Hitch is that, until he opens his mouth, he's Mr Anonymous. Not only would you not pick him out in a crowd, you wouldn't notice him if he was the only person walking along the pavement. He's of middle height and I couldn't even guess his age. He's slim, but wiry from all that heaving around of knocked-off building supplies, and going bald. Hitch refers to this last feature as a receding hairline. It's receded to the back of his head, leaving the top domed and shiny. To compensate, he's grown what's left long so that it hangs round the bare patch like the fringe on an old-fashioned table-lamp. He always wears worn jeans and a washed-out navy-blue tee shirt. I've never seen him in anything else so he must have a wardrobe of these items. He's always cheerful and always on the fiddle. He misses nothing.

He came back as the customer left. 'Gonna move the van, darling,' he said. 'You'll be pleased to hear. And ah—' He fished in his jeans back pocket and took out a grubby wallet. He opened it up, revealing a wodge of notes and some small white cards, one of which he peeled off and handed to me.

'There you go, darling. Stick that up on your board, all right?'

I looked at the card. On it was printed: 'JEFFERSON HITCHENS. ALL PROPERTY MAINTENANCE AND HOME IMPROVEMENTS. PATIOS A SPECIALITY. ESTIMATES FREE. NO OBLIGATION. BEST TERMS.'

I said, 'Ha!' loudly.

Hari keeps a corkboard in the window and, for a pound a week, anyone can leave a notice up there. I added Hitch's. Ganesh came back while I was doing this. I pointed out that Hitch hadn't paid the required pound.

'Don't worry,' said Ganesh. 'I'll knock it off his bill. Don't go upsetting him, for goodness' sake.'

'Me?' I protested.

'Yes, you. You glare at him as if he's just insulted you and that weird haircut of yours bristles even more. Can't you do something about it?' He frowned. 'It looks like a mangy hedgehog.'

'Join the club, why don't you? Let's all insult Fran. I don't like being called darling. If he's going to do it all the time he's here, he's going to get a flea in his ear.'

'Oh, don't make such a fuss,' said Ganesh.

For all he was acting in control, I guessed Ganesh was nervous. It was one thing plotting to go behind Hari's back and get the washroom fixed up. The reality of Hitch on the premises had reminded him that he hadn't Hari's authority and if anything went wrong, the buck stopped there with Gan.

I appreciated his fragile state of mind, but he'd got himself into this and he could get himself out of it. Likewise, he had no cause to be rude about my hair, although by the same token, I'd no right to be rude about Hitch's baldness. A few weeks back, when the weather had still been mild, I'd decided to go for a new look. So I had my hair shaved off at the sides and kept a short brush top and a thin layer at the nape of the neck. I quickly decided I'd chosen the wrong time of year. In the summer, the shaved sides would've been all right. But now, at the onset of winter, it was a chilly style, so I was growing it all out. The result was a bit of a mess, the sides were fuzzy and the brush top was going all ways, some of it sticking up, some falling over. I'd done my best to tidy it up, using gel, and I didn't need reminding I looked as if I'd just had an electric shock. It'd grow out. The sooner the better. Haven't you ever made a mistake like that?

Hitch came back, whistling happily. He was carrying a colour chart. 'If you was to decide on the magnolia,' he said, 'I've got a few tins of that on special offer. Left over from a job.'

I glared at Ganesh but he was refusing to look at me. He took Hitch through to the storeroom so that they could discuss colour schemes in private without my help.

I leaned on the counter and leafed idly through one of the tabloids until my attention was taken by the ting of the bell above the door.

The man who came in was short and Mediterranean-looking. His hair was dark and tightly curled, his features small, his skin olive. He stared at me and said, 'Twenty Benson and Hedges.'

I fetched them off the shelf behind me and turned back to find he'd moved. He'd wandered over to the magazine rack and was

43

studying the titles. I put the cigarettes on the counter and waited. I didn't have anything else to do so I watched him. Gan had told me to watch out for loiterers at the mag stand. They sometimes slipped one magazine inside another and tried to get away with paying for one only. Then there are the ones who're coy about taking down the girlie mags from the top shelf. They spend ages looking through titles on woodwork and computer graphics and finally reach up for one of the dirty dozen with a start of surprise, as if they'd just noticed them and hadn't a clue what they contained.

Somehow, I felt this man wasn't interested in any of the magazines. He was looking all round the shop and I started to get apprehensive. When he started back towards the counter, I glanced down to make sure I knew where the jemmy was in case I had to grab it.

He sought through a handful of coins in his palm. 'Business quiet,' he observed.

'Comes and goes,' I replied. I took his money and rang up the till.

He tucked the packet of cigarettes inside his blouson. 'Nothing exciting ever happens, eh?' He was smiling at me in a way he probably thought charming. He had small white pointed teeth.

'Not since I've worked here,' I said.

'Friend of mine,' he said, 'came by here the other day.'

'Oh, yes?'

'He said there was a bit of a dust-up outside. A chap got roughed up. He came in here.' His English was good enough but heavily accented, with a lisp and Rs which stuck in his throat.

'No one came in here,' I said coldly.

'Perhaps you weren't here, then.' His eyes slid round the store again. 'Anyone else work here?'

'I'm always here mornings,' I said just as icily, 'and I saw nothing.'

The little white teeth flashed. 'That's right, it happened during the morning.'

Ouch. I'd slipped up there.

He was smiling with his mouth but his eyes watched me like a vicious dog waiting for a chance to snap. 'Sure you didn't see anything?' His hand slid into the jacket and came out holding a note. 'Fact is, the man might've dropped something and my friend would like to give it back to him. He thinks he knows where to find him.'

He was offering me twenty quid. Offering any money was clumsy, offering so much was plain stupid. If I'd not been interested before, I'd be fascinated now to know just what he was after. Actually, I was interested—but I wasn't going to let him know it.

'You're wasting your time,' I told him.

There was movement at the back of the shop floor. Ganesh and Hitch emerged from the storeroom, causing me to glance their way.

45

At the same time the doorbell tinged again. I looked round and found the customer had slipped out. I wondered whether to tell Ganesh and decided against it. No point in worrying him.

'All right, darling?' asked Hitch cheerfully. 'No problems? I'll come in tomorrow early, bring along a mate to give me a hand. We'll carry on over the weekend, have it all finished by Monday afternoon.'

'You owe a pound,' I said, 'for pinning up your card in the window.'

'Wish I had you keeping my books,' he said, fishing in his pocket and producing fifty pence. 'Here you are, on account. Give you the other fifty tomorrow.'

'What did you do that for?' asked Gan when Hitch had left.

'Because I don't trust him.'

'I don't know what you've got against Hitch,' Ganesh said. 'You've never liked him.'

'Instinct,' I told him. But truth to tell I had other things on my mind than the washroom. Ganesh could tell Hitch to paint the place purple and put in gold taps for all I cared.

'You haven't found anything in the shop, have you, Gan? Dropped on the floor?'

'What like?'

'Like lost property. I don't know.'

'What've you lost?'

'I haven't lost anything. Oh, forget it.'

'Sometimes,' said Ganesh, 'the way you

46

ramble on, I wonder about you.'

'That's it!' I said crossly. 'I'm quitting for the day.'

'It's not eleven!' he protested.

'It's quiet. You can manage. I'll come in tomorrow.'

'I'm only paying you for the hours you've worked, not for the whole morning.' He sounded pompous and indignant in equal measure.

'On what you pay me, that's no great loss!' I stormed out.

*　　　*　　　*

I don't like quarrelling with Ganesh but the row had been brewing up over the last few days and now it was out and by tomorrow the air would've cleared. I was still annoyed with him, though. To tell the truth, I was feeling annoyed with myself. I really didn't need to get involved in anything. I hoped the little foreign guy asking the questions wouldn't come back. Perhaps I should've told Ganesh about him.

When you're fending for yourself in the city, you develop all your senses like an animal. You get to smell danger and I smelled it now. Nevertheless, I must have been getting careless, because it wasn't until I was almost home that I became aware of a tingle between the shoulder blades which told me someone was following me. Not walking behind me,

47

following me.

I wheeled round. People were surging along, faces set and purposeful, on many the strain of the approaching festive season already showing. I wondered which one it was. None of them looked a likely candidate. Perhaps my nerves were overstretched, firing my imagination. Or perhaps the tracker had been quicker than me and, a split second before I turned, had nipped into a doorway or wheeled round and started back away from me. I moved on, thoughtful.

\*     \*     \*

The rain had packed in during the previous night and a fitful sun had shone all morning, drying up the pavements and streets. Despite that, a puddle had formed in the road outside my flat. Water doesn't usually collect there but the rains had been heavy. I didn't pay it too much attention.

I hadn't seen anything of Daphne since our chat over the bottle of wine. As far as I knew the brothers Knowles hadn't returned, but I was keeping an eye open. Daphne wasn't the only person on my mind. There was Tig. I should let that situation alone; it wasn't my business. But I decided to give it a try. The day was fairly bright, but it wouldn't last long. By four darkness would've drawn in again. If I wanted to find Tig, I had to set out now. I had a quick cup of tea and went in search of her.

I returned to the entrance near to the supermarket where I'd found her, but she wasn't there. I widened out my hunt in slowly increasing circles because I thought it likely she and her partner were working this area. But they appeared to have moved on. Maybe they'd been warned off, either by the law or because they'd trespassed on someone else's turf. At any rate, neither Tig nor the man in the plaid jacket were to be seen.

I decided to give up and for something to do in the remaining short space of daylight, set off for Camden High Street.

Trotting down the Chalk Farm Road, I felt my spirits rise. I like this patch. To my mind, it's the nearest thing to Dickensian London, alive and kicking in all its variety and vulgarity. So, it's getting a tad gentrified with middle-class stores and antiques shops setting up, but it is still reassuringly eccentric and clinging to its pleb roots.

The recent rains had washed it clean. The black horses with glaring red eyes which leaped out from the façade of the Round House gleamed as if some infernal groom had buffed them up. I was lured by the promises of the Circus of Horrors and the Terrordome, but they were closed at the moment. So I went on, revelling in the used-car outlets, cheap clothes shops, the fast food dispensaries and street pedlars. I smiled up at the huge painted

49

figures decorating the upper floor façades of the shops, the giant wooden boots, camouflaged tank, leather-jacketed rocker, silver skull and, why oh why, above the tattoo parlour, a sea of scarlet flames?

I knew that the Stables and the canalside markets wouldn't be open now, but remnants of Inverness Street market could still be in progress and I might pick up something cheap and cheerful there. As stallholders closed up, they were often happy to let you have something virtually at cost. But before I ever got there, I glimpsed a plaid jacket ahead of me and there he was, Tig's boyfriend. I was just in time. Seconds later, he turned into The Man in The Moon pub.

He wasn't likely to be out in a hurry. Tig wasn't with him, but ten to one, she wasn't far away. I guessed they'd staked out a pitch and he'd left her begging while he spent the money on lager. I hunted in earnest now, casting about below the railway bridge and in the environs of the big drive-by supermarket which lay behind the main road, round by the bridge over the canal and at last ran her to earth in the entrance to Camden Town tube station.

She wasn't pleased to see me. 'You again!' she exclaimed, and her pinched face blenched with fury. It emphasised the greenish-black patch on one cheekbone. 'You following me around or what?'

'Time for a coffee-break, Tig,' I said. 'And

don't worry about him. He's in the pub.'

*     *     *

We took our polystyrene cups of coffee down by the dark olive-green canal and found a seat. Tig hunched on her end of the bench, sipping the coffee, eyes fixed on the water swirling sluggishly past, thick as treacle.

'What's his name?' I asked.

'Jo Jo.'

'He the one who beat you up?'

Despite herself, she took one hand from the cup to touch the bruise on her face. 'No one beat me up,' she said. 'It was just a slap.' She straightened up and became belligerent, her eyes, through the rat's tails of greasy fair hair, as cold as the canal's waters. Since the Jubilee Street days, she'd acquired a ring through the outer edge of her left eyebrow. Speaking as one who wears a nose-stud, I'm not criticising, you understand. It was just one more detail about Tig different to the old days. 'Anyway, it was your fault,' she said.

'Mine?' I wanted to know how she'd worked that out.

'The chocolate bar you gave me,' she said. 'He found it in my pocket. He said I'd been siphoning off the takings and spending them on stuff. I wasn't.'

'One lousy sweet?' I gasped. 'He thumped you because you'd bought one chocolate bar?'

51

'I didn't buy it,' she argued. 'You gave it to me.'

'Oh, sorry, excuse me!' I retorted sarcastically. 'I didn't realise that made it all right for him. Yes, my fault, why didn't I think of that?'

There was a silence. She looked away. 'Well, anyway, Fran . . . I didn't mean it wasn't nice of you. But when people try and help they nearly always foul you up more, you know that.'

I let her simmer. We finished our coffee and she slung her cup into the canal where it bobbed away. The old Tig, who'd arrived bright-eyed and bushy-tailed from the Heart of England, wouldn't have dreamed of littering up the place like that.

'Why'd you take up with him?'

'Why do you think?' She shrugged. 'He's not so bad.' She glanced sideways at me. 'If you want to know, I had—a bad experience. I was raped.' She spoke the last words with an awful blankness of voice and expression.

I waited. After a moment, she went on, 'I was on the game at the time, but I hadn't bargained for that. I was stupid. I should have realised—I mean, a regular working prostitute would've sized up the situation and got out of there, but I walked into it, didn't I?'

'It was a punter, then?' I prompted her.

'Yes, or I thought so. I thought he was on his own. He came up to me, youngish guy, bit drunk, City type. It was a Friday evening. He'd been celebrating the end of the week, I thought, and now he was looking for a cheap lay. I went with him to his car—I told you I was stupid—and the next thing I knew, there were two other guys, pals of his. They bundled me into the car and drove me to a house. They were just like him, hooray Henrys, red braces, Italian suits, the lot. Drunk as skunks. They kept me there for, I suppose, a couple of hours while they had their pervy fun. I don't know exactly how long, I just wanted to get it all over with and get out of there alive. My biggest fear was they wouldn't let me leave. But they did in the end.'

'Do you know where this house is?' I asked angrily.

'No, it was dark. I was too scared to take notice, I was watching them, not watching the surroundings. I didn't know what they were going to do next. There were the three of them and I didn't know which one of them to watch. They laughed all the time. One of them was sick, threw up on the floor and the first one swore at him so I guess it was his house and his carpet. Perhaps that's what made him think the time had come to call a halt to the fun and games. At any rate, he told me to get dressed. They got to arguing a bit while I scrambled into my gear as fast as I could. I knew they were arguing about what to do with me. I thought perhaps I could run while they were distracted, and get outside. They wouldn't

53

want a scene in the street.

'But then the first one—I don't know any of their names—he grabbed my arm and shoved me along ahead of him down the hall, out and back into the car. He told me not to say a word or he'd take me straight down to the river and hold my head under till I drowned. The river police pull out bodies every day, he said. I'd just be one more, floating past. I believed him. I sat there almost too frightened to breathe. He drove me back to King's Cross, which was where he'd picked me up. He gave me eighty quid and said, "Don't try telling anyone it was rape, sweetheart. You offered and I paid."'

'Eighty quid,' I said, 'would hardly have covered it even if you'd agreed. That's under thirty quid each.'

'What was I going to do, argue? He tossed me out and drove off. I told you, Fran, I thought they'd kill me. I was just so pleased when he drove off ... Afterwards, though, I couldn't put the whole business out of my mind. I was too scared for the meat trade. So I took up with Jo Jo and we do all right, with me begging and Jo Jo watching out for me. I've had no more trouble with men since Jo Jo's been around.'

'What about the habit?' I asked.

A dull flush stained her pale cheeks. 'I'm clean now, Fran, I swear. That was when I was turning tricks to get the money for a fix. After the rape, I knew I had to break the habit

54

because as long as I was on it, I'd take any risk to get the money. I went on to methadone and now I'm clean.'

I told her that was great, because it was. It had taken courage and perseverance but most of all, it showed that Tig hadn't slid so far down the ladder that she no longer realised how bad things were.

'What about you, Fran?' she asked. 'You seem to be doing all right.'

I explained that I was working temporarily at the newsagent's, just while Hari was in India.

'You haven't cracked it as an actress, then?' She gave a little smile.

'Not yet,' I said. 'I will.'

'Sure,' she said. It niggled.

'I also,' I said, 'look into things for people.'

That made her suspicious. 'What sort of things? What sort of people?'

'Mostly people who can't get help anywhere else. Like a private detective, you know, only I'm not official. I'm not fixed up with a proper organisation or the tax and insurance people would get me. Anyway, I don't do enough work for that. But what I have done has been all right.'

I suppose simple pride must have echoed in my voice, but why not? I'd been reasonably successful, considering.

Tig looked impressed but persisted, 'But what *sort* of things do you do? Say, if someone came to you and told you they wanted something arranged but they couldn't do it themselves, would you do that?'

'I do anything legal,' I said, perhaps not as cautiously as I might've done.

'Should've thought that cramped your style a bit,' said Tig. 'Sticking to the law, I mean. Don't the coppers get in your way?'

'Yes,' I said, adding airily, 'but I can handle them.'

You know what they say about pride coming before a fall, don't you? Tig didn't ask anything else but sat scowling at the canal water and twisting one finger in a lank strand of hair.

'You know,' I said, breaking in on whatever deep thoughts she was having, 'I was really surprised to see you the other day. I thought you'd have gone home long before now, back to where you came from.'

She gave a strangled little laugh. 'I can't go back, not now, not like I am. Can you imagine their faces if they saw me now? No, of course you can't. You don't know them.'

'You mean your parents?'

'They're really respectable people,' she said dully. 'Really decent. My mother's so houseproud she can't even bear to see the streaks the rain makes on the windows. She's out there polishing them off as soon as the rain stops. She's always polishing everything up. A perfect house, that's what she runs, because

56

that's what he likes, my dad. Everything just so. I can't go back, Fran.'

'You could try.' I leaned forward. 'Listen, Tig, sooner or later Jo Jo's going to get tired of you, right? You're certainly going to want to get away from him. Where are you going from here?'

'Don't!' There was so much pain in her voice that I was conscience-stricken at my question. 'What do you think, Fran? What do you imagine *I* think about, day in, day out? How do you think I like facing another Christmas on the streets? Even if Jo Jo and I find a place in a hostel, it'll be for a few days only—and then going back out is worse. I can't get along with these charities and I'm not like you, Fran, a survivor.'

'Pull yourself together!' I said sharply. 'That isn't true and you know it. It took guts to get yourself off drugs and you wouldn't have done that if you hadn't had some other vision for yourself, some idea of getting away from all this—'

Suddenly she struck out at me wildly, sobbing in dry gasps, her fists clenched into rock-hard little mallets. She caught me a couple of times, but I fended off most blows because she was too disorganised and angry to think about targeting them. At last they became weaker and finally stopped. Her hands dropped back in her lap.

For a moment she was still, then she sat up,

tossed back her hair, and turned a stony face to me. 'I've got to go,' she said. 'I'm not making any money sitting here chewing the fat with you.'

'Write to your family!' I urged. 'A postcard, that's all. Call them!'

'How can I? Don't be stupid, Fran.' She sounded weary and exasperated. 'I don't even know what the situation is back home now. Maybe they don't live in that house any more. Perhaps they were so ashamed when I left that they couldn't face the neighbours. Perhaps they've moved. It's the sort of thing they'd do.'

'And perhaps they're still there, hoping that the next time the phone rings—'

'Shut up!' she hissed.

She'd jumped to her feet with the last words and was making to walk off. I knew that if I lost her now, I'd lost her for good. She'd never sit and talk to me again. She was several yards away already, at the foot of the stone steps up to the bridge.

'What have you got to lose?' I yelled desperately.

I thought she mightn't have heard me but she stopped and turned. The light was fading very fast and I couldn't make out her face, only her dark spindly form. Her voice, eerily thin, came through the gloom. It gave me goosebumps. 'They hope I'm dead, Fran. For them, I am dead. Soon I will be dead. We both know that.'

'Rubbish!' I bellowed back. 'You're giving up! This isn't the time to give up!'

'Why not?' She sounded calm, too calm. I had to keep her there, keep her talking.

'Perhaps together we can think of something.'

'You're crazy, Fran. You always were. Don't try and help me. I told you, do-gooders always foul you up.'

'You're already fouled up,' I retorted. 'But you want to get out of this and I might be able to help. Or I can try.' I hadn't a clue how, mind you, and probably I shouldn't be sticking my neck out like that, but I could feel her slipping away, not just physically, but mentally. A few moments back, just for an instant, I'd made contact. 'Isn't it worth it?' I shouted. 'Or do you want to wait until Jo Jo knocks out your front teeth and then goes off with some other girl?'

She swore at me and turned on her heel. I shouted after her, 'You can find me mornings at the newsagent's by the traffic lights, just down from where I saw you the other day. Or leave a message for me there with Ganesh Patel.'

A brief abusive reply drifted back to me through the evening shades.

I let her go and wondered if I'd see her again. I told myself it didn't matter if I didn't. That was life on the streets. People came and went. If anyone vanished it might be because

59

they wanted to. Everyone had that right—to be anonymous, to be spared probing questions, needing to give an account of oneself. It was up to Tig to decide how she wanted to live. In the end, it mattered to no one but herself.

'Not to you, Fran, at any rate,' I told myself aloud. I went home.

The chap was wrong who said no man was an island. That's what each of us is, an island.

## CHAPTER FOUR

'Morning, darling!'

'Hullo, Hitch,' I returned unenthusiastically.

He was on time, I'd give him that. It was just a little after eight. I'd arrived ten minutes earlier and found Ganesh in subdued mood. I fancied he looked relieved to see me. I went to take a last look at the old washroom and I had to admit, it badly needed doing up. Hari really shouldn't complain. I just wished, somehow, it wasn't Hitch carrying out the work. There's always a snag where he's concerned, something he hasn't told you. But for the life of me, looking around the small area involved and the basic fittings, I couldn't see what it was here.

'Go and tell him to open up the back gate, will you, darling?' Hitch wheedled now. It must have got through his thick skull that he wasn't my favourite person and he was wary of me. 'So's Marco and I can bring the new stuff in and take the old out, right? You don't want it coming through here, do you?'

Ganesh came out of the storeroom at that moment so I said, 'Tell him yourself.'

'I'll go and open up,' said Ganesh, who'd obviously overheard. He gave me a very direct look which meant, I knew, don't antagonise the workforce.

Ganesh disappeared to open up the small yard out back and Hitch followed, taking a good look round him as he went. I hoped he kept his fingers to himself in the storeroom.

I was on my own. I fiddled around, tidying the mags and papers, replenishing the bins of packeted snacks and the sweet trays until the bell jingled, the paper chains and tinsel rustled, heralding a newcomer in the shop.

I emerged from behind the rack of Christmas cards and gaped. He was six foot tall and beautiful. His long blond hair was tied back with a ribbon and contrasted with large dark eyes and eyebrows in an oval face with a long narrow nose. His expression was dreamy and serene, suggesting behind it was a mind concentrating on higher spiritual matters. It was as if the Angel Gabriel had just stepped off one of the cards. Perhaps the hair was bleached—I didn't care. He wore an old dark quilted jacket and clean but paint-stained jeans and trainers. He hadn't, alas, brought a message from on high.

'Hitch around somewhere?' he asked. He had a nice voice and was altogether my idea of a Christmas present.

'Out back in the yard,' I croaked, adding in, I hoped, a more normal if incredulous voice, 'You're Marco? I'm Fran.' If he looked like any kind of painter, he ought to be one knocking out some entry for the Turner Prize.

'Oh, right. Can I get through here? Or have I got to go round?'

'You can go through, I'll show you.' I led the way to the storeroom. Perhaps having the Jefferson Hitchens Property Maintenance Company on the premises wasn't going to be so bad, after all.

\*       \*       \*

Oh yes, it was. The rest of the morning was dominated by a deafening banging and clattering from the washroom as the old fittings were torn out. Every customer who came in asked what was going on and I soon had a headache. Brief respite came roughly every hour when Hitch and Marco took a tea-break in the storeroom.

'You know,' I said to Gan, 'not that it's any of my business, but you ought to keep an eye on them in there.'

'I can't spy on them,' said Gan nervously.

'We'll take it in turns,' I said. 'I'll go first.'

I opened the storeroom door and peered in. Hitch was sitting on a plastic chair, reading the *Sun* and drinking from a large souvenir mug celebrating West Ham Football Club. There was an empty crisp packet on the table together with the crumpled wrappings from a bar of turkish delight. Marco was drinking Coca-Cola from the can and reading a Terry Pratchett novel. They glanced up.

'Need some more KitKats!' I excused my presence hastily and grabbed a carton.

'Just the job,' said Hitch, brightening. 'Cheers, darling.'

I handed them out a KitKat each and went back.

'Price of two KitKats, a can of Coke, a turkish delight and a packet of crisps to be knocked off the final bill,' I said. 'You'd better keep a tally. Has he given you the fifty pence owing from yesterday?'

Ganesh looked at me in wonder and reproach. 'I've never known you so stingy, Fran.'

'It's like Aladdin's cave in there as far as Hitch is concerned,' I warned.

Ganesh looked worried and the next time the workers took a break, he was in there like a shot, checking on them.

At eleven, I made coffee for us all, using water from the kettle I'd filled before they started work. Needless to say, the water supply was now switched off. They were quick workers, at least on the demolition side. They'd pulled out the washbasin and the loo and cistern. I'd had to go next door to the petfood shop and ask to use the loo there. This time, as I carried my offerings of coffee to our two creative builders in the storeroom, my nostrils were assailed by a distinctive sickly scent as I opened the door.

'I don't want to worry you,' I said to Ganesh, 'but Marco's smoking a joint in there.'

'What? For God's sake, stop him!' Ganesh looked as if he was going to have a heart attack. 'Anyone coming in the shop will be able to smell it!'

'You stop him,' I suggested. But in the end I was the one who went back in there and informed Marco that smoking—of whatever kind—on the premises was strictly forbidden owing to the high fire risk.

'Sure,' he said, smiling serenely up at me. I found myself smiling back, mesmerised.

'You mean, you gotta shop full of fags and you can't light up?' demanded Hitch, shocked.

'That's it,' I said. With Hitch playing gooseberry, what chance romance? 'The insurance company insists.'

'We'll have a couple of them Mars bars over there, then.' He pointed airily at the box.

By now, I didn't have to tell Ganesh to keep a tally. He was feverishly jotting it all down on a scrap of paper by the till.

'Here,' said Hitch suddenly, 'we found

64

something when we pulled the old basin out, didn't we, Marco? You got it?'

'Yeah.' Marco fished in his pocket and handed me one of those small padded envelopes. 'Jammed down behind the pipes underneath.'

'Thanks,' I said, taking it. I turned it over. It was stuck down with Sellotape. I pressed it cautiously and felt something small, cylindrical, and solid inside. I didn't recognise the shape but the envelope looked clean and fresh. Whatever it was, it couldn't have been there long.

'Dunno what it is,' prompted Hitch, adding virtuously, 'We didn't open it, Marco and me. It's stuck down.'

I forbore remarking that it was a pity the contents of the storeroom weren't stuck down. I retreated into the shop, followed by our workers, and handed the package to Ganesh.

'They found it hidden behind the pipes.'

'What is it?' asked Gan suspiciously.

'How do I know? Open it, you're the manager.'

'I'm not going to open it,' he said. 'It might explode. You read about these things in the papers. Nutters go round shops hiding incendiary devices.' Hitch and Marco backed off a little.

'What would be the point of it going off in the washroom?' I asked. 'It wouldn't set fire to anything in there. Besides, how would he get into the washroom to hide it? The public never goes in there and no one could get past whoever is working in the shop without being seen.'

'You open it, then,' he said.

'All right, I will!'

Hitch and Marco watched with interest and from a safe distance, as I tore open the envelope and shook out what appeared to be a small roll of film on to the counter top. We looked at it. Ganesh put out his hand.

'Wouldn't touch it if I was you,' said Hitch. 'Might be dodgy. You don't want your dabs on it, do you?'

That will tell you quite a bit about Hitch.

'What's it doing in the washroom?' asked Ganesh, bewildered. 'Why should anyone put it there?'

'It might be mucky,' suggested Hitch brightly. 'You know, some feller and girl getting up to things. I mean, things like in that Indian book what tells you how to do it all kinds of funny ways.' Both he and Marco gazed at Gan and myself with a new interest and some respect. 'Never read it myself,' added Hitch with regret.

This irritated Ganesh who snapped, 'Don't talk such nonsense! The *Kama Sutra* is a serious work of great beauty.'

Hitch opened his mouth to ask for further enlightenment but the look on Ganesh's face made him change his mind.

I knew why Ganesh was ratty. It wasn't just that he doesn't like to hear his culture misunderstood (although he grumbles enough about it himself), it was because that's not how things are between him and me. Some people get the wrong idea about that. Hitch wasn't the first. But Ganesh is my friend, not my lover. Not that I couldn't fancy Ganesh, or that he couldn't fancy me. There have been times when we've come awfully close to moving beyond the friendship scenario. But we both know it wouldn't work out if we did. Sex complicates things, in my experience, and for us it'd make life more than difficult. His parents have other plans for him, and I'm not part of them. They like me, or I think they do, even though they obviously fear I'm a bad influence on him and give him dangerous ideas of independence. Ganesh says they like me and they've always acted as if they do. But they simply don't understand me or my life-style, my lack of family or the way I exist from day to day. It's one of those situations. Nothing can be done about it and you just have to lump it. Still, I'm glad to have Gan as a friend because that means an awful lot.

Ganesh went on now in tones clearly meant to dash any remaining fantasies Hitch might have, 'In any case, this doesn't belong to me. Is it yours, Fran?'

'Course not!' I protested. 'I'd have said so. Why on earth should I hide it in the

67

washroom, even if it was mine? Besides, I haven't even got a camera.'

'Well, Hari wouldn't hide it there, would he?' argued Ganesh. 'If he wanted to tuck it away somewhere, he'd put it upstairs. So it isn't his.'

'That makes it no one's,' I pointed out. 'And that's daft. It has to belong to someone.'

'Oh well,' said Hitch, losing interest. 'Makes no difference to me and Marco. It's all yours whatever it is.'

The two of them drifted back to the storeroom. I took Ganesh's arm and propelled him nearer the entrance to the shop, out of earshot.

'It belongs to that bloke!' I whispered excitedly. 'It must do, Gan. You know, the one who stumbled in here the other morning? It must be his and he hid it there. You let him use the washroom to clean up. Someone was after him—after *this*—and he stashed it there to pick up later.'

'Don't be daft, Fran,' said Ganesh, but he looked uncomfortable. 'Anyone could've put it there. Even Hari, though I don't know why.'

'Of course Hari didn't put it there! Why on earth should he? Look, Gan, I didn't tell you this, but someone came in yesterday morning, asking about the guy—and wanting to know if we'd found anything dropped on the floor. He told a stupid tale about a friend of his losing something—and he offered me twenty quid.'

'Fran!' cried Ganesh, agonised. 'You didn't take it?'

'Course I didn't! I didn't say anything, either. Think I'm daft?'

Ganesh glanced at the counter and the roll of film lying on it. 'What do we do with it? Give it to the police? It really doesn't look like it's anything, but if you think someone's after it—'

'We could get it developed first.' I tried to make the idea sound as tempting as possible. 'You know, just to make sure. I mean, we can't go to the police with a blank film or someone's holiday snaps, can we? I'll take it along to Joleen at the chemist's down the road. They've got a one-hour service.'

Hitch and Marco had recommenced the labours in the washroom. Hitch was whistling piercingly as they hammered the old tiles off the walls. As each tile came loose, it fell to the ground with a shattering of ceramic.

'I can't stand much more of this,' I said. 'I'll nip along to the chemist's, anyway. I need some headache pills.'

'We sell 'em here,' said Gan, not losing his business instincts, even in the circumstances.

\*　　　\*　　　\*

I nipped back to the chemist for the developed reel at lunchtime. It was Saturday and the place was packed. Joleen, to whom I'd given the film, was dealing with a customer. Another woman in the shop fetched them for me.

'It says here,' she read from a note stapled to the yellow envelope, 'that most of the film was unused and there were only four snaps on it.' She stared at me curiously.

'Right,' I said jauntily, as if I knew. I paid her and scuttled outside with them.

I couldn't resist taking a peek on my way back to Ganesh, but they weren't very interesting. They showed three men sitting at a table in some kind of garden or possibly a planted area surrounding a swimming pool at a posh hotel. Exotic-looking flowers bloomed on a creeper growing over a whitewashed wall. To the extreme right of the picture, beyond the wall, could be glimpsed a small area of coastline, a beach of sorts, some hinterland and a smidgen of sea. One of the men was mustachioed and swarthy in appearance, one had his back to camera and I could see only dark hair and a sweat-stained grey-blue shirt. The third man, in early middle age, was either fair or grey-haired, it was hard to tell. He looked plump and prosperous, but tough, and wore a multi-coloured leisure shirt. Dark glasses hung on a safety chain round his neck. Holiday snaps, after all, I thought, and felt really disappointed. I don't know what I'd expected.

'Here,' I said, pushing them under Ganesh's nose in a gap between customers. 'What do you make of them?'

'Nothing,' said Ganesh, glancing at them.

'They've got to mean something,' I persisted.

'No, they haven't. Don't tell me that bloke who was in here the other day went to the trouble of hiding those! Four pictures of him and his mates on the Costa Brava?'

'He's not in them,' I objected. 'Not even this guy with his back to camera is him, I'm sure of it.'

'So, he was the photographer. Only he wasn't, because I don't believe they belong to him, Fran. It doesn't make any sense.'

I was peering at the snaps more closely. There was a bottle of beer on the table, label towards the camera.

'If we got this blown up,' I said, 'we could read that label and it'd give us a clue.'

'They are someone's holiday snaps,' said Ganesh patiently. 'And even you can't make out differently. Look at that chap's shirt.'

'It's somewhere warm and holiday-ish,' I mused.

'It might be the Canary Islands,' said Ganesh thoughtfully. Despite his dismissive attitude, I could see he was gradually getting as hooked on this as I was. 'Usha and Jay went there on holiday and this could easily be one of their snaps.'

Usha is his sister and Jay her accountant husband. Jay is doing spectacularly well and now Usha's studying accountancy at evening classes so she can work in his office. The better they do, the more depressed Ganesh gets. I tell him that's nobody's fault but his own. He's got to get out of the retail business.

This wasn't the moment to bring up that delicate subject. Right now the photos had priority. I didn't go along with the Canary Islands theory and said so.

'Well, it's not Bournemouth, is it?' argued Ganesh.

'That doesn't mean it has to be some other obvious holiday spot. Look, see that bit of beach? It hasn't got any parasols or sunbathers on it. And look at the landscape behind the beach. You can only see a bit of it, but it looks as if it's in the middle of nowhere, scrubby-looking trees and dried-up grass. There aren't any skyscraper hotels. The beaches in most tourist resorts are lined with hotels and bars.'

'Ever been to the Canaries?' retorted Ganesh.

I had to admit I hadn't. 'But I've seen pictures. Come to that, I've seen Usha's holiday snaps and they don't look a bit like this.'

Ganesh straightened up. 'So, what do we do with them?'

'If that bloke hid the film,' I reasoned, 'he wanted to keep it safe and my guess is, he'll come back for it. But not until he knows the coast is clear. If he thinks the men who were after him are watching this shop, he won't come here yet. He'll wait. The least we can do is keep the pics and negatives safe until he comes. So I think you should put them somewhere safe while *we* wait.'

'OK,' said Ganesh resignedly. 'I'll keep them for a week and if he hasn't come back for them in that time, I'm going to bin them, right?' He shoved the yellow packet under the till. 'Look, are you going out anywhere tonight? I've been thinking, every other business round here is having a staff Christmas dinner. So I don't see why you and I can't go out and have a decent meal at the expense of the shop.'

'Hari—' I began. I thought it only fair to remind him.

He interrupted. 'I'm the manager while Hari's away and it's my decision that the staff can have a Christmas outing. We're entitled. We've worked hard.'

'Fair enough,' I agreed. 'I'm not doing anything else.'

Ganesh nodded. 'Come back here around eight-fifteen—gives me time to lock up.' He hesitated. 'See if you can fix up your hair before then, can't you? It does look awful, Fran.'

I overlooked renewed criticism as I was being offered dinner.

73

# CHAPTER FIVE

On my way home, however, I caught sight of myself reflected in a window and Ganesh was right. My hair looked awful. A little further along, on the corner, was a small hairdressing salon. I peered in. It didn't look particularly busy. I pushed open the door.

A ferocious-looking woman, who was assaulting a customer with an outsize can of spray, looked up through a cloud of chemicals and exclaimed, 'Gawd, what scissor-happy maniac done that?'

Everyone in the shop, staff and customers, stopped their conversations, magazine-reading, cutting, washing, etc. and stared at me.

Before I could answer, she went on just as fiercely, 'You didn't get that cut here. She didn't get it done here!' she repeated more loudly for the benefit of anyone who hadn't heard.

'No, I didn't,' I said meekly. 'Can you fix it?'

'I dunno . . .' She looked at the clock on the wall.

'I'm going out tonight,' I said pathetically.

'Make the date over the phone, did he?' asked the charmer with the hairspray. 'He'll have a fit when he sees that. Oh well, sit down a tick and I'll have a go when I'm finished

74

here. That hedge on the top will have to come off.'

When I emerged, some time later, I looked like Joan of Arc about to go to the stake. My hair resembled a reddish-brown bathing cap. She'd trimmed the spikes on top back to little longer than the bits at the sides and brushed it all forward to a little wispy fringe on the forehead. I have to admit, though, it looked quite good, certainly better than before.

Because of this I didn't get home until three-thirty and the light had a dirty greyness to it presaging the early dark. But I could see the puddle in front of the house still hadn't dried up. It hadn't rained again and I wondered vaguely about it before my attention was distracted.

The lights were on in Daphne's front window, a room she seldom used, and the curtains hadn't been drawn. Through it I could see, brightly lit, Bertie and Charlie standing close together in deep discussion. Charlie was leaning on the marble mantelshelf and Bertie was puffing on a pipe. They looked the perfect pair of crooks. I couldn't see Daphne. She was probably making the unspeakable duo tea.

I resisted the urge to knock on the door and ask to see her. If she wanted to tell me what they were up to now, she'd tell me in her own good time. But the sight of them there, looking so at home as if they already owned the place, made my new haircut bristle.

I went down to the basement and my own flat, put on the kettle and sorted through my meagre wardrobe. Since I hadn't acquired any new clothes in the past three months—apart from a pair of sock-slippers kindly knitted for me by Daphne and hardly suitable for the 'staff dinner'—it looked like the ankle-length purple skirt I'd got from Oxfam and the ethnic Indian waistcoat again (Camden Lock Market), teamed with a black polo-neck sweater (BHS sale) and my Doc Marten boots, because they were the only footwear I had at that time, apart from a pair of ancient trainers with holes in both soles.

Later, when I'd showered and put it all on, I stood in front of the bathroom mirror to study the effect. I looked a real ragbag. When I was studying drama, we did a production of *Blithe Spirit* and I got to read for the part of the batty medium, Madame Arcati. Now I looked as if I was dressed for the role. I was distracted by a loud ring on my doorbell.

It wasn't even a quarter to eight yet and I didn't think it could be Ganesh. Besides, the arrangement was I meet him at the shop. As I went towards the door, I noticed an envelope lying on the mat just inside. Either someone had delivered it since I'd come home—and I hadn't heard the letter box—or I'd stepped over it in the gloom when I'd walked in. I stooped and picked it up, tucking it in my pocket, before opening the door on the chain and peering through.

It was one of the Knowleses—going by the brown jacket, Charlie. 'Good evening!' he crowed, and simpered at me in a sickly fashion. 'Can I come in for a little chat, my dear?'

'I don't know what about and I'm not your dear,' I said to the crack in the door. It was worse than being called 'darling' by Hitch. At least Hitch did it unconsciously.

'Won't take a mo,' he fluted in a coaxing voice.

I opened my mouth to tell him to get lost, but I remembered this was Daphne's nephew. So I slipped the chain and let him in. He nipped over the threshold and toddled past me, uninvited, into the living room. There he stood, dead centre, with his eyes darting all over the place. He might be related to my landlady, but he was making pretty free here, just as he and his brother had been doing upstairs when glimpsed by me through the window. Only he wasn't anything to me and I objected. Before I could let him know this, however, he added insult to injury.

'You're keeping it very tidy, I see,' he said. 'Quite a little homemaker, eh?'

The sheer rudeness of all this rather took my breath away. But I rallied. 'That what you came to check on?' I still couldn't get over the patronising old git's attitude but I kept telling myself this was Daphne's nephew. Be nice to him, Fran, even if it kills you.

He had slipped his hand into his jacket pocket and took out a small notebook. 'As a matter of fact, I have come to check—not on your housekeeping, dear, oh my, no. Purely a technical point, you might say. I understand from Aunt Daphne that when you moved in no inventory was made.'

I was starting to hyperventilate. I made myself count to ten. 'I signed an agreement with Daphne. The flat was furnished, just as you see it now.'

'Yes, but no detailed inventory was done, no actual list of items. You didn't sign for the individual contents, did you? I thought not. Aunt Daphne isn't a businesswoman, I'm afraid. It does mean that when you leave—' a faint smile hovered on his plump cheeks. He couldn't hide his hope that would be soon— 'it will be very difficult to establish that everything's in order. Now, don't be offended, my dear. This is as much in your interest as in ours. You understand that? So I thought, while Aunt Daphne . . . I thought I'd just nip down and check them off. You've got time, have you, mmn? It won't take us long. For your own protection, you know.' He gave a sickly grin.

There was something more than rotten in the state of Denmark here. But he had already flicked open the notebook and produced a gold pencil. He began to walk round the room. 'Is anything here yours? This little table? No?' He scribbled industriously. 'I see the carpet appears to be new. No marks or stains.' Scribble. 'Now, how about the kitchen? Pots and pans? These mugs?'

'Those are mine!' I snarled.

He crossed them out reluctantly. 'Now what about the bedroom?'

He was sidling towards the door which led into the little windowless bedroom beneath the pavement, formed from a Victorian coal cellar. I didn't follow but stayed where I was in the living room. He hesitated.

'Perhaps you ought to come too, dear. I don't want to list any *personal* items ...' He was breathing, I fancied, rather more heavily than he'd been doing earlier. I was beginning to get the drift of this. I mean, I'm not that thick.

More interested to see how far he'd commit himself than anything else, I followed him into the bedroom. After all, if it came to fumble and grapple, I could take care of Charlie with one hand—or a knee in the groin.

He was standing by the bed and there wasn't much room for more than one person. He wrote something in his notebook and then leered at me, eyes bulging. 'My brother and I were a little concerned when Aunt Daphne took you in.'

'She didn't take me in. I rent the flat,' I said.

'I don't somehow think you pay the full rent,' he retorted silkily.

'What I pay's between me and Daphne. Ask

her.'

He moved up against me, his face as red as beetroot. I hoped the build-up of lust in his creaking loins wasn't going to lead to some kind of seizure. If he keeled over on my bed, it wouldn't be a good situation at all.

'Things may change,' he wheezed, sweating profusely. He had open pores all over his nose. It looked like a pumice stone.

'I'm going to meet a friend of mine in fifteen minutes,' I said. 'Have you listed everything?'

'Now, then,' he said. 'Not so fast, eh? Let's say, for the sake of argument, my brother and I take over control of this house, including this flat. We might want to reconsider your position.' I said nothing and he went on, 'You are aware of your legal position with regard to fully furnished accommodation?'

'Get on with it!' I said crossly.

Unfortunately, the silly old goat misunderstood.

'I knew you'd see reason!' he yelped, dropped the notebook on the bed, and threw his pudgy arms round me.

My knee came up in automatic reaction. He let out a shriek, a gasp, and tottered back, doubled over. I scooped up his notebook and then I grabbed him by his collar. He spluttered and coughed and looked terrified.

'Look, Charlie boy,' I said, 'no fun and games. No deals. Got that? Now take your notebook and go back upstairs. And if I see you down here again, or if you try anything silly now, you're going to come off very much the worse, got it?'

'You little cow!' he gurgled. 'You assaulted me!'

'No, you assaulted me, and if you try anything like that again, I'll scream blue murder and make sure the whole street knows. Now get out!'

He staggered as far as the front door where he turned, straightened up as much as he could, and spat, 'Street is where you belong and I'll see you back out there before you can say knife, you—you trollop!'

Then he bolted before I could reply.

I slammed the door after him. Trollop? I didn't know whether to be angry or laugh. Perhaps I ought to be worried. I thought Daphne would resist their bright idea that she make over the house to the twins. But she was elderly, there were two of them to her one, and blood was notoriously thicker than water.

No time to brood over it now. Thanks to Charlie, I was running late. I pulled on my jacket and dashed out of the house.

\*         \*         \*

'You choose,' said Ganesh. 'Indian or Chinese?'

'Greek,' I said. 'That nice new taverna. The

81

shop's paying, isn't it?'

The taverna was busy and we were lucky to get a table without booking. What they call the chattering classes were well represented in the crowded room, together with well-heeled City types. The general atmosphere was just that bit noisier, the customers just that bit more jovial, more slap-happy, because Christmas was coming. They all felt they had a licence to go out and make merry, even an obligation to. After all, that's what Gan and I were doing there. The Greek staff were taking it in their stride. It was all good business. But since their Christmas wasn't due until January, they were keeping their heads about it.

'Why do people do it?' I asked Ganesh, as I looked around the crowded room. 'I mean, years ago, I suppose people didn't take many holidays or go out for a good blow-out so often and once a year was special. But this lot—half of them are on expense-account lunches all the year round and eat pretty well even when they aren't. They party all year. They take holidays, sailing round the Caribbean or skiing or pretending to be Tuscan peasants or what-have-you. But just look at them. You'd think they'd been let out of the workhouse for a binge.'

'It's truce time,' said Gan. 'You know, bury the hatchet in the ground and not in each other. It doesn't happen often. It's like the old Greeks. They used to call a halt to their wars during the period of the Olympic Games. I read that in a Sunday supplement.'

I had noticed, that since working at the newsagent's, Gan had become a mine of odd information gleaned from a variety of magazines. He could tell you the top restaurants, the season's fashion colour, how much it would cost you to go camel-trekking across the Gobi desert, the world's ten best-dressed men and the best-kept secrets of the stars. None of this was of the slightest use to him, but he just liked knowing it and, if the opportunity offered, telling me.

Over the meal, I told him about Charlie's visit and his grotesque advances. 'I couldn't believe what I was seeing and hearing,' I said. 'Did he honestly think—'

'Course he did,' said Ganesh indistinctly, chewing.

'What's that supposed to mean?' I demanded.

He swallowed. 'Keep your hair on.' This struck him as funny and he fell about giggling for a bit. When he'd calmed down, he went on, 'He doesn't know you. He thought he'd try his luck.'

'Well, his luck ran out.'

Ganesh wiped his mouth with his napkin and pronounced, 'He and his brother won't rest till they've got you out, Fran.'

'Tell me something I don't know,' I muttered.

'Be careful.'

'Am I ever anything else?' At this point, I put my hand in my pocket for my hanky and my fingers encountered the envelope I'd put there earlier and quite forgotten during my encounter with the rampant Charlie.

I pulled it out and put it on the table. Ganesh squinted at it and asked, 'What's that?'

'I don't know. Someone must have put it through my door and I didn't see it when I went into the flat. I hadn't switched on the light and it was pretty gloomy down there. Besides, I was thinking about the twins and how pleased with themselves they looked up there in Daphne's drawing room. I didn't see the envelope until I went to let Charlie in.'

'Well, open it!' he prompted impatiently. 'What does it say?'

'It might be private,' I pointed out, but my fingers were tearing at the seal.

Inside was a single sheet of paper, torn from a pad, and folded over. On it was scribbled:

You were kind enough to render first aid at the newsagent's recently. I need to talk to you. I'll call back tonight at ten, if that isn't too late.
      Yours,
      Gray Coverdale

'Look, look!' I squeaked, jabbing a finger at

the note. 'You said that reel of film didn't belong to him! I told you it did. It must do. What else would he want to see me about? I thought someone was following me yesterday. It must've been Coverdale spying out where I lived.'

Ganesh looked at his wristwatch. 'It's gone half-past nine.'

'Then what are we waiting for?' I jumped to my feet. 'Ask for the bill!'

*　　　*　　　*

We hurried to the flat as fast as we could make it, but it was still going to be after ten by the time we got there. I hoped Coverdale would wait. As we turned into the street I searched the pavements but there was no one about and no strange cars waited at the kerb. The wind whistled chilly round my shaven head and Ganesh hunched his shoulders, sinking his chin into his upturned jacket collar.

'Looks like he's been and gone, Fran.'

'He mightn't have arrived yet. It can't be more than ten minutes past. He might be in the basement.'

The front of the house was in darkness. That didn't mean Daphne was out or in bed, but that she was probably in her preferred sitting room overlooking the back garden. At least Bertie and Charlie would appear to have left.

I began to clatter down the steps to the basement well, Ganesh at my heels, when suddenly his hand gripped my shoulder. 'Hang on, Fran!' he said sharply.

On mid steps we both paused and peered down. The well was gloomy, the yellow sulphurous gleam of the streetlamps only touching the far corner. Yet in the near corner, right up by the flat entrance, the darkness seemed oddly different, blacker and thicker. As I stared, I began to make out a shape, huddled against the door. It didn't move and I tried to tell myself it was only a trick of the shadows.

Ganesh had no such doubts. 'Someone's there, Fran.' His voice breathed the words into my ear. I shivered and leaned over the railing.

'Mr Coverdale, is that you? It's Fran Varady, the girl from the newsagent's. I got your note.'

There was no reply. The shape—I didn't doubt now Ganesh was right that it was human—didn't move. There was something horrible about its stillness. Even a sleeping body in a doorway radiates a kind of life. This gave out nothing.

I moved slowly to the bottom of the steps and waited there, unwilling to investigate any further. Uncertainly I said, 'I'm sorry we're late.' I spoke because I wanted to hear a human voice, even my own, not because I expected an answer. None came. The wind rattled the railings and the streetlamp's yellow pool of light quivered. A few late-falling leaves rustled at my feet.

'Do you think it's a drunk or a down-and-out?' I whispered to Ganesh. 'You know, just thought he'd found a good place to sleep it off?'

Ganesh squeezed past me and walked up to the huddled form. 'Hey, mate?' He stooped. 'You all right, there? Come on, wake up. Can't sleep outside the lady's front door.'

He put his hand on the shape's shoulder and shook gently. Slowly, with a scrape of clothing against the brick wall, the shape tilted sideways, uncoiled and collapsed. No longer a huddle in the shadows, it became a human being, sprawled across the basement pavement at our feet. The man's head, previously tucked into his chest, fell into the patch of streetlight. It shone down on a livid but recognisable face.

'That's Coverdale!' I gasped.

Ganesh dropped on his knees and, his long black hair veiling his face as he crouched over the body, put his fingers to Coverdale's neck. Then he tore at the front of the prone figure's overcoat, trying to locate the heart.

Suddenly he muttered, jerked back his exploring fingers and raised his hand for my inspection. Even in the gloom, I could see Ganesh's palm was smeared with streaks which, though they looked black rather than scarlet in this light, I knew were blood.

'He's dead, Fran,' Ganesh said, his voice shaking. 'Looks like he's been stabbed.'

## CHAPTER SIX

We didn't panic, Ganesh and I, but the situation did develop rapidly into semi-controlled chaos. I raced up the steps to Daphne's front door where I rang the bell and shouted through her letter box until she opened up in visible alarm. I was glad to see she hadn't gone to bed but wore her reading glasses and clutched a rainbow-striped knitted cardigan about her thin frame.

'Fran? What's happened?'

Bearing in mind she was elderly, I knew I should break it gently. But a body in the basement isn't the kind of news which lends itself to being wrapped up in soothing words. I did my best and told her there'd been an accident and I needed to use the phone.

'An ambulance?' she cried, snatching off the reading glasses to see me better. 'Who's hurt, Fran? Not you? I hope it isn't that nice young man from the newsagent's.'

'No, it's not Gan and I don't need an ambulance—I need the police.'

I had to tell her about the dead man, there was no way out of it. She reeled back but, true to form, she rallied fast. Daphne is tough.

'You are quite sure he's dead, Fran? You're not a doctor. Perhaps you should send for an ambulance as well.' She patted the cardigan pockets wildly. 'So silly, I ought to have my other glasses. Perhaps I should come and have a look? I did a first-aid course once. I know how to put him in the recovery position and that sort of thing. We should wrap him in a blanket, but not give him anything to drink.'

All this sounded so sensible that for a moment I even hoped that after all, Coverdale might only be unconscious. But even before the hope took root, I knew it was no more than a desperate wish unlikely to be fulfilled. The recovery position, I explained to Daphne, wasn't going to help Coverdale. Nor was he in need of a blanket. He was dead, all right, and I didn't think it a good idea if she came downstairs to view the body. But I asked for an ambulance anyway.

The paramedics confirmed the diagnosis the moment they arrived. Or as one of them murmured to his mate, 'No rush, this one's a stiff.'

During the few minutes' wait before the ambulance arrived at the door, Daphne had provided tea and brandy in her kitchen for myself and Ganesh. We sat miserably avoiding one another's eye until Daphne, perhaps desperate to talk, took the opportunity to make an apology for which she'd no reason at all.

'This gives me a chance, Fran dear, to say how sorry I was to learn how badly my nephew Charlie behaved earlier today.'

Even with my mind on other things, I was startled. Had Charlie confessed his amorous advances? No.

'He had no right whatsoever to come downstairs without even mentioning it to me and ask you to agree an inventory. He did it entirely off his own bat and I'm very annoyed with him. I told him so. It's absolutely none of his business and I shouldn't have allowed it, if I'd known what was in his mind.'

She hadn't known all that was in Charlie's mind and he certainly hadn't told her about the scuffle in the bedroom. But he had told her about the inventory in case I complained. He could deny the little episode in the bedroom, but he couldn't deny he'd been in the flat. It went without saying that Daphne must guess that Charlie had crept down to the basement without mentioning it to her, because he'd known full well she'd have forbidden it.

'I realised you had nothing to do with it, Daphne,' I said. 'You don't have to say sorry. Forget it.'

Nevertheless, I hoped she didn't, and that it'd have demonstrated to her that Charlie and Bertie were already counting their chickens, and she must be on the watch for further tricks on their part.

                    *          *          *

'Well, at least we know who the poor bugger was,' said DS Parry.

On the heels of the ambulance, a patrol car of uniformed men turned up. Swiftly after that, CID moved in, in the person of Parry, also the police doctor and a posse of photographers.

I had hoped that after my last run-in with Sergeant Parry, I'd seen the last of him. But no, here he was again, sitting in Daphne's kitchen, drinking coffee, still trying unsuccessfully to grow that moustache, still suffering from a shaving rash and with a haircut even worse than mine. His resembled a ginger coir mat.

You wouldn't think, would you, with disadvantages like that, and lacking any kind of charm, Parry could possibly imagine I might be brought round to fancying him? But deep in what passes for his heart, or more likely in what passes for his brain, it seems he fantasises about me. It was Ganesh who pointed this out to me and at first I wouldn't—couldn't—believe it. But I've been brought round to the horrid conclusion Gan is right about this, as about so much else.

Outside, men measured and photographed and crawled round under their arc-lights for clues to put in their plastic bags. The remaining population of the street had turned out to watch and speculate, but were kept back behind a blue and white plastic tape tied across the thoroughfare. Behind the crowd, indignant motorists had got out of their cars to demand why they were being denied access.

Inside this cordon, like a set of plague victims sealed off from normal humanity, we were at Parry's mercy.

He took Daphne's statement first, rightly surmising whatever she had to say would be less interesting than anything he could bully out of Ganesh and me. Daphne hadn't heard or seen anything because she'd been in her sitting room at the back of the house. Parry thanked her with a politeness he never wasted on me, before dismissing her from her own kitchen and turning his attention to Ganesh and me, his preferred prey. Daphne was the starter, we were the main course.

'All right, then, let's have it,' he said. 'You first, Miss Varady, being as it's your flat where the bloke copped it.'

'Not *in* my flat,' I protested vigorously, '*outside* my flat!'

'In your basement,' said Parry, unimpressed.

I told him my version and Ganesh told him his, which was virtually the same. We also had to tell him about the business at the shop when Coverdale—as we now knew him to be—staggered in and I told him about the man who'd come enquiring later.

The *bombe surprise* was Hitch's discovery of the packet behind the pipes of the washroom and the roll of film it contained. This had Parry scribbling like a man possessed, all the while chewing one straggling corner of his moustache, his expression steadily more disapproving.

When he heard that I'd taken the film to be developed, he stopped scribbling and turned puce. 'You did what? Don't tell me, I can guess. You were playing detective again, Fran? Right? How many times have I told you? You got anything suspicious to report, you bring it to us.'

'It wasn't suspicious,' I argued.

'You still oughta have reported it. Where are these snaps now?'

'At the shop, stuck under the till,' Ganesh said.

'Then we'll have to go over there and collect 'em, won't we, son? If they're still there—which I hope they are. If they're not, you two are in a spot of trouble. They're material evidence, they are.'

'Look!' I said sharply. 'We didn't know he was going to get murdered, did we? We offered to call the police when he was beaten up and he didn't want it. What else could we do?'

'You are certain, are you,' Ganesh asked in a very formal voice, 'of your identification? The only reason we're calling him Coverdale, as I see it, is because a note signed in that name was pushed through Fran's letter box.'

Parry gave Ganesh a dirty look. 'Well, no one's identified him yet, if that's what you mean. But he'd got business cards in that name in his pocket and a press pass with his phizog on it. He's—was—a journalist, Graeme Coverdale. Don't worry, we'll track down someone who knew him to take a look at him in the morgue.' Nice.

Parry was tucking away his notebook. 'I think the best thing would be if a constable accompanied you to the shop, Mr Patel, to get those photos and negatives. You'd better stay here, Fran—Miss Varady—until Inspector Harford arrives. He'll want to talk to you, both of you.' Parry gave a sinister leer.

'Who's he?' I asked. Obviously this was a serious crime and they weren't leaving it entirely to Parry, but there was a relish in Parry's voice which suggested Harford would prove some sort of ogre. Parry, by contrast, would be a regular Peter Pan.

'Harford? Oh, he's the blue-eyed boy, he is. Graduate intake, fast-track promotion. He's been to university, has Inspector Harford.' Parry oozed rancour. Even the ginger hair in his ears seemed to bristle. Then he rolled his bloodshot gaze in my direction and added, 'So don't you try giving him any lip, Fran. He's not tolerant, like me.'

On this breath-taking misstatement, he ushered Ganesh out of the door and left me in the kitchen.

94

Daphne put her head round. 'All right, Fran?'

'Wonderful,' I said gloomily. 'I'm waiting for an Inspector Harford, apparently the Met's finest.'

'A car's just drawn up outside,' she said. 'I'll go and spy out the land.'

She pottered off quite cheerfully. Daphne never fails to amaze me and I realised that far from being terrified at the thought of gory death in her basement, Daphne was enjoying all the hullabaloo. This must beat reading about murder in one of the whodunits lining her shelves. This was the real thing.

There was much conversation going on in her hallway. I could hear Parry's voice and another man's, more of a tenor to Parry's bass growl. Daphne scurried back.

'He's here!' she announced, eyes shining. 'And he's awfully young. I suppose policemen do get younger as one gets older, but really, this one looks like a schoolboy. I suppose he's got enough experience for this sort of thing. It hardly seems possible.'

Unfortunately, as she spoke the last words, a new figure loomed up behind her.

'Good evening.' The voice had a noticeable edge to it. He'd overheard. 'My name is Harford. Excuse me, madam,' the newcomer sidestepped Daphne, 'I'd like a word with Miss Varady, if she's up to it.'

He didn't look like a schoolboy, but also he

didn't look all that much older than me, though I suppose he must be. He was chunkily built, with a shock of light brown hair, parted on the side and brushed straight with a ruthless hand. Add to that, a wide mouth, good complexion, blue eyes and, most striking of all, an air of arrogant self-possession. He was wearing an expensive-looking suit and a clean shirt, all pressed and starched, even at this time of night. I wondered if he'd jumped into his car when he'd got the summons, or taken time to shower and change first.

His voice matched his looks, with clean-cut vowels which must have made him something of a novelty at our local nick. In fact, I shouldn't have thought they knew what to make of him at all. I'd have loved to be a fly on the canteen wall.

I met his gaze and found it was studying me in no very generous way. By comparison, my own appearance was distinctly at fault. Harford's gaze suggested he classed me with something brought in by the cat. I was glad I'd had my hair trimmed, but wished I wasn't wearing the assembled contents of a jumble sale stall. If I'd been sitting here in a power suit and stilettos I might have stood a chance. As it was, he'd clearly labelled me riffraff.

'Right, let's get started, shall we?' he said bossily, taking his place at Daphne's table. I felt a fleeting sympathy for Parry.

'The coffee's cold,' I said, to make amends

for Daphne getting us off on the wrong foot. 'I can make some more.'

'We won't worry about coffee.' His tone put me firmly in my place. 'Now, I've had a quick word with Sergeant Parry and glanced over your statement and Mr Patel's. But I'd like to hear it from you.'

'Starting from when?' I asked.

'From the incident at the shop where I believe you're employed.' He made it sound as though I sold sex aids and porno videos.

'It's just a newsagent's,' I said. 'And I work mornings only.' He said nothing, only sat there looking fit, sharp and unpredictable, like a police dog. So I went through it all again, about the stranger, whom I now knew to be Coverdale, how someone had come to the shop enquiring about him, how Marco and Hitch had found the envelope containing the film and how I'd taken it to be developed. This last, as expected, proved the stickiest bit.

'Why did you take the film to be developed?' he asked.

'There might have been something on it to tell us whose it was.'

'But you realised it had been hidden by a total stranger. Why did you think you'd recognise anything on the film?'

'I supposed—we supposed—it'd been hidden. We didn't know it for sure. We didn't know what sort of pics they were. They looked like holiday snaps.'

'Why should someone want to hide holiday snaps?'

'How should I know? I'm not the detective, you are!' I retorted unwisely.

He froze. The blue eyes bored into me. 'Just answer the questions, Miss Varady, if you don't mind.'

'I do mind. I've been through this already for Parry.' I realised I was doing badly but his attitude was niggling me. He was managing to make it sound as if I was hiding something.

'Tell me about this evening.'

I told him how I'd found the note but hadn't read it until I was in the restaurant with Ganesh.

'Ah, yes, your boss, Mr Patel, had taken you out to dinner. Does he often do that?'

'It was our staff Christmas dinner,' I said tightly. Now it was my friendship with Ganesh he was managing to make sound seedy. 'We went to a Greek restaurant.'

'Food any good?' he asked suddenly.

He must think I was stupid. 'I had the moussaka and Ganesh had something which was mostly chickpeas. He's a vegetarian. You can check at the restaurant. The waiter's name was Stavros. He had it on a label pinned to his shirt.'

Harford's face twitched. He leaned forward slightly. 'You still have this note?'

'I gave it to Parry.'

'Ah—' He paused and straightened up.

'You're something of an old acquaintance of Sergeant Parry's, I understand.'

'We've met. Strictly official.'

'Yes . . .' Harford tugged at his crisp white cuffs. 'You do seem to attract trouble, Miss Varady. I made a few enquiries before I came over here. Not your first brush with murder, is it? Or three murders, to be exact, not to mention a kidnapping.'

'I don't go around collecting corpses,' I said wearily. 'I wasn't involved in the others. I just happened to be around and got drawn in.'

'The bodies just drop in your vicinity?'

Was this meant to be a joke? He wasn't smiling although there was a sort of rictus round his mouth. If he was joking, it was at my expense.

'I can't tell you anything else,' I snapped. 'Go and enquire about Coverdale, if that's his real name. That's your lead, for goodness' sake. Parry says he was a journalist. Find out what story he was working on. I bet it's connected with that.'

'I think we can manage our own investigations, thank you!' His face had reddened. 'I—we don't need advice from you.'

'It seems to me you're wasting time, sitting here with me,' I countered. 'Look, Coverdale said in his note he'd come back at ten o'clock. Ganesh and I were here by quarter past ten, but Coverdale was already dead. So he couldn't have been dead long. What does the doctor say?'

'That's police information.' The red flush had now crept up his throat. He looked about to explode.

'Well, I reckon it couldn't have been more than fifteen—twenty minutes. Someone followed him here.'

'That's supposition.'

'Or was waiting for him when he arrived,' I mused. 'It's dark in the well. Someone could have been hiding down there.'

And Ganesh and I had just missed him. It was an eerie thought. A few minutes earlier and we could have met the killer coming back up the basement steps, knife in hand.

'We've thought of that!' Harford was getting really annoyed. 'Just leave the detection to us, will you? Don't start pretending you're Miss Marple.'

'Miss Marple? *Miss Marple!*' I fairly bounced in my chair with rage. 'Do I look like some old girl who snoops on her neighbours? How about a murder weapon? Have you found it?'

'Look, I'm asking the questions.' He was getting flustered now. That 'I'm-in-charge' air was slipping. Now it was more 'it's-my-cricket-bat-and-I-say-who's-out!' 'Let's get back to Coverdale.'

'That's what I was telling you to do,' I muttered.

'Thank you!' he retorted sarcastically. 'Did

100

you see anyone else in the street when you arrived? Anyone walking, driving, anyone apparently going into a house.'

I said we hadn't. I was sure. I'd been scanning the scene for Coverdale and I'd have noticed anyone else.

'How,' asked Harford, 'did the killer know he'd find Coverdale here?'

'He followed him,' I said patiently.

'All right, so how did Coverdale learn your address?'

'Someone followed *me* from the shop yesterday, I'm fairly sure of it. It could've been him.'

'But you didn't see him? He didn't approach you?'

'Of course he didn't. Someone else might have been watching me. He had to be careful.'

'Not careful enough, it seems,' said Harford as if the whole thing was entirely my fault.

Luckily we were interrupted. A tap at the door heralded Parry, looking pleased with himself. He brandished a yellow envelope.

'Got 'em, sir. Got the snaps and the negs.'

Harford rose to his feet with dignity. I got the impression he wasn't sorry for the interruption either.

'Good man,' he said. 'Thank you for your time, Miss Varady. We'll talk again.'

Parry gave me a triumphant wink.

'Do you know, Daphne,' I said, when they'd left, 'I never thought I'd say it, but I think I'd

101

rather deal with Parry than with Inspector Harford.'

'He's a very handsome young man, isn't he?' said Daphne sentimentally.

I'd noticed that, but I wasn't going to let it influence me. Women of Daphne's age, I told myself, were susceptible to young men of Harford's ilk. Not so yours truly.

Eventually, after all the photographs were taken, everything measured up, and documented, they dismantled their lights and Coverdale's body was removed, leaving behind a sinister chalked outline, over which I had to step to return to the flat at one in the morning. They really didn't want me returning to the flat at all. They said I'd be interfering with a scene of crime. I pointed out I wasn't going to sleep in the basement well, but in my flat, in my bed—and Coverdale hadn't crossed my doorstep. I can't say I relished the idea of going into the flat, let alone sleeping there alone that night, but I insisted as a matter of principle, even though Daphne offered me a bed.

'Don't touch anything, right?' Parry warned.

'He wasn't ever in my flat,' I repeated, I don't know for what number of times.

'We'll just check, shall we?'

Parry followed me into the flat, also stepping over the chalk outline, and stared around. 'It don't look touched,' he admitted.

'It's not. Now can I be left in peace in my

own home? I've had a very trying evening.'

'Just mind how you go in and out. Don't touch anything in the stairwell. Although we'll want your dabs for elimination. Bloke will come round tomorrow for 'em.'

'Where've I heard that before?' I muttered.

They were still scurrying around out there when I went to bed, and in a way that was comforting. I still went to sleep with the light on.

\* \* \*

'Hitch looked in this morning and turned the water off again,' said Ganesh plaintively. 'He said he and Marco will come over later and install the new loo and washbasin ready for tomorrow morning.'

It was Sunday morning and he'd arrived around nine. That's classed as daybreak on a Sunday in my book at the best of times and after a disturbed night, I'd hoped for a lie-in. I wasn't dressed or ready for visitors and had to open the door in my Snoopy nightshirt.

'Turn it on again,' I said grumpily, padding back inside.

'I did and it spurted out the hole in the wall where the washroom tap used to be.'

'But you must be able to turn off the washroom plumbing separately.'

'Well, I haven't found a way to do it. Can I use your shower?'

'How much are they charging you to come in on a Sunday?' I asked. 'Or haven't they said?'

'Hitch is a mate,' Ganesh defended him. 'He's doing it so's we don't have to keep running round to the petshop on Monday morning every time we want to take a leak. You know how you grumbled about that.'

'That's right, blame me. Go and take your shower.'

I trailed back to the bedroom and tugged on jeans and a sweater. Ganesh was still locked in the bathroom when I came back, and outside the window, in the basement, the police were back and still searching around. There was a guy fingerprinting the doorway and the windowsill. Like it or not, I was living on a scene of crime. I made coffee against the splashing of water from the bathroom and handed Ganesh a mug as he emerged, his long black hair dripping. I could've made coffee for SOCO outside, but I drew the line at that. They were causing me enough disruption.

'Got a hair dryer?' Ganesh asked.

'Do me a favour,' I said. 'With a haircut like mine? What'd I do with a hair dryer?'

'I'll catch cold,' he said sulkily.

'I'll turn up the gas fire. Gimme that towel.'

He sat in front of the gas fire grumbling as I towel-dried his long hair briskly. 'Ouch! Ow! That's my ear, Fran!'

'Oh, shut up or do it yourself!'

'He grilled me again, too, you know,' said Ganesh, emerging from the towel. 'Harford, I mean. He went bananas over those negatives. Said we should've turned them in straight away. But there wasn't anything on them for us to need to do that.'

'Conceited snooty prat.'

'Got your back up, then, I see. I thought he seemed bright enough. He's probably worried you won't take him seriously.'

'I do take him seriously. He's set to be a real pain. What else did he ask you?'

'Kept making me go over the same thing over and over again. I began to wish we'd just chucked those photos away.'

'Harford would love that,' I said. 'I wish I knew who the rich-looking guy in them is. He must be the one who was after Coverdale to get them back. Why is he so worried about them? They don't show anything criminal, just three guys having a drink.'

'Perhaps it's to do with the other two men in the pictures? I know you can only see one's face. Perhaps this other man is the one who wants the negatives back.'

I shook my head. 'No, the dark one is just a regular thug. The light-haired man with the bright shirt is the important figure. He's the one we've got to worry about.'

Ganesh put down the towel and stared at me in concern. 'We've got to worry?'

'Yes, of course we have. He doesn't know

105

where the film is and he's still looking, right? I bet whoever killed Coverdale went through his pockets and didn't find it. They know Coverdale ran into the shop to escape his pursuers the other day. They'll find out pretty quick I work there. Coverdale was ringing my doorbell when his killer found him. What would you make of it all, if you were him?'

Ganesh looked unhappy. 'I should've warned Dilip. He's looking after the shop this morning.' They were open for the Sunday newspapers until noon.

'Dilip's built like a brick barn,' I reassured him. 'He can look after himself.'

A ring at the bell announced that the fingerprint guy whose visit Parry had promised me, was ready for me. He took my prints. 'Are you the bloke who was with her last night?' he asked Ganesh. 'Right, let's be having yours as well.'

'My father,' said Ganesh emotionally, scrubbing black ink from his fingertips when the man had gone, 'must never know about this.'

'It's routine, calm down,' I said, old hand at this sort of thing as I was by now.

But Ganesh carried on fretting and said he ought to go back to the shop and make sure Dilip was still in one piece. I walked out of the flat with him, through the SOCO, and up to pavement level, ducking under the police tape which still cordoned off my basement. Across the road, someone was taking photographs of the front of the house. He didn't look like a copper and I suspected he was press.

The road was open to traffic again and, as we emerged, a taxi drew up and out popped the Knowles brothers. They were wearing identical blazers today, with some badge or other on the breast pocket, but by now I could tell them apart, having had the chance to view Charlie so close at hand in my flat. He had the coarser skin and slightly less hair, but he did have his own teeth. Bertie, I noticed now as he bared them at me in rage, didn't.

'We knew it!' they cried in unison. 'Nothing but trouble! Poor Aunt Daphne! A victim of her own kind heart.'

'What are you talking about?' snapped Ganesh, who was in no mood for this sort of thing. 'Who are these people, Fran?'

'Oh,' I said with a sigh, because this was all I needed. 'Allow me to introduce Bertie and Charlie Knowles, Daphne's nephews. I did mention them to you before.'

'And who,' asked Bertie icily, 'is this gentleman?'

'He's Mr Patel. I work for him.'

'Work? Indeed?' said Bertie nastily.

'Murder!' Charlie moved in, practically salivating with revenge. He flung out a hand towards the basement and the boiler-suited figures down there. 'To think poor Aunt Daphne, a solitary, defenceless lady of mature

107

years, could have had her throat cut. And all because of you.'

'We shall insist,' said Bertie, 'that you leave these premises at once! Aunt Daphne cannot be left at risk.'

'Hey!' said Ganesh indignantly. 'She didn't do anything. It was all a bit of bad luck.'

'Luck?' Charlie sneered. 'I'd say it was your seedy lifestyle and unsavoury connections leading to violence, crime and God knows what else. From the start we told Aunt Daphne she should never have taken in a person like you, straight from the street.'

'I wasn't living on the street, I was in a council flat,' I told them. I was glad they hadn't seen the flat in question, a condemned high-rise in a block from hell. It was the second of such flats I'd had. The first had been trashed by neighbourhood kids. Before that, I'd always lived in squats. I have what the council likes to call 'low priority' on the housing list, i.e., no clout at all.

'We shall, if necessary, take legal steps,' chimed in Bertie. 'Aunt Daphne must be protected.'

At this juncture, the door at the top of the steps flew open and Daphne appeared. She might be frail and in her seventies, incongruously clad in jogging pants and Fair Isle socks, but she radiated authority.

'Charles, Bertram!' she called. 'Stop that at once!'

The twins fell silent and shuffled, shamefaced, like a pair of five-year-olds caught throwing stones.

'I will not permit you to harass Francesca,' went on Daphne majestically. 'She has had a frightening experience for such a young girl. I apologise, Fran. Bertie and Charlie—inside!'

She withdrew and the Knowles brothers scuttled up the steps after her, their voices chiming in duet.

'Horrified to hear—so pleased to see you unharmed—a dreadful experience—not safe in your own home—warned you about that girl—change all the locks . . .'

The door shut on them, cutting off further accusations against me and lurid scenarios of what might have happened.

'Weird,' said Ganesh.

'I just hope they don't frighten Daphne,' I said. 'She's been fine till now.' I glanced down at my feet where the puddle in the gutter still hadn't dried out and seemed to my eye to have got bigger, spreading out into the road.

'It didn't rain last night, did it, Gan?'

'No,' said Ganesh. 'Does it matter?'

'I was just wondering,' I said.

'I'd have thought you got something more to wonder about than the weather!' was his reply.

# CHAPTER SEVEN

I walked round to the shop at lunchtime, mainly to avoid having to watch the SOCO scrabbling around in my basement. What's more, I had a feeling Parry was going to turn up at some point and I really couldn't cope with him again so soon. Parry's best taken in small doses.

Outside the house, a notice had appeared, tied on the lamppost. It informed passers-by that a serious incident had occurred, giving time and date, and requested anyone who'd seen anything unusual in the vicinity to notify the local nick. I doubt anyone could've seen what was going on in a dark basement well. It made a nice, ironic touch, though, considering the yellow Neighbourhood Watch notices which sprouted in several windows up and down the street. Since none of the neighbours had called the police last night, they'd all been confining their watching to their television screens, presumably.

Two of the local good citizens were standing before the notice, looking serious. 'Time for a meeting, Simon,' said one.

That was par for the neighbourhood. Not good on action, but dab hands at meetings.

They were just closing up the newsagent's when I arrived at twelve, as was normal for a

Sunday. Dilip was standing in the doorway with Ganesh.

You can't miss Dilip. The impression he gives is that he's as broad as he's tall. He has a walrus moustache and immensely powerful shoulders. His normal job is running a hot-dog stall and he never has any backchat from the punters.

'No trouble?' I asked hopefully.

'No trouble,' growled Dilip. 'But a kid came round asking for you.'

'For me?' I was startled.

'Young girl, skinny, looked like she was going to peg out at any minute.' Dilip doesn't approve of skinny people. He thinks everyone ought to be built on the same lines as himself.

It had to be Tig and I was taken aback. I really hadn't thought she'd get in touch with me. I wondered what had happened to prompt her change of heart and asked if she'd left a note.

He shook his head. 'She said she'd come in again some time.'

It was a pity and might prove an opportunity missed for good. When someone's in Tig's situation, there may only be the one moment when they're prepared to allow anyone to help. Miss it and it's gone. From within the shop came a loud clatter and clang and the sound of Hitch swearing.

'Got the workers in, I see?' I observed.

' 'Sall right,' said Dilip. 'I locked them out of

111

the storeroom and they didn't argue.'

He took himself off. I followed Ganesh back inside in time to see Marco stagger in from the back yard carrying a lavatory pan. In his arms, it looked like a piece of modern sculpture. 'Hi!' he said, smiling serenely at me. I smiled back, all silly.

'See,' said Ganesh. 'It'll be all fixed up by tomorrow. All they'll have to do is slap a bit of paint round and finish fixing the wall tiles. It's going to look really good. Come and see what they've done already.'

They'd put in the washbasin and new extractor fan and I had to admit the place was shaping up very well. I still felt a niggle of unease, though about what specifically I couldn't say, but dismissed it, telling myself it wasn't my problem.

'Where's the old stuff?' I asked.

'Taken that to the dump, darling,' said Hitch. 'Don't you worry about that. I've taken care of it.'

\*       \*       \*

Ganesh and I went upstairs to the flat over the shop and made sandwiches. We'd talked ourselves to a standstill about Coverdale, so we talked about Tig instead. I explained her situation and why I was worried about her.

'She ought to go home,' said Ganesh.

'It's not as easy as that.'

'Still the best chance she's got.'

*     *     *

I set off back to the flat when I judged the SOCO team would've left. They had, and taken away the plastic tape, but I'd forgotten the press. A couple of bored guys in raincoats, sharing a Thermos, leaped into action as I appeared and cornered me at the top of the steps down into the basement.

'Fran, is it? Could we have a word?'

'No,' I said, trying to get past.

Fat chance. 'We understand you found the body. Did you know him? Why was he in your basement? Had you arranged to meet him? What's his connection—'

'For crying out loud,' I said wearily. 'How the hell do I know? I met him once. I don't know how he wound up dead in my basement.'

They exchanged glances. 'Look,' one of them said confidentially. 'He was a journo, right? Like us. He had to be on a story.'

'If he was,' I said, 'I don't know what it was.' A thought struck me. 'Here,' I said. 'You'd know which paper he worked for. It must know what he was up to.'

'Forget it,' said one of them. 'He was freelance, was Gray. He had quite a reputation.'

'Oh?' I said encouragingly. 'What sort of reputation?'

113

'For news,' said the other. 'He dug up some great stories. He could smell 'em out. Knew how to sell 'em, too, to the highest bidder. Editors were ready to give their eye-teeth for some of the stories Gray Coverdale ran to earth.'

He sounded wistful. The thought seemed to have slipped him by that digging out another great story might just have got Coverdale killed. It did seem to occur to them both, however, that they were giving out more information than they were getting.

'Come on,' they wheedled. 'At least tell us how you met him. Go on, it can't hurt.' Two false smiles beamed down on me.

'Are you crazy? The police would go ballistic if I talked to you.'

'Just general background, you know, something we can take back to our editors. Give us a break.'

They sounded pathetic, ill-used, at imminent risk of the sack if I didn't give them any information.

I was rescued, if that was the word, by a car drawing up. They swung round eagerly.

'Right,' said Inspector Harford. 'The lady's got nothing to say. Got that? Nothing.'

*     *     *

I had to ask him in. I had little choice. Watched by the two presshawks, we descended

114

the basement steps and I conducted him into the living area of my flat, a largish room with the tiny kitchenette and bathroom off it.

'Nice place,' he said, taking a good look. 'You're lucky. How did you find it? I'm trying to find a new place. Where I live now means too much time lost travelling.'

'I wasn't just lucky,' I said. 'I helped someone out—and later he helped me out. He's a friend of Daphne's.'

'That wouldn't be Monkton, would it? The old guy whose granddaughter was found hanged in a squat over by the river, Rotherhithe way?'

'Well, you seem to know all about it,' I said sourly. But he must do, of course. He'd mentioned it in passing the first time we'd met. This wasn't my first encounter with violent death and he wouldn't forget it.

Through the small window at the far end of the living room could be glimpsed Daphne's back lawn. Due to the sloping topography, it was at eyelevel. Immediately outside the window was a sort of ditch, enabling light to get in. So I shouldn't look out on to the bare earth wall of the ditch, Daphne had disguised it, not very well, as a rockery. Unfortunately, the plants hadn't flourished in the sunless, damp ravine. All to be seen were lumps of rocks jutting through mud and suggesting a half-hearted archeological excavation. Sparrows hopped about on them, searching. I

115

was in the habit of chucking crumbs out through the window for them.

Inspector Harford had moved to this window and was studying the uninspiring view.

'You've got no door out into the garden, then?' He peered through the glass, craning his neck upwards at an unnatural angle which is what you had to do to see anything more of the garden.

'Not as such. My landlady's told me that if I want to sit out there in summer I can. But I'd have to go through her place. I could climb through that window, I suppose, by way of a short cut.'

I really shouldn't have said that bit about climbing through the window. It was just a casual remark, a feeble joke, but he took it very seriously. He rattled at the catch, pushed open the window, which had hinges at the top of the frame and appeared to be making calculations. Eventually he let it drop back into place and secured the latch before turning round.

'I didn't,' I said sarcastically, 'stab Gray Coverdale on the doorstep, shut myself in and lock the door, go through this room, out that window, climb over all the garden walls between here and the end of the street, come back along the pavement and "find" his body.'

He sat in my pine-framed easy chair, rested his hands on the wooden arms, and said, 'I didn't suggest that.'

116

'You looked as if you were working on it.' I stared at him resentfully. To be truthful I was surprised to see him. I'd expected Parry. I'd imagined Harford would be at home recovering from a roast Sunday lunch, or doing something healthy and outdoor. He wasn't wearing his suit today, but M & S chinos, peacock-blue Puma sweatshirt and navy suede Nike trainers. He obviously wasn't a man who held much truck with brand loyalty.

'Why should you kill Coverdale? He was a man you'd hardly met, so you said,' he asked, managing to imply I'd been economical with the truth the last time we'd met.

'That's right, I scarcely knew the man. On the one occasion I did meet him, I didn't know his name.' I paused. 'He definitely is Coverdale, then?'

He nodded. 'A relative was found to make the identification.'

I imagined the scene and it was a gruesome picture. Then I wondered who'd potter down to the morgue to identify me if I turned up dead. I didn't fancy Daphne being asked to do it. I supposed it might be Ganesh. I don't have any relatives. After my mother walked out when I was seven, Grandma Varady moved in and looked after Dad and me. Dad died first, which was odd because he wasn't old and he didn't think he was ill. He'd long had what Grandma called 'a delicate stomach' but the list of foods he couldn't digest got steadily

117

longer. It turned out he had stomach cancer and by the time that was found out, it was inoperable. Grandma and I soldiered on pretty well for a year or so, but Dad's death had hit her hard and she never came to terms with it. Her mind grappled with it in vain until she descended rapidly into a half-world. She didn't so much die as fade out, and then I was on my own—out on the street because the landlord didn't want me in the property. I was sixteen and alone. I've been on my own ever since.

My mind had been drifting, thinking all this. I realised Harford was watching me closely.

'Well, go on then,' I said.

He frowned. 'You didn't answer my question.'

'You didn't ask a question,' I said, and realised straight away that of course, he must have done, but I hadn't heard it.

I apologised. 'Sorry, I was thinking—you know about someone having to look at his body and say they recognised him. That's a pretty lousy job.'

'Yes, it is.' He glanced towards the curtain of plastic strips covering the entry to the kitchenette. 'Shall I make us some tea?'

I supposed I should have offered him some. I started to get to my feet, but he waved me back and took himself off and returned minutes later with tea in two mugs. 'Do you take sugar? I couldn't find any.'

'I probably haven't got any.'

He sat down again. 'How are you feeling today?' He'd changed tactics. I was getting tea and the bedside manner now.

'OK.' I thought about it and decided to unburden myself of the thought which had been nagging at me since Coverdale's death. 'I can't help feeling a bit responsible for what happened, because I didn't read his note straight away when I found it. If I had, I'd have been here at ten when he came back—and not turned up with Gan, late. Too late.'

'Why didn't you read it?' He sipped from his mug, his eyes watching me.

'I was distracted. Someone else was here.' He raised his eyebrows so I told him. 'One of Daphne's nephews.'

'Mr Charles Knowles or Mr Bertram Knowles?' he asked unexpectedly.

'You've met 'em, then.' I was surprised, but really oughtn't to have been. We couldn't have something like this happen without the brothers scurrying round to put in their fourpenn'orth. 'It was Charlie.' I wondered if he'd ask what Charlie had wanted.

He nodded. 'They sought me out to express their concern about the murder and their aunt's safety and, frankly, about your presence on the premises.'

The miserable pair of shysters. They didn't lack brass neck. I leaned forward, slopping tea, and declared, 'Well, let me tell you something about Charlie and Bertie, they're creeps and

119

they're con men. They're trying to persuade Daphne to give them this house. *Give* it to them! Just like that. They've told her some spiel about letting her stay on, which has to be a load of rot. I don't believe them. Is it illegal for them to suggest that to her? If it isn't, it ought to be. Can you stop them?'

He shook his head and put his empty mug on the carpet by his feet. 'That's a family matter. Naturally they're concerned about an elderly relative. They're partners in a firm of solicitors, I understand, so I'm sure they know the law. I wouldn't, if I were you, go about suggesting that they had ulterior motives. Not unless you have concrete evidence. If they got to hear of it, you could be in trouble.'

'I thought,' I said bitterly, 'one was supposed to report anything suspicious.'

'There's nothing suspicious in suggesting she think about avoiding inheritance tax. Anyone would do it.'

People with the sort of background he no doubt had did it. People like me, who had nothing to leave and no chance of inheriting so much as a rusty watch chain, had no such worries.

'As a matter of pure hypothesis,' he was saying, 'if anyone who wasn't a registered financial adviser were to urge Miss Knowles to invest money somehow or other, that might be a different matter. But as it is, I wouldn't meddle, Fran. You'd probably end up burning your fingers.'

I felt my face flame as I told him that I wasn't meddling. I was concerned for my landlady. His attitude made me angry. I didn't like his familiar use of my Christian name and I was doubly infuriated to think the brothers had been complaining about me to him. Then it occurred to me that here I was, complaining to him about *them*.

'However,' he was going on, 'since you're so keen to report anything suspicious, I'm surprised you didn't report the incident at the newsagent's when Coverdale came into the place, injured.'

So we were back to that again. 'We explained all that. He didn't want us to do it.' I decided it was time I took charge of this conversation. We were in my flat, after all. 'Have you studied the pics? Do they mean anything to you?'

I hadn't expected much of a reply to this, just an official brushoff, but it had an extraordinary effect. 'I don't want you talking to anyone about those photographs!' he snapped. 'That's one reason I'm here today, to make that absolutely clear to you. I don't want you even to mention finding them. Their existence has to be kept secret, right?'

Hold on, here. I'd hit a nerve. 'They do mean something to you!' I gasped.

He'd reddened. 'We're investigating. But I mean what I said, Fran. You're not to talk about those pictures to anyone at all, not the press, not your landlady, not to your friends. You're not to say what's in them or describe the people they show. It is standard practice not to reveal everything in a murder investigation,' he added belatedly.

'All right, all right, keep your hair on.'

He simmered down and looked a tad embarrassed. 'It's important, that's all. Police investigations can get completely buggered by gossip.'

'You'd better speak to the builders, then. They found the packet with the film in it. Hitch—Jefferson Hitchens—and one of his—' What was Marco? Hardly a registered employee with all the paperwork, National Insurance contributions, tax and all the rest of it, involved. 'Some chap who was helping him out,' I finished.

'We're on to that, thank you,' Harford said primly. 'Someone's gone to see them.'

Parry, ten to one. Harford had wisely left it to someone who'd fare better on that territory. Now he sat back in the chair and changed the subject completely. 'Parry tells me you trained as an actress, Fran.'

It seemed like he knew so much about me, he could've written my biography. Didn't they have anything else to chat about down the nick? 'You keep calling me Fran,' I said coldly. 'I don't remember telling you that was OK.'

He flushed. 'Sorry,' he said stiffly.

'And I don't see how my having been on a Dramatic Arts course matters to you, either. I was—but I didn't finish it.'

'Why did you drop out?' he countered.

I could have explained about Grandma Varady dying and the landlord throwing me out and all the rest of it, but I didn't see why I should. 'I just did,' I said.

'Pity you didn't stick to it.' He had that superior note in his voice again.

'My business, not yours.' I was getting more and more fed up. But as I spoke, it occurred to me that if he knew I'd had stage training, he might be wondering how convincingly I could lie. 'Did you come here just to tell me not to talk about the photos?' I asked icily.

He hesitated. 'That—and to ask you not to talk to the press at all.' He held up his hand to stem any indignant rebuttal I might make. 'Yes, I know—they were pestering you and you were refusing to be drawn, which was quite right. They'll hang around for a couple of days but they'll soon get bored and move on if you don't help them out. If they get no news story here they'll go and find something else.'

'Unless,' I said, 'they've got wind of what Coverdale was up to.'

He started to get worked up again, flushing to crimson. 'If you, or your pal Patel, screw this up for me, I'll throw the book at you both, remember that.'

There was no reason why I had to sit here

and let him insult me. 'If you've finished,' I told him, 'I think you'd better go.'

He hesitated but got to his feet and made towards the door. Determined to see him well off the premises, I accompanied him up the basement steps to street level. The two pressmen had gone—or were hiding in a doorway until he went.

Harford looked up and down the street, perhaps checking it out for the missing reporters. Then he said unexpectedly, 'Someone been washing a car out here?'

'Not that I know of.'

'Just, there's a lot of water in the road here.'

He'd noticed it too. Perhaps I ought to mention it to Daphne. Harford was sliding behind the wheel of his own car. I'd imagined he'd be driving some powerful flash motor, but he'd climbed into an elderly Renault. I watched him drive off and decided not to bother Daphne about the growing damp patch outside. She had enough on her plate.

The rest of the day passed off without incident. I didn't see either of the Knowles twins nor did any more coppers decide to make nuisances of themselves. I turned in early. I had to be at work the next day.

\*　　\*　　\*

It was a pleasant Monday morning, quite mild, with pale sunshine lending quite a cheerful air to everything. Even with all the outstanding unsolved problems, I felt quite cheerful too, until I turned the corner into the street where the newsagent's stood—and saw the police car parked outside the shop.

It wasn't quite eight. I wondered how much hassle of witnesses constituted police harassment. We must be getting near the dividing line. Geared up for battle, I threw open the door and marched into the shop, ready to defend Ganesh's rights. What I saw stopped me in my tracks.

Ganesh sat on a chair in the middle of the shop. His head was bound in thick white bandages and he looked badly shaken. Nevertheless, he was doing his best to answer the questions of a policewoman who hovered over him, notebook in hand.

'Gan!' I shrieked.

The policewoman jumped round as if stung and nearly dropped her notebook. She was a strapping blonde with legs like a footballer's in her black stockings. She jammed her hat back on her head and scowled at me.

A second copper, who'd been prowling round behind the counter, came rushing out and tried to bundle me back out of the door on to the pavement. I resisted.

'Shop's closed, miss. Didn't you see the notice on the door?' He took my elbow in the approved manner.

'Leggo!' I snapped, wedging myself in the

125

doorframe, my back against one upright and my boots braced against the other. 'I work here. What's happened to Ganesh, to Mr Patel?'

He was unwilling to let me back inside but was obliged to check my claim. He looked over his shoulder. 'That right?' he called towards Ganesh. 'She work here?'

'Yes . . .' said Gan faintly.

The copper reluctantly stood back to let me in.

I hurried over to Ganesh. 'What's happened, Gan? Who did that?' Had someone tried to hold up the shop? First thing Monday morning was a hell of a time to try it. So little business would've been done, the takings would be negligible. But thieves weren't always logical. The culprit might've been a psycho or desperate for just enough money for a fix. I felt sick with rage and anger.

'Last night,' Ganesh mumbled. 'Intruder . . . down here. Heard a noise. Went down to see what was going on, got laid out by some joker, whoever he was, and ended up in casualty.'

'We think an attempt was made to burgle the shop,' the policewoman said. 'Perhaps you could take a look round, if you work here, and see if you notice anything missing. What's your name?'

She didn't like me, I could tell. I told her my name.

Ganesh, fidgeting, said, 'I don't think

126

anything's gone. I looked in the storeroom and the cigarettes are still up there behind the counter. There wasn't any money in the till.' He met my eye as he spoke. I knew what he was telegraphing. Don't mention the photos or Coverdale's death. These were ordinary uniformed coppers and they might not know.

The male officer walked through the shop and disappeared out back somewhere. The woman asked, 'Shop alarm in order, sir, as far as you know? Only it appears not to have gone off. Isn't that odd?'

I fancied Ganesh looked shifty, and had just decided it must be a look of pain, when he said, 'Fact is, I might've forgotten to set it.'

'Forgotten?' She was both surprised and suspicious. So was I.

Luckily she was distracted by the return of her partner, bare-headed and breathless. 'I reckon he climbed over the rear wall. Back door's open, but not forced. Who's got a key?' He stared at Ganesh.

'No one,' said Ganesh indignantly, and then put a hand to his injured head. 'Ow! Look, no one has a key but me.'

'You ever have the key?' The copper turned an accusing eye on me.

'Never!' I told him.

The law looked at one another. 'Chummy might've been clever with locks,' said the one who'd come in from the yard. 'But if he was, he wasn't your run-of-the-mill break-in artist.

Force entry, grab goods, get out. That's the usual style. You say he never took nothing?'

Now they were both looking at Ganesh and disbelief was written all over their mugs.

'You say, sir,' said the policewoman, 'that you collided with this intruder on the stairs?'

'I was coming down,' Ganesh said. 'And he was hanging about there, right by the bottom step.' He pointed towards the door which opened on to the staircase leading up to the flat overhead. 'I started to say something like—I dunno—who're you? Then he lashed out.'

'He'd got that door open, then?' The male copper scratched his head. 'Like he was going to come upstairs?'

'He might've been.' Ganesh sounded wary.

'And how long did you say you were unconscious?' The copper was consulting his notebook in a theatrical manner.

Ganesh told him he hadn't said because he didn't know. He hadn't looked at the clock before coming downstairs. He thought he must have been out some time and then it had taken a while before he was *compos mentis* enough to ring for an ambulance. 'Because I realised I'd been hurt,' he said. 'I was bleeding.'

'Yes, sir. Your call was logged by the ambulance service at ten minutes to five this morning. You must have been unconscious a long time. What do you suppose the intruder was doing in that time?'

'How,' muttered Ganesh, 'should I know? I was out cold. Perhaps he'd left.'

The woman took up the questioning. 'You've got to see it looks a bit odd, at least to us. I mean, more chance of his being caught if he went upstairs to the living accommodation, wasn't there? You might've come round and rung us, or got out of the shop and raised the alarm. Easy enough for him to help himself to a few thousand ciggies and a load of first-class stamps down here, wasn't it? But he's not touched a thing, either here or upstairs.'

'He could've printed himself out a few lottery tickets for nothing, while he was about it,' said her partner. Must have been the canteen comedian.

'Oy!' I said, thinking it was time I took a hand. 'It's not funny.'

It wasn't. They didn't believe Ganesh's version of the night's events, that was clear. They'd turned their steely gaze on me. The male officer smirked.

The woman said in a cajoling voice, 'Now, sir, you're sure this wasn't a domestic?'

'I'm not married!' Ganesh's voice rose and again his words turned into a yelp and he put a hand to his bandages.

'You live nearby, do you?' The man gave me the sort of look they give you when they're trying to convince you they know the truth and you might as well speak up and save time. It usually means they know sod all and are hoping you'll be stupid enough to tell them. 'Weren't here at all last night, were you, miss?'

I gave them my address and informed them I'd been at home all night, thank you. Unfortunately, I couldn't give them a name of a witness who'd verify that. I lived alone. Yes, alone.

They received all this with a world-weary air. 'We know it's embarrassing,' said the policewoman, 'but best to tell us exactly what happened. Wasting police time is an offence. Now, you had a bit of a quarrel, did you?'

'We didn't quarrel!' I yelled, losing my cool. 'I wasn't here and I certainly didn't bash Gan over the head!'

'Well, if it isn't our own Calamity Jane! In trouble again, Fran? Can't leave you for five minutes, can I?'

We all turned to the door. Sergeant Parry stood there, grinning like the Cheshire Cat, the pale sun playing on his ginger stubble.

'Nothing here for plainclothes,' said the policewoman. 'Who sent you over? Just a break-in, nothing taken, so he says.' She glanced at me. 'Possible domestic.'

' 'Sall right,' said Parry. 'You let me take care of this one. I'm already on this case.'

They exchanged glances. The policewoman shrugged, closed her notebook and gave me a dirty look. They took themselves off.

Parry shut the door, checked that the closed sign was showing, and came back into the room.

'Right,' he said. 'What's been going on here?'

Before Ganesh could begin to tell his story again, there was an interruption. From the back yard came a loud but tuneless whistling followed by the clatter of noisy entry. Hitch arrived and stopped, surveying the scene. Marco appeared behind him, saw Parry, and melted back out of sight again, probably to shove his private grass supply down the nearest drain.

Hitch had also identified Parry. 'Got the strong arm of the law here, I see. Sergeant Parry, I do believe. What's up? Can't keep away from us?' He turned his attention to Ganesh in his bandages and then to me. 'Hullo, darling. Been knocking the poor bloke around again, have you?'

## CHAPTER EIGHT

'It was a joke,' I said wearily. 'It's Hitch's idea of a joke.'

We were sitting upstairs in the flat, Parry, Ganesh and myself. Ganesh was drinking tea and swallowing aspirin, and looked as if he ought to be lying down quietly in a darkened room. Parry was walking round the place examining everything, and I was sitting in the

131

basketwork chair suspended from the ceiling, a sort of Indian equivalent of a rocker.

Hitch had been sent home, Parry warning him yet again to keep his mouth shut or else. Marco had vanished without being sent.

'That's all right,' said Parry. 'I didn't think you and him—' he nodded at Ganesh— 'had had a barney. Or at least, I didn't think you'd taken up GBH. Give it time, eh?' He grinned at me. He needed to see a dentist and get a scale and polish.

I decided that if ever I were tempted by a spot of grievous bodily harm, it'd be directed at Parry.

'By the way,' I said, 'before we start on any other business, I'd be glad if you'd stop telling everyone my private history. I'm not some villain whose past form is everyone's to know.'

'Ah,' he returned, unabashed. 'You've had a visit from his nibs, haven't you? How'd you get on with the boy wonder?'

'He was making a lot of fuss about those photos, but he wouldn't tell anything about them.'

'Nothing to tell,' said Parry unconvincingly.

'Do me a favour. Why tell us all to shut up about them, then? Me, Gan here, Hitch, Marco . . . Last night's intruder was looking for that film they found in the washroom, wasn't he? Don't say you can't be sure. *I'm* sure. Who *is* the guy in the prints?'

Parry grinned mockingly. 'That's for us to

know and you—'

'To find out,' I finished.

He glowered and shook a sausage-like finger at me. 'No! No detective work this time, Fran! I mean it. You've already interfered and messed up enough. You had no business getting that film printed up. You could screw things up badly for us. What I was going to say was, for you to keep quiet about.'

'I'll have to keep quiet, won't I?' I said sarcastically. 'Seeing as I don't know anything and you won't tell me.'

He nodded. 'And that's the way it stays. You keep your trap shut—unless, of course, there's anything you've forgotten to tell us. Now's your chance if there's something you want to get off your chest.'

Here Parry appeared sidetracked and allowed his bloodshot gaze to rest on the front of my sweater. Dream on, I thought. That's as far as you're ever going to get.

Parry caught my eye, flushed and turned to Ganesh. 'All right, then, let's have your story again, from the top.'

'He ought to be lying down,' I protested. 'He can't keep going over it again and again. He's concussed. Anyone can see that.'

'He can go and lie down all day, once he's told me his story.'

'No I can't!' mumbled Ganesh, whose eyes were beginning to look distinctly unfocused. 'I gotta open up the shop.'

133

'Shop's closed for the day,' said Parry. 'Fingerprint guy is coming over to dust the back door and all around. Your visitor last night was a professional. He knew all the wrinkles and he had help. Of course, if you hadn't forgot to set that alarm . . .' Parry oozed suspicion. 'Funny coincidence, that.'

'Listen,' muttered Ganesh, propping his head in his hands. He sounded deeply despondent. 'There's something I've got to tell you about the alarm.'

'Oh, yes?' Parry sounded ominous. 'What's that, then?'

I saw Ganesh take a deep breath and wondered what on earth he was going to say. My heart sank. It had to be bad news.

It was. I couldn't believe my ears.

'A fake?' yelled Parry, when Ganesh had stopped speaking. He wrestled for control, gave up and, breathing heavily, glared at us both in a way which made me seriously alarmed for his mental and physical health.

Ganesh, totally dejected, mumbled, 'Not my fault. My uncle—'

'Your uncle is a bloody idiot!' yelled Parry.

'Hey, wait a minute!' I broke in. I was really worried about Ganesh by now. I'd never seen him look so ill. 'I don't know what's gone on here, but yelling at Gan won't help. He's not fit, right? He's got to go and lie down.'

Before Parry could object, I grabbed Ganesh by the arm, hauled him up from the chair and propelled him into the bedroom.

'Lie down, right?' I ordered. 'And stay there until Parry's gone. I'll handle it. I'll see to everything. I'll open up the shop when the cops are out of the way and everything. *You are sick!*' I gave him a shove in the direction of the bed and retreated, closing the door firmly behind me.

Back in the sitting room, Parry was waiting and now having only one person to vent his fury on, advanced on me, flecks of spittle flying as he spoke.

'Of course it didn't go off last night, did it? Because it wasn't set? No. Because the sodding thing's a dummy, a phoney! The bloke who owns this crummy shop is too damn mean to pay for proper security, so what does he do? He rigs up what he hopes will fool a burglar. Does it? Does it hell. A professional break-in artist was always going to rumble it straight away—and one did, didn't he?'

Silently I cursed Hari. One positive thing came out of this, however, I thought. I no longer had to worry that Ganesh was going to get it in the neck for having the washroom done up. Hari deserved to be made to pay. He could hardly grumble, however much Hitch charged for whatever kind of job he did. If Hari hadn't been so penny-pinching, Gan wouldn't have got knocked cold.

But that was for the future. Right now, I had to calm down Parry. Things were looking

135

bad for Ganesh. I let myself drop into the chair vacated by Gan near the table, and rested my elbows on the red chenille tablecloth. 'OK, I agree with you, for what it's worth. But making a fuss about it now isn't going to get us anywhere, is it?'

Reason was wasted on Parry who stormed over, put both palms on the table and loomed over me.

'You can't dismiss it just like that, you know. When I got here, Patel had already reported the break-in to the uniformed boys. I don't think—correct me if I'm wrong—he told them that all he'd got out there on the wall was a painted tin box without a perishing bit of wiring anywhere near it! That's wasting police time, that is. That's withholding essential information. That's actively misleading police enquiries, that's—'

'Oh, shut up!' I snapped. 'He'd been bashed on the bonce. He wasn't thinking straight. He was dozy—'

'There,' Parry interrupted sarcastically, 'I agree with you. Dozy is one word for it. I can think of others. If he's lucky, that bang on the head will have knocked some sense into it.' He paused. 'Here,' he said at a new thought, 'I bet the insurance company doesn't know about that little setup. That could be an attempt to defraud. Strikes me, your mate is in a lot of trouble.'

'He isn't,' I insisted. 'Hari is. You can't

blame Ganesh. It's not his fault. He only works here. He's not stupid, he's in a difficult situation. Hari is his uncle. He couldn't shop a family member to the insurance company, could he?'

'Why're you so bloody loyal to him?' Parry demanded.

Taken aback, I retorted, 'Because he's my friend, and everything I said is true.'

'Yeah, yeah.' Parry chewed the end of his ragged moustache. 'I've been a good friend to you and all, seems to me. Fat lot of thanks I've got for it.'

'When?' I gasped.

'I've stood between you and a lot of trouble. You could've been charged with interference in investigations before now, if it weren't for me.' He managed a sickly leer. 'And you're going to need me again, this time, aren't you, if your pal Patel isn't to be dropped in the brown stuff? I don't have to put this dummy alarm business in my report, you know. You think about it. Only don't take too long. I'll be filing the report as soon as I get back to base.'

I met his bloodshot gaze and held it. 'Do you know,' I told him, 'I don't know which of you makes me want to throw up more—you or Charlie Knowles.'

Parry flushed, then grinned evilly. 'That old feller been patting your bum?'

'Something like that.'

'Dirty old devil.'

137

'Well, he's not the only one living in hopes, is he?' I snapped back.

Parry straightened up and shook a yellowed fingernail at me. 'One of these days, you'll wish you'd been nicer to me, you'll see.'

'At your funeral,' I told him.

'Very funny. We'll see who laughs last, eh?'

'Listen,' I'd had enough of this, 'why can't you and Harford let it be known you've got the negs and pics? That would take the heat off the rest of us.'

He shook his head. 'No way.'

'Oh great,' I muttered. 'Ganesh gets laid out senseless. I could be next, or Hitch or Marco as well, I suppose.'

'We've warned the two cowboys fixing up the washroom. But to lay it on the line, if chummy approaches either of them, they'll pass the buck so fast, it'll be a blur. All they did was find a sealed package. They gave it to you and Sleeping Beauty in there.' He nodded towards the bedroom door. 'They saw nothing, no negatives, no prints. Not like you, eh? You went running along to the chemist and got the film developed, didn't you? Not smart, Fran. Take my advice—it's official—don't go opening the door to anyone you don't know, right? If anyone comes here to the shop, or to your flat, or makes any kind of approach, phone call, anything, you let us know straight away. It's in your interest, remember. Do yourself a favour, Fran. Wise up.'

'I told you, someone already came to the shop, asking.'

'Yeah, well, you didn't give him the right answer, did you? He came back last night. He didn't get any joy then, either, so he's got to keep trying.' Parry leaned forward again. 'He needs that film.'

'Who does?' I countered.

The only reply to that was a spiteful grin. Parry walked to the door. 'Oh,' he said, 'I'm still not sure whether to put that dummy alarm in my report. Let's say, I'm holding that as a sort of guarantee of your future behaviour, Fran.'

I told him to get out, but he'd already gone.

*     *     *

I didn't get the shop open until after three in the afternoon, just in time to sell the day's *Evening Standard*, a few packets of ciggies and a couple of girlie mags. In between, I had to keep nipping upstairs to check on Ganesh, who was sleeping so soundly I began to worry if I ought to wake him up. He might be in a coma for all I knew.

Everyone who came in the shop wanted to know why we'd been closed earlier. Since several of them had seen the police cars outside first thing, I had to put out some kind of story. I said there'd been an attempted break-in, but the intruders had been disturbed and fled empty-handed. That was true, as it happened.

Every listener to this story told me we'd been bloody lucky. They were right.

At six, I shot the bolts across and went upstairs to check on the invalid. Ganesh, to my great relief, had woken up and was moving around the kitchen in slow motion. I opened up a tin of soup and made toast, but he wasn't very interested.

'You ought to see a doctor,' I said.

But he wasn't having that. 'I'll be fine tomorrow.'

'Gan?' I had to mention it. 'About that dummy alarm.'

He waved both hands, fending off the question and the look on my face. 'I know, I know.'

'I'm not blaming you. But you ought to get your family on to Hari. He had no right to leave you here with nothing but an empty mock-up on a wall for protection.'

A hunted look crossed Ganesh's face. 'You haven't let my family know about this, have you?'

'Relax, of course I haven't.'

'Only they'd write to Hari and he'd be back from India on the next flight. He'd say it was my fault. He'd never leave me in charge again. He must never know anything about any of this, Fran!'

'All right, all right!' What with the coppers

140

telling me not to talk and Ganesh joining in, I might as well take some kind of Trappist vow and be done with it. I went back downstairs and reopened for business.

*　　　*　　　*

I left around eight. Ganesh had promised to go to bed early and I'd promised to be at the shop at seven the next morning to help with the papers. I hoped my rusty old alarm clock did its stuff. Sometimes it just sat sullen and silent. I ought to get a new one, but normally I had no need of a morning alarm. I never seemed to stay in employment long enough.

A thin drizzle was falling. The pavements were wet and the light from bar and café windows threw yellow strips across them. Through the windows I could see the Christmas decorations strung around walls and ceilings, lots of glittering tinsel, paper bells and plastic holly. It looked really festive and made me feel sad. Everyone was getting into holiday mood. People were going out for the evening, hurrying past me, chattering and laughing. They'd stop, study a menu fixed up outside a place perhaps, decide against it and move on, or go in, whichever. They were out to enjoy themselves.

I never went out in the evening. I never went anywhere and the one recent time I had gone, for our staff Christmas dinner, I'd come

141

home and found a body in the basement. Why does this happen to me? Why doesn't it happen to other people?

I began to think about Coverdale and his unfulfilled wish to talk to me. The more I thought about it, the more uneasy I became. His killers would want to know why he'd been keen to see me. They'd checked the shop because they were thorough. But what they'd decide in the end was that either Coverdale had given me the film—or I'd found it and Coverdale had come round to see me and get it back. This was what probably had happened. Either that, or he'd come to tell me where he'd hidden it and to ask me to get it for him. He wouldn't have risked returning to the shop in case the guys after him were watching. They were watching him, as it happened, rather more successfully than he'd realised.

So, whichever way you cared to look at it, the villains were sure to reckon I was the link to the negs. The police had embargoed the news that they had them. I was left, staked out like a goat in a clearing, waiting for the tiger. Or even several tigers.

It wasn't a cheery thought and it made me highly nervous. I kept looking over my shoulder and wondered if I ought to go straight home, or adopt some devious route, designed to throw anyone following off the trail. But if they'd killed Coverdale outside my front door, they didn't need to follow me to find out where I lived. They knew.

I still kept looking back on principle. So busy was I doing it, that when someone stepped out of a doorway in front of me, I almost collided with them and just about jumped out of my skin when a voice said, 'Fran?'

'Oh God, Tig,' I gurgled. 'I nearly had a perishing heart attack.'

*      *      *

'What's the matter with you, then?' asked Tig.

I hadn't wanted to hang about in the street and neither had she, so we took refuge in a nearby café, a narrow-fronted establishment that ran back a long way like a tunnel. It was crammed with marble-topped tables. In the summer, they moved some of the tables out on to the pavement, but this time of year, only a lunatic or a polar bear would sit outside.

Tig and I had retreated to the furthermost end of the room from the door with our espressos.

'I'm scared Jo Jo will look in and see me,' Tig had explained, leading the way. She now gave me curious scrutiny. 'Who're you trying to avoid?'

'Don't ask,' I said. 'I'm not allowed to say.'

She shrugged. She didn't care anyway. She didn't look any better or healthier since I'd last seen her. The dark shadows under her eyes

143

were worse, the pinched look more pronounced and there was more than fear of Jo Jo in her eyes. There was a deeper fear and it had driven her to seek me out. I waited for her to tell me what it was.

She went at it a roundabout way. 'I came to the shop yesterday, where you work, Sunday morning. There was an Indian guy there, big bloke. He said you weren't working, not Sunday. They'd got the builders in. They were working Sunday. They moonlighting?'

'No, self-employed. Dilip told me you'd been. I hoped you'd get in touch again. Sorry I missed you.' I sipped the coffee. I was glad of it. My nerves needed settling.

Tig shifted on her wooden chair and it scraped on the tiled floor. 'Yeah, well, I'm sorry I gave you an earful last time.' She rubbed her thin hands together. The fingertips were blue and the nails dirty. She needed a bath.

I asked, 'You sleeping rough, Tig?'

She twitched. 'Look, did you mean what you said? About doing anything legal?'

'Ye-es,' I said, not at all happy.

'OK, then, I'm hiring you.' I must have looked as if I'd been hit with a sock full of wet sand because she added irritably, 'Well, you said you were a private detective and you worked for people who couldn't get help anywhere else. That's me. I can't go anywhere else, so I've come to you. I want you to get in

144

touch with my family for me. Like, act as go-between.'

I knew I could only blame myself for this. I'd urged her to go home. I'd offered to help if I could. It had been a spur-of-the-moment thing. If I'd given it any thought afterwards, which I hadn't, I would've decided, with relief, that she wouldn't take me up on it. And I'd also told her I took on jobs for people. I'd boasted about it, to be frank. Which just goes to show you've got to be ready for the unexpected, and if you don't want to be reminded of something you've said, keep your mouth shut.

'Well?' She was leaning across the table, her pinched face flushed in anger and her whole attitude a bad case of aggro. People at a nearby table gave us alarmed looks. They probably thought we were about to start a fight on the floor. 'Or was it just a load of crap?' she went on. 'All that what you told me? You made it all up? You've never done any jobs for no one.'

'Yes, I have!' I was moved to defend myself. 'I was surprised when you asked, that's all.'

'Are you going to do it?' She leaned back now, fixing me with a very direct stare.

'All right,' I said. 'What do you want me to do? Phone them?'

'No, go and see them.' She was fumbling inside her jacket and pulled out a roll of dirty notes secured with an elastic band. 'See this?

It's my emergency cash. All I've got. Jo Jo knows nothing about it. There's enough there to buy you a day return ticket, rail, from Marylebone to Dorridge. That's where they live. There's a train every hour—I checked it out for you. Leaves Marylebone quarter to the hour. Coming back, leaves Dorridge at forty-eight minutes past the hour. Any money left over you can keep for your fee. I don't know what you usually charge, but this is all I've got, so take it or leave it.'

She was going too fast for me and my fee was the least of my worries. 'Who lives there, your parents? Where's Dorridge, for crying out loud? It sounds like porridge.'

'It's on the way to Birmingham, before you get to Birmingham, just before Solihull. It'll take just over two hours to get there and the same back, so you'll have to go early in the morning.'

'Hey, hold on.' She'd got it all planned, it seemed, but I had questions to ask.

A streetwalker came in out of the cold. She was just starting the evening stint and was all dressed up nice in a fake fur coat and patent leather stilettos. She wasn't young, in her forties, a bit blowsy with bottle-blonde hair and too much make-up. The Italian waiter evidently recognised her because he gave her a secretive sort of smile and, without her having to ask, yelled down the café to the guy on the espresso machine, 'Hey, give the lady a

146

coffee!'

She didn't pay for it. I guess she'd already paid.

Tig, watching the same scene, said scornfully, 'Why'd guys pay her? They can pay someone like me half the money and I'm half her age.'

'Then watch out for the pimps,' I said. 'They don't like competition on the same patch.' I didn't mention that the professional tart had certainly taken the trouble to shower before she went to work. Some punters, though admittedly not all, might be put off by Tig's appearance and the whiff of street doorway.

My companion shrugged again. 'Well, I'm not on the game now, anyhow. I told you, I don't do it any more, not unless I'm really skint, you know, and some old feller comes up and asks. They bloody well nearly always are old, the ones who like really young girls.'

'I know,' I said, memory of Charlie still fresh.

'Still—that sort don't give no trouble.' Her gaze darkened. She was thinking of her treatment at the hands of the City types who'd gang-raped her.

My mind was working overtime. If I went on this errand for Tig, it'd take me out of London for a whole day. That would mean, in present circumstances, a whole day without having to look over my shoulder and jump at shadows. I liked the idea of that. On the other hand, with

Ganesh in his fragile state of health, I couldn't leave him to manage on his own in the shop. I'd have to go on a Sunday when Dilip could help out doing the morning papers.

'We need to talk serious business,' I said. 'If, and it is only *if*, I do this for you, there are things I need to know. For starters, why you left home in the first place and why, all of a sudden, you want to go back. And it's no use clamming up on me. I'm not going into a situation like that blind, OK? Another thing, I can't just get on a train and go to this Dorridge place. Suppose I turned up and your parents had gone out for the day? Or like you said before, they might've moved. I'd have to phone first and make an appointment. They're going to ask questions. Also, does Jo Jo know what you're planning and what's he likely to do when you take off? Follow?'

'He can't,' she said quickly. 'He doesn't know what I'm going to do or where my family lives. I've never told him where I come from and he hasn't asked. You don't, do you?'

She was right. The homeless respect one another's privacy and the right to keep stum about an individual's past. If you want to tell everyone, fine. If you don't, they don't press you. It's a rule.

She hunched over her empty coffee cup. 'If I tell you, you'll do it?'

'I'm not bargaining,' I told her. 'I'm telling you my terms. Take it or leave it.'

148

The waiter was giving us funny looks. I told Tig to wait and went up to the counter to get us another couple of coffees. Thanks to the lay-out of the place, it would be difficult for her to slip past me and out while I was away from the table. But I kept an eye on her, in case.

She'd taken the time given by my absence to think it over and had reached a decision. 'All right, I'll tell you anything you want to know. I'll give you the phone number and you can ring them. But if you do, you're not to say where they can find me, right? The last bloody thing I want is them driving down here.'

'Understood.'

'I'll write their names and address and phone number down for you.'

Neither of us had a bit of paper though I had a stub of pencil. There was a card on the table telling customers of some Christmas offer the café was running—coffee, choice of sandwich and a cake for £2.50, something like that. Tig turned it over and wrote on the back.

'Their name is Quayle, Colin and Sheila. My name's Jane, really. That's what you'll have to call me when you talk to them.' She pushed the card towards me. She'd written it all down, with address and phone number.

A thought had struck me. 'You need to send a personal message, or tell me something that I couldn't know about you or them unless I knew you well. I mean, I've got to convince

149

them I really am speaking on your behalf.'

She gave an odd little smile. 'All right. Wish my mum a happy birthday. It's her birthday tomorrow.'

It was personal, all right, but I wished she'd thought of something else.

Tig found giving out the practical details easier than the next thing she had to tell me. I could see her bracing herself. 'Jo Jo and I,' she said, 'we had a place to doss but we lost it. The last few nights, we've been sleeping over Waterloo way, in an underpass. You know the place? It's under the road system, a big empty space. There used to be lots of people sleeping there. Most of them have gone now, moved out. They're building there now. But there's still space to doss if you haven't got anywhere else. They try and move you on, of course.'

I nodded. I knew the place she meant. It had been the site of Cardboard City, that squatters' camp in the maze of subterranean walkways between Waterloo and the South Bank complex. I'd never slept there but I'd been there in its heyday, looking for someone or just passing through. Each inhabitant had had his space, with his sleeping bag and plastic carriers of personal belongings, his dog, his transistor radio—some even had a scrap of dirty carpet down and a broken old armchair or two. Some were young, some old, some in sound mind and some way out of theirs. Some had been there years. When I was at school, our art teacher had been keen on the painting of a guy called Bosch who'd turned out stuff which looked as if it had all been painted when he was as high as a kite—but which she reckoned was symbolic. The old Cardboard City had put me in mind of one of those paintings by Bosch—a world of weird things which were normal to those caught up in the nightmare.

But even down there the homeless hadn't been secure. The area was being developed, as Tig said—luxury flats and a monster cinema going up. The debris of the streets was being swept up and moved elsewhere as the men in the hard hats and their equipment moved in.

Tig was avoiding my eye, her face turned down, her stringy fair hair falling forward. Her voice was muffled. 'Coupla nights ago,' she said, 'someone died there.'

People do die on the streets. I waited. There had to be more.

'It was a girl, about the same age as me. She was sleeping right near us. She'd got a little dog. Nice dog, friendly. Some people have those big dogs that go for you. Jo Jo had one once and I was glad when he sold it on to someone. You had to watch it all the time or it'd have you. Anyhow, this girl, I didn't know her name or anything, but I'd talked a bit to her that evening. I'd made friends with the dog and that's mostly what we talked about, the dog. Later she went off somewhere and she

151

didn't come back until after midnight. She'd had a couple of drinks, I could smell the booze—and I guess she might've got hold of some stuff and been shooting up somewhere. Sunday morning, she never got up. Never stirred. No one bothered much at first. But then the dog started whining and sniffing at her. I got a really bad feeling. I went over and shook her shoulder. She was cold already. Her eyes were open and bulging and her jaw had fallen open and stiffened like that. She looked horrible. It was the scariest thing I ever saw in my life. Like a horror film only worse, because it was real.'

Tig shook back her hair and looked up, meeting my gaze firmly. 'And I thought, that's me. That's how I'm going to end up and pretty soon. It's true, isn't it?' She stared at me defiantly.

'Unless you do something about it,' I said.

'Right. That's what I thought. I won't like it, I won't like going home and facing them: Perhaps they won't even have me. But I've got to try because it's the only way out I've got. Some people get out of it other ways. They get a permanent place to live and they get a job. Like you, you've got out of it. You always were smart. But that's not going to work for me. I haven't time enough for that. I get out now or by spring, I'm dead.'

'Don't worry,' I said. 'I'll do it.'

She relaxed and I felt a stab of unease.

152

She'd be relying on me. Supposing I messed the whole thing up? Said the wrong thing on the phone? It'd be Tig's lifeline snapping. I forced the worry away but I did venture, 'You could ring them yourself and then I could go up—'

'No!' Her voice was fierce. 'I won't talk to them until—They'd ask too many questions.'

They were going to ask me questions, but I took her point. 'So, why'd you leave in the first place?' I asked. 'Just general.'

She shook her head. 'I told you what my mum's like, everything so perfect. Dad's worse. It didn't matter how hard I tried at school, he'd find some subject I'd done poorly at, and ask, what about that? I went to a good school, they paid—private.'

'So did I,' I said glumly. 'Until it threw me out.'

'Well, then, you know how it is. Parents have spent money and they want results, don't they?'

She was turning the knife in my conscience, though she didn't know it. Her parents had probably found the money without too much difficulty, but Dad and Grandma Varady had really scrimped to send me. When I'd been expelled, they hadn't moaned, just sympathised and rallied round. But I knew I'd let them down and would have it on my conscience to my dying day. For Tig, it was different, however. She'd worked hard, apparently, but it hadn't been enough.

'He—my father—kept talking about university,' Tig was saying. 'But I didn't want to go to university. He said I'd never get a really good job without a degree. He kept on and on. Then there was Mum with her "you-can't-go-out-looking-like-that" and "be-careful-to-make-nice-friends"! And, of course, "you-don't-want-to-be-thinking-about-boys-you've-got-your-studies".'

Tig shook her head and leaned forward, her pale face flushed. 'Look, I know it doesn't sound so bad, talking to you now. They weren't beating me up. Dad hadn't got his hand in my knickers, there was nothing like that. It was just day in, day out, pressure. I couldn't get away from it, not there. So—I left.'

Everyone's got their reasons. It doesn't matter whether they sound good or bad reasons to anyone else. They're good enough for the person concerned.

'You see,' Tig said sadly, 'how hard it is to talk about going back. How disappointed they'll be, how shocked, horrified. I don't know if they can cope with it. That's why you've got to find out first.'

'I'll really do my best, Tig,' I promised. 'Honestly, I will.' I hoped I hadn't bitten off more than I could chew.

# CHAPTER NINE

With all the trouble I was causing Daphne at the moment, I didn't feel I could ask to phone long-distance to Dorridge from her place. I don't mean I wouldn't pay her. I always paid for my calls from Daphne's. But I might find myself explaining about Tig. Daphne would be interested and I was pretty sure, sympathetic, but she'd worry about it. Besides, I needed time to think out what I'd say. The more I thought, the less I liked the whole idea.

The next morning, I explained it all to Ganesh. He was feeling better and had got rid of the bandages, but still had a large plaster on his head. I told him to sit on a stool behind the counter and stay there. I'd do any running around and would stay all day till closing time. At least I was spared Hitch and Marco creating havoc in the washroom. It seemed they couldn't come in and finish today.

'He's got a problem with his supplier over the floortiles,' said Ganesh.

I made no comment on this, but privately decided they were both keeping clear of the place while there was any chance of running into the police on the premises. Neither of them, I fancied, liked answering questions. Instead, over our coffee-break, I explained about Tig.

'You ought to have steered clear of that,' said Ganesh. 'No way are you going to come out a winner. Tell her you've changed your mind.'

'You told me you thought she ought to go home,' I protested.

'I know I did. I still do. But I didn't mean you should set it up. Families,' said Ganesh, who knew about these things, 'are tricky.'

'It's her only chance, Gan. She's right. She's not really a survivor. She looks sick. She's had to take up with the awful Jo Jo just to get protection. She's got to get out fast.' I added sadly, 'And I did offer to help.'

'More fool you,' said Ganesh. His sore head was making him grumpy. But his thinking was still clearer than mine. 'Look at it from the point of view of her people,' he went on. 'They will have been waiting to hear from Tig for months. Suddenly, out of the blue, they get a call from a complete stranger who claims to know their missing daughter. The stranger wants to come and see them and arrange the daughter's return home. What does that sound like to you?'

'A scam,' I said miserably.

'Too right. The first thing they'll want to know is, what's in it for you?'

'My fee,' I said. 'And it won't be much once I've paid the train fare out of what Tig gave me.'

'Who cares about your couple of quid fee

156

from Tig? She's got no money—there's no point in you trying to get it from her. The Quayles will think you want money from *them*—because from the sound of it, they're pretty well set up. So, they'll be expecting you to ask them to pay you for acting as middleman. They won't believe you if you say you don't want anything. Look, who knows what they'll think? Maybe that you've got Tig locked in a cellar and don't mean to let her out until the Quayles have coughed up a really big amount. You'll turn up in this place, what's it called?'

'Dorridge.'

'Are you sure you've got that right? You'll turn up and find a police reception committee. At the very least, they'll call their solicitor. You know what I think you should do? You should tell Harford about it, ask his advice. At least, tell him what you're going to do so that you're covered if the Quayles turn nasty.'

'I can't!' I exclaimed in horror. 'Not Harford! He'd sneer. Besides, it's nothing to do with him. Nor have I got Tig's permission to bring the police into it—and I wouldn't get it. Tig would just disappear if I mentioned the cops.'

'How about Parry? He's a pain in the neck but he'd know all the ropes in a case like this. Don't the police deal with missing teenagers? Hey, it might even be illegal for you not to tell them about her.'

157

'It's not illegal to go missing if you're overage,' I pointed out. 'And if a person's over sixteen, the police won't do anything, either—not unless it's suspicious circumstances. She's got to be more'n sixteen. She was fifteen in Jubilee Street, and that was months ago. She's probably seventeen and anyway, she was only ever just a runaway. There's hundreds of them out there, up and down the country. The coppers don't want to know about another one.'

Ganesh tried another tack. 'They might not want her back. She's been a lot of trouble. They may think she's dishonoured them.'

'I don't think they're worried about honour, not from what Tig says. They're worried about respectability.'

'Well, same thing, isn't it?' he said. I began to feel this was one of the times when Gan and I found ourselves heading for a culture clash. It didn't happen often, but there was no way round it when it did.

'Look,' I said patiently, 'she hasn't run away from an arranged marriage. She just pushed off because of the pressure.'

'Don't think I don't know what that means,' said Gan testily. 'You want to know about family pressures? Try my lot. But have I pushed off to live rough on the street?'

This was getting me nowhere. I asked if I could use the phone. He told me to help myself and suggested I phoned from the flat upstairs. There was no one in the shop and he could manage. I think his head was hurting and he was fed up with talking about Tig. If I wanted more trouble, I was welcome to it. He was washing his hands of it.

*      *      *

I went up to the flat and sat in front of the phone for five minutes before I picked up enough courage to dial the number Tig had given me. It rang several times during which I went over what I'd rehearsed in my head—and decided none of it would do. I'd have to improvise.

It was still ringing. They were out. My heart lifted. I was about to replace the receiver when a woman's voice, breathless, asked, 'Hullo? Yes?'

'Oh, hullo,' I said stupidly. 'Is that Mrs Quayle?'

'Yes . . .' The voice was wary.

'My name's Fran Varady. I'm a friend of T—of Jane's.'

There was a silence. I could feel her gathering up her wits, steeling herself to deal with this. She asked in a careful way, 'Were you at school with Jane?'

I understood what she was getting at. If I was an old school pal who'd not been in touch for years, I mightn't know that Jane had left home. If that was the case, Mrs Quayle could

159

invent some reason for Jane not being there and falsely promise to deliver a message.

'No,' I said. 'I'm phoning from London. I know Jane here.'

There was a gasp and a bump. After that came such a long silence I began to be afraid she'd fainted. I was anxiously repeating her name when she came back on the line.

'I'm sorry—it was such a shock. I—I had to sit down. You know Jane? Where—Why isn't she on the phone herself? Is she all right?' Panic began to enter her voice.

If I didn't watch out, I'd have a hysterical woman on the other end of the line. 'She's all right,' I said firmly. (I wasn't being untruthful. Tig's situation was grim. But she was in one piece and walking around, clean of drugs, and in street terms that was certainly all right.)

Her voice shaking, Mrs Quayle began to ask questions so fast, I couldn't have answered any of them if I'd wanted to. 'Where is Jane? What's her address? Why isn't she calling herself? Who are you? Where did you get my home number? Did—'

I managed to get a word in at last. 'Mrs Quayle, I'm sorry it's been such a shock, but if you'll let me, I'll try and explain. Tig—Jane would like to come home—'

'But of course she can come home! She always cou—'

I cleared my throat loudly and Mrs Quayle fell silent. 'She's too embarrassed to call you herself, so she asked me. Mrs Quayle, Jane's been living rough. Things haven't been easy for her. You ought to know that.'

'You said she was all right!' she retorted suspiciously.

'She is—but she can't—she doesn't want to go on living as she is now.'

Mrs Quayle was cudgelling her brain back into working order. 'Is my daughter in some kind of trouble?' Her voice was sharp.

'Not with the law, if that's what you mean,' I said. 'But things are difficult for her and she doesn't want to come to the phone and have to answer a lot of questions. Can't you understand that?'

'I don't know,' she said. 'I don't know who you are or even if you really know Jane.'

I had to play the one card Tig had given me. 'She asked me to wish you a happy birthday, by the way. She said it was today.'

Mrs Quayle moaned. It was a heart-breaking sound. I felt a louse. Ganesh had been right and I ought to have told Tig I couldn't do this.

'Mrs Quayle?' I asked. 'Would you like to talk this over with your husband? I can ring again.'

'Oh, no, please! Please, don't hang up!'

Now she was terrified she'd lose the one indirect contact Jane had made after so long. She truly didn't know what to do, poor woman.

'I will call back,' I promised.

161

'Can't I have your number? Can't I call you?' She was getting frantic. 'Look, you must tell Jane that of course she can come home. Daddy and I—'

'Jane thinks I ought to come and see you, Mrs Quayle. There's a lot I have to explain. She isn't the same girl who left you. She's changed. You've got to understand that. She can't just walk back in the way she walked out. I'm sorry if I sound brutal—but it's true. You'll have to be prepared to make, well, adjustments. It'll take time to pick up the pieces.'

She was quiet, thinking about it. Fretfully, she said, 'I wish Colin were here ...' Then, making up her mind, 'When can you come?'

'Sunday, if it's all right with you? I can't come in the week, I've got a job.'

I should have said that earlier, mentioned that I was in employment, not skulking on street corners. It must have sounded reassuring.

'Oh, of course, we don't expect you to take time off from your job. Yes, come Sunday.' She sounded quite enthusiastic.

I told her I'd be there Sunday morning and to talk it through with her husband but not to get het up. She still wanted my phone number but I refused and I'd taken the precaution of withholding it from the system in case she dialled 1471 as soon as I put down the receiver.

162

*    *    *

'Well, you'll have to go now, won't you?' said Ganesh when I repeated the conversation to him.

After that, we didn't talk about it again. I could see he wasn't feeling well. I couldn't get him to go upstairs and rest, even though as the day wore on, he showed no willingness to do anything but sit in the storeroom, drinking coffee or dozing off with his head on the table. I managed on my own somehow, and at eight I closed up shop, checking the back premises were secure and the shop door bolted. I left the lights on low as added security. Then I confronted Ganesh in his storeroom retreat.

'What time is it?' he asked and looked bewildered when I told him.

'I've closed up. Can you manage to open that antique of a safe Hari's got upstairs for me to put the cash in?'

He stumbled upstairs to the flat and we managed to stow the cash away. I don't know what else Hari had in that safe; I could only see bundles of paper. But it seemed to me crazier than ever to put a dummy burglar alarm on the outside of the place if Hari had anything at all he wanted protecting.

'As soon as I've gone, will you go to bed?' I demanded.

He promised he would and followed me

163

down the other flight of stairs from the flat which led to the separate street entrance beside the shop window.

'Promise, Ganesh?'

'Swear it, Fran.'

'I'll come early tomorrow, OK?'

I stood outside and listened to him lock and bolt this door, too. He hadn't completely lost his presence of mind. When he'd done that, he opened the letter box and addressed me through it.

'Fran, if by any chance when you get here in the morning the place is closed up because I've overslept or something—ring the bell on this door. It makes a helluva row.'

I set off home. Or at least, that was my intention. But I hadn't got a dozen steps from the shop when I heard my name hailed and recognised Harford's voice. I stopped and turned with a sigh.

'I thought you quit work at eight,' he said. 'I've been waiting.'

'Don't you lot ever quit work either? I had to close up, Ganesh isn't fit.' I glanced round. 'Waiting where? You can't park here.'

'I've been sitting in that grubby little coffee place over the road, by the window.'

'Police surveillance now!' I muttered.

'Look,' he said, 'I'm off duty, right? I need to talk to you. I thought we could go and have a drink.'

I squinted up at him in the poor lamplight.

He still wore the suit, but had taken off his tie and unbuttoned the neck of his shirt. He looked and sounded genuine, wasn't sneering, and was even acting friendly. It had to be a trick.

I debated whether or not to go along with this. Nothing obliged me to go with him. On the other hand, if he'd been sitting over the road in Lennie's Drop-By Café (known jocularly among the locals as the Drop-Dead Café), he must want to talk to me about something that mattered.

'All right,' I conceded. 'There's a pub round the corner.'

'There's also a little Italian restaurant,' he said. 'It might be nicer. I checked it out earlier.'

I'd walked into that one. But it was getting late and I was hungry. We went to the Italian place.

It was nice, with green-checked tablecloths, a green-tiled wall behind the bar, real flowers in the vases and, inevitably, Christmas decorations.

'I eat Italian a lot,' he said. 'I hope you like it.'

'I eat anything,' I said ungraciously. Because I'd let him outmanoeuvre me didn't mean I had to go all sweet and girly. Anyway, it's not my style.

He leaned his elbows on the table, propping his chin in his hands, and stared at me

165

thoughtfully. After a minute of this, I got fidgety.

'Something wrong?' I asked.

'No—nothing. Why did you cut your hair so short? I mean, it looks great—but it's a nice colour and it'd probably suit you longer.'

Heaven help us. Compliments from the Met. Was I, by any lunatic chance, being chatted up here? I opened my menu and took a quick look. Nothing was cheap but the *penne al tonno* was reasonable.

'I'll have that,' I said, pointing to it. 'And I pay my own way, right?'

'Fine. I'll buy us a bottle of wine. You did agree to a drink.'

When the wine had arrived and he'd poured us a glass each, I said, 'Look, Inspector—'

'My name's Jason.'

'Well, Jason, I'd like to know just what I'm doing here. I can't believe you're desperate for a date.'

He smiled. It transformed his face and if Daphne'd been there to see it, she'd have been bowled over. Not me, I'd like to make clear.

'Something tells me we've got off on the wrong foot, Fran. Obviously, we met in rather difficult circumstances—over a corpse.'

'Yes, what about the late Gray Coverdale?' I sipped the wine, which was rather nice. 'We're here to talk about him, I suppose? We don't have anything else in common.'

'Yes—and no. We might have more in

common than you think. At least we could try and find out. I'd like to talk about you a bit. Or you can quiz me if you want. I'd like us to be friends. There's no point in glaring at each other like a couple of cats squaring up over territory. I thought we could bury the hatchet. It'd make life a lot easier.'

Friends, us? I spelled it out carefully. 'Just because this is a murder investigation and I found the body, doesn't mean that I've given up all right to a private life. Ask me about Coverdale and I'll tell you what I know—although you know it already. Anything else, *Jason*, is off limits. None of your business.'

'Why've you taken a dislike to me?' he asked, disconcerting me. 'Is it because you don't like coppers? A lot of people don't—or so I've been finding.' He frowned. 'I include respectable people. I never expected to be popular with villains, but I have been shocked, since I joined the force, by the general distrust shown by Joe Public. We're protecting them, for God's sake! We're not the enemy.'

'You should have thought about that before you joined the police,' I pointed out. 'If you wanted to be popular you should've formed a pop group. Why did you join the police, anyway? Couldn't you have got a job in the City or something like that? I should've thought that'd be more your mark.'

'Why?' He sounded offended. Then he hunched his shoulders. 'I could've gone for

167

banking or something, I suppose. A lot of guys I know have done that. I just wanted something else, not just making money.' He fidgeted in an embarrassed way. 'I don't want to sound a pseud or big-headed, but I wanted to feel I was helping people, making a difference. I wanted to be able to think that what I was doing really mattered in the community. That somehow the world around would be a smidgen better for my efforts. I didn't just decide for all those high-minded reasons,' he added defensively.

'They sound all right to me,' I said.

He relaxed. 'The police force offers a good career structure for a graduate these days. It has to be more interesting than sitting at a desk. You meet a lot of unusual people ...' Here he grinned at me and saluted me with his glass.

'What am I? A freak?' I snapped.

'Of course not. I think you're, well, bright, very attractive and probably fun if you'd get that chip off your shoulder. We could be friends, if you'd be prepared to give it a try.'

'Chip?' I goggled at him. 'Me? Chip?'

Fortunately the pasta arrived. We must have been equally hungry because conversation flagged while we concentrated on eating.

When we'd pushed our plates aside and Harford had refilled our wine glasses, he asked, 'How's Patel today, by the way?'

'A bit groggy. Could be worse.' I eyed him.

'Do you think the guy who attacked him will come back?'

'Not tonight. We've got a patrol car keeping an eye on the place, just in case. I'm more worried about you, Fran. He—the man who's looking for the film—may think you have it or can get hold of it.'

'Thanks, I worked that one out for myself. You're still not going to let the public know you've got it?'

He shook his head. 'Once he knows that, he'll vanish. As long as he thinks he has a chance of recovering it, he'll hang around and we'll get him. Don't worry.'

'Look,' I told him, 'I'm not thick. I do realise what you coppers are up to here. Ganesh and I are decoys, right? You're waiting for whoever-it-is behind this to get in touch with one of us—or failing that, Marco or Hitch. As I see it, the least you can do is offer us adequate protection.'

'We've got it all under control,' he assured me.

'Have you, heck. Why's Ganesh staggering round concussed if that's the case?'

'That was a slip-up. It won't happen again. We're keeping an eye on you, Fran.'

I supposed I had to take his word for it. I toyed with my glass. 'Why did the person who tracked Coverdale to my place kill the poor bloke? That was stupid if the tracker wanted the film back. He's not going to get it off a dead man, is he?'

'My guess is, he panicked. Or he threatened Coverdale with the knife but Coverdale took him on. There was a struggle and the stabbing was accidental.' He hesitated. 'I looked over your flat when I called round the other day and it's a pretty secure place. I don't think anyone could get through that little window on to the ditch and the lawn—but don't leave it open at night. I realise this time of the year you probably wouldn't. If it's got a weak point, it's not having burglar bars on the basement window. I saw you had safety locks on the window and a chain on the door and that's fine, but why don't you talk to your landlady about getting burglar bars sometime?'

I'd previously thought my flat secure, but this kind of talk was making me nervous.

'You sound pretty sure he'll come back.'

'His employer will insist. He's a worried man.'

'But I'm not to know who he is, this worried Mr Big?'

Harford looked serious and shook his head. 'No kidding, Fran. All discussion of those photos is embargoed.' Without warning, he made a jump of subject. 'You and Patel go back some way, or so I understood Wayne Parry to say.'

Wayne? Parry's name was Wayne? Had his mother liked cowboy films? And just how much gossiping was done about me down at the nick? 'Ganesh is my friend,' I said coldly.

'Just that, a friend?' His eyes met mine and there was no mistaking what he meant.

That made me angry. I leaned over the green-checked table. 'Listen, saying someone's a friend is saying a lot. I don't chuck the word "friend" about. A friend is someone who's there when you need him. You never have to explain yourself to a friend. You can have a stand-up row with a friend and when the dust settles, you agree to differ and you're still mates. I don't know what your background is, but I bet it's pretty comfortable. You've probably got a lot of people you call friends. But friends are thin on the ground when you're down and out. I wonder, if you ever find yourself really up against it, as I've been lots of times, whether your friends will still be there for you the way Ganesh has always been there when I've needed him.'

He was looking down at his clasped hands on the cloth as I spoke, avoiding my eye. As I fell silent, I realised that something had changed. The atmosphere had plummeted well down the scale and the chill factor had set in. He looked up and the good nature had gone from his face. He was back to the sneery cold look again. He signalled to the waiter.

'You'll want to get back home,' he said.

Now what had I said that had really upset him? Something had. I'd touched a nerve. I remembered what he'd said about the public not supporting the police and wondered if he found himself got at from all sides. I couldn't imagine he got on easily with the other CID people and as for the uniformed bluebottles, they probably wrote rude limericks about him on the bog wall. By my words, I'd made it clear I excluded him from my world, too. Well, if he was a misfit, it wasn't my problem. But to have accused me of having a chip on the shoulder was a bit rich.

'I pay my whack, like I said,' I told him, dragging my purse out from the neck of my sweater. I keep it on a leather string under my top clothing. I've always kept my money tucked well away. It's because of the sort of company I'd kept for too long and the crap places I'd lived—before I got the flat.

After the snug warmth of the restaurant, outside was really miserable. We stood on the pavement in the drizzling rain. I hunched down in my denim jacket, Harford stood with his hands in his pockets and a truculent expression on his face. 'Do you want me to walk you back?' he asked.

Put like that, how could a girl accept? 'I don't need an escort,' I told him sourly. 'Thanks for the wine.'

I don't know whether he watched me walk away. I didn't look back. *Brief Encounter* with a modern twist. You wouldn't catch me going for a drink with a bloke I didn't like again.

# CHAPTER TEN

I didn't sleep at all well. My brain was too busy. It was only partly because of Harford's words about security at the flat. I'd checked everything and thought I was safe. Just to make sure of that little garden window, I'd blocked it by taking the medicine cabinet off the bathroom wall, and wedging it in the window space. It looked odd and was inconvenient, taking the light, but if anyone tried to get through the window, he'd dislodge it and it'd fall down with a heck of a noise.

As I lay there, drifting in and out of sleep, my mind ran on Coverdale, whom I'd hardly known, but who'd died just outside my door. Ganesh and I had rescued him from his pursuers once, but in the end it hadn't helped the wretched man. It did, however, leave me with a feeling of responsibility towards him— quite unnecessarily as I told myself, but hard to shift.

I speculated irritably about the perverseness of Fate. I remembered the story in which a merchant's told he's going to meet Death the next day, so he travels to Damascus to avoid it only to find Death has travelled there too. Coverdale had cheated Death at the shop, only to meet the Grim Reaper in my basement. I supposed there was a sort of sense in that.

Coverdale had presumably poked his nose in where he shouldn't. He'd been an investigative reporter and that'd been his job. It had risks attached and they'd caught up with him. But me, why had I been dragged in?

In the end, I decided Ganesh was responsible. He'd allowed Coverdale to use the old washroom. He'd decided to get Hitch to rip out the fittings. So that settled that. It was Gan's fault.

I turned my thoughts to the fair-haired man in the photo and wondered where he was and what he was doing. His heavies were incompetent. They'd picked up Coverdale and lost him again the day he'd stumbled into the shop. Then one of them had contrived to kill the poor bloke before they'd found out what had happened to the—

I sat up in bed. 'Buck up your ideas, Fran!' I said aloud. Just because Harford thought Coverdale's death might have been unintended in a struggle, or because the killer had panicked, didn't mean that was how it had been. I was forgetting—and Harford was, too—that *Coverdale* hadn't known Gan and I had recovered the film any more than the villains did. Coverdale thought the film was still hidden in the washroom at the shop. He had come to the flat to ask me to retrieve it for him. When threatened by the knifeman, had he confessed this? If so, having told the knifeman what he wanted to know, Coverdale himself had then become expendable. In fact, he'd become too dangerous to leave alive. No accident, then. No panicking assailant. Coverdale had been murdered deliberately by a cold-blooded killer and any further knowledge he'd had about the fair-haired man in the pic had died with him.

It explained why the searcher had next tried the shop. It wasn't because he was blundering around, hoping to strike lucky, but because he'd been told, by the man who'd hidden it, that the film was there.

He must have had a terrific shock when he saw the washroom with the partly installed new fittings. Coverdale hadn't known about that, either. Coverdale would've described the old washroom and the exact spot he'd stashed the packet with the film in it. The searcher had realised that someone else must have come across the envelope when the old fittings were torn out. But what he didn't know was what the finder had done with it. Had he or she simply chucked it in a waste-paper basket? Or kept it? The intruder had started up the back stair leading to the flat with the intention of searching there, but that's when he'd met Ganesh on the staircase. I wondered how long Gan had lain unconscious. Long enough for the intruder to complete his search? Hari's flat was a tip. Needles in haystacks would hardly have come into it. On the other hand, it was easier to search for something if you knew what it was, than if you didn't, if you see what I mean.

Having reached these various conclusions, it was difficult to get back to sleep at all. I looked at the clock and saw it was gone five. In an hour's time, Ganesh would be taking delivery of the morning papers—if he'd woken up. I got up, made some tea, showered, dressed, and set out for the shop.

It's surprising how many people are out and about just before six in the morning. The streets were quite busy, traffic already building up. People were bound for work, forming queues at the bus stops and hurrying into the entrance to the tube station.

Ganesh was at work already, taking in the stacks of newspapers, apparently much recovered, and surprised to see me.

'I told you I'd come early,' I said.

'You can give me a hand to put these out, then.'

I hate handling newsprint. You get filthy. I concentrated on the quality broadsheets, because that print is less likely to mess up your hands. As we worked, I told Ganesh about my encounter with Harford the previous evening, and also what I'd worked out about Coverdale's death. I didn't tell him how I'd concluded that our involvement was all his fault. I'd save that for later.

Ganesh agreed. 'What's more,' he said, 'I've been thinking over the business of that dummy

176

alarm. That's typical of Hari and very bad thinking. Penny wise and pound foolish, that's the old fellow. I think I'll get a proper system installed before he gets back. It's for his own good and protection, not to say mine.'

It certainly made sense, but what with that and the new washroom, Hari's profits were in danger of disappearing fast. I felt a bit sorry for the poor old boy, holidaying out there in India, blissfully unaware what his nephew was up to.

When we'd finished the newspapers, I washed my hands in the nice new washbasin, and went down the road to the French bakery to buy us *pains au chocolat* for breakfast. I felt we needed a little treat and chocolate is supposed to cheer the spirit.

We needed cheering because the master craftsmen were back.

'Coppers not hanging around?' asked Hitch, putting his head round the doorjamb. He spoke in what passed, for him, as a whisper. I thought he'd have been good at stage asides, clearly audible to the audience.

Told they weren't expected, as far as we knew, he edged in and took a good look round the place to make sure, just in case Parry jumped out from behind the cold drinks cabinet. 'Got the back door opened up? Marco's bringing the tiles in. We can finish it all off by lunchtime. You all right today, sunshine? How's the old napper?'

Ganesh said he was fine, thanks, and glad they could finish the job today. He went to open up the back door.

Left alone in the shop, I sold three newspapers, a tube of throat lozenges and a packet of disposable cigarette lighters, all to the same person, a brickie from a nearby construction site. If he cut back on the ciggies he mightn't have needed the throat sweets but I was more intrigued by what he was going to do with three papers. I asked.

'I buy 'em for me mates,' he explained hoarsely.

I didn't follow up the questioning although I was tempted. Two of the papers were downmarket tabloids but the third was the *Financial Times*.

After he left, trade, such as it was, fell off completely. From the rear of the premises came the muted roar of Hitch's normal speaking voice.

The doorbell tinged and I looked up.

'Hi,' said Tig, edging in nervously. Like Hitch earlier, she took a good look round. 'I thought I'd drop in and ask how you were getting on—you know, if you'd rung my parents.'

She looked worse than ever this morning. Her features had a nipped, chilled look and her lips had gained a blue tinge.

'You want a cup of coffee, Tig?' I offered. 'Things are quiet and the kettle boiled only a few minutes ago.'

She accepted, nursing the warm mug in her skeletal fingers and pressing it against her cheeks. She wore a dirty dark-coloured donkey jacket and a red scarf wound round her neck. Her hair was lank and straggly. I'd have to clean her up before I sent her home. Provided, of course, that I managed to bring off that little project successfully.

I explained about the phone call to her mother and that I hoped to go to Dorridge on Sunday.

'Not till then?' She sounded disappointed.

'Oy,' I protested. 'I'm doing my best. But I've got other commitments, you know. Ganesh—the manager here—got bashed on the head the other night.'

Tig didn't ask how or why. Getting done over happened to everyone from time to time in her world. But she still looked restless and I guessed something had happened to worry her.

'Is it Jo Jo?' I asked, because that seemed the most likely explanation.

'He's getting really nosy,' Tig said. 'I'm afraid he'll get one of his moods when he thinks someone's plotting against him. He doesn't really trust anyone, not even me. He freaked out over that chocolate you gave me and if he knew about this, he'd go completely ape. I don't mean most of the time he isn't OK. But he can be scary.'

179

Scary, as in being a headcase. 'You've got to leave him, Tig,' I said firmly. 'Right away. I mean, as of now. Don't go back.'

'Where'm I going to go?' she asked. 'I gotta kip somewhere.'

That put me on the spot and I had to offer. 'You can come to my place until you go home. It'll be all right. I'm on my own there.'

And what if she didn't go home? Was I to be landed with her indefinitely? I didn't fancy the idea.

She wasn't exactly leaping at the offer, either. 'I dunno,' she said. 'What about my gear? Jo Jo's minding all our stuff.' Shrewd of him. Standing guard over Tig's few belongings might be enough to keep her by his side. If so, time to show him he was mistaken.

'Then ditch it. It's not worth the risk going back for it. You couldn't sneak it away without his noticing. Have you got anything you can't leave behind?'

She was nodding. 'Yes, sort of. There's— there's one thing I've got to go back for.' She put down the empty mug. 'Tell me where your place is. I'll come over this evening, about nine. Jo Jo's got something on tonight, got to go and see a mate on business. I don't know what sort, he didn't say.'

Something connected with drugs, I shouldn't be surprised. Jo Jo didn't look the type to have scruples. I still didn't think it a good idea for her to return to him in the meantime but I could see she was adamant. I told her where I lived. As I finished speaking, there was the sound of Ganesh returning.

Tig said quickly, 'OK then, see you later, this evening sometime.' She was gone in a second.

I debated whether to tell Ganesh of this latest development and decided not to. He'd say I was getting in deeper and it was a really bad move. And what on earth was Tig carrying around with her that was so valuable she had to risk Jo Jo's violence to go back for it?

*       *       *

Ganesh said I could go at twelve if I liked. He was feeling better and Dilip had promised to come round for an hour around six when things tended to get busy.

I set off down the pavement and reached the chemist's shop where I'd taken the negatives to be developed. It occurred to me that my houseguest would be unlikely to bring a range of bathroom toiletries with her; from the look of her, soap might be a novelty these days. Poor Tig, once the dedicated tooth-brusher. Well, if she was going to stay with me, personal hygiene wouldn't be an optional extra. It'd be a basic necessity.

I pushed open the door of the shop. Things were quiet. One of the two regular assistants had gone to lunch and the other, Joleen, was

181

leaning on the counter, reading *Black Beauty and Hair*. Her ambition was to be a beauty consultant with her own salon but selling cough mixtures and contraceptives in our local chemist's was as far as she'd got. I sympathised with her stalled ambitions, being in the same boat myself. I collected a bar of soap and a bottle of showergel from the open shelves and took them over to her.

'Hi, Fran,' she said. She held out her hands towards me, backs outward, so I could admire her purplish-red nails. 'What do you think?'

'Very nice,' I said.

'It's a new range. This shade's called Smouldering. Chip-proof. You ought to try it. I could do your nails for you. I'm a trained manicurist, you know.'

'Believe me,' I said, 'given my lifestyle, I wouldn't need chip-proof varnish, I'd need bomb-proof.' I put my purchases on the counter.

'Two ninety-five,' said Joleen, stabbing at the till with her vampire talons. I paid. She put the items in a plastic bag and propped herself on the counter again for a chat.

'Mike, he does the developing out back—' she indicated the rear of the premises— 'he hoped those holiday snaps he did for you the other day were all right. He had a lot of trouble with them. It was some kind of foreign film, wasn't it?'

'Probably,' I said cautiously. 'They weren't

mine. I got them done for a friend.'

'He had a coupla goes at them, as you'll have seen. The first lot came out really rubbish colours. The second lot were better, but he wasn't really satisfied. He said to tell you he couldn't do better—only it wasn't me gave them back to you, was it?'

'No, it was the other woman ...' I said slowly, my brain grinding into gear. 'Joleen, what do you mean, as I'd have seen?'

She stared at me. 'He put both lots in the envelope, so you could see he really tried.'

'Hang on,' I said carefully. 'Are you telling me he took *two sets of prints from that film*?'

'Sure. He put them both in the envelope, like I said.'

'No,' I said, 'he didn't.'

'Oh.' Joleen thought about it and shrugged. 'He meant to. Must've changed his mind. Well, like I said, the first lot were no good anyway, so you wouldn't have wanted them.'

'But I would!' I said hastily. 'The friend— the person who asked me to get the film developed—he's lost the original negs now and can't get any more pics printed off. He'd like some copies to send to the other guys in the pictures. So, if the first prints are still out back somewhere, yes, I'd, I mean he'd, like them— even if the colour is duff.'

Joleen looked doubtful. 'They've probably been chucked out by now. I'll go and ask.'

She sashayed into the back room on her

platform soles, her beaded braids swinging, and giving the impression she wasn't wearing an awful lot under that crisp white overall.

She came back a few minutes later carrying a metal wastepaper bin. 'Mike says, sorry, he meant to give them to you with the others. If they're still anywhere, they might be in this bin.'

The bell rang signalling a new customer. 'Here,' Joleen thrust the bin at me, 'take a look for yourself.'

She moved off to dispense corn plasters and E45 cream to an elderly woman.

I set down the bin and riffled through its contents eagerly (which distracted the elderly customer who gave me a funny look). Please, please ... I was whispering to myself. Bingo! Right at the bottom, only one of the snaps— the other three must be lost for good. But one was better than none. I fished it out. The colours were bad, all right; no wonder Mike hadn't wanted to send these out. I'd have asked for my money back. The fair-haired man at the centre of the scene appeared to have had an orange rinse. But the images were clear enough.

'OK? Got them, then?' Joleen was back.

'Got one. Thanks, Joleen. I—My friend will be really chuffed.'

' 'Sall right,' she said cheerfully. 'Do you want a lipstick, free? I've got a box full of tester samples here, discontinued lines. Most of them have got quite a bit left.'

'Keep on smouldering, Joleen!' I called as I left the shop, and she let out a great shriek of a giggle. In the plastic bag I now carried the soap, the showergel, a half-used burnt sienna lipstick, which Joleen reckoned was my colour—and best of all, a luridly hued picture of Mr Big. It might prove dangerous property—but on the other hand, it might come in useful.

*　　　*　　　*

I got back to the flat mid-afternoon and sat on my sofa looking round the place, thinking my newly won privacy and independence were about to be invaded by Tig. I'd lived in squats and was used to sharing space and been grateful, often enough, when I'd first found myself on my own, to be offered shelter by anyone. I knew I couldn't have done anything else but invite Tig to stay, but it was harder to accept the reality than I'd imagined it would be. I'd got used to being on my own. This was my place. I lived here. I told myself not to be selfish but I'd got selfish. We all do the more we have. Anyone can be generous with nothing. Having Tig here to share would be good for me.

I did wonder if I ought to mention Tig to Daphne, because if she saw her going in and out, she might wonder. But I was perfectly entitled to have a friend to stay and anyway, I didn't think Daphne would mind. Charlie and Bertie, if they found out, would object strongly and it'd give them a weapon against me. I'd be accused of filling the flat with undesirables. But Tig wasn't going to stay long, or not if I had anything to do with it. It was, after all, up to me. I now had a perfect reason for fixing things up with the Quayles.

Tig didn't come until almost ten that evening. I was beginning to wonder if she'd managed to get away from Jo Jo or if he'd discovered her plan. When the bell rang, I called through the door, 'Who is it?' Because I now had a list of people I didn't want to see, including the Knowles twins, Inspector Harford, Wayne Parry and the killer of Gray Coverdale.

'Tig!' called back her voice and this was followed by a scrabbling sound and I heard her urge, 'Stop it.'

Had she brought someone with her? I opened the door cautiously.

'I'm here, then,' said Tig. She glanced down. 'I had to bring Bonnie. I hope you don't mind.'

I looked down. At Tig's feet sat a small brown and white rough-haired terrier, head on one side, ears pricked, gazing up at me expectantly.

'This is what you had to go back for,' I said. 'Bonnie.'

'That's right. OK if we come in?'

186

I let them both pass. Tig lugged in a bulging haversack which she dropped in the middle of the carpet. She looked round critically. 'Nice place, but why is the bathroom cabinet stuck up there where a window ought to be?'

'I'll tell you about that later,' I said.

Bonnie had started on her own tour of inspection, trotting round the furniture, sniffing out everything.

'She won't pee on the carpet, will she?' I asked nervously.

'Course she won't. She's really good. She belonged to the girl who died, the one I told you about. You remember I told you I got talking to that girl about her dog? Well, this is the dog and someone had to take her on. I had to bring her with me here. I couldn't leave her behind with Jo Jo, because he'd only sell her on to someone and I feel, you know, I've got to see she's all right.'

She felt about Bonnie the way I felt about Tig herself, so I understood. Bonnie came towards me and stood right in front of my boots, still looking up at me expectantly. She was mostly white, with a brown patch over the right eye and the ear above it. On that same right flank she had another large brown patch and a brown tip to her tail. On the left-hand side she was white all over—except for the tail tip. Looking at her from the right side or the left was like looking at two different dogs—on the one side a brown and white one and on the other, a white one.

'What about her food?' I asked.

' 'Sall right, I brought some.' Tig delved in the haversack and produced a tin of some dog food or other. 'She's no trouble, really.'

My attention had moved to the haversack. 'I see you've brought all your gear. Jo Jo will know straight away when he gets back that you've taken off.'

'Don't care. I've done it now. Can't go back.' She looked round. 'Where do I sleep?'

'On the sofa.' I indicated it. She was right. She couldn't go back and I couldn't tell her to leave. Like it or not, I was stuck with her.

There was something else I had to draw her attention to right away. 'That's the bathroom,' I said, pointing. 'You can have a shower. Why don't you take one now and I'll make us some sort of supper?'

'OK,' she said. 'It'll be nice to have the use of a proper bathroom again.'

Bonnie gave a short excited bark.

'Yes,' I told her, 'we can bath you, too.'

While Tig showered, I put bathing Bonnie into practice. I ran warm water into the kitchen sink, scooped her up in my arms and stood her in the pool. She didn't mind being picked up, but she was doubtful about being stood in the water. She sniffed at it, had a go at drinking it, and then looked at me reproachfully.

'Sorry, but it's for all our benefit,' I told her.

I wet her all over and, careful to avoid her eyes, lathered her up with some washing-up liquid. She cringed miserably, her ears flattened and her tail drooped. By the time I'd finished rinsing her off, she looked like a drowned rat.

I'd found an old towel which I wrapped round her and lifted her to the floor. My intention was to dry her off, but she had other ideas about that, wriggled out of my grip and scuttled off. She then shook herself vigorously, waterdrops flying everywhere, showering the carpet and furniture.

'Oy,' I ordered. 'Stop that and come here—'

I set off in pursuit with the towel, but Bonnie was quicker than me, adept at squeezing through small spaces and, just when I thought I could grab her, putting on an extra spurt of speed and slithering through my grasp.

After five minutes of this, I was breathless. Bonnie—who'd regarded the chase as a great game—was wagging her tail and barking at me to keep going.

'Game's over,' I told her, collapsing on the sofa. Bonnie now came over to me and allowed me to pat her. The chase had pretty well dried her coat which was now quite silky, with a tendency in the longer hair to wave. Instead of smelling of grubby dog, she now smelled of lemon fragrance from the washing-up liquid.

'Hey,' said Tig, emerging from the bathroom, 'she looks pretty good.' Tig was looking an awful lot better, too, with her hair washed and a fresh look to her skin.

I hauled myself off to the kitchen to clean out the sink. I splashed a bit of bleach round to kill any germs or bugs which might have dropped off Bonnie. Then I turned my attention to supper. Having houseguests looked like turning out to be a lot of work.

I'm not a cook and when I opened my store cupboard, I realised I wasn't much of a housekeeper either. It held half-a-dozen eggs, the rest of the packet of pasta from last week, two tins of beans, a half-squeezed tube of tomato paste and some bread. I made us scrambled eggs and toast.

Tig ate it up appreciatively and while we dined in style, Bonnie gobbled up her dinner from a dented tin dogbowl Tig had brought with her. They were easy to please, I'll say that.

'How will your parents take to Bonnie?' I asked.

Tig looked over the rim of her coffee mug. 'Well, there might be a bit of a problem with that.'

My heart sank. 'Problem?'

'Yes, my mum's so houseproud, I told you. She doesn't like animals about the place. She says they shed hairs. So, um, I don't think I can take Bonnie to Dorridge. I thought, well, you might like her—or you could find a nice home for her. She deserves a nice home,' added Tig pathetically.

The pathos worked on old gents, not on me. 'Forget it,' I said robustly. 'I am not taking in Bonnie.'

There was a clatter from the kitchen and Bonnie appeared, dragging along her empty tin dish. She dropped it in front of us and barked.

'There,' said Tig. 'She's telling you she wants a drink of water. She's ever so clever.'

I went to fill the dish. 'This is temporary,' I said to Bonnie as I set it down. 'You are just passing through, right?'

Bonnie gave an excited little yelp and fixed me with that expectant look. I was beginning to recognise it. It was the canine equivalent of Tig's Little Nell act. Resist me and have me on your conscience for ever, it said.

'Don't push your luck,' I told her.

We all three settled down cosily for the night, quite soon after supper. It had been a long day for all of us.

As I've mentioned before, my bedroom was the adaptation of a former Victorian coal-cellar under the pavement, and reached by a short passage from my basement living room, through the basement itself. The bedroom was, of course, windowless, although some light managed to get in through an opaque toughened glass panel in the ceiling, i.e., the
191

pavement above, which replaced the former metal cover of the coal chute. I retired for the night in this tomblike little room, leaving Tig and Bonnie curled up together on my blue rep sofa in the living room.

Exhausted, I went out like a light. I was woken at some ungodly hour by a hand shaking my shoulder.

'Fran?' Tig's voice came as little more than a breath in the darkness. 'Wake up and don't make a noise.'

I was awake in an instant, every instinct straining. I couldn't see Tig but knew she was there by the bed. I also heard the sound of something struggling and realised she must be holding Bonnie in her arms.

'What is it?' I sat up and swung my legs to the ground. My foot bumped against her leg and she moved back. The struggling sound was renewed together with a muffled whine.

Tig shushed the little dog and I guessed she had one hand clamped over Bonnie's muzzle to stop her barking.

'Someone's trying to get into the flat,' she whispered.

## CHAPTER ELEVEN

Together we edged back into the living room where enough light seeped through the basement window from the streetlamps outside to reveal Tig's silhouette. In her arms Bonnie wriggled like a creature berserk, desperate to be allowed to do her job and see off any intruder.

He, the visitor, was at the basement window. The curtain was drawn and all we could see was his fuzzy outline and upraised arms as he worked his way round the frame. These were old houses and didn't, alas, have double-glazing, just old-fashioned single-paned windows in a wooden frame. He must have recced beforehand and had probably thought entry would be a doddle. Now he was probably realising that safety catches must be in place on the inside.

I felt slightly sick and was glad I'd wedged the medicine cabinet in the garden window. He'd have squeezed his way through there in a few seconds. The thing was, who was he?

'Do you think it's Jo Jo?' I whispered, not that I thought it really was. But there was an outside chance.

Tig dismissed it. 'No ... he doesn't know I'm here. That guy at the window's not big enough for Jo Jo, anyway. Is it that bloke you were so scared of the other day?'

Tig hadn't been so wrapped up in her own problems that she'd forgotten the fright she'd given me when she'd stopped me in the street.

'Sorry,' I murmured. 'Should have warned you this might—'

Tig hadn't got a free hand but used her elbow to jab me painfully in the ribs as a sign to keep quiet. We waited.

He'd moved away a little from the window but had now returned and began to do something down in the right-hand corner of the window pane. There was a faint squeaky scratchy noise.

Bonnie, frustrated to the point of madness, tried to tear her muzzle free of the restraining hand and renewed her efforts in Tig's arms, both of which were now tightly wrapped round the terrier's frantic body.

Whoever he was, he was a pro and had come prepared. He was cutting a hole in the glass. Tig leaned towards me and put her mouth to my ear.

'When he gets his hand through, you pull back the curtain and I let Bonnie go, right?'

I nodded, though she probably couldn't see it. There was a pause in activity at the window pane and then a soft tap. The small circle of glass fell inward but was prevented from falling to the ground and shattering noisily by the sticky tape he'd fixed to it to prevent this. He knew his stuff. We watched, horrified yet fascinated, even Bonnie stopped wriggling. Through the thin curtain, we saw a hand emerge through the hole into our space, and fingers feel about for the safety catch. It was like one of those old horror movies, you know, *The Mummy's Hand*, but I was beyond being merely scared, I was almost paralysed with fear.

He's not in yet, I reassured myself. And there are two of us, three with Bonnie.

'Now!' breathed Tig.

I leaped forward and yanked back the curtain. Bonnie, released, exploded out of Tig's embrace, flew at the hole in the window pane and sank her teeth into the searching hand. There was a scream of surprise and pain from outside. I dashed to the wall and switched on the light.

He was pressed against the window, his face contorted in pain and rage, but I recognised him as the little fellow who'd come to the shop. He was mouthing oaths in some foreign language, possibly Spanish or Portuguese. I'm not well up in either of those, but I knew it wasn't Italian. I could see his small white teeth and his eyes were like a wild animal's. I thought, this is the man who killed Gray Coverdale, and if he gets in here, he'll kill us for sure for doing this to him.

He was trying to get his hand back through the hole, but Bonnie, true to her terrier instincts, didn't let go but hung on grimly. Blood was dripping down the windowsill. Suddenly he pushed his hand forward, instead of trying to tug it back towards him, then jerked it viciously back again. It must have hurt him, but it hurt Bonnie too as her nose crashed into the cut edge of the glass. She yelped and fractionally loosened her grip.

Tig and I both yelled at her to let go. We didn't want her injured. Further confused, she dropped to the ground. The man pulled his free hand back through the hole a split second before Bonnie recovered enough to grab it again. Gripping injured fingers to his chest, he bolted out of the basement. We could hear the soft thud of his feet running away along the pavement.

Tig was kneeling on the floor trying to examine Bonnie's nose. Bonnie, cheated of her victim, was yelping and squealing, in no mood to stand still for a medical. She got loose and hurled herself at the front door, barking furiously.

We dragged her away and calmed her down. The side of her muzzle was scratched but she was otherwise unharmed. The blood on the windowsill was the intruder's. Serve him right.

'I'm really sorry, Tig,' I said. 'I should have explained things to you before you came here.'

'What's going on, then?' asked Tig. She disappeared into the kitchenette and could be heard switching on the kettle. We'd both come down in the world but we'd both been brought up on traditional lines and knew the golden rule: whatever the emergency, get the tea brewing.

Bonnie ran back and forth beneath the window sniffing at the carpet and from time to time, putting her paws on the sill and sniffing along there. She was reliving her victory over the would-be intruder in her mind. Probably, like many humans, she was garnishing it with a few extra heroics, although to my mind, she'd been quite heroic enough.

'The other evening,' I explained to Tig when we'd got our mugs of tea and settled down on the sofa on top of Tig's sleeping bag, 'a man was murdered out there, in my basement.'

Tig sipped at her tea and eyed me through a fringe of hair. There was a new air of friendliness about her. She'd woken up next to a body: I'd come home and found one on my doorstep. We had something in common.

'Why?' she asked.

'He'd come to see me because he thought I might have something a lot of people seem to want—or that I knew where it was.'

'Have you got it?'

I shook my head.

'You oughta move out of this end of town for a bit,' said Tig, after thinking this over.

'OK, I'm going to Dorridge on Sunday, remember? The thing is, you'll be here and he might come back.'

'I've got Bonnie and anyway, he won't try anything like that again now he knows the dog's here. She kicks up a real racket.'

Yes, she did. I wondered whether Daphne had heard anything. Her bedroom was on the first floor, which put her two floors above us here. It overlooked the garden and it was possible she'd slept through the whole thing undisturbed. I hoped so. I was less sure about the neighbours and their Watch Scheme which, after Coverdale's murder, must have gone into top gear.

'Tig,' I said. 'I'm going to have to report this to the police.'

She sat up, alarmed. 'I'm not staying here if the pigs are going to be crawling round the place!'

Bonnie got excited again at the tone of her voice and began rushing round the room, yelping.

'Calm down!' I begged them both. 'Look, you don't have to be involved. In the morning, first thing, we'll go upstairs and explain things to Daphne, my landlady. She'll have to know. I suppose the damaged pane can be fixed on her buildings insurance. I'll ring the police from her place. They *have* to know, Tig—Daphne will want to tell them—and anyway, the—this thing everyone wants, the police have—the police are interested. I'll ask Daphne if you can sit up there in her kitchen while whoever the police send does his stuff down here. You won't have to see them, the coppers. They won't see you. Not that it matters if they do see you does it? You're not wanted for anything?'

She shook her head. 'I just don't like the pigs.' She fidgeted about, undecided. 'Your landlady won't like me. Respectable old girls don't.'

'Daphne isn't like the others,' I assured her, and hoped I was right.

As I spoke, we heard the sound of a car turning into the street. I jumped up and switched out the light. Tig grabbed Bonnie again. Bonnie, hoping for a replay, took a dim view of this and whined pitiably.

I stood by the damaged window and peered up. I could just make out the top of the car as it cruised past.

'Neighbourhood Watch must've phoned through to the cop shop,' I said. 'It's the law, taking a look.'

'Shit,' muttered Tig.

We waited and after a while, we heard a regular plod's footstep approaching. From time to time it stopped and then moved on. He was checking out the basements. He reached mine and leaned over the iron railing. The beam of a torch flashed across the window. I heard him swear and call out to his partner. 'Sorry,' I said to Tig. 'He's spotted it. You hide in the bedroom, take your stuff with you, and leave Bonnie out here.'

The officer was descending my stairwell, flashing the torch around. He shone it on the broken window again and turned aside to ring my doorbell. Tig had scuttled into the bedroom and there was no way I could ignore the summons. Bonnie was barking her head off.

I picked her up, switched on the light, and opened up. 'Good evening, officer,' I said, although it was the middle of the night.

'Evening, miss …' He looked rather startled. Perhaps it was the Snoopy nightshirt which had shrunk in numerous washes and was now little more than a long tee shirt. He dragged his eyes away and peered past me. 'We received a call a little while back from one of your Neighbourhood Watch members, old gent living opposite. You seem to have had some damage to a window pane. You know about that?'

I had to let him in. 'Someone tried to break in. My dog saw him off.'

Bonnie, in my arms, was behaving very badly. She clearly didn't like the police, either. Someone had taught her they were the enemy. She was growling ferociously, lips rolled back to bare her teeth, and the hair bristled along her spine. The encounter with the would-be intruder had given her a taste for blood.

'Yes,' said the copper, eyeing her nervously, 'she looks a real little scrapper. Did you call us?'

'I haven't got a phone. I was going to call in the morning.'

Pounding feet announced his partner. The first one turned to him. 'This is the place, all right. Dog drove chummy off.' He turned back to me. 'You on your own here?' He was eyeing the nightshirt again.

I said I was and they expressed some concern. I pointed out I had Bonnie, who, faced with *two* coppers, was doing her nut, longing to be allowed to get at 'em. I gripped her muzzle as Tig had done earlier. She spluttered, enraged.

'I've had a good look up and down the road, but he's gone,' said the newly arrived copper.

'We'll try and block up that gap for you,' the other said, 'and send someone round in the morning. You'll have to make a proper report then. OK?'

I promised them I'd be waiting. They were really rather nice, better than average anyway. It must have been the Snoopy nightshirt. They taped cardboard over the holed place and advised me to leave a light on.

'I'd offer you a cup of tea,' I said. 'But I'd have to put the dog down.'

They took the point.

When they'd driven off, I released Bonnie who, having had the last word in a defiant barking session, sat by the front door hopefully, waiting for the next arrivals. I opened the bedroom door and called to Tig that she could come out.

Tig sidled out, her white face defiant, as though she anticipated what I was going to say.

'You see,' I said. 'It was all right.'

'I don't like the pigs,' she said obstinately.

\*　　　\*　　　\*

201

Daphne didn't let me down. Although she was clearly upset at the attempted break-in, she greeted Tig kindly and said how nice it was to meet one of Fran's friends. I saw Tig calm down under this civilised reception, but she remained wary and sat huddled in the corner of Daphne's kitchen, while we rang the police to see when they'd be coming round, and waited for them to turn up.

In the meantime, Daphne provided toast and coffee and made a great fuss of Bonnie.

'What a brave little dog and so lucky your friend had brought her along.'

Bonnie accepted all this praise as no more than her due, her stumpy tail thumping the ground.

Tig continued to sit awkwardly in the corner of Daphne's kitchen, her eyes studying every detail of the fixtures and fittings. I wondered what she was thinking.

'I'll get the glazier in today straight away,' said Daphne. 'And perhaps I'd better get a burglar-proof grille put in down there.'

'Inspector Harford's all for those,' I told her. 'But I don't fancy being locked in a cage, Daphne.'

'It's only at night or if you're away,' she pointed out. 'You can pull them back and forth, or so I understand. I didn't mean the fixed sort.' A thought seemed to strike her and she frowned worriedly. 'I suppose I can keep this from Bertie and Charlie.'

Oh blimey, the dreaded duo. I'd forgotten them. They'd love this.

'Who're they?' asked Tig, breaking her silence.

Daphne explained they were her nephews. 'And always so worried about my security, as they call it. Inclined to fuss, really, but it's all very well meant. Perhaps I can get the glazier to come quickly and get it all fixed up before they find out.'

There was the sound of a car drawing up outside and a door slammed.

'That'll be the police,' I said. 'You stay here, Tig.'

* * *

Parry was just climbing the steps to Daphne's front door as she opened it. He said, 'Morning, ma'am,' to her and, glimpsing me in the hall behind her, added less graciously, 'What's going on, then?'

We took him down to the basement and explained. He examined the window and sighed. 'I'll get the fingerprint boys over *again*. You say you can describe this bloke, Fran?'

I gave him a pretty good description: small, dark curly hair, Mediterranean appearance and foreign accent, injured hand. 'So you ought to be able to pick him up.'

'You may not have noticed it,' said Parry

203

sarcastically, 'but the streets of London are littered with blokes speaking with foreign accents.'

'Tourists, I suppose,' said Daphne.

Parry gave her a jaundiced look. 'Yes, ma'am, and every petty crook and thug who likes to pop across the Channel. We make it easy for 'em these days.' I put Parry in the Eurosceptic camp. But then, I imagined Parry was sceptical about everything.

'When will these fingerprint experts come?' asked Daphne. 'I want to ring the glazier.'

'When they've got a minute,' muttered Parry to me. 'Seeing as they've got other things to do besides spend half their lives at this place or round at your mate Patel's.' He turned back to Daphne. 'I'll just take a statement from Miss Varady, and I'll be off.'

Daphne took the hint and left us. When we were alone, Parry took out a notebook and biro. 'I can't leave you for five minutes, can I?' he grumbled. 'I come in this morning and what do I find? Overnight you've had a break-in. First Patel, now you.'

'That's right,' I said. 'And the man who tried to break in here last night was the same man who came to the shop fishing for information about Coverdale.'

Parry, poised with pen above notebook, gave me a sharp look. 'You're on the level with this, Fran? You'd better be.'

I could have thumped him. There's just no

getting through to Parry. 'I am sure!' I said tightly. 'So we know what he was after, don't we? Why don't you just release the information that you've got the flippin' negatives?'

'Been decided higher up,' he said. 'It's embargoed and it stays that way. We've all got to lump it. Right, let's have the rest of your statement, then.'

When I'd given it, he asked, 'Where's the dog?'

'Upstairs with Daphne.'

Parry wasn't stupid, despite his manner and general appearance. 'Since when have you had a pet pooch, then?'

'I'm looking after her for a friend.'

'Friend wasn't with you, then, last night?'

'Your boys were here,' I said. 'They talked to me. They saw the situation. You've got my statement. Now, if you don't mind, I've got to go to work.'

\*     \*     \*

I went to work. I didn't tell Ganesh about my overnight visitor. He had enough worries. Instead, I excused my lateness by telling him I'd overslept. At least Hitch and Marco had finished the new washroom and, I had to admit, it did look good.

'See,' said Ganesh. 'The old chap won't be cross, not when he sees it.'

Looking at the shiny new tiles, the extractor fan which worked and sanitary fittings which didn't assault the would-be user, I had to admit Hari ought to be pleased. I still thought he'd make a fuss about the cost. Ganesh said that had been very reasonable. He'd haggled a bit and Hitch had brought it down. I privately thought that if Hitch had reduced the quoted price, it was because he'd increased it in the first place to allow for this. Still, it did seem mean to quibble. Hitch and Marco had done a good job and deserved to be fairly paid.

*      *      *

I did wonder, when I got home at lunchtime, whether I'd find Tig still there. I was relieved to hear Bonnie bark as I clattered down the basement steps. I noticed that the glazier had been and I had a new window pane. The putty was still soft.

'I've been out,' said Tig. 'You know, to walk Bonnie and get out of the way of the guys who came to fix the window. I brought us in some lunch and more dog food for Bonnie.'

'Watch out for Jo Jo,' I warned her. 'He might come back to this patch to look for you, seeing as you were working the area earlier.'

She'd brought in fish and chips. She heated them up in the oven and served them up to me on a tray. She obviously wanted to work her passage. I appreciated that. Tig had been no trouble in the old days, back in the Jubilee Street squat, because she'd always done her fair share. Reminded of her then, and seeing her miserable state now, I felt sad and worried. What would her parents think when they saw her? How could I prepare them?

We were washing up when the doorbell rang. Tig, who'd been chatting in quite a friendly way, was immediately back on the defensive, hissing, 'Who's that?'

'Hang on,' I said. 'I'll go and see.'

I peered out the nice new window and was rewarded with the sight of Jason Harford, who'd left the door and was prodding at the new putty in a critical way. Behind me, I heard the bathroom door click. Tig had taken refuge, dragging Bonnie in there with her.

I kicked Tig's rucksack behind the sofa out of sight and threw her sleeping bag after it. The coast clear, I let him in.

'You all right, Fran?' he asked, looking and sounding genuinely concerned. If we'd parted coolly on the last occasion, he appeared to have forgotten.

'As you see me,' I said. Behind the bathroom door, Bonnie was barking at the sound of a strange voice. 'I've shut the dog in there,' I explained, 'because she's been a bit overexcited since last night. She thinks she's got to see off any stranger.'

'Lucky you had her here,' he said. 'Parry said you're looking after her for a friend.'

'That's right.' He was standing in the middle of the room, fidgeting about, looking round him. He had his sharp suit on today and still didn't look your average CID man. I wondered again to what extent, if any, he fitted into the police scene. 'I made a statement,' I said, prompting him to explain his visit.

'Yes, I know, I read it. We've put out a description of the man you recognised. But he'll have gone to ground. I was going to suggest you came over to the station and took a look at the mug shots. He might have a record.'

'I can't come now,' I said. 'Maybe tomorrow.'

'I thought I could give you a lift over there now—' he began.

'I told you, tomorrow! I've had enough of coppers for one day, right?' I was beginning to sound like Tig.

I saw his features stiffen. The man was really sensitive about being disliked for what he did.

'Nothing personal,' I said wearily. 'But I'm sick to death of this whole business.'

He nodded. 'I understand that. Tomorrow, then.' He hesitated. 'Oh, by the way, you might like to know you weren't the only one to be burgled last night.'

If this was an attempt to console, it was cack-handed. I realised there must have been numerous break-ins of one sort and another in the Greater London area during the previous twenty-four hours.

'Don't get me wrong,' he went on hastily, noting my expression. 'What I meant was, a Mrs Joanna Stevens who lives in Putney came home last night to find someone had been in her house. Local police notified us because Mrs Stevens is Graeme Coverdale's sister.'

Light dawned. 'Oh,' I said.

'Coverdale used her house as a base in this country.' Harford's interest in property led him to reflect. 'That's a nice area. All those houses in Shaker Lane where she lives are big detached places. Four beds, quiet street, front shielded by laurel hedges, trees in the back garden.' He pulled himself together. 'Mind you, a burglar's dream. She's a widow with just one married daughter, so she was happy to give Coverdale a home. He wasn't there all the time, always coming and going, according to her. But one bedroom was kept as his and he left all his spare clothes, books, personal documents, that sort of thing there. Yesterday evening she went out as she always does to a church women's group. A friend called by to pick her up and off they went. When they got back, she invited the friend in for coffee. As soon as she got through the door, she says, she knew someone had been there.'

'There was a hole in a window?' I said.

He shook his head. 'No, different *modus operandi*, suggesting a different man. The
209

same, perhaps, who broke into the shop. Nothing appeared to have been taken, just like the shop. There was little sign of disturbance, again just like the shop. But Mrs Stevens is a house-proud lady living alone and it didn't take much to attract her notice. A crooked mirror over the mantelpiece. Ornaments not facing straight forward. Coats on the hanger in the hall bunched together. When she went into the downstairs cloakroom she found the toilet seat had been left up. So she knew, she said, a man had been there—and he'd used the loo. She was more annoyed about that than anything else, I think.' Harford grinned. 'Anyway, we'd already been there and searched Coverdale's room ourselves with her permission, so backed by her friend, she rang her local station. They took a bit of convincing, as nothing was missing, but she urged them to get in touch with us. We didn't take any convincing.'

It wasn't good news. The unknown man behind this needed those negs desperately. He, or his employees, would be back. But I said, 'Thanks for telling me, anyway.'

'Look, Fran . . .' He'd flushed pink. 'I was going to come round and see you anyway, because the other evening at the restaurant . . . it didn't go the way I'd wanted it to. I mean, I wanted us to be friends, but we parted, well, a bit coolly. It was my fault.'

I hadn't expected an apology and it took me

aback. I told him it wasn't anybody's fault. No one struck up pally relationships over a corpse.

'I really hope this will all be settled soon,' he said. 'Perhaps we can be friends then?'

His persistence niggled me. He couldn't be that naïve. 'Look,' I told him, 'you lot have pegged Gan and me out to dry. You won't release news of those negatives and as long as *they*—whoever they are, and you won't even tell me that—think Gan or I have them, we're both looking over our shoulders and waiting for more break-ins. It's time you spoke up.'

He looked unhappy, rubbing at his shock of hair. 'It's not my decision, Fran. Left to me, I'd do it, take the heat off you and Patel. There is a good reason for it, trust me.'

'It'd better be good,' I said sourly.

He hung around a few minutes more, perhaps hoping I was going to offer him coffee. I wasn't going to do that. I was afraid, apart from the fact that Tig and Bonnie couldn't stay in the bathroom indefinitely, that he'd wander into the kitchenette and see two plates, mugs, etc. He took the hint eventually and left, looking down in the mouth.

I tapped on the bathroom door and told Tig she could come out.

Bonnie rushed out and scrabbled at the front door. Tig emerged looking more frail and yet more determined than ever. She avoided my gaze and went past me in silence.

'OK, you can stop sulking,' I said crossly. 'I

didn't know he was going to come.'

She'd found her gear behind the sofa and still neither speaking nor looking at me, began to stow it away in the rucksack. Bonnie ran over to her and put her front paws on the sofa, head tilted, her bright worried brown eyes asking to know what this meant. Tig's hand dropped absently to the little dog's head and then she carried on rolling up the sleeping bag.

My heart sank and I asked her what she was doing, knowing the answer.

She looked up, two red spots staining the white skin on her cheekbones. 'I'm getting out. I'll come back after Monday to see how you've got on with my people—but I'm not staying here. The place is crawling with bloody pigs. One lot here in the middle of the night, two lots here today. Every time anyone comes to your door, it's a copper, either in uniform or plainclothes. I might just as well have taken Bonnie and myself down to the nick and asked them to give me a bed in a cell for a few days. I'd see fewer of 'em down there than I've seen here.'

'It's not my fault,' I began, 'I don't want them here, either.'

'Then why're you so bloody thick with them?' she retorted.

I drew a deep breath. If she left, I wouldn't see her again. Jo Jo might find her, or she might go back to him, but she wouldn't come back here. Any trip I made to Dorridge would be for nothing. Pleading with her would do no good. I had to meet the problem head on. After all, it was her problem, not mine.

'Go on, then,' I said as brutally as I could. 'Run. That's what you do best, isn't it, Tig? Run?'

She looked up at me in surprise. Bonnie pricked her ears and looked puzzled and alarmed at my change of manner.

As they both stared at me, I went on, 'You didn't get on with your family, so you ran away from them. Where did it get you? Nowhere. You took up with Jo Jo and that didn't work out, so you ran away again—here. Now you're going to run yet again. Where to this time? You can't keep running, Tig, you've got to stand and face your problems. You've got nowhere else to go now. You've got to get a grip.'

Her lips moved stiffly as if she forced them to form sounds. 'I told you—I just don't like pigs.'

'So, how are you going to get on when you go home, back to your parents' place? People there, Tig, won't run at the sight of a copper even if they've done nothing. People there won't hide every time a stranger comes to the door. People there won't assume everyone's an enemy, or just won't like them—as you said Daphne wouldn't like you. Why shouldn't she?'

She stared at me for a brief moment, her

213

face working soundlessly, her eyes blazing with unexpressed emotion. I braced myself for an earful of abuse, but I was caught out when, without further warning, Tig launched herself at me.

'Bitch!' she yelled. She wrapped both arms round me, pinning my arms to my side. The combination of the impact and being unable to balance myself left me helpless. I stumbled back, slipped and crashed to the floor. Tig threw herself on top of me, pummelling me with both fists and all the time, sobbing, 'Bitch—bitch—bitch!'

Bonnie darted around us hysterically as we struggled, not knowing whose side to take, and nipping indiscriminately at any bit of body within her reach. I managed to thrust Tig off me and roll aside. She scrambled to her feet and aimed a kick at me, but that was her undoing, because I caught her foot and twisted it. She yelped and crashed down to the floor where she scrabbled to a sitting position, her back against the sofa, and glared at me, her eyes bright with tears.

'All right,' I panted, taking advantage of the standoff to regain my feet. 'What's all this about?'

'You—' she gasped. 'You should bloody know—'

I interrupted her. 'Yes, I know. I understand why and how you've got like this, Tig, not trusting anyone, not even me. I know why

214

you're scared of the police—'

She shook her head. 'You don't—you don't know . . . You know sod all.'

'All right, I don't know it all!' I was hanging on to my own temper here, more angry with myself than with her, because I didn't know what to do or say. 'Don't you see, Tig?' I pleaded. 'If you're to go home and get back into a different sort of life, which is what you say you want, then you've got to get over all these hang-ups. I'm sorry about the place crawling with coppers today, but it's not my fault, is it? It's because that guy tried to break in. I don't like them round here any more than you do, but I don't freak out. I deal with it and get rid of them.'

'You're you and not me,' she muttered.

'I'm not saying it's going to be easy,' I told her. 'But if you can't hack staying a week in my flat, how do you think you're going to cope with being home again with your family and dealing with them?'

I thought she might have another go at me, but instead she got up, smoothed back her hair, and with her back to me, resumed her packing.

I thought, I've blown it. She's taking off and that's that. I won't see her again. But after a few moments during which she struggled inefficiently with the rucksack, she chucked the whole lot to the floor and sat down on the sofa, head hanging, her wispy fair hair veiling

215

her face.

'OK, now, Tig?' I asked tentatively.

'I've been thinking about it, too, Fran, you know,' she mumbled. 'I'm not the same person I was when I left home. How can I go back? They won't understand, my parents. They'll expect me to walk in just the same little girl who walked out. That's how they think of me, their little girl. I don't think I can cope with it and I don't think they can. Perhaps we'd better scrap the whole thing.'

I hunkered down in front of her and took hold of her hands. They were icy to the touch. Bonnie jumped up on the sofa beside her and pushed her muzzle into Tig's side, wanting to add her own comfort.

'We made up our minds to do this, Tig, you and I. You asked me to go to Dorridge and I said I would. Neither of us is going to welsh, right? It's a pact. I'm going there on Sunday, and you're going to wait here until I come back. No one's saying this'll be easy, but it's like you said. It's your one chance. Don't muff it. Don't just duck out and run.'

She looked at me miserably through the curtain of hair. 'All right. I'll stay. But you'll have to tell them the truth, Fran. You'll have to tell them everything.'

'Sure,' I said encouragingly. It was all right promising. How I was going to manage that interview, I hadn't the slightest idea. In the meantime, however, I had other fish to fry.

'Come on,' I said. 'We're going out.'

'Where?' She was immediately suspicious again.

'Putney. We're going to do a bit of investigating. I want to know what's going on and there's only one way I'm going to find out and that's by doing it myself. Just wait here a tick while I nip up and ask Daphne to let me take a look at her A–Z.'

'You leave me out of this, whatever it is!' Tig burst out. 'You start going out there and pestering this woman he was talking about, the one who had a break-in, and you'll have all the coppers you want round here. But you won't have me! I don't know what you're into, but you're not involving me, right?'

'Take it easy. I won't involve you. I'll have to go and see this Mrs Joanna Stevens on my own. She'd be worried if two of us turned up. All I want is for you to come out to Putney with me, and hang around while I call on her. I'm not leaving you here on your own, Tig. You'll start brooding about going home and get into a state—and before you accuse *me* of not trusting *you*, let me tell you, that's not it. I just think you're better not left alone this afternoon. We'll leave Bonnie in charge of the flat.'

# CHAPTER TWELVE

We got out to Putney and found Shaker Lane all right. That was no problem. But I did have two other problems to deal with, before I ever got near Mrs Stevens. One was that the early dusk meant light was already fading by the time we got there. That worried me. I didn't want to knock on Mrs Stevens' door in the dark. She might be even more unwilling to let me in than I anticipated she'd be anyway. The other problem was Tig, who grumbled and threatened to desert all the way there. I wouldn't have brought her along if I could have safely left her back at the flat in the mood she was in. However, when we actually reached Shaker Lane, she bucked up a bit and started to get interested.

'This is it, then?' She looked up and down the road. The word 'lane' was a misnomer. Probably there had been a lane there once, donkey's years ago, but any trace of a rural path had disappeared. The road was as Harford had described it: prosperous. The houses pretty well all answered the description of Mrs Stevens' he'd given me. I wondered which was hers. 'What are you going to do now?' Tig asked.

Good question. 'Come on, Tig,' I said. 'Back to that little shopping precinct.'

The precinct in question wasn't much more than a row of shops and a paved area with a couple of wooden seats around a depressed-looking tree. It lay off the bottom end of Shaker Lane and we'd walked through it on our way there. I'd noticed, as we did, that it contained a florist's.

'They cost a lot of money,' said Tig, as we stood outside the shop, surveying the bunches of blooms in buckets. 'You could go inside and distract the assistant and I'll nick a bunch, if that's what you want.'

'It's not what I want!' I said firmly. 'I thought you wanted to stay out of trouble, Tig? You've got a funny way of going about it. We'll both go in.'

'I want some flowers to take to a lady who's bereaved,' I told the assistant. 'Only I haven't got much dosh. What can you let me have?'

The girl cast an eye over me and nothing she saw disproved my claim to be broke. 'Someone round here, is it?' she asked.

'A Mrs Stevens. She lives in Shaker Lane.'

'Oh, right!' She brightened. 'Several people have been in buying flowers for her. Her brother, wasn't it? He got knifed. Horrible, only it didn't happen around here, thank goodness.' She stared at us with increased curiosity.

'That's right,' I said, not parting with any more info, something which clearly disappointed her. 'So, what have you got?'

'Well, we've sold quite a lot, like I said, on account of her,' said the girl. 'And it's getting late in the day. You can have any of that lot, half price.'

I said fair enough, and parted with the cash for two bunches of freesias and some ferny stuff. They smelled nice and when I put them all together, they looked a lot.

'You don't know what number her house is, do you?' I asked. 'I had it written down but I left the bit of paper at home.'

'Hang on,' she said, going to the counter and opening a ledger. 'It'll be in the order book. She came in asking about wreaths. Yes, here it is, number fifteen.'

'See?' I said to Tig, as we left the shop. 'All you've got to do is haggle a bit. You don't have to nick 'em. And I found out the number of the house as well. That's being a detective.'

'They've got loads of them,' said Tig. 'They wouldn't have missed them. You could've gone in asking about the house number while I pinched some.'

It occurred to me that, if and when Tig got home to Dorridge, rehabilitating her was going to be a job and a half. Thankfully, it wouldn't be mine.

'You stay here,' I said. 'Sit on one of those benches. I won't be long.' If Mrs Stevens wasn't at home, or if she shut the door in my face, I'd be very quick.

It was darker by the time I got back to

number fifteen, but someone had switched on a light downstairs, so I was in luck there. I rang the doorbell.

After a few minutes, it opened on the chain. I could just make out a woman's face, pressed against the crack. 'Yes?' she asked cautiously.

'Mrs Stevens? I've brought some flowers.'

'Oh, wait a tick.' She pushed the door to. I heard her unhook the safety chain. It reopened and I could see her properly in the hall light.

I judged her quite a bit older than her brother, a stocky woman of middle height with greying hair cut short and glasses. She reached out a hand for the flowers. 'Is there a card?' she asked.

'I'm not delivering them from a florist's,' I explained, hanging on to the bunch. 'They're from me personally. My name's Fran Varady. I—I knew your brother slightly.'

'Oh?' She hesitated, looking me up and down. 'Well, you'd better come in, then.'

That got me over the doorstep. I handed over my flowers in the hall. She thanked me and murmured something about just putting them in the sink for a moment. Then she disappeared into, presumably, the kitchen. I looked around. It was all very neat and tidy. The cloakroom, in which the incriminating loo seat was to be found, was off to my left. To my right I could see, through an open door, a comfortable sitting room.

221

Mrs Stevens returned and ushered me in. We took facing armchairs and studied one another. She was wearing a dark green dress with a cowl collar which did nothing for her, but was presumably a sign of mourning. She wasn't in any way remarkable—a middle-aged woman like thousands of others—and that a close relative should have been knifed in my basement seemed incongruous. I wasn't quite sure how I was going to break that bit of news to her, about it being my basement, or even if I should.

She spoke first. 'Are you a journalist?' When I denied this, she went on, 'Because my brother, being freelance, knew a lot of press people. I thought you might be one of them, a reporter or something.'

I supposed I did look disreputable enough to represent one of the more downmarket tabloids. 'I'm not sure,' I said, 'whether to call him Graeme or Gray.'

'His name was really Graeme, of course, but he's—he was always called Gray, right from childhood.' She faltered slightly.

Feeling bad, I told her sincerely that I was very sorry for her loss.

'I'm sure he always took unnecessary risks,' she said. 'He was always the same, even as a boy. There was a twelve-year age gap between us so I was the older sister who had to keep an eye on him. He arrived rather late in my parents' marriage and they found him a handful. He was always better with me. Giving him a home here seemed natural. Although he was hardly ever here.' She paused. 'May I ask how you know Gray, if you're not a journalist?'

'He came into the shop where I work a little while ago. He sent a note saying he wanted to see me again—but—' I searched desperately for the words, but she made the connection.

'Are you the girl he was trying to see, when he—when he was killed?' She leaned forward.

I admitted it and decided to throw myself on her mercy. 'Look, Mrs Stevens, I'm really sorry to bother you. I don't know why such a dreadful thing happened to Gray. I don't know what sort of thing he'd got into, but whatever it was, I think it may affect me. In fact, I'm sure of it. I know your house was broken into last night. Someone tried to get into my flat last night, too, only I had a dog in the place and the intruder was scared off.'

'Oh, my dear!' she said, then, 'Would you like a cup of tea?'

I thought of Tig hanging about in the cold down at the shopping precinct. But the offer of tea meant Mrs Stevens was prepared to talk. I accepted.

'I'm afraid,' she said, when she'd brought the teatray, 'I really know nothing either. Gray didn't confide in me. I told the police all this because they were asking, too. He used to go on trips a lot, but often didn't say where he'd been. Sometimes he'd let me know when he was coming home and sometimes he'd just turn up. He was like that. I realise—I realise that this time he must have been doing something dangerous.' She paused and looked down at the cup and saucer she held on her lap. 'The police asked if anything had been taken from his room, but I had to tell them, I'd no idea. I didn't know what Gray kept up there. When I first called the police—the local police—they didn't want to believe I'd had a break-in. They said the place was all too tidy and nothing was missing. I told them, tidy maybe, but not tidy enough! Then there was the downstairs toilet. He'd used it, I know, because he left the seat up. Do you know,' she was getting heated at the memory, 'the young policeman who came actually laughed when I told him that!'

'I believe it,' I said.

'I told him, I didn't think it was funny. Someone had definitely been in my house! Anyway, I could sense it, if you know what I mean. I just felt someone had been in while I'd been out. I still don't think they'd have taken me seriously if I hadn't told them about Gray's death. Then they got on to the other police— the ones investigating Gray's murder. They came out here and they were very sympathetic.'

'When did Gray come home this time? Had he been away long?' I asked.

'He'd been away about a month. Quite early

224

on, he sent me a postcard from Switzerland, from Zürich. After that I didn't hear a thing until he turned up in his usual way, just a week before he died. I had a phone call from the station half an hour before he arrived to let me know he was on his way. I just had time to go up and make up his bed. He was very suntanned. I asked if he'd been skiing or something like that in Switzerland. He said, "I'll tell you—"' She broke off and fumbled for a handkerchief. 'He said, "I'll tell you all about it one day, Jo!" and that was all he said.'

I waited while she dabbed at her eyes and nose. 'I hate doing this,' I told her, 'but can I just ask, did he seem different in any way when he came home this time?'

She considered this as she tucked away the handkerchief. 'I must say, he did seem pleased with himself. But one morning he smartened himself up—because to be frank, he was a very untidy dresser—and said he was going to have lunch with a contact, he called it. When he came back,' she paled at the memory, 'he had a dreadful black eye! I asked what on earth had happened. He said, he'd tripped getting out of a car and hit his head on the kerb. I didn't know whether to believe him or not.'

I reflected that Gray Coverdale had been a practised liar. He knew to put an element of fact in his story, in this case, his abrupt exit from the Mercedes. Even a smidgen of truth adds confidence to the liar's voice, and it's always difficult to disprove a story that's partly true. I wondered what sort of journalism he'd gone in for. The sort that tracked down MPs in secret lovenests and interviewed the partners of men who'd been convicted of lurid crimes, I suspected. It all made sense. I was willing to bet he'd been following up some kind of dodgy story—only this time his luck had run out.

'I'd better go,' I said. 'A friend's waiting for me. I'm truly sorry about your brother. I expect the police will get it sorted soon.' I didn't believe any such thing, but you've got to say it. 'Would you mind,' I went on, 'not mentioning my visit to you to the police? They're sort of fussy.'

'Oh, that's all right,' she said. 'I won't say a word. They did tell me not to talk to journalists, but then, you're not a journalist, are you?' She gave a rueful smile. 'I'm used to not talking about Gray's business, partly because I knew so little about it, and partly because he wouldn't have liked it. Poor Gray. My father wanted him to be an accountant, you know? It would've been a lot safer.'

I made my way back to the shopping precinct, wondering whether Tig would still be there. It was quite dark now and had got a lot colder. Some of the shops, including the florist's, had closed up for the day, but a supermarket was still open and brightly lit. No one was sitting on the benches. I wondered whether she'd gone off to find a coffee or perhaps gone into the supermarket to buy a can of Coke or something. At least, I hoped she'd buy it and not try and slip it in her jacket, but by now, I realised I couldn't rely on her. As I approached the store entrance, I heard a familiar voice.

'Got any change?'

My heart sank. There she was, hanging by the exit, wearing that tragic look and waylaying shoppers. I grabbed her and hauled her away.

'What do you think you're doing?'

'Hullo, Fran,' she said. 'You were a long time and I got bored. I thought I could get back the money you spent on those flowers, but they're a stingy lot round here. I only made just over a quid. We could try somewhere else.'

'We're going home,' I said. 'Before you get us both arrested!'

\*       \*       \*

The two days left before my trip to Dorridge passed off uneventfully, to my great relief. I worked extra hours at the shop because we were really busy now, Christmas being so close. We did a brisk sale in festive cards, decorations and wrapping paper, boxes of chocolates, all the things people pour out money on, grumbling all the while about how expensive a time of year it is. Tig behaved herself (or as far as I knew she did). She walked Bonnie by the canal and didn't encounter Jo Jo. With luck, he'd found himself another girlfriend by now. He hadn't looked to me the sort who'd pine.

I did go over to the nick to look at their book of criminal mugshots. At first they left me alone to study it but after a while Parry came in and asked if I wanted a cup of tea. I said yes, please. He brought it in a polystyrene cup and hung around for a few minutes until I told him he was distracting me. After that I had more time alone until Harford turned up.

'How's it going, Fran?' He took a seat beside me.

Normally I'd have given him the same treatment I'd given Parry, but by now, I was getting bored with looking at one broken nose, cauliflower ear and schizophrenic stare after another, so I took a break and said I was sorry, but really, so far I hadn't seen anyone remotely like the man who'd tried to break into my flat.

'Keep trying,' he encouraged. He moved his chair a little closer, his knee not touching mine, but not that far away either. Hmm, I thought. Now what?

He'd begun to turn the pages. 'Was he anything at all like this one, or this? You know, a year or two can make a difference and some of these mugshots are quite old.' He leaned towards me. He smelled quite nice, of expensive aftershave, unlike Parry who always seemed to niff of sweat, high-tar cigarettes and cough lozenges. He was also starting to

228

confuse me. One minute I was getting the big freeze, the next he was trying to be friends. Well, I was prepared to be friends. I'm prepared to be anyone's friend. But, don't get me wrong on this, I'm not desperate for a shoulder to lean my head on and I like to know where I am with people. If Harford would stick to being snooty, it would be easier. At the moment, it was like the 'nice cop, nasty cop' scenario, all rolled into one man. I wondered if he'd quite got the hang of it.

I told him I really was trying, and we persevered onward through the book. Parry reappeared in the doorway midway and, seeing us with our heads cosily together, gave us a funny look.

'Yes, sergeant?' asked Harford crisply, looking up.

'Just come to see how she's getting on, sir,' said Parry, his look now indicating that he thought Harford was getting on all right, even if the identification exercise wasn't. 'OK, Fran?'

'All right, thank you!' Harford answered for me. Parry gave me a reproachful glance and left.

I did wonder vaguely whether Harford's hand might eventually stray to my knee, but he had more style than Parry—or Parry's interruption had put him off. We reached the end of the book without a word or move which could have offended a Victorian dowager.

'No,' I said. 'Not even allowing for old pics, blurred pics or plastic surgery. He's not there.'

Somehow, I wasn't surprised, and I could see that neither was Harford, who closed the book, looking resigned.

'If he's foreign,' he said, 'he might have arrived in this country only weeks ago. In fact, he probably has.'

I asked him why he was so sure of this. He replied evasively, because the man hadn't had time to get into trouble yet officially.

'No form,' as he put it, sounding a little self-conscious as he used this well-worn scrap of police jargon.

'Well, I've done my bit as good citizen,' I said, standing up.

'I'll run you home,' he offered. I nearly accepted, but then I remembered Tig back at the flat. If I turned up yet again with a plod in tow, she'd freak out. 'Thanks,' I said. 'I'll walk. I've got a spot of shopping to do.'

I did fancy he looked a little disappointed. But perhaps I was only flattering myself.

\*     \*     \*


So Sunday dawned and Tig and I went over to Marylebone for me to catch the Dorridge train. It was early morning and none too busy at the weekend. Being at Marylebone awakened memories in me, however, and I found myself looking around the place, my

230

eyes searching for ghosts.

'Who're you looking for?' asked Tig, ever suspicious.

'Someone who won't be here. I met an old wino here once, Albie Smith, he was called. I was just thinking about him.'

Tig wasn't interested in my past life. She pointed up at the smart computerised arrivals and departures screen, new since my last visit, and drew my attention to the platform number which had appeared alongside my train time.

'It's in, you'd better go on.'

I don't know why she was in such a rush. At that time of the morning and on a Sunday at that, it wasn't going to be full.

'Don't make a fool of me, Tig,' I said, before it drew out. 'Be here when I get back.'

'Promise,' said Tig. Bonnie, attached to a length of string and sitting on the platform at Tig's feet, gave a short bark of support. The train drew out and she waved at me. I had to trust her.

I sat back and reflected that even if I was successful in fixing up Tig's return, she'd declared herself unable to take the dog with her. I was going to be left with Bonnie on my hands. Still, getting Tig *off* my hands would be a start.

It was a long journey, much of it through nice countryside, but my head was filled with the forthcoming meeting with the Quayles. If Ganesh was right, I'd be met by a reception committee, probably including their solicitor and a magistrate or two who just happened to be their good friends. According to Ganesh, I oughtn't to be surprised to find a tactical response unit in body armour.

Tig had given me precise instructions on how to find the house. She hadn't described the place itself, but I'd guessed it would be a lot like Shaker Lane back in Putney, and it was. The house was thirties-built with bay windows and, even in winter, the front garden looked neat and cared for. Every other house in the street looked the same. Some had cars in the drive and all of them were polished and new. I felt out of place and apprehensive. There hadn't been that much money left over from Tig's savings once I'd bought the train ticket, and my fee was negligible. I was earning it several times over.

I approached the glass porch and rang the bell. The front door on the further side was opened almost at once. She must have seen me hovering outside as I sized up the place. We stared at each other through the porch door, then she came towards me and opened it up.

'Miss Varady?' she asked.

Her voice trembled. She was a small, slightly built woman and I could see Tig in her. Mrs Quayle must have been in her forties but had hung on to her figure. Her hair was done by a hairdresser, the grey rinsed away, and her very fine skin, starting to become lined as such skins do, was carefully made up.

I acknowledged my identity and said I was glad she'd agreed to see me. I wondered where Colin Quayle was.

She ushered me inside. The hall gleamed with new paint, new-looking carpets and shiny furniture redolent of the sort of perfumed wax you spray from a can. It made Mrs Stevens' place look scruffy. I had the feeling I ought not to come into contact with any of it, but shimmer across space a few inches above the ground in a sort of levitation experience.

As it was, I clumped my Doc Martens way into a painfully tidy drawing room (there was no other term for it) and sat down in a velvet upholstered armchair with snowy white, starched, crocheted protectors to save the soiling touch of the human hand. I could certainly see why Bonnie wouldn't be welcome in here.

'Coffee?' asked Mrs Quayle, still nervous. She stood in front of me, eyeing me in much the way the coppers had eyed Bonnie, as if I'd bite given half a chance.

'That would be nice,' I said, because I felt that was the answer she wanted. Still no Mr Quayle. I asked, 'Isn't your husband going to be here?'

'He's gone to church,' she said. 'He's a sidesman today. He'll be here shortly.'

She scurried out to make the coffee. I leaned back uneasily in my chair and studied the room further. There were china figurines of Edwardian belles on the mantelshelf and a photograph of a little girl in a ballet tutu.

I thought of Tig as I'd last seen her on the platform at Marylebone, in worn jeans, Doc Martens like mine, a grubby donkey jacket and holding on to a piece of string with a scruffy terrier attached.

Mrs Quayle was coming back. I got up to help her with the tray and she mumbled thanks. The coffee was in a cafetière, the cups were bone china, the spoons were proper coffee spoons with enamelled plaques at the end of the handles depicting flowers. There was a plate of homemade shortbread biscuits.

'Do you take sugar, Miss Varady?' She was observing the niceties in a desperate way, clinging to form as a drowning man might cling to a wooden spar.

I told her I didn't and asked her to call me Fran.

'I'm Sheila . . .' she said, handing me a cup of coffee. It slopped in the saucer. I felt sorry for her and wished I could put her at her ease. She was wearing a three-piece woollen outfit in a respectable, muddy brown: long skirt, sweater and long sleeveless jacket. It looked expensive. Her fingernails were painted a brownish-orange to team with it and matched her lipstick exactly. My feeling of pity for her increased. When Tig had walked out, this poor woman had been left with nothing to do but polish the furniture, visit the hairdresser and shop for painfully smart but respectable outfits. But how would she cope with Tig's return?

'Is Jane—You've seen Jane recently?' she asked now, leaning forward slightly, her eyes pleading.

I told her I'd seen Jane that morning and she'd been fine.

'I still don't know why she couldn't come herself,' Sheila Quayle said fretfully, and I recognised the tone of voice of the woman on the phone. She felt all this was unfair. She'd lavished care and attention on her family, her home, and in keeping herself looking nice. Her reward was this: desertion by her only child and a temporary desertion by her husband who, just when she needed him, was away doing his own thing. He'd left her here, facing a total stranger and one of an unknown species at that, begging for details.

She then floored me with a question I hadn't anticipated. 'There isn't a baby, is there?' There was a world of dread in her voice.

I gawped at her. 'No,' I said foolishly.

She flushed, her tissue-fine skin turning a dull rose-red. 'Only, these days—I mean there are so many single mothers and I thought, perhaps the reason Jane didn't come home— or even, the reason she'd left . . .'

I sighed. Since Tig had left, her mother had

sat here asking herself, why? To her way of thinking, this perfect home couldn't be at fault. That must be nonsense. Her daughter had been working hard at school, so that couldn't be it, either. Sheila Quayle had come up with the only other thing she could think of. Explaining was going to be much more difficult than I'd imagined in my wildest moments.

'There's no baby,' I said, underlining the fact.

She looked relieved but then that fretful expression came back. 'Then I really can't see why—'

We were interrupted by the sound of a car turning into the drive.

'Colin!' exclaimed Mrs Quayle as beleaguered drivers of wagon trains cried out 'The cavalry!' She jumped up and darted out into the hall to brief him as we heard his key turning in the lock.

She'd shut the drawing-room door behind her, but I could hear the slam of the front door and the muffled conversation which followed. The drawing-room door reopened.

He was a big, red-faced man in a houndstooth-checked suit worn over a mustard-coloured felt waistcoat. His shoes were highly polished brogues. The initial effect was that of a country squire rather than a businessman. At second glance, it was less convincing, all too new and too well pressed. It was a good suit, but I guessed off the peg. The shoes were top of the range, but likewise off the shelf, and the flashy gold wristwatch jarred. Such country gents as I'd come across—like old Alastair Monkton—wore suits of incredible age but beautiful cut and made-to-measure shoes cracking up with wear. When they wanted to know the time, they consulted ancient half-hunters which had belonged to their grandfathers.

I wondered about Colin's origins and guessed they'd been pretty ordinary until money had enabled him to move, as he'd probably term it, 'up' in the world. Perhaps the outfit was a sort of passport. Not all self-made men wore their success easily.

He didn't offer to shake hands but stood before me, towering over me, while he scrutinised me in a way no gentleman would do, as Grandma Varady would've said.

'You're the girl who phoned, then?' he challenged. 'The Londoner.'

I resisted the temptation to exclaim, in stage Cockney, 'Cor, swelp me, guv! Sit down and rest your plates of meat. Have a cuppa Rosie Lee.'

Sheila said nervously, 'Her name is Fran.'

'Oh, is it?' he retorted disagreeably. He lowered himself into the opposite chair and glanced at the coffee tray.

'I'll get you a cup!' his wife said at once, and darted off into the kitchen again. It was a telling moment—at least, it told me a lot.

He placed his hands on the chair-arms and I wondered if the crocheted covers were because this was his habit. His hands, I noticed, were large and coarse for all they were carefully kept. I decided the country suit had been chosen because it flattered his general build and style. I wondered, my fancy wandering as it's apt to do, how he looked when he and his wife went to a formal do and he was required to get togged up in a tuxedo. Like one of the door bouncers, probably. I liked the image and allowed myself a smile.

He interpreted it badly.

'While my wife's out of the room,' he said bluntly, 'I'll ask you a straight question, to which I want a straight answer. What's your part in all this? Also, if you think I'm paying you any money, you can forget that idea right now. So you needn't sit there smirking and looking pleased with yourself! You'll find me a hard man to fool and I'm impervious to sweet talk.'

Yes, he was a nasty bit of work and Ganesh had been right. He was the sort who put a price on everything and assumed everyone else did the same. He'd calculate success by financial reward. This house and its contents were proof, as was his well-dressed wife and—until a couple of years ago—his pretty daughter whom he'd sent to private school and ballet lessons. These things, which people could see and admire, these things only mattered.

I realised, with a stab of shock, how angry Tig's defection must have made him. His bubble of success had been punctured, his wealth rejected. His daughter had chosen God knew what sort of street life in preference to this. Could he ever really forgive that? I wondered.

'I don't want your money,' I said sharply to him. 'Jane asked me to come on her behalf. I'm doing it as a favour to her.'

His mind ran on the same lines as his wife's. 'She doesn't need anyone to speak for her. She could pick up the phone. She knows where we are. I'm not convinced you're on the level. I'm not even sure my daughter sent you. Why the dickens should she? She only had to pick up the phone,' he repeated doggedly.

Sheila was back, carrying a cup and fresh coffee in a little individual cafetière. She set them down with a clatter on the tray and took a seat nearby, smoothing her skirt over her knees. The action drew the eye to her manicured hands. Even diamond rings and nail varnish don't entirely distract from a looseness of skin on the knuckles and brown liver spots. I wondered briefly if it were possible she was older than her husband and all this care with make-up and appearance was to keep at bay the inevitable, the day when he'd look at her and decide she was no longer trophy wife enough. Time to trade her in as he'd do with his car. She was fixing anxious eyes on me. But though she didn't look at him, it was to her husband she spoke.

'Fran assures us there's no baby.' There was relief but also a hint of triumph in her voice, as if they'd argued this point over and over, she denying the possibility, he insisting. She wasn't daring to say, 'I told you so', but she couldn't quite keep it hidden.

'There'd bloody better not be,' he said. But he, too, looked relieved. 'Right, speak up. Where's my daughter? Supposing that you know and aren't just stringing us along. You'll be sorry if you are. I promise you that.'

'In London, staying at my place at the moment.' I ignored the threat though the impulse to get up and march out was strong. But if I did, Tig would be lost, and he'd be convinced he was right, I was conning them and he'd frightened me away.

'And what sort of place might that be?' His manner and voice were both insulting.

'I've got a basement flat in a perfectly respectable street, as it happens,' I replied, goaded into letting my anger show.

'And how do you pay for that? Got a job? Or just a welfare scrounger like the others?'

I was pleased to be able to say yes, I had a job. I worked in a newsagent's. I knew I had to get a grip on this conversation or I'd find myself sitting here being bullied by Colin until

240

I was thrown out by him.

'Well,' I said briskly, putting my cup back on the tray, 'you'll be pleased to know T—Jane is fine. She has lost a lot of weight—'

Sheila let out a gasp and put orange fingernails to her lips. Her husband gave her an irritated glance.

'Has she been ill?' he asked me.

'No—but she's been living rough.'

Sheila moaned. Colin Quayle gave her another cross glare. 'Stop whimpering, Sheila, for God's sake. If you've got something to say, say it.'

He didn't give her any chance, however. Turning to me, he went on, 'By living rough, do you mean under arches, in doorways?'

'Recently, yes. Not all the time. She's had different places to live. At one time she shared a squat with me and some others.'

'I thought you said you had a flat!' he snapped at me.

'Before I had the flat, I lived in several different places. Look,' I was getting seriously annoyed with him, 'do you want me to tell you about Jane or not?'

'Don't take that tone—' he began but, to my surprise, was interrupted by his wife.

'Let her speak, Colin. If you keep interrupting her, we shan't learn anything.'

He looked startled but fell silent. I took up my tale.

'Jane would like to come back home, but

241

you'd need to be prepared—if she does come—for a lot of changes in her. She's had some bad experiences. She's had a rough time. She doesn't trust people any more. She's afraid of the police.' His eyes bulged and his mouth opened, but before Colin could speak, I hurried on, '*Not* because she's any reason to be, but because of the sort of life she's been living. The police have harried her and other homeless people like her. She's—she's been attacked during her time on the street. She's been hurt. Besides, she's had to do things on the fringes of the law . . .'

They were both staring at me in frozen horror. I knew I couldn't tell them that at one time Tig had been on the game, much less about the gang-rape.

I said, 'Like beg.'

'Beg!' Sheila screamed.

'Beg?' Colin took up the cry. Perhaps they'd have taken the idea of rape with less horror. His voice rose. 'My daughter? Begging on the street? For pity's sake—why didn't she just pick up the phone and ask us to come and get her? Or to send some bloody money? God, if it were only the money—'

'She—she was scared to,' I said, and thought I understood well why.

'My daughter begging . . .' He pulled out a handkerchief and mopped his face. 'Bloody hell. If people get to hear about this . . .'

Oh yes, that's what worried him.

242

Prosperous, successful Colin Quayle the church sidesman—whose daughter stood on London streets with her hand held out to passers-by, asking if they had any change.

I said loudly, 'So you see, if she comes home, there will have to be a lot of give and take. You'll have to make allowances for her experiences, for the change in her. She's got to learn to live this sort of life again.' I indicated the room around us, but my heart was sinking as I spoke. Could Tig do that? Readjust to this? Especially with a blockhead like Colin around, a man as sensitive as Attila the Hun. 'It's going to be hard for all three of you,' I went on. I pointed at the picture of the child in the tutu. 'You've got to forget that.'

Sheila whispered brokenly, 'She was a lovely little dancer. She won prizes. You don't know what it's been like, Fran, since she's gone. I've hardly slept. I lie awake all night thinking of her. I think of her all day long. Every time the phone rings, or there's someone at the door, I've thought, perhaps it's Jane. I wait for the post . . .' She seemed to remember her husband. 'Colin has, too, haven't you?' she asked him.

Colin didn't answer that directly. He was afraid of showing even that allowable human weakness, I judged. I felt sorry for the man, really. He was in a sort of prison he'd made for himself, keeping up a set of unreasonable standards. The trouble was, he'd tried to

243

impose those standards on Tig.

Now he asked grimly, 'Who attacked her?'

'Who knows?' I replied. 'That's how it is on the streets.'

'Is she on drugs?' he asked next. He was tactless but not stupid. He knew there was a lot I wasn't saying.

'She was.' I tried not to look at Sheila, who was swaying in her chair. 'But she's clean now. That took some doing. She's got courage.' I leaned forward. 'All she needs is some support and help. She can do it, she can get back into regular life. It won't be easy, but she can do it if you'll help. She does—will need—a lot of help. She hides behind the furniture when strangers come to the door. She thinks everyone is out to get her.'

They looked at one another and then both sat in silence.

'Dr Wilson could help,' Sheila said to her husband at last. 'He's known Jane since she was little. Perhaps a—some visits to a therapist.'

'I don't need some trick-cyclist telling me my daughter's crackers!' Colin growled. For him, having to turn to a psychiatrist would be another admission of failure. Frankly, I thought he was the one who needed the shrink.

'It might be a good idea to ask your doctor for advice,' I said. 'Anyway, T—Jane needs to go on some sort of proper diet to build her up

244

again and, in my opinion, she won't last much longer if she doesn't.' It was make or break time. 'So,' I said, 'what do I tell her? Can she come home or not?'

Colin began, 'We need a bit of time—'

Sheila, again surprising me, broke in. 'Of course Jane can come home. This is her home. It's always been her home. She's our only child, Fran. Without her, what do we have? Nothing.'

Colin blanched. It was as if she'd hit him. He struggled for his former bullish self-composure. 'Yes, better tell her to come. If she's ill, of course, she must.' He made another effort. 'I can drive down and collect her.'

'I'll put her on the train,' I said. 'You can pick her up at the station.'

There was a release of tension in the atmosphere now the decision was taken.

Sheila stood up, picked up the tray of used cups and asked, 'Would you like to stay to lunch?'

I ignored the glare of baffled fury Colin directed at his wife. I had no wish to stay here longer than I had to, anyway.

'Thanks, but no. I've got to get back. It's a long journey.' I got to my feet.

'I'll see you out, just let me pop this into the kitchen.' She trotted out.

Colin grunted but that was his only attempt at further communication. He had nothing more to say to me and stayed where he was as Sheila saw me to the front door. On the step, she touched my arm and said, 'Thank you.'

'It's OK,' I said. 'I'd like to think Jane was getting her life back together again.'

'Oh, yes,' she whispered, 'to think Jane will be home again. It's the best Christmas present I could've imagined. I've prayed for it. I honestly thought God wasn't listening, but He was.'

There were tears in her eyes. 'You will be prepared for changes?' I repeated anxiously. I really wondered how they'd cope.

But Sheila, I'd already decided, had hidden depths. 'We'll manage,' she said firmly. 'Jane and I always had a good relationship before.'

It didn't seem to occur to her that if it had been as good as all that, Jane would have been able to talk through her problems at home.

She had put her hand in the pocket of the woollen jacket and produced a small package wrapped in a paper napkin. She put it in my hand. 'Shortbread, for the journey.' She gave an apologetic smile. 'I'm sorry you're not able to stay for lunch. Have you got enough money to buy something?'

'I'm fine,' I assured her, 'but thanks for the biscuits.' There was nothing else to say but to wish her good luck, and put distance between myself and that house as fast as I could.

\*       \*       \*

I felt really relieved as the train drew out, as if I'd put down a heavy weight I'd been toting along ever since Tig had turned up at the door with Bonnie. I'd done what I'd said I'd do and got away relatively lightly. My part was over.

A metallic rattle announced there was a trolley service on this line. The guy came along, hauling his load as I'd been hauling my symbolic one. He stopped and asked, without much show of interest, if I wanted any refreshments. I bought a coffee (black, white or cappuccino?) off him and unwrapped my shortbread biscuits. But somehow, although I was hungry, I couldn't eat more than one of them. I wrapped the others up again and put them away to give to Tig later.

Supposing Tig was still there when I got back. I'd raised Sheila's hopes and I couldn't bear to think of them being dashed. No, I would *not* worry about that. It wasn't my concern. I'd done my bit. You don't have to save the world, Fran!

A previous traveller on this train, who'd sat on the opposite seat to mine, had left bits of his Sunday newspaper behind, including the magazine supplement. To take my mind off Tig and her family, I reached for it, and sipping my coffee, opened it up.

'BRITAIN'S MOST WANTED MEN!' screamed the heading to the story which made centre pages. A row of smudged mugshots or

247

heads taken from paparazzi snaps formed a border to the article which was, it seemed, about criminals who'd eluded the law successfully—the Mr Big figures of the underworld, who lived it up with flash cars and flashy girlfriends while the foot soldiers, who took the risks, did the time. I ran my eye down the rogues' gallery with only minor interest.

Then I saw it—saw him. His hair was darker in this pic but a bottle of bleach had since taken care of that. There he was and not a shadow of a doubt of it. Not sitting in a jazzy shirt in the sunshine as he'd been when the snaps Coverdale had acquired were taken. No, here he was leaving what looked like a nightclub, caught in the glare of the flashlight as he made for his limo. His name, I learned at last, was Jerry Grice.


## CHAPTER THIRTEEN

At least, the article informed me, as I scanned it eagerly, that was one of two or three names he'd operated under. A warrant had been issued for his arrest in connection with a raid on a City bank vault which had netted an undisclosed sum in gold ingots and other valuables in safety deposit boxes. No one could ever be sure just how much the raiders had got away with, because many of the deposit box owners had been strangely coy about the contents, but the gold alone had made it a major robbery. Of the gang, most had been picked up and several gaoled. Grice alone remained at large and, more importantly, he knew where the loot was. Virtually none of that had been recovered.

Ironically, Grice was described as being not a violent man, but a planner, an ideas merchant. The journalist was being deliberately naïve, I thought. If you're in charge, you don't need to be violent yourself. You've got underlings to do that sort of thing for you, the actual orders issued by middle-ranking thugs in your employ. That way, Grice and others like him kept their hands clean. They were the clever clogs who got clean away with the dosh, while other mugs got banged up, and snoopers like Coverdale got dead.

I sat back, the cooling coffee in my grip, the magazine lying open on my lap. Coverdale had set his sights on tracking Grice down and thanks to Mrs Stevens, I knew he'd started in Zürich, home of the numbered bank account. Shrewdly, he'd tracked the money, because that would lead him to the man. It'd led him to a tropical location where he'd not only found Grice, but managed to get the photos as evidence. Then Coverdale's plans had gone disastrously wrong. What, I wondered, had Coverdale meant to do with the information? He hadn't handed it over to the cops. Had he envisaged some mega-deal with telly or a top magazine or newspaper, his name blazoned over everything? I didn't know, probably never would know, what Coverdale had wanted to do. He didn't get to do it, that's all I knew. Except that now I knew too what the police were playing at.

Grice's minions had failed to recover the negatives. Not knowing they were in police hands, he must be growing increasingly frustrated and angry—and very worried. Sooner or later, by police reckoning, he'd come back to take care of it himself. That's what they were waiting for so patiently; that was why they wouldn't reveal to the public that they held the negatives. They were forcing Grice's hand, confident that he'd show.

It wouldn't be difficult for him, after all. With that amount of money to play with, he could buy himself a false passport in any nationality he chose. He could hire a private plane to fly him in and out to a deserted air-strip or field. Heck, if SOE could fly agents in and out of Occupied Europe during the last war, then a seriously big-time crook like Grice could buy himself an away-day any time he chose. He'd probably done it a dozen times before, cocking a snook at detectives and half-a-dozen other concerned agencies.

So what made it so different, from the cops' point of view, this time? Why were they so sure this was their great chance to get him? Partly, I told myself, because this time they knew roughly when to expect him and a network of underworld informers must have been put on alert. But mostly, because this time they knew whom Grice would contact. He'd contact me.

By now, we'd rocked gently into the tunnel immediately before Marylebone Station. I was startled into awareness. The journey had passed with me deep in thought. I rolled up the magazine carefully and set out for home. To tell Ganesh or not, that was the question. On the whole, my instinct was not. On the other hand, there was nothing like a little insurance. If only one person knows (viz., Coverdale) he can be taken out. The more people who know, the more difficult it gets.

It was growing dark by the time I reached the house. The window of my basement flat was in darkness but a light was flashing around in the basement itself and indignant voices floated upwards on the cold air. I could also hear muffled, furious barking.

'She must be there, Charles. I'm sure of it. At least, the damn dog is. Ring again.'

I leaned over the railing. Bertie and Charlie had obviously heard about the break-in and come down in force to remonstrate with me. One of them was holding a torch to the window and trying to see in. The other was by the door, trying, for some reason, to see through the letter box. I toyed with the idea of calling the police or running across to the

Neighbourhood Watch fanatic opposite to report prowlers. It was a nice idea, but I didn't need more hassle with the duo than I already had.

'What on earth are you doing?' I asked in a dignified way.

There was no way either of them could look anything but caught red-handed. The one by the door jumped up as if on a spring and the one by the window swung the torch round and shone it up into my face.

I shielded my eyes with my hand and snapped, 'Put that out!'

Rather to my surprise, he did. While I still had the advantage of surprise, I added, 'And come up here if you want to talk to me. I'm not coming down there.'

They huffed a bit, but climbed up the stairwell and arrived on the pavement. By the light of the streetlamp, I could see the one with the torch was Bertie. He was trying to shove it away in a battered briefcase he carried as if it'd suddenly become red-hot.

'We wish to speak to you,' said Charlie, getting his presence of mind back first.

'Go on, then,' I said. 'But don't waste my time.'

'Look here!' he began. 'You shouldn't take that tone with us, really you shouldn't! It's most unwise. We have genuine cause for grievance, as you very well know. Our aunt continues to be put in danger by your presence and we have come to insist—'

His voice was rising in indignation and Bertie, who'd been glancing uneasily at Daphne's windows, cleared his throat and took charge.

'Quite, Charles, quite. But not, um, here in the street perhaps? My dear,' he turned a sickly smile on me, 'can't we go down to the flat and discuss all this in civilised fashion, eh?'

'No,' I said. 'The flat is my home and I don't choose to allow either of you into it. Nor do I want you prowling in the basement. You've upset my dog.'

'We don't see anything in your lease which allows you to keep animals!' squawked Charlie.

'There's nothing in it says I can't. Anyway, Daphne knows Bonnie is there and she doesn't mind.'

Bertie, growing even jumpier, suggested we might, then, perhaps repair to a hostelry, as he put it.

'I'm not going into any pub with a couple of old goats like you two,' I said. 'I've got my reputation to think of.'

'That's slander!' gasped Bertie.

'No, it isn't. You ask your brother. He's got difficulty keeping his hands to himself and for all I know, you're the same. You're two and I'm one. I wouldn't feel safe. We talk here or, if you don't hurry up, we don't talk at all.'

Bertie had been distracted enough to turn

to his brother. 'Charles? What's she talking about?'

'No idea,' bawled Charlie, oblivious to how many people might hear him. 'She's *non compos mentis*, if you ask me. Clearly not of sound mind.'

'You . . .' Bertie lowered his voice, shuffled a few steps away and drew his brother aside. 'You haven't . . ?' he whispered hoarsely.

'Of course I bloody haven't!' snarled Charlie.

'Not for want of trying,' I called.

They turned an angry but united front to me. 'It seems very strange to us,' said Bertie, appointing himself spokesman, 'that Aunt Daphne, after living safely and undisturbed in this house for forty years, should suddenly find the police virtually camped on her doorstep. First a murder, then an attempted break-in— what next, I wonder? There was also, we understand, a previous unpleasant affair which necessitated numerous calls at the house by the constabulary. You can hardly blame us for our concern. We do not, and cannot, consider you a suitable tenant in the light of all this. We have the safety of an elderly, frail lady to consider.'

'It's for Daphne to decide,' I retorted. 'And anyway, she hasn't been bothered, or not much, by the police. I have and I can cope.'

'Don't doubt it,' muttered Charlie. 'Practice makes perfect, they say.'

254

Bertie sidled up to me like an evil old owl. 'Tell me, my dear, what was the intruder after?'

'How should I know?' I snapped.

'But we think you do, eh? Yes, we think you do. Consider it. He didn't attempt to break into our aunt's house. He chose your flat—yet a look through the window, or a few minutes reconnoitring beforehand, would've told him you were unlikely to prove a rewarding target.'

'It's a basement,' I pointed out. 'They're always likely targets. No one could see him trying to get in.'

'The police,' Bertie insisted, 'seem to have made several visits and do not, in my experience, usually spend so much time on a failed burglary. One visit to take a statement and perhaps some fingerprints, would normally be enough.'

'So, what was he after?' growled Charlie, thrusting his unattractive mug into mine.

'Dunno,' I said. 'A rapist, perhaps?' I met his piggy little eyes accusingly.

Charlie stepped back. 'Come along, Bertram,' he said. 'We're wasting our time.' He turned back to me with a final shot. 'You've had your chance to discuss this, as my brother said, in a civilised manner. Very well. So be it. We shall have to see what may be done under the law.'

They marched off up the street, side by side, rigid with outraged dignity.

I wasn't too worried, because unless Daphne chose to evict me, there was little they could do. But they had a point. I couldn't go on causing this kind of disturbance. The entire neighbourhood would be signing a petition to get me out before long.

*       *       *

I let myself into the flat and switched on the light. Bonnie, who'd been lurking behind the door, began to jump up and down, whining an excited welcome. I picked her up, tucked her under my arm, and called out for Tig.

There was an upheaval behind the sofa and Tig crawled out on her hands and knees, her face concealed by a curtain of tangled hair. She got to her feet.

'I've been stuck behind there ages!' She glowered at me. 'They were at the door and looking through the flamin' window before I had a chance to hide in the bedroom or bathroom. All I could do was duck down behind there. They wouldn't go away. They kept ringing the ruddy bell and shouting through the letter box. You get a lot of visitors, don't you? And they don't mind insisting on coming in.'

'You could,' I said, irritated and tired after a long and difficult day, 'simply have answered the door and told them I wasn't here.'

'Answer? Not likely. They looked a real pair

of weirdos.' She swept back a mess of hair from her eyes. 'So, how'd you get on, then?'

'OK,' I said. 'I'll tell you all about it later. I'm going to have a cup of tea first. I need it.'

When I emerged from the kitchenette, minutes later, with two mugs of tea, Tig was sitting on the sofa, reading my magazine. She tossed it aside and took one of the mugs.

'You saw them?' She sounded eager but nervous.

'I saw them.' I fished out the packet of shortbread. 'Here, your mum gave me this to eat on the train.'

Tig took the folded napkin and unwrapped the shortbread. She sat looking at it. 'You shouldn't have brought it,' she said in a muffled voice. 'Were they all right? Not ill or anything?'

'In blooming health, but been worried about you. They thought you might've been pregnant when you left.'

Tig burst out laughing. 'I bet that was Dad's explanation! I can imagine him shouting at Mum that it was a woman's business and she ought to have noticed and Mum denying the whole thing.'

'You weren't, were you?' It occurred to me that perhaps the Quayles' suspicions might not have been unfounded.

'No, of course I wasn't. When would I get a chance to get knocked up? I never went anywhere, never dated a boy. Dad thought

257

they were all rapists—well, perhaps he wasn't far wrong at that.' Bitterness touched her voice.

'I thought your mum quite nice. A bit nervy.' I wanted to take her mind off her terrible experience.

'And my dad?'

'Wasn't so keen on him.' I couldn't politely say more but I didn't need to. Tig had given me a look of perfect comprehension but made no other comment.

'You can go home any time,' I said.

'You told them about the time I was on drugs?'

'I did. Not about your being on the game, though. They could only take so much and frankly, I don't think they need to know that.'

Tig fed a piece of shortbread to Bonnie, held out one to me which I took, and ate one herself. 'You think I'm doing the right thing, Fran? I know you said so before, but you hadn't met them then. It's one reason I wanted you to meet them. Do you still think I'd be doing the right thing in going back?'

'I still think you'll be doing the right thing, but I understand it won't be easy. You'll have to give each other time.'

Tig wiped the shortbread crumbs from her shirt. 'Did they say anything in particular? You know, did they make any conditions?'

I realised that the Quayles hadn't stipulated any rules beforehand. Perhaps they hadn't thought of it or perhaps they weren't quite so narrow-minded as I'd imagined. 'They mentioned a Dr Wilson.'

'That old boy? He's still practising? He must be eighty.'

'I warned them you'd lost weight—and I told them you'd been attacked while sleeping rough. That's all I said, no details.'

Tig looked away from me and muttered, 'Yes, sure.' After a moment, she said, 'I'll go tomorrow, then.'

I was startled enough to show it and she gave a wry smile. 'Strike while the iron's hot, that's what they say, don't they? I don't want to give myself too much time to think about it. I'll talk myself out of it if I do. It's all right if I leave Bonnie here, then?'

'Look,' I said, 'we'll have to phone them first so your dad can pick you up at the station.'

She was shaking her head. 'No. I don't want any contact with them beforehand. We'll start quarrelling on the phone and everything will just, you know, get screwed up. I'll just go. It'll be all right. If no one's in, I'll sit on the doorstep till they get back. Give the neighbours something to talk about.'

I imagined the neighbours would have plenty to talk about all right.

'Don't mess up that magazine,' I said. 'I haven't read it yet.'

*     *     *

I ran up to the shop first thing the next morning and explained to Ganesh that I had to go with Tig to the train. 'Not just to see her off, but to make sure she's really gone. I'll come back later.'

So Tig, Bonnie and I found ourselves at Marylebone again, only this time, our roles were reversed. Tig got on the train and I stood on the platform with Bonnie on her string. Bonnie lay down and put her nose on her paws. Her eyes looked up, rolling from side to side, and her expression said, 'Oh, are we doing this again? Is it going to be regular?' I thought that both she and I hoped not.

Tig had been in a funny mood since getting up. She hadn't said much although from time to time she'd looked as though she was about to speak, but then thought better of it. I couldn't blame her for being unsettled. I could only guess at how she must be feeling. The Quayles would probably be horrified when they saw her but even after only a few days with me, she was looking a lot better and taking more trouble with her appearance. She'd combed back her hair and secured it with one of those big spring grips. It suited her. I wondered if my hair would ever grow that long and how many months it would take, starting as it did from near zero.

She was standing in the open doors of the

260

Chiltern Lines Turbo, studying me carefully in the way she had. I'd got used to it, mostly, but it was still unsettling.

'Something you've forgotten?' I asked.

Indecision flickered across her face before she seemed to take a deep breath and to have made up her mind to say something. 'Fran—' she began. Someone pushed past her and she moved aside, back into the carriage. When she reappeared something, some resolve, had gone out of her. 'I was just going to say, thanks.'

'No problem,' I said. But it occurred to me that wasn't what she'd been about to say and I wondered, if the other passenger hadn't intervened, if she'd have spoken out loud at last what had been on her mind since breakfast.

'You didn't get much of a fee,' she went on. 'When I get some more money, I'll send you some.'

'No, you won't,' I told her. 'We're quits. You've given me Bonnie.'

There was a whistle down the platform, a warning buzz from inside the train and with a pneumatic hiss, the doors slammed together. Tig, on the inside, waved at me as it drew out. I waved back.

'Just you and me then, Bonnie,' I said to the terrier. She jumped up and wagged her stumpy tail. 'You know, we're going to have to get you a proper lead,' I went on. 'This piece of string doesn't do anything for either of us.'

*     *     *

I rattled homeward on the bus with Bonnie sitting on my knees, attracting much admiration and petting, and looking as if butter wouldn't melt in her mouth. In the small hours of the morning, I'd thought out what I was going to do next. Not having the encounter with the Quayles looming over me had freed up my mind considerably.

I went to the flat first, collected the magazine, and the photo Joleen had unearthed for me, and made my way to the shop.

Hitch was there, leaning on the counter. 'Hullo, darling,' he greeted me. 'What's this then?' He meant Bonnie. He stooped to scratch her ears. 'This is a Jack Russell, this is.'

'It's a dog,' said Ganesh disagreeably. 'And they're not allowed in the shop. I've got a sign outside that says so.'

He was right. A yucky thing it was too, a picture of some soulful animals and the legend 'Please Leave Us Outside'.

'If I let you bring that one in,' Ganesh went on, 'I'll have to let everyone bring their dogs in. Loads of people round here have got dogs and some of them are big.'

Ganesh, you'll have gathered, isn't a dog-lover. Shop hygiene rules aside, he just doesn't like them and they don't like him. I leave it to

262

you to work out which dislike sparked the other. All I know is, perfectly placid dogs, which had been rolling at the feet of little children moments before, would turn into snapping, snarling throwbacks to the wolf as Ganesh approached. Even Bonnie, catching the tone of his voice, made a soft growling noise in her throat.

By way of distraction, I asked after Marco. Hitch informed us he'd gone to the continent for a few days' holiday. I asked where.

'Amsterdam,' said Hitch. That made sense. Though his being away in the clouds half the time would've dulled my pleasure in Marco's company, I was still sorry we hadn't made it even to first base. I had fancied him.

'Catch rats, them little dogs,' said Hitch cheerfully, bringing things down to earth. 'Bloody good rat-catchers. Couple of people down our street, when we was kids, kept terriers like that. We used to pull up the manhole covers and drop the tykes down the sewers. They had a great time down there chasing rats. Then we had to squeeze down after 'em to get 'em back. Catching them was a job and a half down there. It was dark and stinking, all you could do to breathe. Had to watch where you put your feet, too. Do you know, a lot of them sewers are Victorian? Lovely bit of brickwork, wonderful workmanship, real skill.' He shook his head sadly. 'Kids don't have fun like that no more.

It's all telly and computers stuffing their heads with rubbish. They learn nothing. They don't take no healthy exercise.'

I explained that Bonnie wasn't used to being left alone and for today at least, I'd had to bring her. I took her into the storeroom and tied her up. She didn't seem to mind that and settled down happily on some flattened cardboard, with a clean plastic container of water, home from home.

When I went back Hitch and Ganesh were wrangling over payment of the bill for the new washroom. Ganesh wanted to write a cheque: Hitch wanted cash.

'It's easier, is cash,' wheedled Hitch. 'I can just stuff it in me back pocket. Cheques I've got to put through the books. I'll have to charge you VAT.'

'Don't tell me,' said Ganesh, 'that your turnover requires you to register for VAT. Not unless you've been putting in new washrooms from here to Battersea. I've got to put it through our books to show Hari what I've spent.'

In the end, Hitch took the cheque, though he clearly didn't have any confidence in such a method of payment. He trailed away looking as if Ganesh had given him a wad of Monopoly money.

'I told you to watch out if you were going to deal with him,' I reminded Ganesh.

Ganesh replied loftily that he could take

care of business matters, thank you. He wasn't without experience.

It was time to dent his smugness. I unrolled the magazine and opened it out flat on the counter.

'What is it?' Ganesh peered at it suspiciously. 'Do we sell that one? It looks like one of those Sunday supplements to me.'

'It is. Just look at the photos, will you? Any of them mean anything to you?'

Ganesh scanned the pages, hesitated at Grice's picture, then moved on. After a few moments he sighed. 'I know what you want me to say, Fran. You want me to tell you that this one—' he tapped Grice's pic— 'is a bit like the chap in those photos Coverdale left in the old washroom. I agree, there is a faint resemblance, but that's all there is. Don't start leaping to conclusions. You know what you are.'

I ignored that. I took out the print from the chemist's and put it beside the one in the magazine. 'Look again. Imagine him with bleached hair and perhaps four or five years older.'

Ganesh gasped and jabbed a finger at the print. 'Where did you get that?'

'It was in the darkroom waste bin, down at Joleen's place. Never mind how I got it. Look again and be honest.'

'It looks like him,' agreed Ganesh sulkily. 'But I'd better be wrong and so had you. From what it says here, he's bad news.'

'Coverdale's body in my basement's already told me that,' I retorted.

Ganesh closed the magazine and leaned his palms on the counter. 'So what are you going to do? Move house?'

'How can I? Talk sense. What I'm not going to do is spend my time jumping out of my skin every time someone walks up behind me, stay frightened to go down alleys, and sleeping with the light on. This has got to be settled. I'm going to take this down to the copshop and see what Harford and the others have to say.'

'You're mad,' said Ganesh simply. As I walked out, he added on a panicky note, 'Hey, don't leave me here with that dog!'

'You've got to get over this phobia of yours,' I called back. 'I won't be long.'

\*         \*         \*

'Hullo,' said the desk officer when I walked into the station. 'You again?'

Honestly, there are professional safe-crackers, muggers, even streetwalkers, who see less of the inside of the nick than I do, though I only get as far as the front desk, and occasionally an interview room. I've not yet been tossed in the cells. Give it time.

I told him I wanted to see Inspector Harford or, failing that, Sergeant Parry.

'Can't be done,' he said. 'They're in a

meeting. Know it for a fact. Saw 'em all going up there ten minutes or so back and they gave out they wasn't to be disturbed.'

'What, all of them?' If they were, it had to be something important and I'd got a funny feeling crawling up my spine.

'You tell them,' I said, 'that Fran Varady is out here and I know who the man in the photos is.'

'What man in what photos?' he asked, being a simple bluebottle who didn't get taken into the confidence of CID.

'Tell 'em!' I instructed him. I sat down on an uncomfortable bench by the wall and picked up an ancient copy of *Police Review* lying there. It was that or a dog-eared copy of the *Sun*. From the corner of my eye, I saw him lift up a phone.

When he put it down, he called across, 'The inspector will be down in a minute or two.'

'Fine,' I said, calm and collected. The biggest mistake I could make now would be to storm in there ranting and demanding protection. I was a member of the public and I didn't have to do anything or go along with anything they'd dreamed up, if I didn't want to.

There was a clatter of feet on stairs nearby. Harford rounded the corner, face flushed and, contrary to his usual crisp business appearance, a little dishevelled. He jumped down the last three steps and marched over to me.

'What's all this?' he asked disagreeably. So we were back in that mode again, were we?

'Jerry Grice,' I said.

His face turned white. He glanced over his shoulder towards the desk and the officer manning it who was stirring his coffee.

'Don't say names like that out loud!' Harford hissed, stooping over me. He straightened up and recovered some of his aplomb. 'I think, in the circumstances, you'd better come upstairs and join us. We're just discussing that matter and we meant to call you in, anyway.'

'Oh, were you?' I asked sarcastically.

He retorted in like tone. 'Yes. So you've saved us the bother, haven't you?'


## CHAPTER FOURTEEN

It was a meeting all right. The tribal chiefs had gathered for a powwow and the air was suitably thick with smoke. There must have been a dozen or so people in the room, perched on table corners, or leaning against walls, amid a litter of polystyrene cups, sweet wrappers and overflowing ashtrays. Most were men, two or three women and at least one who'd have doubled for either. I recognised Parry amongst them, and a couple of the

268

others whom I'd seen before, but not a thin-faced man with grey hair and a grey complexion to match. He was the only one seated at a desk and everyone else hovered around him.

'This is Fran Varady, sir,' said Harford to him. To me, he whispered, 'Superintendent Foxley.'

His manner indicated I was being accorded an audience equal to that with a Chinese emperor. I wondered if I was expected to fall down and bang my head on the floor in obeisance, or merely retreat from his presence backwards. Well, I wasn't one of those struggling up the police promotion ladder. I was a free spirit and felt this was the moment to underline it. Apart from which, I'd choke if I had to stay in this foul atmosphere longer than a few minutes more.

'Do you think,' I said to Foxley, 'we could have a window open?'

There were looks of shock and bewilderment on all faces. They were quite unaware of the fug.

'Open it,' said Foxley without looking round. Some minion obeyed, creating a gap finger-thick, through which some of the haze began to seep.

'Sit down, Miss Varady, won't you?' Foxley offered and, again, an underling pushed a chair forward. 'Your arrival is perhaps timely. Can we offer you some coffee?'

I'd drunk their coffee on previous occasions and declined politely. I could see Parry in the background. When I'd walked in, his ginger eyebrows had shot up to meet his hairline. They hadn't far to travel. Now he was engaging in an elaborate pantomime, asking what on earth I was doing there.

'What's the matter, Sergeant?' asked Harford tersely, catching a particularly extreme example of Parry's mugging.

Parry mumbled some reply and buried his face in a cup.

'We've been having a case conference, as you can see,' Foxley went on to me. He didn't show surprise at my refusing the coffee. He probably understood and sympathised. 'We are not yet in a position to make an arrest with regard to the murder in your basement, but we're closing in.'

Closing in? Coppers said things like that in the old black-and-white movies I watched late at night. After someone says it, old-style black police cars race through deserted streets, sounding sirens fit to bust and alerting every villain for miles around that they're on their way. I had hoped police methods had advanced since then. Possibly the methods had—lots of technical wizardry and forensic leads—but not the approach.

Harford, standing behind and to one side of my chair, cleared his throat and said, 'Miss Varady believes she's made a discovery, sir.'

He sounded nervous.

'Miss Varady knows she has,' I corrected him. I pulled out my magazine and opened it. They all leaned forward, peering at the page of mugshots. I tapped the relevant one. 'Jerry Grice,' I said. 'That's the guy in the snapshots, isn't it? Give or take a bottle of bleach.'

Someone at the back of the room said, 'Shit.' Another said wearily, 'Bloody press.'

Parry turned purple and his eyes bulged at me.

'I told you not to muck about—' he began.

Foxley glanced over his shoulder and Parry fell silent. 'Yes, Miss Varady, that's right,' the superintendent said evenly. 'And you understand I'm sure, why we don't want to advertise the fact that he's the man we're after.'

'I understand,' I said. 'But I don't like being pegged out as decoy.'

He raised sparse eyebrows. 'Did we do that? I wouldn't say so. We have been keeping a friendly protective eye on you, I admit that.'

'Rubbish!' I retorted robustly.

Since Foxley was clearly the big cheese round here, my attitude was causing ripples of emotion round the room. I detected, on different faces, disapproval, anticipation and even glee. Parry looked about to faint.

'Someone tried to break into my flat the other night and if I hadn't had a dog on the premises, he'd have got in.' I did my best to sound like an outraged citizen. The very least they owed me was an apology.

The superintendent merely looked irritated. 'An oversight.'

I dismissed this with, I hoped, visible scorn. 'You bet it was an oversight. So, from now on, you include me beforehand when you want to use me. Otherwise,' I added on a brainwave, 'I'll take my case to the Police Complaints Committee.'

Parry turned aside towards the window to hide his reaction to this. His shoulders were twitching. I didn't know whether from laughter or despair.

Foxley didn't snarl 'Feel free!' though it obviously hovered on his lips. Instead he gave a strained grimace and advised me that we hadn't got to that stage yet, surely?

I wasn't going to push the point, to tell the truth. But it did no harm to let them know I was seriously displeased.

Foxley had got the message. He leaned his elbows on his desk and placed the tips of his fingers together. 'I sincerely hope that you won't let a misunderstanding damage what I hope could be a profitable collaboration. The fact is, Miss Varady—' this was accompanied by his bleak smile. He was doing his best to be charming, but he wasn't cut out for it. I awarded him a point for trying—'the fact of the matter is, we need your help. Now, of course, you don't have to say yes. You don't have to do anything unless you decide to help. It's your decision and no pressure will be put on you. But I'd be grateful if you'd just let me explain.'

Had Ganesh been there, he'd have told me to say no, and get out of there as fast as I could. But I reckoned it would do no harm to listen. A bit of police goodwill wouldn't come amiss. 'Go on, then,' I said.

Foxley launched into a seamless narrative which led me to believe he'd done this sort of thing before. I wondered briefly what had happened to others, such as myself, who'd been talked into helping in just such circumstances.

'Your magazine article will have told you why we're after Grice. He's been giving us the runaround but the net is closing.' (Did he, too, watch old films?) 'We believe that Grice will shortly be arriving in this country. There is an underworld rumour to that effect. We have it from a normally reliable source.'

I wondered about the 'source'. Say what you like, the professional grass earns his money. He probably wouldn't be in the business if the police didn't have some hold over him, but all the same, it's a risky enough trade to undertake in whatever circumstances. Rumbled and he's done for. His body is washed up and deposited on a Thames mudflat. The river police go out and scoop it up and add it to the statistics. If anyone enquires, and it's unlikely anyone will, a dozen people will testify to how depressed the late unlamented was, and how he'd spoken frequently of ending it all.

'Grice needs to recover that strip of negatives and any prints made from it, Miss Varady,' Foxley said. 'His hired help has bungled the job. He can't afford another body in a basement. Above all, you see, he seeks to avoid publicity. Pictures in magazines, murder reports on the evening news, police enquiries such as the one set in motion by Coverdale's death, all these things are anathema to Grice. Successful big-time crooks, you have to understand, view themselves as successful businessmen. It irks them that they make the money but can't spend it except in the society of underworld characters. They want out of that world. They're social climbers. They long to be on the Town Hall invitation list. They hanker to join the world of Rotary dinners and mornings on the golf course. In a word, they want to be legit. A respectable businessman is probably how Grice is passing himself off somewhere and the worst thing that can happen to him is that his new friends learn the truth, depend on it. It makes him vulnerable now in a way he wasn't when he was just a villain. He's displaying an Achilles' heel, you might say.' Foxley paused and then asked me, 'You know what that is?'

Prat, I thought. 'Yes, I do know,' I said

aloud, crossly. 'I went to a good school, you know. Achilles' mother dunked him in the river Styx to make him invulnerable but forgot about the heel she held him by.'

'That a fact?' asked Parry, looking interested. 'I didn't know that. You'd think the poor little bugger would've drowned.'

Foxley gave him a dirty look and me an only slightly less dirty one. 'Your education wasn't wasted then, I see.'

He scored a hit, if only he knew it, but I wasn't going to let him see it.

Foxley regained his position effortlessly. 'To return to Grice. He'll try negotiation. To put it bluntly, he believes you have the film Coverdale hid—or you are in a position to obtain it. We are confident he'll offer to buy it off you.'

Oh, they were, were they? 'What if I tell the truth and say you lot have what he wants?' I asked.

His smile grew wider but no pleasanter. 'In Grice's world, people don't speak the truth. Why should he believe you? We haven't released any statement about the photographs. They are worth money. You could take them to a newspaper. They'd pay you well. Probably that was what Coverdale intended to do. Why should you not do the same? Grice will make you a pre-emptive bid, that's all.'

'An offer I can't refuse,' I said caustically.

'That's right.' His mouth stretched in a

genuine grin. 'Got it in one.'

I thought it over, but not for long. 'What do you want me to do?'

There was a palpable relaxation of tension all round. This was what they'd all been in a huddle discussing before I arrived. How to get me to co-operate in this. Well, here I was, putting my head on the block. I had about as much choice as one of Henry the Eighth's wives. Grice was on his way and I was his target anyway. Either I worked with the police or it didn't bear thinking about.

'Good!' Foxley sat back in his chair. 'I'm glad we've got all that sorted.'

'What sorted?' I protested. 'What am I supposed to do?'

They'd been discussing that one, too. I got an encouraging nod.

'It's highly unlikely that Grice himself will approach you in the first place. An underling will do that. He'll tell you the deal. You agree, saying you don't have the negatives to hand, but you can get hold of them. You have one condition only, you'll only hand the negatives over to Grice himself. His representative will argue. But you stand firm. You say you don't trust intermediaries in view of what's happened before. They know they've screwed up and they'll take the point. So you say you want to be sure the deal's gone down as planned and the only way you can do that is for Grice to be there. It's likely Grice himself

276

feels the same way. He'll want to be sure, too. The only way he can be is by collecting the negatives from you himself. Say you'll meet Grice wherever he wants, provided it's a public place in broad daylight. You'll bring the negatives. He brings the money. Straight swap. You then let us know where the exchange is to take place and we'll pick him up.'

Just like that. I must have looked unconvinced.

'He needs those pictures badly, Fran,' Harford said, beside me.

I fully realised that. Something on those pics not only betrayed Grice's location, it betrayed his current game. A project he'd planned carefully and executed beautifully had been thrown into jeopardy by Gray Coverdale, the man who took risks. Even Coverdale's death hadn't made Grice secure. Only getting his hands on the film could do that.

Foxley was speaking. 'Oh, another thing. You make your own way to the meeting place. On no account get into a car. Just make it clear to them that you're broke, you have no interest in Grice's business, and your entire aim is to make a little cash. They'll believe that.'

I had an idea this last remark was probably insulting but I let it pass.

'How much money do I ask for?'

'They'll make an offer. I doubt it'll be extravagant. You can look a little disappointed if you like, but accept it. If you try to haggle, things might get nasty. It'll be enough to tempt someone in your circumstances, don't worry, but they won't make the mistake of dangling huge sums before your eyes. They'll calculate you're not a person used to dealing in large amounts of money and too many noughts could turn your head. You might decide that anything worth that much could find a higher bidder, and attempt a double-cross. Oh, and Miss Varady—' he wasn't smiling now and his eyes reminded me of a dead fish— 'you wouldn't try that, would you? A double-cross, I mean. I wouldn't take it kindly. You'd find trying to be clever at our expense wouldn't pay you, Miss Varady.'

'Do me a favour,' I said wearily. 'All I want is for this business to be over and done with. One small point you seem to have overlooked . . .'

'Yes?' The sparse eyebrows shot up in genuine surprise. Parry, in the background, looked affronted.

'I don't *have* the negatives,' I said. 'You do. If I do go to meet Grice, he won't hand over an envelope of dosh without checking first that I've given him the kosher goods.'

There was a pause. 'When the deal's set up, we'll let you have the negatives.'

They would have as many prints as they needed, anyway. But then Grice might be concerned about prints, too. I pointed this out, though not mentioning the extra print I'd got from Joleen's waste bin.

'A fair point.' Foxley nodded. 'We'll put a set of prints in with the negatives. You swear to them that's all there are.' He gave his thin smile. 'I hear you're an actress, Miss Varady. I'm sure you can make it convincing.'

If only some casting agent somewhere had the same confidence in me.

*       *       *

Foxley's parting instructions were not to discuss this with anyone, understand? Anyone at all.

Parry made a move to escort me out, but Harford was ahead of him. He led me downstairs, through reception and out on to the station steps, where beneath the overhead lamp he made a very neat speech.

'I want you to know, Fran, that I admire your courage. It's really brave of you to agree to this and we're very grateful.'

That was easy on the ear, but I'd expected something of the sort. Now, however, Harford unbent sufficiently to add, 'The super's an old miseryguts but he's really chuffed that you're playing along with us in this. I don't want you to worry. Everything will be all right, I promise. I'm making it my personal responsibility to see nothing goes wrong. Whatever else happens, I'll be looking out for you.'

It was nice to think I had someone to look after me but since their priority would be to nab Grice, I couldn't help but be less than completely convinced all eyes would be anywhere but on the main prize.

He noticed the indecision on my face. 'What's worrying you?' he asked anxiously.

'Nothing,' I told him. 'I was just waiting for the spotlight to shine on us and the unseen choir to strike up.'

Concern faded in his face and the touchy look came back. He straightened up, stiff and wooden as a toy soldier.

'Relax!' I told him. 'It was a joke. I watch too many old films in the early hours of the morning.'

He looked faintly embarrassed and managed a smile. 'You see,' he said, taking my hand and squeezing it. 'You can even joke about it. That's what I mean, Fran. You've got guts.'

Another explanation would be that I was missing a few marbles but I just gave a noble smile back because it's not often someone tells me I'm a heroine, and it was nice to bask in approval for once.

Harford still had hold of my hand and I found I didn't mind too much. If he'd just get the chips off both shoulders, we might even get along quite well.

'We'll have the place completely covered,'

he was saying. 'As soon as Grice has taken the envelope, we'll move in on him.'

'Look,' I said, 'he's going to be suspicious, you know. He hasn't stayed out of gaol this long by making silly mistakes.'

Harford leaned towards me earnestly. 'Let me tell you something, Fran. Sooner or later, they all make mistakes. They get to think they're invincible, you know? They're too used to calling the shots and getting away with anything. They really get to believe they can't be caught.'

'Grice thinks he can get caught,' I said. 'That's why he wants those photos back. The person who thought he could get away with it was Coverdale. Instead he got himself into something nasty and it caught up with him in my basement!'

Harford's hand, holding mine, gave a convulsive twitch before he let my fingers drop. 'Don't forget, tell us the moment he makes contact.' He turned on his heel and ran back up the steps into the station. A couple of uniformed men coming out gave me a curious look.

\*     \*     \*

I went back to the shop to collect Bonnie. Both she and Ganesh welcomed me with flattering enthusiasm.

'Well, how did you two get on together?' I

asked heartily. 'Friends?'

'I needed to go in the storeroom,' Ganesh said with emotion. 'And every time that animal growled at me. I had to keep feeding it crisps. It was the only way I could get past.'

Bonnie, sitting on her cardboard bed, thumped her tail. She looked pleased with herself.

'So?' Ganesh prompted. 'How did you get on with your police mates, then?'

'We're not mates. I told them it was Grice in the pics. They admitted it was. They told me not to discuss it with anyone.'

'Well,' said Ganesh. 'Now I hope you're satisfied and you'll leave it alone.'

I was glad I hadn't told him any more about the setup I'd agreed to back there at the nick. Gan wouldn't think me a heroine. He'd say I was nuts and make no bones about it.

A customer came in and he left me to go and deal with him. I untied Bonnie, called out goodbye, and set off slowly homewards, Bonnie pattering beside me.

Light was fading already. If I was to meet Grice in daylight, it would have to be quite early in the day to make sure of not being caught by gathering evening shades. I wandered down my street, lost in this and other depressing thoughts, and was almost at the house before my eye was taken by a glitter on the pavement ahead, just outside Daphne's front door. I approached wonderingly and

282

gazed down at a silver patch of water which ran across the pavement slabs, over the kerb, into the gutter, and down that to the nearest drain. The silver patch had its origins in a tiny spring which had forced its way up between slabs. Around it were some painted marks which hadn't been there earlier. Bonnie sniffed around and tried to drink the spring. It bubbled up her nose and she jumped back and barked at it. Daphne's door opened and light beamed on me.

'Oh, Fran,' my landlady called. 'I've been watching out for you. The water board has been to inspect it and they're coming first thing in the morning to mend it. Unfortunately, they've got another emergency on and couldn't deal with it straight away.'

'But it's coming up through the pavement,' I pointed out.

Daphne came down the steps to view it. 'So it is. That's new. It wasn't doing that earlier when the water-board men came. There was just a lot of water seeping out. I have been worried. You know, there was a big puddle out here which never seemed to dry up? I assumed it was the aftermath of the rain, but it did seem odd.'

I told her I'd noticed it, too. We told each other we should have got in touch with the water board earlier.

'But they are coming in the morning,' Daphne comforted us. 'If it gets worse before

283

bedtime or if they're late in the morning, I'll be on the phone straight away.'

She returned indoors. I dragged the fascinated Bonnie away from the spring, picked her up and carried her down the basement steps. As I felt for my key, she wriggled and growled.

'It's only water,' I told her. 'We'll go out and look at it later, see if it's worse, OK?'

I pushed the door open. Bonnie's growls intensified. In my arms, her body was stiff. The ridge of hair had risen along her back, the whites of her eyes showed and her ears were flattened.

A nasty sick feeling gripped the pit of my stomach. I peered into the darkness of the flat. There was complete silence but an odd feel to the place, something I could only sense. Bonnie sensed it too and to her it meant another presence. I stretched out my hand for the light and flipped it on. I could see into my living room and it was empty. Nothing looked as if it had been disturbed. Leaving the door open, I edged in. I put Bonnie on the floor and remaining by the exit, ready to run, watched to see what she'd do.

She ran round the place, nose to carpet and fetched up by the curtain and plastic strips which covered the entrance to the kitchenette. Here she stopped, pricked her ears and began to bark in short repetitive bursts.

That was enough for me. No way was I

284

going in there unaccompanied. If I had to go back to the shop and wait for Ganesh to finish there and come back with me later that evening, so be it. But I couldn't leave Bonnie here with whatever danger threatened. I called to her but she wouldn't come. She remained in front of the curtain, barking, alternately rushing forward a little, then scuttling back as if caution tempered her combativeness.

I edged in a little further. 'Bonnie—come here, come on.' I crouched and whistled to her, but she was deaf to my urging.

The curtain shimmered, rustled and parted, and a man stepped out into the room. In my guts I felt sicker than ever, even though the dog's behaviour had told me he must be there. Bonnie hurled herself forward but the next moment yelped shrilly as she was propelled across the floor by a well-aimed kick.

'Hey!' I darted forward, heedless of the fact that I was distancing myself from the open front door and my escape route. 'Don't hurt my dog! She's only small.'

'Shut the door,' he said. His voice was low, cold, expressionless. 'Pick the dog up and shut it in another room. If you don't, I'll kill it.'

He meant it. I closed the front door behind me. I was shut in now with him, at his mercy. Bonnie wasn't easy to catch. She skittered round my outstretched hands, her eyes fixed on the intruder, still barking. At last I managed to grab her and shut her in the

285

bathroom. In there, she began to scrabble at the door and keep up a noisy protest.

My visitor had remained by the kitchenette, his hands folded in the stance of the professional bodyguard. He was a big fellow in a dark suit, balding but with his remaining fairish hair tied back in a ponytail. His skull appeared to be perfectly round like a football. He wasn't so young—I supposed him in his forties—but as solid as a brick barn. I hadn't seen a Mercedes car on my way home—but no doubt that was parked nearby, possibly in the next street.

'Switch the light out,' he ordered in the same expressionless tone he'd used throughout our short conversation. For all that, it was an educated voice. 'And sit down there—on that sofa. We're going to have a talk.'

## CHAPTER FIFTEEN

Once I'd switched out the light, the basement room was plunged into gloom, made worse by the fact that the medicine cabinet still blocked the small garden window. Ridiculously, I found time for a spasm of embarrassment. He had probably seen and guessed the reason for that pathetic attempt at barricading myself in. Totally futile, as it turned out. This fellow hadn't needed to break in by burglars' methods as had his Spanish-speaking colleague. This was the man who'd got into the shop, and, on the night the Spaniard (as I thought of him) had been trying to get in here, had effortlessly entered Mrs Stevens' Putney home. There he'd drawn a blank. Here the Spaniard had also been unsuccessful, thanks to Bonnie. He hadn't even got in. Ponytail had been forced to come here and try himself. I fancied a hierarchy was emerging. This sinister intruder, with whom I shared the darkness, was Grice's lieutenant, entrusted with his messages and orders. The other guy was a regular foot soldier. That Grice had sent his right-hand man suggested Foxley had been correct. Grice was taking personal control, albeit at one remove. Foxley would be pleased about that. I wasn't so sure.

I glanced towards the window. Up there, out in the street, it was still comparatively light, that steel-grey moment before dusk falls. Down here, I could barely see my visitor.

He had moved, taken a chair over by the television, which put him between me and the only exit. As my eyes adjusted to the poor light, I could make him out better but he was still little more than a silhouette.

I couldn't see his face and was glad of it. His voice was frightening enough.

Though Foxley had warned me that someone would contact me soon, I hadn't—and Foxley hadn't—bargained for it being as soon as this. As a result I was unprepared. In stage terms, I hadn't had time to learn my lines or rehearse. The interview would have to be conducted off the cuff. It would have to be a *tour de force* of improvisation. If I got it wrong, if he guessed I'd been primed by the cops or that I was uttering the smallest lie, he'd kill me. I found I was holding my breath and forced myself to breathe as naturally as I could in the circumstances, but my chest was rigid and it felt as natural as being in an iron lung must be. Even Bonnie had fallen silent. From the bathroom came only an occasional whimper and desultory scrabble at the door. She, too, was listening.

'Do you know why I'm here?'

I started. I hadn't expected a question. It was a clever one, straight to the point. It allowed for no evasion. If I lied, he'd know straight away.

'I can guess, I think,' I said. My voice sounded as if it were being forced out of a bag, like piped icing. 'Is it to do with the roll of film?'

'Yes.' I'd given the right answer. There was a touch of approval in his voice. I'd be a fool to bank on it. 'Do you have it?'

'Not here,' I croaked.

'I know you don't have it here,' he replied, now sounding reproachful.

Of course he knew. He'd used his time to search the place, just as he'd searched the house in Putney. It didn't look upside down because only careless, amateur searchers (or those bent on vandalism) leave a place looking as if it's been done over. The professional has been through your gear and you never know it. Mrs Stevens had guessed only because she was super-tidy and he'd made the error of leaving the loo seat up.

At the thought of him, searching methodically through my gear, the sick feeling returned. He'd been through everything, my clothes, including my underwear. My bed, looking under the mattress and inside the pillowslip and duvet cover. In the bathroom, unscrewing my tube of toothpaste and tin of talc. In the kitchen, shaking out the contents of the coffee jar, the packet of tea. Everything had been touched by him and soiled by him though he'd left no sign, not even a fingerprint, that was for sure.

'You've searched,' I said dully. 'Did you search the flat above the shop, too? After you knocked out my friend?'

'The Indian guy? He didn't have it.'

Yes, he'd calmly stepped over Ganesh's prostrate body and gone through Hari's flat. That must have taken a bit of time. There are a pile of papers to do with the business up there. At any moment, Ganesh could've regained consciousness but, thank God, he hadn't.

'How did it come into your possession? Did

289

Coverdale give it to you?' Ponytail asked next.

'No, he didn't. He hid it in the old washroom at the shop the morning he stumbled in. The morning you—He was being chased. The washroom's been renovated since. That's when it came to light. It was in an old envelope, tucked behind some pipes.'

He thought that over and must have accepted it. His voice went back to being expressionless. 'The person I'm representing would like the film. Can you get it?'

'Yes.' That was true. Foxley had promised that.

'He is a fair man and will pay you for your trouble. A thousand pounds. That's a lot of money. I'm sure you can use it.'

Yes, I could. But I'd rather earn it a different way. Come to that, the police would take it off me in due course, even if all went according to plan. They'd say it was evidence. I wondered if I could argue the case for being allowed to keep it. Then I thought wryly, why worry about that, Fran? A chance would be a fine thing.

'A thousand?' I said wistfully. It wasn't difficult to get the tone right. It came naturally.

'That's right. You agree?'

I hesitated. I wasn't acting. It was real. I was about to take the plunge. 'Yes, all right. I know you've been looking for the film but—but what about the bloke you—who was found dead outside my door here? I don't want to end up the same way. Don't take this wrong, but how do I know I can trust you? Look, I want to trade, but I'm not going to agree to hand over the film to you in some place, say like this flat here, where it's just you and me, like this. I'm not trying to be difficult. I'm trying to look after myself.'

I felt his anger though he hadn't moved. I hurried on. 'I'm not trying to shake more money out of you. You can have the film for a grand. That's fine by me. But I want to hand it over to—to the person you're representing, himself. That way, I'll know he's got it and that nothing's gone wrong. See, you say you represent him, but maybe you don't. Maybe you represent someone else. I don't know, do I? I give the film to your boss or no one, right?'

'You are not in a position to make conditions,' he said tersely.

But actually, I thought he was bluffing there. I was. I had the negs—or knew where they were. I was prepared to play along and return them for a grand in cash. They didn't want more trouble either, according to what Foxley had said. I hoped he was right. 'Look,' I said, 'just explain that to your principal, will you? You're right, I could use the money. I don't want the film. It's no use to me.'

He was hesitating. 'My principal may wish for some evidence that you do actually have access to it.' Sarcasm entered his voice. 'Since we don't know we can trust you, either.'

Tricky. I could hardly send him down the nick to ask. But if Grice himself were to come, he'd have to be persuaded. I gambled. 'I did get it developed,' I admitted.

At my words, he moved. He was across the room and towering over me in a split second. Bonnie, in the bathroom, began a determined attempt to scrape her way through the door, whining hysterically. He snatched me up off the sofa in a single move, holding my arms in a painful grip. I hung between his hands like a rag doll, helpless and wondering if I hadn't made the worst mistake of my life. But he had to know. If I handed the goods over, they'd know at once they hadn't got a film but a set of developed negatives. Explaining that if they were unprepared would be well-nigh impossible. They'd be sure it was a double-cross.

'Hold on!' I gasped. 'I'm not making trouble! When I got it printed up I didn't know, did I, that it'd be of interest to you? I thought it might tell me whose it was, but it didn't. I didn't—don't—know the people in the snaps. I only ever wanted to give the stupid thing back to its owner and if you want it, you can have it!'

He dropped me. I fell back on the sofa in a heap like the victim of a session on the rack. I was sure my shoulders were both dislocated.

He still loomed over me.

'Where are the prints?' His voice was low and harsh.

'With the negs. Except one I've got here in my pocket. I meant to—to put it in a safe place with the others, in case the owner came asking, you know. Somehow it got left out. Look, it's only a holiday snap, what's the fuss?'

I was doing my best to sound thick, but I wasn't sure he'd bought the explanation. He held out his hand silently.

I fumbled in my pocket and gave him Joleen's print. He took it to the window and held it so the street lighting fell on it. I heard him give a little grunt. He put it in his inside pocket and turned back.

'How many of these prints do you say you have?'

'Four. Most of the film was unused, I swear. There were only four pics on it. You've got one print there, the three others are with the negatives, but not here. Look, I nearly threw them away! They're not interesting or anything.' I crossed my fingers beneath the cushion.

'The prints must be returned with the negatives, including any blanks that you may still hold. If we were to find you had held any back, we would be seriously displeased.' The threat in his voice when he said that would've chilled anyone's blood. It froze mine.

'Look,' I said pleadingly, and that wasn't

acting, either, 'I really do want to give you the lot, get rid of it all, get the money, and then hear nothing more about it. I swear, I never wanted to get involved in any of this in the first place.'

That all rang beautifully true because it was. He was convinced at last. 'Very well. I'll tell the person I represent what you've said. I'll be in touch with you again. You'll speak to no one meantime.'

He stepped towards the front door, it swung open and he was gone, just a shadow on the basement steps. Despite being a large man, he moved almost silently, like a panther.

I got up by dint of pushing myself off the sofa with my hands. My legs were like jelly. I stumbled towards the bathroom and opened the door. Bonnie rushed out but I had no time for her. I staggered to the washbasin and threw up violently.

When I'd retched myself just about inside out, I went back to my living room and tried to think straight. I ought to let the cops know that someone had been in touch, but I was afraid to leave the flat. They knew I had no telephone here and they might be watching to see if I went to phone anywhere else—or went to see anyone else. I couldn't involve Daphne, and a public telephone box would be a dead giveaway. I'd have to wait until Ponytail got in touch again with details of the exchange arrangements.

*　　*　　*

Going to bed that night took some effort of will. To begin with, there was the picture in my head of Ponytail searching through the bedding. It wouldn't go away although I stripped pillowcase, sheet and duvet cover and put them to wash. Even if I'd been able to push away that image, the pain in both upper arms reminded me of my visitor. I showered, hoping that would make me feel better, and eventually crawled into bed around midnight. Bonnie hopped up on the duvet and settled down by my feet. I had discovered that Bonnie liked sleeping with people. I suppose it was because her original owner had been living rough.

In my bedroom under the pavement, sometimes I could hear feet walking overhead. Mostly it was a silent little cubbyhole, at times uncomfortably tomblike. Although there was a ventilation grille in the door to prevent my suffocating, I always propped the door open. I just didn't like being shut in there.

Perhaps Bonnie and I were both exhausted by the day's turn of events. At any rate, we both fell asleep.

I was awoken by a whining in my ear and opened my eyes to realise Bonnie was on the pillow, standing over me. She licked my face.

I sat up, startled and confused, wondering if

295

this was a dream or, if not, what on earth was happening. Above my head, feet stamped back and forth. There was the noise of a powerful motor, something like a pump. Lights flashed across the overhead glass circle like the strobe lights in a disco. Voices were shouting and behind it all was an eerie trickling noise like running water.

Before I had time to work it out, someone began to thump furiously on the front door. The bell jangled. Bonnie jumped off the bed and landed with a curious splashing sound. I swung my feet out and yelled, 'Ugh!'

I had put them down, not on the carpet, but in a couple of inches of icy water.

The hammering on the door increased. As I ran out into the living room, splashing through more water, I heard a man shout, 'We'll have to break the window.'

'No!' I shouted back. 'I'm awake! Wait!'

I unlocked the front door and pulled it open. It flew inwards, propelled by a build-up of water on the further side. I lost my footing and fell back, landing on my backside in an icy cold wet mess.

A torch flashed over me and a large figure in yellow oilskins hauled me to my feet.

'Burst watermain, miss!' he bellowed. 'Emergency evacuation. Get some clothes on, grab any valuables and get out of here—right away! Don't switch on any electricity.'

I splashed back to my bedroom, ankle-deep

now in the flood. Luckily my jeans and sweater were on a chair, high and dry, but my boots, which I'd left on the floor, were filled with water. I grabbed my only valuable, Grandma Varady's gold locket, together with my purse and the envelope which held my birth certificate and the only photos of my family I had left, and stuffed them into my jacket. Then I waded out into the living room.

They'd set up emergency lighting outside and it beamed down into the room. In it, I could see a lake all around me, with furniture sticking up like islands. But all I could see of Bonnie in the rising water level was her head, with wavelets lapping at it. Her eyes looked up at me in bewilderment, asking whether she was supposed to swim for it now. I snatched her up and, with soaked dog under one arm and waterlogged boots in my other hand, sploshed my way back to the front door. As I did, Bonnie's tin dish floated past. I scooped that up, too.

The fireman had come back. He was waiting by the door and seized my arm. I was propelled through the mini swimming-pool which my basement had become, up the steps to street level, and found myself in the full glare of the temporary lights.

It was all go up there. There was a fire engine and another vehicle. A huge hose snaked across the pavement. People were working feverishly everywhere I could see. The tiny spring we'd inspected earlier had burst its corsets, flooding first the pavement and then, as drains proved unequal to the task, pouring down basement steps to gather at the bottom in lakes which had forced their way under my front door and those of my immediate basement neighbours.

Daphne's door opened and she scurried down the steps. She wore her usual jogging pants and sweater but in addition gumboots, a raincoat and a sou'wester. She was better equipped than I was. In her arms she held a large tin box.

'Oh, Fran dear!' she wailed. 'They say we've got to go to the church hall. I don't know why we can't stay in my place—that's not threatened.'

'The electrics, ma'am!' called the nearest yellow oilskin.

I realised that there were several police cars parked nearby. An officer appeared to escort us to one of them and we sped away through the night.

\* \* \*

A group of us, about fifteen souls in all, inhabitants of the affected properties, huddled round a pair of portable Calor Gas stoves in St Agatha's hall. Bonnie, having shaken herself fairly dry, had taken the best place in front of one fire and curled up.

We basement dwellers had rescued a peculiar mix of valuables. One man had brought out an oil-painting. There was a crop of video recorders and home computer terminals, two guitars, a porcelain rococo clock and a cat, yowling miserably in a travelling cage. Bonnie had shown brief curiosity in that, but as it was safely locked away and couldn't be chased, lost interest. Otherwise, we looked typical refugees. We'd been handed blankets and mugs of tea by two stalwart ladies who'd appeared from somewhere. They were in the best of spirits. One said she was the vicar's wife. The other one informed us she was Brown Owl. They were obviously friends and lived for this kind of occasion.

At first, we, being British, affected an equal jollity, showing the spirit of the Blitz and so on, though we stopped short of the Vera Lynn songs. But it didn't last. Before long, we put our heads together and began to grumble about the water board, the incompetence of the council, the level of council tax, and those of us from basement properties, about where on earth we were supposed to go to, when the water was pumped out.

Clearly, none of the basements would be habitable. Carpets and furniture would be ruined. Electrical wiring would have to be checked. Insurance companies would have to be contacted. It would take weeks for the last dampness to evaporate, encroaching mould would need to be cleaned away, and then the business of redecoration would start.

A computer buff was sure he'd lost all his work. His floppy disks had got wet and, ohmigod, he didn't dare imagine what had happened to his hard-drive. Someone else had only just finished painting and decorating.

'And a week before Christmas!' groaned yet another.

A young woman burst into tears and declared she'd lost all the Christmas presents for sure. They'd been piled up in a corner. Everyone else turned to comforting her.

I brooded alone. I hadn't lost any Christmas presents because to date, I hadn't bought any and no one had sent me any, either. But it did seem likely I'd lost all my few possessions and worse, was left with nowhere to go. I had no family and no money for hotels.

Daphne, divining what was in my mind, tapped my arm and whispered, 'Don't worry, Fran. We'll be able to go back to my house once they've checked the wiring is safe. With the steps, the water couldn't rise to the level of my door.'

I hoped that was true.

'You can stay with me until the basement is fit to live in again,' she went on.

I thanked her, but said that wasn't on. 'It could be months,' I pointed out. 'I couldn't doss at your place for so long. It wouldn't be fair. There's Bonnie. Anyway, what about your nephews?'

'Oh, blow my nephews!' said Daphne.

But I couldn't stay with her for that length of time. Apart from all the other considerations, the flood had thrown a major spanner in Foxley's plans. When Ponytail came back, if he did, he'd find the flat empty and locked up.

'I'll go down the housing department in the morning,' I said, 'and ask for emergency accommodation. They can't refuse me, surely.'

They mightn't refuse, but they'd stick me in some God-awful hole of a place for sure. And what about Bonnie? Few places accepted animals.

'I might ask you to look after Bonnie for a bit, if you would,' I ventured.

'You listen to me, Fran!' said Daphne firmly. 'We're only days away from Christmas and I won't hear of your turning to the council at a time like this. I have a four-bedroomed house and I insist you stay with me—at least until New Year. Then we'll talk it over. In any case, I'll look after the little dog. She's no problem.'

Bonnie, in front of the gas stove, twitched her ears.

'We won't be able to use the tap water,' said a man gloomily. 'It'll be contaminated. They'll bring one of those water tankers round and we'll have to fill plastic containers.'

'I drink a lot of bottled water, anyway,' Daphne said. 'At least I've got a supply of that in.'

'Shops round here will soon run out of that,' said Jeremiah.

It was four in the morning. I pulled my blanket round my ears and wondered how my boots were drying. One of the stalwart ladies had stood them upside down on newspaper to drain, near to the fire. My co-refugees kept giving them mistrustful looks.

'The freezers will have shorted out!' screeched the young woman who'd lost her Christmas gifts. 'The turkey will be ruined!'

They all began again to talk about insurance. I didn't have that, either. That was to say, I supposed Daphne's house insurance took account of the building, but my personal possessions, well, that was another matter. Not that what I had was worth insuring. But that meant that, by Sod's law, I had neither the goods nor a cheque on its way in the post. The less you have, the more you have to lose at a time like this. I tried that line of argument out on the computer buff, but he didn't take the point at all. 'A year's work!' he moaned repeatedly.

I left him alone with his misery.

\*　　　\*　　　\*

Daphne and I had steeled ourselves to finding

a mess, when we returned home just before ten, but neither of us had anticipated the level of destruction in the basement flat. The water, before they'd pumped it out, had reached a level of some forty centimetres. A tidemark round the walls confirmed it. The old rep sofa had soaked it up like a sponge and would have to be thrown out. The telly would probably never work again. It hadn't worked well before. The pine coffee table might be salvaged. The carpet was ruined. Both bathroom and kitchen tiles had lifted. Worst of all, sewage had contaminated the water and the place stank. Bonnie picked her way fastidiously across the wreckage and returned with the bloated body of a dead mouse which she deposited at our feet.

'Come on!' said Daphne briskly. 'We'll move everything we can upstairs.'

It took us the rest of the morning, carrying the heavier items between us, up my steps, Daphne's steps and down her hall to the utility room at the back where we stacked them up. Some things we couldn't move, like the bed and the cooker, so they had to be left. The water tanker had turned up and so I also hauled plastic jerry cans back to the house to stock up. My arms, thanks to Ponytail's embrace, had ached before. Now the muscles shrieked protest at every movement. So busy were we, it wasn't until Daphne spoke of making something for lunch that I realised I'd quite forgotten about Ganesh and that I was supposed to have been at the shop. I went round to explain.

'I heard about it,' he said. 'It was on local radio, breakfast-time, with the traffic news. Motorists to avoid your street. I wondered if you'd been affected and when you didn't come in, I realised you must be. I'm really sorry. I was going to pop round later to see you.'

'You bet I'm affected,' I said. 'Flooded out and homeless again.'

He frowned. 'You can stay here until Hari gets back.'

'No, I can't. One of your family might turn up and find me and there'd be hell to pay. Daphne will give me a bed, at least until after Christmas.'

The bell jangled and Hitch came into the shop. He looked cheerful. 'Hullo, darling!' he hailed me. 'I hoped I'd find you here. I've been down your street and I saw your place was one of the ones flooded out. Here, you take my card and give it to the old girl who owns the house.' He thrust one of his business cards at me. 'You tell her, when she's getting quotes for the insurance, to come to me. I can give her a very good price for fixing that flat up.' He lowered his voice. 'And if you was to fancy lilac paint for the walls, I've got a job lot of that.'

I took the card without comment.

'Gan,' I asked, 'I need to use the phone up in the flat, OK?'

I left him with Hitch and ran upstairs. My luck continued out. I couldn't contact Foxley, Harford or even Parry at the nick. They passed me to someone I'd never heard of, called Murphy, and I had to tell him that Grice had been in contact.

'Himself or one of his boys?' asked Murphy, not sounding particularly interested.

I explained and he said, 'Fine, I'll tell the super. Let us know when he gets back to you.'

Then he hung up on me. I glared at the phone. For two pins, I'd have rung again and called the whole thing off. Then I remembered I couldn't.

Hitch had left when I returned to the shop. I told Ganesh I hoped to be into work the next day as normal, but he said if I needed to mop out the flat, he could manage. We left it at that.

I dropped Hitch's card in the waste bin on my way out.

\*　　　\*　　　\*

I arrived back at the house in time to meet Daphne, who was just taking Bonnie out for a walk. An old leather dress belt in sky blue was looped round Bonnie's collar as a lead. 'Better than a bit of string, anyway,' said Daphne, setting off down the street.

I let myself in, went out into the kitchen and was just about to make coffee, when the doorbell rang. I froze. Had Ponytail tracked me down already? I crept into the front room and peered out the window. I was afforded the fat rear view of one of the Knowles brothers. I had just decided to let him stew out there, when he turned and saw me.

'Open the door!' he shouted. It was Charlie.

I opened up and he stormed in, passing me rudely and marching through to the back sitting room.

'Where is my aunt?' he demanded.

'Tied to the nearest railway line,' I said wearily. 'She's gone out.'

He huffed a bit, then made up his mind. 'Then we have time for a little talk.'

'I've nothing,' I said, 'to say to you.'

'Dare say not! Useless trying to justify yourself!' He was marching up and down Daphne's sitting room now, preparing to hold forth at length. 'But I've got a few things to say to you.'

'You're not going to blame me for the flood, are you?' I asked cheerfully, not because that was how I felt, but because I wanted to annoy him.

'This is not an occasion for levity,' he retorted. He had fetched up before the fireplace and stood there on his stubby legs, with his hands behind his back and his brogued feet planted apart.

'You're telling me,' I returned. 'That was my home.'

306

'No,' he said. 'It was, is still, part of Aunt Daphne's home. You were merely the tenant. Where is the other girl? The one with the dog? You had no right to sublet.'

'She was a friend staying a day or two and she left before all this happened.'

Charlie made his way to an armchair where he plumped himself down, his hands on his knees. 'And when will you be leaving?'

I took the opposite chair and braced myself for the outburst which must follow my reply. 'After Christmas. Daphne has asked me to stay here until then.'

I had been expecting Charles to rage, but instead he looked triumphant. He leaned forward and hissed, 'Staying here, indeed? I knew it! You just listen to me, young woman! I saw this coming, you know. So did my brother. We knew you were trying to work your way into our aunt's confidence. You think you've managed pretty well, eh? Well, it hasn't gone unremarked. We know what's what.' Here Charlie tapped the side of his pudgy nose. 'Don't count your chickens, that's all I have to say to you. We'll have you out of here before you can say knife!' He slapped his knees and sat back, looking pleased with himself.

I hit back by leaning forward myself and hissing back, 'Yes, and I know what's what, too! You're trying to gyp Daphne out of this house. You may be interested to know that I've already mentioned my concerns to a police officer I happen to know.'

Charlie collapsed in his seat as if I'd reached across and felled him with an uppercut. His eyes bulged, his face turned purple and I began to be seriously alarmed. Just when I was thinking that, revolting though the idea was, I might have to go over there and loosen his tie and unbutton his shirt collar (actions which he'd no doubt misconstrue), he found his voice, pitched low and full of real hate. The words hung in the air between us, each issuing distinct on a puff of breath.

'You-go-too-far!'

'Just remember,' I said, 'I'm on to your little game.' And I imitated his earlier gesture, tapping my nose.

Charles rose to his feet, straightened his jacket and tugged at his cuffs. 'You will be very sorry for all this. I shall come back later when I hope to find my aunt at home and have some private conversation with her. Don't make yourself too comfortable and don't trouble to see me out. I can find my way.'

I let him go. After a moment or two, it did occur to me that it was taking him a long time to walk down the hall, but just as I was about to go and investigate, the front door slammed. I went to look out the window and saw him marching away along the pavement. If I hadn't been so preoccupied with other matters, I'd have worried about him more.

# CHAPTER SIXTEEN

The following couple of days passed uneventfully. Normally, that would be a plus. In this case, it meant that Ponytail hadn't contacted me with the reply to my offer to meet Grice. Uncertainty heightened my nervous state to the point where I jumped out of my skin at every ring of the doorbell or phone, every time a customer walked into the shop, every time a car slowed by me as I walked along the pavement. I took to hugging the buildings, so that it would be more difficult for someone to bundle me into a vehicle. I scurried home to Daphne's at the end of the day and, apart from walking Bonnie round the block at top speed last thing at night, didn't put my nose out of the door till morning.

A person can only go on like that for so long without it becoming noticeable.

'Are you all right, Fran?' asked Daphne. 'I know you're upset about the flat, but even so, you don't seem your usual bright self.'

'Winter blues,' I told her.

Ganesh, too, had noticed my jumpiness. 'What's going on?' he asked.

'Nothing,' I told him, but he didn't believe it.

'All I can say is, I hope you haven't done something stupid, Fran. This hasn't got anything to do with that whizz-kid inspector, has it?'

'You know what I think of Harford,' I told him.

He snorted. 'I know what you thought of him when you first met him. It strikes me you might be changing your mind about him.'

I told him that was rubbish.

All the same, I felt a pang of disappointment when, Daphne having told me at breakfast-time the following morning the police were on the phone for me, I picked up the receiver to hear Parry's unmistakable tones. I did think Harford might have rung himself.

'Hi, Wayne!' I greeted him, just to let him know that his secret was out.

He answered grumpily, asking if I had anything further to report.

Whispering furtively into the receiver, I told him no more contact had been made and I was still awaiting confirmation of arrangements. I felt perfectly ridiculous saying things like this, as if I'd escaped from a spy thriller.

'You let us know what they are, straight away!' he ordered.

I needed to explain the call to Daphne. I put my head round her door and said, 'They haven't got any lead on my break-in yet. They don't suppose they will.' I didn't like telling her fibs.

'It all seems rather less important now than

310

the flood,' said Daphne. 'But it was nice of them to ring and let you know their progress, or lack of it.'

She didn't know the half of it, that was the trouble. I wrestled with my conscience for the rest of the day. What would happen if Ponytail turned up on my landlady's doorstep? Poor Daphne would be totally unprepared. But ignorance was probably better in her case. Safer, certainly. I just hoped he'd contact me some other way.

That night, as we sat in her kitchen over a bottle of wine, I ventured, 'Have you had any callers today?'

She sighed. 'Only the boys. I wasn't going to tell you because I know you don't get along with them. I must confess,' went on Daphne, lowering her tone as one about to confide a startling secret, 'I am beginning to find them rather tiresome myself. I always found them unnecessarily fussy. But I believed—still believe—their hearts are in the right place. And they are, you see, my only family left.'

Who needs families? I thought, not for the first time, although mine hadn't been like that and I still missed Dad and Grandma. It was getting late. I said good night and went up to bed.

Bonnie bounced ahead of me. I had put an old blanket over the end of the bed to save the counterpane from dog hairs. An attempt to get Bonnie to sleep in a basket which Daphne had unearthed from somewhere, had proved doomed. Bonnie remained firmly convinced that we all slept together in a heap.

It must have been around three in the morning when she woke me, licking at my face and whining as she'd done on the night of the flood.

I sat up, bewildered for the moment, and thinking myself back in the flat. It was pitch dark in the bedroom. Daphne believed in thick lined curtains for winter. Bonnie slid off the bed, landed with a muffled bump on the carpet, and ran to the door where she whined again.

I thought, damn it, she wants to go out. She'd never done this to me before. Her late evening walk usually enabled her to last out till morning. I got out of bed, pulled on the old dressing gown my landlady had lent me, opened the door and made for the stairs.

I didn't want to disturb Daphne and hesitated to put on the light. Out here on the landing, streetlighting shone through an uncurtained window. I scooped up Bonnie and began to make my way downstairs with her tucked under my arm, the other hand clinging to the banister in case I lost my footing. Halfway down she began to struggle.

'Stop that!' I ordered her quietly. But she whined and then growled.

At the same moment, I heard a slight noise from the hall below. Immediately I clamped my hand over her muzzle and froze where I was on the stair. Oh my God, I thought. It's Ponytail! He's let himself in just as he did at the flat.

I didn't want to face the man but even less did I want Daphne to come face to face with him. I made my way down the remaining stairs as quickly as I could, Bonnie squirming beneath my arm.

The intruder had moved from the hall and was in the drawing room at the front of the house. More streetlight falling through the transom above the front door let me glimpse the erratic beam of a torch which was being flashed around in there. By now, I'd got a grip of my nerves and my brain was functioning better, too. If it was Ponytail, surely he didn't intend to search this large house, belonging to someone who had no connection with Coverdale, on the off chance I'd hidden the negatives here? I had told him I was prepared to hand them over. All he had to do was tell me where and when. Wasn't it more likely that, whoever was in that room, he was no more than a common thief?

I crept up to the door and cautiously stretched my hand through the gap, feeling for the light switch. He was on the further side of the room now. He stumbled over a piece of furniture and I heard a muffled 'Blast!' That wasn't Ponytail.

I switched on the light and dropped Bonnie

to the floor.

Then everything happened at once. Bonnie rushed across the floor, barking. The burglar let out a high-pitched shriek, stumbled back and fell over, bringing down a little table over which he'd been bending. It was one on which Daphne kept a display of small silver antique items—spoons, salt dishes, pillboxes, that sort of thing. All these items spilled from the table as it crashed to the carpet, and rolled away in all directions. The burglar had become tangled up in the table legs and flailed about on the floor like an upturned tortoise. If you've never kept a tortoise, I can tell you that, once turned upside down, they can't get the right way up again, and lie there with all four legs working uselessly. Our intruder was, I was now able to see, somewhat tortoise-like in shape; round of body and short of leg. He was wearing dark pants and sweater and a ski-mask over his head. This round woollen head, with just two eyes showing, enhanced the tortoise impression.

Bonnie wriggled through the obstacle and grabbed the burglar's trouser cuff in her strong little jaws. She began to worry it, growling ferociously. I could see she was having the time of her life.

'Let go, you wretched brute!' came in a howl from the ski-mask. He struck out at Bonnie with his torch.

'Don't you hit my dog!' I shouted. I darted

across and snatched the torch from him as he waved it wildly in the air. He was trying to kick out his snared leg and shake Bonnie off. No chance.

'Fran! What's going on?'

Daphne had appeared in the doorway holding a walking stick in businesslike fashion.

'Call the police, Daphne!' I gasped. 'Before he shakes Bonnie off!'

'No!' yelled the ski-mask frantically. 'Don't, I can explain!'

There was something familiar about that voice. Daphne and I must have recognised it at the same time. She put down the walking stick and I pulled Bonnie away.

Released, the intruder sat up and began to disentangle himself from the table legs. I reached over and pulled off the ski-mask.

'Bertie!' exclaimed Daphne. 'What on earth do you think you're doing?'

\*       \*       \*

'If you weren't so obstinate, Aunt Daphne,' said Bertie a little later, 'Charles and I wouldn't have to resort to desperate measures.'

We had righted the table, picked up the silver objects and retired to Daphne's kitchen, the centre of operations in this house. Bertie sat on a wooden chair, his ski-mask lying on the table. His exertions, and being imprisoned

315

in a woollen hood, had left his face very red and sweaty and his thinning hair ruffled. He was clearly conscious of the ridiculous figure he cut in his black polo-neck sweater and new-looking black jeans. Had he gone out and bought these items of clothing specially for tonight's expedition? No doubt he'd decided that was what house-breakers wore. Also on the table lay a dark blue canvas shopping bag.

'I don't know what you're talking about,' said Daphne. 'And how did you get in, Bertram?'

He looked sullen, crossed and uncrossed his short legs, and confessed, 'Charles took the spare key from the hook in the kitchen when he called round the other day. You weren't here.' His small angry eyes fixed on me. 'She was!' He pointed a stubby finger.

'I thought he took his time letting himself out,' I said. 'I should have escorted him to the door. Why did he send you? Why didn't he come back himself instead of sending you in, all togged up like The Shadow?'

'I don't owe you any explanations,' snarled Bertie.

'You owe me several!' Daphne told him. 'I hardly know where to start. Why did Charles take the key? Why have you embarked on this ridiculous escapade? If I, and not Fran, had heard you and come downstairs, I'd have been frightened out of my skin!'

'But I didn't mean you to hear me!'

316

protested Bertie. 'For crying out loud, I didn't know she'd brought a blasted dog with her. It wasn't here when Charles came the other day. We thought that other girl, the one staying with her—' the finger jabbed at me again—'we thought she'd taken the dog away with her.' Bertie smoothed his hands over his ruffled hair and attempted some of his former confidence. 'If we'd known about the dog, we should have thought of something else.'

'I think,' said Daphne, 'that you've both taken leave of your senses.'

'I can explain, Auntie,' said Bertie. 'If you'll let me. But I don't choose to do it in front of that girl.'

'I hardly think,' said his aunt icily, 'you are in a position to make conditions. You've given Fran a terrible shock. You owe her an explanation as much as you owe me one.'

'Well, all right.' He folded his short arms awkwardly over the polo sweater. 'Charles and I have repeatedly told you that we think this house quite unsuitable for a lady of your mature years, living alone. Not only is there the responsibility, there is the security aspect. The recent and regrettable flood has, we hope, brought home to you the extent of the responsibility a house of this size carries with it. We wanted to underline the security aspect, or lack of it. She—' finger jab—'suffered a break-in, or an attempted one, at the basement flat. It gave us the idea to stage one

317

here, in the house proper. All we thought we'd do was break in, just the one of us. We cut cards to decide who. My intention was simply to remove some small items. Then, in the morning, Charles and I would have called round openly, returned the articles missing, and pointed out to you how easily an intruder could get in.'

'An intruder wouldn't normally have a key,' I said.

'Bloody hell,' said Bertie. 'Neither my brother nor I are professional house-breakers. How on earth should we know how to get in without a key?'

'And what,' asked Daphne, 'if before you had called round, I had called the police?'

'Ah,' said Bertie, looking smug. 'Thought of that. We knew you didn't use this room much, never went in it from one end of the week to the other, unless we came. We knew about the collection on the table. I was just going to take one or two things. It was highly unlikely, even if you'd glanced in, that you'd have noticed.'

I'd been listening to all this with growing scepticism. 'Or,' I said now, 'Daphne might have been tempted to think I'd pocketed them—or I'd let in some accomplice to make off with the lot and anything else he could find. I can't see why you needed to bring that shopping bag if all you were going to remove was a couple of teaspoons.'

'Yes,' said Daphne grimly. 'You're sure this

wasn't some ridiculous plan to get rid of poor Fran?'

'Look at the company she keeps!' squawked Bertie. 'When Charles called round the other day, he found her here alone. She could have gone through the place and taken every pocketable valuable you have, Auntie! We really think you're out of your mind to have invited her to stay here! I'm surprised the police haven't warned you. Or have they? For goodness' sake, surely you can see we've acted in your interest, Auntie?'

'This is enough!' Daphne ordered. 'I won't listen to another word of this rigmarole. Where is your brother?'

'He was waiting round the corner in the car,' said Bertie miserably. 'But he's probably pushed off home by now.'

'Hardly very loyal of him,' said Daphne. 'But I suppose I shouldn't expect Charles, or you either come to that, to be anything but cowards.'

Bertie opened his mouth to bluster but thought better of it.

'You had better go,' said his aunt. 'Kindly do not call round in the morning, or telephone, or even write. It will be a very long time before I want to see or hear anything of either of you again.'

Bertie got to his feet, picked up his ski-mask and shopping bag, and hovered uncertainly.

'Well?' Daphne asked.

'Look here,' he said. 'If Charles has left me here in the lurch—I mean, I've got no transport.'

'Walk!' Daphne and I said together.

Bonnie barked in support.

When Bertie had taken himself off, Daphne fetched the bottle of wine we'd started that evening and poured out a couple of glasses.

'I really can't believe it,' she said, taking a swig. 'The worst of it is, one doesn't know whether to laugh, cry or just scream in frustration. Whatever did he think he looked like? That silly sweater and the ski-mask! Oh, my God!' Here Daphne let out a great hoot of laughter.

I was rather taken with the image of them cutting cards to see who would take the risk. I was sorry it hadn't been Charlie I'd trapped in the drawing room. That would've been sweet revenge for having been cornered in my basement bedroom by him.

Daphne sighed. 'I blame their upbringing. Their mother, Muriel, was a very odd woman. She dabbled in the occult.'

'Cripes,' I said, impressed.

Daphne waved her wine glass dismissively. 'She never took up anything properly. I always say, if you're going to do anything, do it thoroughly. Muriel fiddled round the edges, as it were, with things. Spiritualism, what she liked to call "white magic", oriental philosophies, whatever took her fancy of the moment. She was very beautiful, you know. That often means trouble. People forgive things of a beautiful person they wouldn't forgive in someone as plain as a pikestaff. She had a dreamy, slightly loopy way with her, which passed for charm. A lot of men fall for that kind of thing. My brother, Arnold, did. But then, he hadn't a jot of imagination himself. Believe me, Fran, I've met so many beautiful women who've been unstable. Arnold should've taken a grip on things, but he never did, of course. Putty in her hands.' Daphne snorted. 'You see, you can't blame the boys for turning out as they have. The atmosphere in that household was always unreal. I never had any looks and really, I thank God for it. I feel I've been spared so many complications.'

We'd finished the bottle. I added it to the pile of empties which had been growing in the corner since I'd arrived.

'I'll take these to the bottle-bank in the morning,' I said.

Daphne gazed at them as if she'd only just seen them. 'Goodness, I know the boys have been calling round rather more frequently than usual, but I never encourage them to linger. I mean, a glass or two is all I offer them. You and I, we couldn't have polished off all that lot, could we?'

I thought we probably could've. It was now almost five in the morning. It hardly seemed worthwhile going back to bed for me. Daphne went off but I stayed downstairs and fed myself and Bonnie on Weetabix. At six, I showered, dressed and walked round to the shop.

*    *    *

'Early bird!' observed Ganesh, staggering indoors with a load of newspapers which had been delivered to the pavement outside.

'Not much choice.' I told him about the events of the night.

'I warned you,' he said, 'those two wouldn't rest until they got you off the premises.'

'Daphne says their mother was a white witch, no kidding, Gan.'

He looked worried. 'You oughtn't to meddle with that sort of thing, Fran. You never know.'

'I might even take it up,' I returned. 'Nothing else seems to work for me.'

'Don't even joke about it!' he urged. He cleared his throat, preparing, I realised, to make a speech.

'You'll have to move out of there right after Christmas now,' he said, 'even if the council won't give you temporary accommodation. If you won't come here, you can sleep in Hari's lock-up, I suppose, until he gets back. But you can't stay with Daphne. Weird as the Knowles brothers are, and dodgy with it, they're Daphne's nephews and it's not for you to come between her and her family.'

322

'Even if they're trying to cheat her?'

'It's a family matter, Fran!' he said obstinately. 'She's not a fool. She knows what they're like. It's up to her whether she puts up with them or not.'

I supposed he was right. Daphne had to make her own decision. Like Tig, she had to accept her family or reject them. Once she made up her mind, she had to live with the decision, same as anyone else.

*    *    *

Ponytail rang the shop at a little after eleven that morning. What with one thing and another, plus being tired after a disturbed night and the shop being busy, I'd even managed to forget about the wretched bloke for an hour or two.

When the phone rang, I answered, luckily. I afterwards wondered, if Gan had answered, whether Ponytail would just have hung up and tried again later.

'Miss Varady?' He didn't offer to identify himself but I recognised his voice at once. Even down the phone line, it gave me the shivers.

I croaked, 'Yes?'

'Tomorrow, twelve noon. At the statue of Nelson Mandela outside the Festival Hall cafeteria.'

He hung up.

'Who was that?' asked Ganesh.

'Nothing—someone wanting the chemist's. Gan, is it OK if I go upstairs and make a call from there?'

He said, 'Sure,' but gave me an old-fashioned look. He knew something was going on and I was keeping secrets. But one of Gan's many good points is that he doesn't badger me. If I don't choose to tell him, he lets it go. He knows it's one of the unspoken rules of our friendship.

I rang the police station and, thank goodness, got hold of Jason Harford. 'I need the negatives and snaps,' I said. 'Like as of now.' I repeated the message Ponytail had given me.

'I know the place,' Harford said. 'It's always pretty busy. Damn. There's umpteen ways in and out and it'll be difficult to stake it out. It's right by the Hungerford footbridge and look how many people go back and forth over that. We can't close it off. It'd be obvious and cause chaos.'

'He chose it for a reason, I suppose,' I said sourly. 'How you go about it is up to you. Just give me the negs. I give them to Grice and he gives me the money. That's all I'm contracted to do. Whatever else you're planning, make sure I'm clear, out of the way, before you do it. Grice has a very unpleasant minder.'

'Don't count on the money,' he said. 'What time are you leaving the shop today?'

I told him, probably at one. 'But don't come here, for God's sake. He might be watching.'

'Relax,' he urged. 'We've got it under control.'

All right for him to talk.

I walked out of the shop just before one feeling as if I were walking across red-hot coals. No cars lurked on the double yellow lines. The usual cross section of humanity surged past. A ragged, lunatic-looking old fellow, grasping a wad of badly printed leaflets, was trying to stop passers-by and press one of his scraps of paper on them.

'Bargain sale,' he urged in a piping voice. 'All quality goods. Fire-damaged stock.'

Most people hurried past. A few took a leaflet, perhaps to placate him, and dropped it to the pavement almost at once, turning the immediate surrounds into a litter-bug's dreamscape. A crisp wind blowing straight down the street picked them up and tossed them around, before bowling them off in all directions. They fluttered out into the road and were flattened by double-deckers. They fetched up in shop doorways. One had even been carried by an updraught clear up into the sky like a tiny kite.

'Here you are, dear!' He lurched at me, greasy old raincoat flapping. His feet were wrapped round with plastic bags. Of a pair of trainers, all he had left were the soles, tied on to the wadded bags by string. His hair was long and unkempt. He might have been anything from just an old alkie to a lost soul condemned to care in the community. No wonder people scurried past.

I felt sorry for the poor old devil. He was probably being paid a pittance to stand out here for a couple of hours, kept going by the hope of getting enough out of it for a couple of cans of lager. I didn't want a bargain video recorder, 'fire damaged' being an euphemism, I suspected, for 'hot', but I hesitated.

He moved in front of me so I couldn't walk on. I cursed myself for the momentary weakness which had let him latch on to me. I knew from experience that people like him were often difficult to shake loose again.

'Go on, love,' he persisted, pushing his face into mine. Close to, he wasn't nearly so old nor so decrepit. His eyes met mine and sparkled with something which might have been intelligence or just malice. He pushed a couple of leaflets into my hand. 'Buy yourself something nice. Dead cheap!'

I said, 'Yeah, why not?' and thrust the leaflets into my pocket.

I didn't take them out again until I was safe indoors. I wasn't surprised to find I had not two leaflets, but one leaflet and a brown paper envelope.

I opened the envelope and shook out on to Daphne's kitchen table a strip of negs and four prints I recognised as old friends.

The police had kept their side of the deal. Now I had to keep mine.

## CHAPTER SEVENTEEN

Ganesh and I went out together to eat that evening. Given my guilty conscience, I wouldn't have chosen to go out with Gan that night of all nights. But he called round to the house just after eight to ask if I'd eaten and if not, whether I wanted to go out.

'We might have better luck this time,' he said. 'And not find a body lying around in your basement.'

I nearly told him he shouldn't count on that and the body might be mine—but he wouldn't have thought it funny and neither, come to that, did I.

'Is this another staff Christmas dinner?' I asked. No harm.

'No, it isn't,' he retorted. 'We can't take two staff outings! You'll have to pay your own way. Or I'll pay, if you like,' he added generously.

As it happened, Daphne had gone to see a friend and I was on my own and hadn't got round to making a sandwich—my idea of cooking dinner. So we went, having established that I'd pay my own whack. It was one thing to let the business pay, quite another to let Ganesh shell out. I don't mean because he's broke, but that's not the way our friendship works. He has lent me money in the past when I've been completely cleaned out or needed it urgently, but I've always paid him back. 'Neither a borrower nor a lender be,' as Mrs Worran used to say.

She was our neighbour when Dad and Grandma were alive. She belonged to some exclusive sect, so exclusive that if they were the only ones saved, Heaven must be a pretty empty place, just a few Mrs Worrans rattling around up there. She had a stock of such slogans, one for every occasion. They were uniformly negative. She also had a stock of badly printed tracts which she would post secretively through our door late at night, as if we didn't know they came from her. Once, at the age of ten, when I unfortunately fell off my bike into her privet hedge making a large hole, she shot out and told me that the way I was going, when the sheep were divided from the goats, I'd be in the wrong half of the draw for sure. When I was expelled from school, she was in her element. Even after Grandma died shortly after Dad, and I was left quite alone, Mrs Worran informed me by way of encouragement that she was sure I'd manage all right. 'The devil knows his own,' she said, which at the time I found rather obscure and never have quite worked out.

We left Bonnie shut in the kitchen. She took a dim view of this. We could hear her howling as we closed the front door. She probably added tonight's desertion to the list of things she had against Ganesh.

We ended up in a local burger bar where we both ordered the vegeburger. Ganesh is the vegetarian, not me, but somehow I'd gone off the idea of meat. It made me think of dead things. The vegeburger seemed to consist mainly of beans. On top of everything else, when I went to meet Grice the next day, I'd have wind. Not but what the very thought of going to meet Grice was enough to give anyone wind.

It gave me a chance to explain to Ganesh, however, that I couldn't come to work the following morning. 'I'm sorry to let you down,' I said. 'But something's come up. It's just one of those things. Perhaps you can get Dilip to come in for a couple of hours.'

'You know,' said Ganesh, 'I don't interfere and I'm not about to start. But I want you to know that I know you're up to something and I just want you to be careful.'

'I'll be careful,' I promised. You bet I would.

'And you tell Harford,' he went on grimly, 'that if anything goes wrong with whatever it is, I'll be round to see him.'

'You've got a thing about Harford,' I said.

'I haven't. You have.'

'Rubbish!' I snapped through a mouthful of beans. 'You said the same thing about Parry. Really, Gan, you're turning into a real old matchmaker.' (I knew that would annoy him. That's why I said it.)

'I didn't say you were keen on Parry,' argued Ganesh. 'I said he was keen on you. And he is. So I was right. But you're not likely to fall for him, are you? Let's face it; he's gross. Harford's got education and prospects and is a good-looking bloke. Of course you're interested. But if it's led you into making silly decisions, it's not a good thing. That's all.'

I told him it was a good thing he'd finished his burger or I'd have shoved it down his throat.

*　　　*　　　*

The next morning turned out clear and bright, one of those winter days when the weather seems to have got it wrong, and spring is trying to get in early. The pale sunshine, the pleasant breeze, and the cheerful look on the faces of passers-by, all combined to mock me and the way I felt, which was like a woman on her way to the block. *'Tis a far, far better thing*—No, it wasn't. It was about the stupidest thing.

I began my long walk across the Hungerford Bridge shortly before twelve. Down below me on the Embankment I could see Cleopatra's Needle looking lonely and out of place, just like me up here really. The narrow walkway on the bridge was busy with people going in both directions. They slowed as they passed an old boy who was flying a kite from this vantage point. He was good at it. The kite, which was made of some silvery material, was way up high out over the water and he controlled it very niftily with what looked to me like a converted fishing reel. It shimmered around up there, dipping and diving, catching the eye of nearly everyone. Many stopped to take a second look, unsure whether it was a bird, a helicopter or—there's always one hopeful—a UFO. Then they saw the old man and knew it was a kite. I envied the kiteman his peace of mind as I walked on.

The river sparkled to my left and the view, if I'd been in the mood to admire it, was suffused with that pearly light which hangs over the Thames on days like this. The great dome of St Paul's, where the river sweeps round to the right, hung suspended above the buildings around it. Sometimes when I've seen it, I've really wished I could paint. I don't mean I aspire to being a Canaletto, just I'd like to be one of those hobby painters who can knock out a reasonable watercolour to hang on the wall and show off to their mates. But whenever I've tried, the result has looked like one of those expressive but out-of-sync efforts you see pinned up in infant schools. Even when I was in infant school, I couldn't get it right. I always got more paint on myself than the paper and in the end, they took the poster paints away and gave me crayons. I didn't like the crayons.

They were too much like hard work.

To my right, the trains rumbled and clanked in and out of Charing Cross Station, along the parallel rail bridge. I wished I was on one of the outward bound ones, going anywhere.

Ahead of me lay the South Bank complex, with its galleries, theatres and concert halls, its presence heralded by the line of fluttering blue and white flags along the riverside. I wondered briefly if I was ever going to make a career in the performing arts, or whether I'd no more hope of that than I had of painting in oils or flying a kite. I really did think I had more talent at acting than the other two. Everyone has a talent to do something, Grandma Varady used to say. It's finding it. (You see, Mrs Worran wasn't the only one with slogans. The difference was, Grandma's were intended to encourage you.) Finding this talent and making it work for you are two different things, however, as I've since discovered. Grandma's talent, she reckoned, was in making a very good strudel. She tried to teach me how to do it and, guess what, I couldn't do that, either. Flour and butter everywhere, stewed apple stuck to the pan, the air pungent with burned sugar. Result: a stick of pastry you could've knocked a hockey ball around with.

I wondered at greater length if I was even going to make the return journey back across the bridge this afternoon. In my pocket, the envelope with the negs was burning a hole.

The Hungerford Bridge that morning seemed more like that bridge in Berlin where they used to exchange spies. I imagined finding a couple of heavies with long overcoats and trilby hats waiting for me on the other end. Come to think of it, that wasn't such a wild piece of imagination. God alone knew what I was going to find. Hopefully a well-organised snatch brigade from the Met. The problem was that in my experience, the police never seemed that well organised, more a case of trusting in the endearing British habit of muddling through. Grice, on the other hand, I was sure was organised to the nth degree. I began nervously to study the expanse of concrete promenades on the further side and the festival pier extending a long finger over the choppy khaki water. Was one of the strolling figures Grice?

In the angle where the walkway comes to an end and the flight of steps down to the bank starts, a young bloke was sitting on a grubby blanket, asking passers-by for change. No one gave him any. Even the tourists could tell he was fake. Probably they thought he was a professional beggar. I knew he was a cop who'd ousted the regular pitch-holder for the day. Cripes, I thought, is this amateur the best Foxley could come up with? I just hoped Grice wouldn't walk across this way and see him. Talk about dead giveaways. I don't know what betrays undercover coppers—the way they stand on their big flat feet or their haircuts perhaps? This one just didn't look hungry enough. But mostly, I think, I rumbled him because he hadn't got the voice right. Beggars repeat the same question of passers-by like a mantra, with dulled hope, resignation and not quite buried resentment. This guy sounded altogether too chirpy, as if he was selling flags for charity.

'You're rotten,' I muttered to him, as I passed.

'Sod off,' he managed to mutter back before I was out of earshot.

It was oddly comforting to know that, despite my present co-operation, nothing had really changed in my relationship with the rozzers.

I clattered down the steps. No going back now. There were always people around this large pedestrianised area, even in winter, especially on a fine day like today. I walked down the side of the Festival Hall to the cafeteria. Through its glass walls, I could see a few people having coffee. A young couple right by the door leaned across the table, gazing into one another's eyes. There was a whole world around me, living normal, peaceful lives. What had I done to be excluded from it?

Curiosity killed the cat, Fran, I told myself. You had to go and get that film printed up. You couldn't just have chucked it in the bin, could you?

The concreted area between the cafeteria and the rail bridge saw only a few visitors. I made my way to the larger-than-lifesize bronze head of Mandela on its plinth. No one stood by it and I felt a spurt of ridiculous optimism. Perhaps Grice wasn't going to show. Then I looked beyond it, up the short flight of steps to the higher level of walkway.

A burly figure stood up there, a man, with his back to me. He was leaning over the parapet and holding up a camera as if he were taking photographs of Waterloo Station's wonderful Victory Arch. The trouble was that from there he couldn't see it, only the topmost line of stonework, a couple of flags, and the legend 'Waterloo Station'. The rest was obscured by the grimy yellow brickwork of the rail bridge reaching down into Concert Hall Approach. Thoughts floated through my head in a discouragingly logical progression.

a)    He was no photographer.
b)    He was no tourist.
c)    He might be an anorak obsessed with Victorian railway arches.
d)    He was far more likely to be Grice.

As I neared, he turned and, pointing the camera down towards me, began taking snaps in my direction. He was prosperous in appearance, wearing a belted pale grey waterproof jacket and one of those little green felt Tyrolean hats. The angle he'd chosen allowed him to frame me in the viewfinder as I walked towards him. I heard the faint click as he pressed the button. He'd got a record of me, should he need it again. Nice thought.

He moved again, slipping rather incongruous shades on his nose, walking towards me, descending the flight of steps and pausing at the Mandela bronze. Slowly and deliberately he turned his body sideways on to me, apparently intent on getting a shot of Mandela from the best angle.

I had no doubt now this was Grice, who'd sussed out the area and taken up his position before I arrived. My heart sank to my boots. What did I do now? Walk up to him? It wouldn't do to look too familiar. I couldn't hail him by his name because I wasn't supposed to know it. In the end, I stopped by the plinth and stuck my hands in my pockets, as if I was waiting for someone.

Then someone else did turn up. Ponytail. My heart plummeted. I should have expected that he'd be on hand. Grice would hardly have come without his minder. He'd been close by near the top of the spiral stair which led down to Concert Hall Approach and, my eye distracted by the snapping camera, I hadn't seen him at first.

I was suddenly struck by an idea which I at first rejected and then decided wasn't so fantastic after all. Down that spiral stair, across the York Road, through the subway and Grice would be at Waterloo Station and the Eurostar Terminal. A few minutes' walk only. Was that what Grice had done? Come in on Eurostar, specifically to make this exchange? Having made it, he could just retrace his steps and get on the next fast service to the continent. It was so easy. I wondered if the cops had thought of it.

Ponytail moved to Grice's side and murmured something in his ear. Grice let the camera fall to hang from the strap round his neck. I swallowed with difficulty; my throat had clammed up. Where was Harford and his team? So far, all I'd seen was one phoney beggar back there on the bridge, nowhere near enough to be any use. He was presumably backup in case Grice took flight that way. I glanced round nervously, hoping Grice didn't think I was looking for help, just being prudent. The couple in the cafeteria had left their table and were coming out through the exit, hand in hand and still lovey-dovey. Grice was coming my way.

'Miss Varady?'

His voice was surprisingly pleasant. I'd been expecting a thug like Ponytail. But of course, Grice wasn't like that. Foxley had told me Grice was probably living a blameless life somewhere, masquerading as a respectable businessman, pillar of the community.

'You have something for me, I think,' he went on courteously.

I couldn't see his eyes through the shades. What I could see of his hair beneath the ridiculous hat looked reddish. He'd been at the bottle of colour again. He probably had one to match every photo in his selection of passports.

I fumbled for the envelope in my pocket and dragged it out. 'What about my money?' I forced myself to ask.

Grice glanced at Ponytail, who brought another envelope from his pocket. Grice held out his hand.

'I'd like to check the contents first, if I may?'

'Feel free,' I mumbled hoarsely, handing it over.

He opened it, riffled through its contents, held up the strip of negatives to the light, then looked at me. 'This is the lot? You're sure of that, are you?' His voice was no longer quite so pleasant.

'Yes,' I whispered, because it was a lie. I had removed the duplicate of the print I'd given Ponytail, otherwise there would have been one extra to the four I'd claimed existed.

Some tremor in my voice must have betrayed me. Between the brim of his hat and his shades, his broad forehead puckered into a frown. I felt his suspicion radiate in my direction. Fear made me speak up.

338

'Look,' I said, 'I don't know who you are and I don't care. They're just some blooming holiday snaps. He said you'd give me a grand.' I tried to sound both bolshie and dim. It must have worked.

The frown smoothed out. A slight smile touched his face. He turned to Ponytail. 'Give her—'

*'Oy! You! I bloody know you! Where's my woman?'*

Grice swore. Ponytail swung round, his hand moving inside his jacket. I goggled and nearly passed out.

At the top of the spiral stair, just climbed up from the street below, was a tall bearded figure in a plaid jacket and woolly hat. Jo Jo.

I had forgotten, in admiring the lay-out of this place as I walked over the bridge, just how close it also lay to the network of underpasses which offered shelter of a kind to the homeless. This was where Tig and Jo Jo had been reduced to sleeping, before desperation had sent Tig to me and consequently, back to the Midlands and the claustrophobic high-tension comforts of the Quayle household.

Jo Jo lurched forward, brandishing a clenched fist. 'I saw you talking with Tig! Where's she gone? What've you—'

Belatedly he realised he'd walked in on something he'd rather not be anywhere near. He broke off and turned to run back down the spiral stair. But a bunch of other guys were running up it, blocking it. Others had appeared round the side of the cafeteria from the direction of the river. The male half of the young lovers stopped cuddling his girl and shouted, 'Police! Stay where you are!'

Not bloody likely, as someone else said. I ran.

Jo Jo, unable to scuttle back down the stair to Concert Hall Approach, wheeled round and raced after me. We reached the corner of the cafeteria building neck and neck and made the turn right in unison. But Jo Jo wasn't interested in me any longer, only in escape. Jointly we negotiated the trestle tables set out for snackers, like a pair of runners in an obstacle race. After that, Jo Jo easily outstripped me. I could see him legging it ahead in great strides past the Queen Elizabeth Hall and Purcell Room. He reached the flight of steps leading down to the lower level and suddenly veered right between the blocks of concrete architecture towards the Museum of the Moving Image, making for the steps which led up on to Waterloo Bridge. From there, by turning right on the bridge and keeping going straight ahead, he'd be safe in the warren beneath the Bull Ring in no time. There were probably half-a-dozen blokes looking just like him in that general area.

I clattered down the steps and plunged on past the National Film Theatre. Beneath Waterloo Bridge, open-air second-hand

340

bookstalls had been set up today. Long trestle tables barred my path. There were a lot of people there, sorting through the volumes. I dodged around them and thought I was clear when a dotty old girl with her nose in a book she'd just bought, stepped straight in front of me. I leaped to one side, slipped and crashed to the pavement.

The woman with the book yelled and dropped it. A couple of men by the bookstall left what they were doing and came running. I saw they were headed for me and didn't look friendly. They probably thought I was a fleeing mugger and had made a grab for the woman's bag, slung over her shoulder. I was about to be the subject of a citizen's arrest. A crowd began to form round me. I'd be lucky not to be duffed up as well.

I scrambled to my feet but before I could get away, a pair of hands grasped my shoulder. 'Leggo! I haven't done anything!' I squawked and hacked backwards at my captor's shins.

'It's me, Fran, it's me!' shouted Jason Harford's voice in my ear.

I froze and then, as his grip relaxed, turned. 'It's me,' he repeated breathlessly.

I was pretty out of breath too. I'd a stitch in my side and my chest ached as I dragged air in and out.

'Police!' Harford called to the two men. 'Under control. No problem.' People began to drift away, already deciding that whatever it was, they wanted no part of it. The mention of the word 'police' has that effect. Even the pair of gung-ho types keen to nab me seconds before, were deciding that, after all, they didn't want to be witnesses to whatever it might be.

'Grice ...' I gasped, pointing a trembling finger over Harford's shoulder back the way we'd come.

'We've got him.'

'His minder, big guy with a pony—'

'We've got him too, don't worry. The only guy we haven't got is that loony in the woolly hat who came barging in. Who was *he*?' Harford asked indignantly.

'Nobody important. Just someone who thinks I did him a bad turn. Did you get Grice's camera?'

'His camera?' Harford scowled at me, not understanding.

'He took a picture of me. For God's sake, get the film out and destroy it! I've had enough trouble from bits of film left lying around!'

'Will do.' He grinned. 'Well done, Fran. Foxley will be pleased.'

I told him, rather impolitely, I didn't care whether Foxley was pleased or not. Never, but never again, would I agree to help out the cops. It was not my style. It was against all my principles.

'Do your own dirty work,' I said in one of my more printable phrases.

'You were always safe,' he said

reproachfully. 'I said I'd look after you, Fran.' He put his hands on my shoulders again, but gently this time. 'And I will, you'll see.'

I am not good at handling this sort of occasion. I said, 'Oh, right . . .' and felt a fool. Fortunately, just then Parry turned up.

'Excuse me, sir!' he hailed Harford sarcastically. 'Can you come back to the control van? Mr Foxley would like a word.'

'I'll see you later,' Harford said hastily. He gave my shoulders a last squeeze and hurried away.

'Want a lift home, Fran?' asked Parry, when he'd gone.

I told him no thanks. I just wanted to get away from it all and be alone, like Greta Garbo.

'Going out with him, then, later, are you?' He jerked his head back to indicate the direction Jason Harford had gone in.

'Maybe,' I said.

'Watch yourself,' said Parry. 'He's got every WPC on the Force in a tizz. Still, he's a bright boy. He's going far, as they say.'

The depressed look which had accompanied these words was wiped from Parry's face as he added, 'You didn't half get a move on when you went belting like the clappers out of it back there. I thought you were going to break some record. They need you in the Olympics, they do.'

'Oh, go and arrest someone,' I said wearily.

He'd persisted in offering the ride home, 'in an unmarked car', until I eventually got through to him that he was wasting his time.

Instead I sat by the river for a while until my heartbeat had got back to normal and my legs were functioning again. Then I walked back, over Waterloo Bridge this time, cut through Villiers Street to The Strand and down into Charing Cross tube station. There was a lot I didn't understand, but it no longer mattered. I'd never even got my fingers on the envelope with the thousand in cash in it. That did rankle and I brooded darkly about it all the way home.

*     *     *

Bonnie was pleased to see me, jumping up and squeaking. I was pleased to see her, to be back in one piece, to have it all behind me. A distant rattle of typewriter keys pinpointed Daphne's location. The great masterpiece was being worked on again. Perhaps one day I'd get to read a bit of it.

'Only me, Daphne!' I called. A faint cry replied. The keys rattled on.

I went upstairs, stripped off and soaked in the bath. Feeling a lot better when I got out, I did my best to dress smartly (for me) though the best I could do was a repeat of the clothes I'd worn the night Coverdale had died. Hardly a good omen. To compensate, I applied the stub of lipstick Joleen had given me. Jason Harford had said he'd be round later.

I went down to the kitchen and was making a cup of tea when the phone rang. 'I'll get it!' I called out and went into the hall.

'Fran?' asked a female voice when I picked it up. 'It's Tig.'

I was surprised, though I'd wondered if she'd get in touch and let me know how things were going. I decided I wouldn't tell her I'd seen Jo Jo. It might lead to complicated explanations and anyway, she didn't need to know it. I told her Bonnie was fine, and asked her how things were.

'Mum's gone shopping,' she said. 'I had to wait till she'd gone out to call you. She gets suspicious if I use the phone.'

That didn't sound too good. 'How's your dad taking it?' I asked.

'Dad? He's gone.'

That threw me. 'Gone where?'

'Gone. Shoved off. He couldn't hack it, my being back and being "no longer his little girl" was his way of putting it. He's sleeping over at his office on a put-u-up.'

That was a turn up for the books. I hadn't anticipated that. Poor Sheila. She'd got her daughter back and lost her husband. 'Perhaps,' I said, 'he'll come back when he's got it sorted in his head. I expect your mum is upset about it, his taking off like that.'

'Not really,' said Tig. 'She just says we don't need him because we've got each other back again now. It's awful, Fran. She follows me round the house. She doesn't want me to go out. If I do, she wants to come with me. If she goes out, she wants me to go with her. I had a real barney with her earlier, because I wouldn't go to the supermarket. She's driving me nuts. I can't stand it. I'm going to have to leave again, Fran.'

'Give it time!' I urged. 'You've only just got there. You can't push off just before Christmas. It'd break your mum's heart. She'll calm down. Your dad will come back. He's bound to turn up for Christmas dinner. It's all been a shock for them. The strain's bound to show a bit.'

'Yeah,' said Tig. 'It's doing my head in for sure. But that's not what I'm phoning about. Look, Fran, I owe you. I know that. Even if it doesn't work out here, it's not your fault. You really tried. You did everything you said you'd do. If I screw up now, it's my problem. The thing is, there's something I wanted to tell you before, you know, before I left London, but I was scared to. I didn't want trouble. I still don't. But now I'm up here, away from it, it's not so bad and anyway, like I said, I owe you.'

'It's something I'm not going to want to hear, isn't it?' I said. The last fading beam of daylight moved away from the transom above the front door as I spoke.

'Yeah,' she said. 'You won't want to hear it, I reckon. But I couldn't be easy in my mind with you not knowing.'

So she told me, as I stood there in the darkening hallway, with Bonnie sitting at my feet and Daphne tapping away at her old upright in the background.


# CHAPTER EIGHTEEN

Jason Harford arrived just before seven. He'd changed out of the suit and was back in chinos with a casual shirt and leather jacket. He stood on Daphne's doorstep in the lamplight, with his hands in his pockets, smiling at me.

'You look nice,' he said. It must have been Joleen's lipstick.

I told him he looked pretty good himself, which was true.

'So, can I come in?'

'Sure.' I stood aside to let him pass. He hesitated in the doorway and leaned forward as if he was going to kiss me, but I slipped past him to close the door.

'No landlady?' he asked glancing around.

'Gone to see a friend, be back later.'

He wandered down the hall, studying the pictures and knick-knacks. 'It's been a great day,' he said over his shoulder. 'You've no idea how much Foxley's wanted to nail Grice. Grice is denying ordering anyone to kill Coverdale, of course. He says his "former associate", as he puts it, panicked and stuck the poor guy. After that, says Grice, he gave the killer his marching orders and doesn't know, surprise, surprise, where to find him now. Still, we've got Grice himself and he'll be angling soon to cut a deal. It's looking good. The super's as pleased as punch. I told you he's normally a sour old git. Right now, he's dancing on the ceiling.'

'Got it sewn up, then,' I said. 'Congrats.' I hadn't meant to sound frosty, but I did.

'Don't get me wrong. I don't mean anyone's going to make any deals with Grice,' he went on hastily, 'but it's been made clear it's in his interest to co-operate. He knows he's going to gaol, but he doesn't want to stay there any longer than he has to. The other guy, the one with the ponytail, has a record of violent offences and my guess is, he'll talk if Grice doesn't. There's a way to go yet but we'll get there.'

'No honour among thieves,' I said.

'Lord, no!' Harford looked quite shocked. 'Every villain I've ever come across would double-cross his own grandma.' He tapped the Victorian barometer, something Daphne had told me you shouldn't do. It upset it. 'You should listen to them volunteer to squeal when the heat's turned up.' He pointed to the barometer. 'Just like this. Guaranteed to be affected by current conditions.'

I wondered just how many villains he had met. His meteoric rise through the ranks to date, which niggled Parry so much, didn't seem to me the best way to build up a close acquaintance with the criminal world. In textbooks, maybe. In the flesh, less so.

Now, Parry, who had met hundreds of crooks in his day, would probably have said many villains were good family men, crime being their gainful employment, as they'd see it, and their families being chips off the old block. We're talking the professionals, of course, and not the bash-old-ladies brigade whom most of the regular type would abhor.

'That sort,' Parry had told me once, 'and the pervs who meddle with little kids or murder 'em you wouldn't believe how difficult it is to protect 'em from the other prisoners, once they get inside.'

It also crossed my mind, as I listened to my companion's optimistic forecast, that Parry would also have shown less confidence in the judicial system's ability to put Grice away. Perhaps Harford was showing a little lack of experience there, too.

If so, it wasn't the moment to suggest it to him. He'd abandoned the barometer. 'Time to go out and celebrate. I thought we might try the Italian place again. The food's good and this time, we might manage to talk.' He grinned.

'We need to talk,' I said. 'But perhaps we ought to do it here before we go out.'

He raised his eyebrows.

'You said,' I reminded him, 'that you'd explain to me why Grice was so anxious to get the negs back.'

'Oh, that, sure. I owe you the full story. You're right. We don't want to be talking shop over the spaghetti.'

'That's right,' I said. 'Come in the kitchen.'

At some point during the day Daphne had cracked open another bottle. It stood on the shelf with the cork sticking out at an angle. It was a Chilean Cabernet Sauvignon. I was going to have to keep my eye on Daphne. Among the bottles I'd taken to the bottle bank earlier, had been wines from France, Germany, Australia, Bulgaria and California. Daphne was making a boozer's world tour. I poured Jason a glass and half a glass for me and we settled down, either side of the big pine table. He picked up his glass and held it up in salute. I gestured towards mine but didn't pick it up.

'This is a nice kitchen,' Harford said approvingly. 'Mind you, this is a bloody good house. I thought so when I first came here— and met you. I'm not surprised the two old boys are after it. Any more trouble with them, by the way?'

'I think,' I said, 'they've been dealt with for the time being.'

'That's all right, then. I told you not to worry.' He leaned on the table. 'I remember that evening very clearly, when I first came here. I've thought about it a lot.'

'You looked at me,' I said, 'as if I'd been scraped up out of a blocked drain.'

'I was scared of you,' he said. 'You looked so tough and assured. It wasn't long, of course, before I rumbled your true nature.' He raised his glass again.

'My true nature,' I told him, 'is to be awkward, obstinate and bloody-minded. Nor am I about to forget that I was treated by your lot in all this as though I were expendable.'

'Hey!' he protested. 'That's not true! I admit we weren't as efficient as we might have been, all the time, but no one wanted *you* harmed. You know *I* didn't, don't you?'

'I don't suppose any of you wanted me harmed,' I said. 'Because without me, you wouldn't have got your hands on Grice.'

He pushed the glass aside. 'We're grateful, all right? But we were reasonably confident that, sooner or later, we'd find Grice.'

No, you weren't, I thought, but he could safely claim so now.

'It might have been a *lot* later, mind you,' he was saying, 'and we were bracing ourselves for that. But, you know, in the end a man like that has to break cover. Damn it, Fran, what's the use of the money if he can't spend it and live life to the full?'

'They never found Lord Lucan,' I pointed out. 'And when it came to tracking down Grice, poor Coverdale did an awful lot better than you. He did find the man.'

'And once he'd done it, he should have come straight to us!' Harford was getting nettled at all this criticism. 'If he had, he'd be alive today. And look here, Fran, we're saddled with always having to go through official channels. Coverdale got his information by God knows what means not open to us!'

I decided I'd made my point and could let it go. 'So where was Grice all the time? Where were the snaps taken?' I asked.

Harford's irritation was replaced by a smug grin. 'Cuba!' he said and laughed at my expression. 'On the level. I can see you think it'd be the last place on earth, but you've got to update your ideas. The leisure industry shifts huge sums of money around the world. In and out of different currencies, developing one playground for the rich after another. Grice may have first thought of Florida as a place to invest his money, but the Americans are canny. They don't like unknowns who turn up with huge sums to invest and no track record. They suspect organised crime and would've rumbled Grice straight away.

'So Grice looked around and saw Cuba.

352

They desperately need hard currency. Cuba's broke but ambitious, keen to develop its tourist industry. The country's so run down it's having to start from scratch but it's making up for lost time. It's already getting to be the in place to holiday. The jet set are going out there for sun and sea. Everywhere else is getting overrun with plebs and package tours. If you've got a lot of money and you want to spend some of it in Cuba, they'll be delighted to see you and prepared to make sure you have the holiday of a lifetime. So when Grice turned up under a different identity, and proposed a joint venture in the tourist market for which he'd put up the bulk of the finance, they didn't ask too many questions of him. He was what they'd been waiting for. Officially, capitalism is still out of favour. But Grice knew how to present his package. He claimed to be a wealthy European socialist. There are several French and Italian communist millionaires. The Cubans bought that, or pretended to. He was wined and dined, lodged in a government guest house—which was where Coverdale ran him to earth and, at a guess, bribed a servant to take those snaps.'

'And was about to tell the world where Grice was doing business.' I frowned. 'It was risky for Coverdale, but I'd have thought Cuba a high-risk investment for Grice.'

Harford spread his hands. 'Hey, before the revolution, fortunes were made in Havana out of hotels, casinos, nightclubs ... Some pretty shady operators ran much of it then. Grice meant to run it this time round. The Cubans probably hoped his involvement meant otherwise; they want tourists but not the bad old days back again. Grice played that up. He presented himself as a financier with sound principles. Not just a money man and definitely not the Mob—which is what the Cubans would have been most worried about. No, he was a regular Mr Clean.'

I thought about this. 'So you've got Grice,' I said. 'And you think you know where he's stashed the money. But that's not the same thing as getting it back, is it?'

'Give us time,' said Harford with confidence.

I thought privately that the only one getting time would be Grice. But they couldn't lock him up for ever, even if they did manage to pin responsibility for Coverdale's murder on him. Good lawyers (which Grice must have) would make sure they had trouble doing that. No lawyer, and I doubted any accountant, could get that money back. Grice wasn't an old man. I judged him forty-two or -three at the most. He could sit it out. Besides I still wouldn't have put money on his definitely going to gaol. Maybe the authorities would get lucky. Maybe Grice would.

I had other things on my mind. So did Harford, who was in buoyant mood. 'Are you ready to go out and eat yet?'

'Not just yet.' I leaned my elbows on the table. 'Parry says you're destined for fast-track promotion. I suppose you're already on your way.'

He looked surprised. 'Why bring that up now?'

'Perhaps you should have thought about a different career,' I said.

He frowned, puzzled and a little angry. 'What are you on about, Fran? You're not one of these people with a down on the police, are you? The last thing I'd have thought you was bigoted! I suppose you've not always seen eye to eye with authority. I can understand that, but hell, that's not my fault. I know we met over a professional matter, but from now on, couldn't you try and see me as a normal person?'

'I'll always have difficulty,' I said. 'My problem is this. I'll always have in my mind that girl you and your two mates kidnapped over by King's Cross, took to the house belonging to one of you, held there for at least two hours and raped.'

I didn't think a room could go as quiet as that kitchen. The only noise was the faintest zizz from the fridge. All colour had gone from Harford's face, draining out as I watched.

He said, 'What the hell is this? What bloody stupid sort of joke is that?'

'No joke, Jason,' I told him. 'It was never a

joke. You put her through a nightmare. She'll never forget it. She was abused, she was hurt, she was terrified. She thought you were going to kill her. The one who drove her back to King's Cross—I know it wasn't you—he threatened to take her down the river and hold her head under.'

'Who told you all this—this nonsense?' he whispered.

'I have a lot of friends out there on the streets, Jas,' I said. 'You forgot that.'

He ran his tongue over his lower lip. The expression in his eyes, watching me, was both hard and unpredictable. I felt a stab of fear, the faintest echo of what Tig must have felt.

'Then one of your *friends* lied to you,' he said.

'I don't think so.'

'Where is this girl?' He leaned forward so suddenly I couldn't help but recoil. 'You put her in front of me and have her repeat her story! She bloody won't, you know!'

'Of course she won't, Jason, you know that. You've always known that. You won't find her now. She's out of your reach.'

'I bloody well will find her! What's her name?' The fury spewed out of him now. He crashed his fist on the table. Bonnie, who'd been listening uneasily, jumped up and barked. Harford looked down at her. 'There was another girl here for a while, wasn't there? You kept her hidden away but the workmen

356

who came to fix the window saw her and the scene of crime boys glimpsed her too. They said she was acting oddly. She had that dog. She left it here with you.'

'You see,' I said. 'None of you ever even asked her name. She wasn't human, she was just a thing, picked up off the street like garbage. Something to be used and chucked back in the gutter.' All the scorn I felt for him must have filled my voice. 'Only,' I said, '*she* wasn't the garbage. The three of you were that.'

He'd gone quiet again, leaning back in his chair. His features were frozen, his body tense, only his fingers drummed nervously on the table top.

'Why'd you go along with it, Jason?' I asked. 'Did you want to prove you were still one of the lads, despite being a copper? Was that it? Or was it a night out with old mates from university days—the ones who'd got City jobs—and it turned into something you hadn't anticipated and hadn't got the guts to stop?'

'You've got it all wrong!' He was shaking his head in disbelief, not at the outrageousness of my tale, but that this could be happening to him. 'I'm not proud of it. But it wasn't the way she told you. She was just a little tart and she was paid . . .'

'She was a barely sixteen-year-old kid down on her luck and desperate for money. She was paid a miserable eighty quid for two hours of horror. Twenty-five quid each, Jason. A quickie in a street doorway would've cost you that. A real professional prostitute would've cost you more.'

He stood up abruptly, the chair legs screeching on the tiled floor as he pushed it back. 'I take it dinner's off, then?' he asked coldly.

'You bet,' I said.

He put both palms on the table and leaned over me, his face dark now and threatening. His eyes held a mix of hatred, fear and desperation. I held my breath and hoped I hadn't judged it wrong.

'I swear, if you ever breathe a word of this—' he began.

'Calm down, Jason,' I told him as evenly as I could. 'No one would believe me. Just as you, all three of you, always knew no one would believe the girl if she was brave enough or daft enough to talk. You're safe. At first it really sickened me to think you'd got away with it so completely. But then I remembered what you've forgotten, Jas. You forget that besides yourself, your victim and now me, two other people know what happened that night. That makes five, and that's too many to keep a secret for ever.'

I saw alarm and then suspicion in his eyes. 'Who else? I don't believe you.'

'The other two guys involved with you. They

know.'

He was staring at me, surprised, puzzled, not getting the message. I explained it to him.

'You think you can rely on them because you were all in it together. Wrong, Jas. You're a copper, remember? You're a copper destined for high things! Real senior rank. And one day in the future, just when you think it's all going swimmingly for you, one of those mates of yours is going to come to you and ask a favour. He'll tell you he's in a mess and you, his friend, can help him out. It might be any kind of jam. Fraud? An unreported fatal traffic accident? Perhaps he'll have picked up another girl for the same kind of games, only this time things may have gone really wrong and she's dead. Whatever it is, he'll come to you for help in some form or other. Perhaps for inside information on just what the police know or don't, or to request a report to be misplaced, a connection deliberately not made, information not passed on or a junior copper persuaded to tear a page out of his notebook. He may ask, tip me off, Jas old pal, if the police get close, so I can hop the country. You're a mate, you won't refuse. You won't be able to refuse, will you? Because he'll have the dibs on you.'

He was shaking his head.

'I know what's in your mind,' I told him. 'You're thinking, he won't be able to shop me because he'll be shopping himself. But when it

359

happens, he'll already be in trouble and a little more old scandal won't make it that much worse for him. But you, you'll have everything to lose. So when I said you were safe just now, I meant, for the moment. After all, you were telling me that there was no honour among thieves. I'd be willing to bet there's none among rapists. Like you said, when the heat's turned up, every man's for himself, right?'

He looked like a man in the middle of a bad dream hoping he'd wake up and afraid he never would. He walked slowly to the door and as he got there, I called, 'Inspector?'

He turned unwillingly. 'Yes?' His voice and face were stony. But I wasn't afraid of him any more. The fight was kicked out of him for the time being. He'd bounce back, outwardly anyway. But from now on, if I'd done any justice by Tig, he'd never go near any of his old mates again. He'd be alone, living with that niggling fear at the back of his mind, every achievement soured. Or I certainly hoped so.

'I've been homeless,' I said. 'And after Christmas I'll be homeless again. My old grandma used to say there were all kinds of people in every walk of life, and that's true. Good and bad everywhere. But I reckon there are fewer rats out on the street than there are living in comfortable houses.'

He was silent, then he said, 'It's a pity, Fran. I really liked you.'

He went out and I heard the front door

close. I went and checked he'd really gone. I knew I had pushed him close. But I'd been taking a calculated gamble. I reckoned that at heart he was a coward. Only a coward would have stood aside and let all that happen to Tig—even worse, joined in. He'd chucked out the window everything he'd claim to stand for as a police officer. All that talk, I thought, remembering our conversation in the Italian restaurant. All that blather about making the community a better place and helping people. He'd sounded as if he'd meant it and I'd been taken in. Perhaps he had meant it. Perhaps he really thought the lapse, as he probably viewed it, with Tig hadn't mattered because she was nothing, just a street-dweller with a drugs habit she was financing by turning tricks.

Faced with the truth about himself and what he'd done, he'd folded. I had to admit there'd been a moment back there when he might've grabbed for my throat, but his brain had clicked in. I'd counted on his being bright enough not to do anything so dumb. Policework had taught him how murderers are caught. Parry, for one, knew he'd come here tonight. I'd probably mentioned it to Daphne before she went out. His fingerprints were all over the kitchen and he couldn't have been sure to clean them all off. Even so, I'd probably come as near to the edge that day as I'd ever want to be—twice.

'Cats have nine lives,' I said to myself as I

poured my undrunk glass of wine down the sink. I hadn't touched it while he had been here. I'm fussy whom I drink with. I think I've told you that before. 'How many do you think you've got left, Fran?'

*      *      *

I hadn't wanted to believe Tig at first, although somehow, as soon as she began to speak, I'd had a premonition of just what she was going to say.

'I didn't know one of them was a copper,' her voice, echoing down the line from Dorridge, had said. 'Not until he came to your flat that afternoon. I caught a glimpse of him as he passed the window on the way to your door. I hid in the bathroom, you remember, but I took a peek through the door, just to make sure. It was him, all right.'

'You are positive about this, aren't you, Tig?' I'd asked.

'What?' asked Tig. 'Do you think I'm ever likely to forget their faces, any of them? I didn't tell you straight off, Fran, and I'm sorry. But I didn't know how thick you were with him. You seemed to be getting on really well with all the rozzers. I didn't know how far I could trust you. I didn't want you fingering me to him.'

'You think I'd have done that?' I'd been incredulous.

'I didn't know you wouldn't. Look, Fran, don't be angry. I was scared. That's why I went for you. I was in enough trouble. I didn't want more. If he'd found out I'd told you about it, he'd have started looking for me, to shut me up. Maybe even to shut you up, too. Knowing some things is dangerous. Out there on the streets, I've seen all sorts of things—some really bad. But I've never talked about any of them, not once, not even to another street-dweller. You don't, do you? You see nothing. You hear nothing. That way you stay out of trouble and that's all I wanted to do. But after I got back here, I started thinking about it. You might really be starting to like him. He's a good-looking guy. He was being nice as pie to you. You had to know what he was really like. I wouldn't want anything bad to happen to you.'

Bad things had happened to me all my life, one way and another, but Tig had done her best to spare me one thing. I said, 'Yeah, I understand, Tig. Thanks.'

I fancied I heard her sigh in relief. There was a faint noise in the background and the echo of a woman's voice, querulous.

'Oh bugger it,' said Tig hastily. 'Here's Mum back from the supermarket and wanting to know who I'm talking to. I'll have to ring off.'

I could hear Sheila's voice now, shrill and frightened.

'All right, Mum!' Tig said crossly. 'It's only Fran. You remember her, she came here. I'm

363

just calling her to let her know I'm OK.' Her voice came more clearly as she put the receiver back near her mouth. 'I've got to go. But I've got to ask, Fran, were you beginning to like him?'

'Not really,' I said. It was a lie. 'Cheers, Tig. Take care.' I hung up.

I'd sat for a long time in Daphne's rocking chair, following that call, with Bonnie curled up in my lap. At first I'd been so angry my stomach had churned. I'd wanted revenge for Tig, for myself. I'd wanted to race round to the police station and face Jason myself. Face them all, tell them all—Parry, Foxley, the lot. I could imagine their faces, horrified, disgusted but not at what he'd done. No, at my effrontery in suggesting such a thing of one of their brightest hopes. No one to back me. No proof. No Tig.

I could hear, in my head, Foxley's dry pinched tones, saying, 'There is no record of any complaint being made at the time. You are unable to produce the young woman who is making these claims. How do you know she isn't lying? How do you know, supposing that some incident of some kind took place, that her story isn't gross exaggeration? Do you expect me to accept an identification made through a crack in a door? The unsubstantiated word of a street-dweller? An amateur prostitute and drug addict?'

Then anger had died back and I'd gone

364

through it carefully, testing to see if there was something I could do. Eventually it occurred to me that the one thing in my power was to let him know it wasn't a secret, what he'd done that night. Others knew and he'd never be safe. He wasn't only evil; he was stupid. I'd been wrong about thinking him bright. Mrs Worran would have called him a 'whited sepulchre' and she'd have been right. Game and match to you, Mrs Worran.

## CHAPTER NINETEEN

It was Christmas Eve. Throughout the country little kids were looking forward to Santa coming down the chimney or squeezing through the radiator somehow. I'm glad I'm not a mum trying to explain that one. As for me, I opened the door and found I'd got Sergeant Parry standing on the doorstep.

'Happy Christmas,' he said, leering.

If recent events hadn't already made it difficult to get any seasonal feeling going, the sight of Parry's straggling moustache and beady eyes would've nipped in the bud any enthusiasm I had worked up. He was wearing the oldest and dingiest green jacket I'd ever set eyes on. It was the sort which is meant to be waxed but all the wax had gone and the side pockets had bulged and sagged. He probably wore it when he wanted to blend with the crowd but something about it, something about all of Parry, screamed 'Copper!' Under it I could see he was wearing a peculiar hand-knitted pullover in cable stitch. It had to have been a present from some elderly female relative. Even a first glance at the front of it showing between the open sides of the waxed jacket revealed several pattern mistakes, cable twists going the wrong way and lots of bits of purl where it should've been plain, and the other way round. Whoever had knitted it, she'd either had poor eyesight or one eye on the television. But who am I to criticise? The only thing I've ever knitted was a Dr Who scarf, and that was when I was about twelve. It took me a year and was out of fashion by the time I'd finished it.

I wasn't feeling kindly about policemen anyway. The showdown with Harford might've been the main reason, but I had others. I'd had time to review my recent co-operation and to decide that whatever might happen to me in the future, nothing would persuade me to stick out my neck like that again. I'd had little choice because Ponytail had been coming for me anyway, but you know what I mean. On reflection, I should've told Ponytail the police had taken the negatives and let him get on with it. That walk over Hungerford Bridge was burned into my memory. As for Jason Harford, I'd nearly made the worst mistake of my life there. It just goes to show you should trust your instincts. I hadn't taken a shine to him when I'd first met him and I should've stayed that way. Still, everyone can be a fool sometimes and I'm no exception. There's no shame in doing something daft provided you don't repeat it and I certainly meant never to repeat it.

'Whaddya want?' I asked sourly.

'Come to see you're all right,' he told me with oily insincerity.

I spelled it out. 'I don't want to see or talk to any coppers. I've had it up to here—' I indicated my throat— 'with rozzers and their dodgy ways. If Foxley wants me to do anything else, you go tell him from me to take a running jump.'

'Oy,' said Parry, looking hurt. 'I've always been straight with you.'

If he had, it was only because subtlety wasn't his strong point. Over his shoulder, I could see the old fellow from the house opposite standing on the pavement, doing a bit of neighbourhood watching. The number of times Parry had been round here lately, he must know it was an officer of the law on the doorstep. For this reason only, I decided to let Parry in.

'Ah, Sergeant!' called Daphne, passing through the hall. 'Season's greetings to you!'

'And to you, ma'am,' he said. He made what was probably meant to be a bow, leaning forward without bending, and inclining slightly to one side like the Tower of Pisa.

'You are always sickeningly polite to her,' I told him. 'Not that I'm objecting, but you never give me that sort of treatment. Aren't I a citizen? A member of the public?'

'Miss Knowles is a lady,' he said, affronted.

'Oh, thanks. What do you want?' I asked again more firmly.

Parry's blotchy skin turned even more unattractive with a dull flush. 'As it happens, I brought you a Christmas present.' He put his hand in one of the bulging pockets and brought out a small package. It was wrapped in red paper with green reindeer on it, all stuck down with Sellotape.

'What is it?' I asked suspiciously. Parry pretending to be Santa was just not on.

'Go on, then, open it,' he said, looking all pleased with himself.

I did and found a rather squashed box of Maltesers. He hadn't broken open his piggy bank, that was for sure. Even though I like chocs, I was anything but delighted because the last thing I wanted to do was accept presents from Parry. I had a horrible feeling it might be leading up to a request for a date. It gave 'not if he was the last man on earth' a whole new meaning. On the other hand, it was Christmas and I didn't want to seem churlish. Goodwill to all men, and all that.

'Thanks,' I said hollowly. 'It's a nice

thought. I appreciate it. But if I accept it, it's only because I'm taking it as thanks for risking my neck recently to help you nab Grice. And remember to tell Foxley,' I added, 'what I said just now. He needn't bother to ask me to save police bacon again. Not a chance. The more I think about it, the more I'm sure I was bonkers even to consider it.'

'Oh, we can do a bit better than chocs for that,' said Parry. He lowered his voice confidentially. 'I do believe, no letting on I've told you, now! I do believe Mr Foxley is going to ask if you can be given a reward from public funds. Probably about fifty quid. How about that, eh?'

'Fifty quid?' I squeaked. 'Fifty—If Jo Jo hadn't turned up when he did, I'd have got my hands on a grand from Grice!'

'But you'd have had to give that back,' he pointed out.

I knew it. I put the chocolates down on the hall table. 'Well, I hope you have a very nice Christmas and I'll wish you a Happy New Year as well, while I'm about it—because I don't suppose I'll be seeing you for quite a while.'

'Don't count on it,' he said. 'But I get the message. Still, while I'm here, I'd better give you the news. Which do you want first? The good or the bad?'

So he hadn't just come to bring me his box of chocs. 'Tell me the bad,' I invited. 'Why not? It's Christmas Eve. Finish it off for me completely.'

'Don't be like that,' he said. 'It's just I thought you ought to know your pal Inspector Harford has asked for a transfer. If you don't know it already, that is.'

'He's not my friend,' I told him. 'And I didn't know it. It makes no difference to me.' I tried not to sound too relieved.

Parry twitched his ginger eyebrows but also looked, I fancied, relieved. It occurred to me the chocs had been intended to soften the blow of what he'd feared would be devastating news for me. Was there a sensitive streak well hidden in the man, after all? On the other hand, he might just be fishing for information.

'There's me,' he said, confirming this last suspicion, 'thinking you were getting along pretty well with Wonderboy. You couldn't hazard a guess as to why he's suddenly decided to love us and leave us, could you?'

'Not a clue.' But I wasn't surprised. Harford had decided not to stay around here where there was a chance he might walk into me again. He was going to cut and run. He was going to find out, eventually, that he couldn't keep running. No one can, whatever the reason. Even his victim, Tig, had found that out. I'd been a bit hard on her, but it'd been for her own good because she deserved a helping hand. As for Harford, I felt nothing but scorn for him.

'I thought he might've confided in you.'

Parry gave his rictus grin. 'Must have been something *I* said, then. Tell you the truth, Fran, I'm glad you're not upset or anything. It's a bit sudden, his deciding to move on. I fancy Mr Foxley's not too pleased. Caused a bit of gossip in the canteen.'

'What doesn't? seems to me,' I retorted. 'What's the good news?'

Parry's manner changed and became more official. 'It's good in the sense it clears up a problem for us—for you, too, maybe. It's not so good for the bloke concerned. I'm talking about Coverdale's killer.'

'You've got him?' I couldn't believe it.

'In a manner of speaking,' Parry replied cautiously. 'We've got him down the morgue, so I suppose you could say we have him. He's a stiff.'

I sat down on a nearby chair. Parry grinned down at me evilly. 'Got his name, too. Miguel Herrera, Spanish national, wanted by the French police. Description answering the one you gave us of the herbert who tried to break in here. Half-healed bites on the fingers of his right hand, probably made by a small dog of the terrier type. You haven't got to worry about him any more, Fran.'

'What happened to him?' I asked.

Parry shrugged. 'He got into an argument in a pub night before last. When he left at the end of the evening, the other bloke in the spat was waiting outside for him with a crowd of his

371

mates. Kicked his head in and ran off.'

'So, how'd you tie him in with Coverdale?'

'When we tried to ID him, his fingerprints matched some we lifted at the scene of the murder and sent to Interpol. Knife found lying near Herrera's body showed the same fingerprints on the hilt and the blade's the same size and shape as the fatal wound in Coverdale. This Herrera johnny must've pulled it to defend himself outside the pub, but didn't get the chance to use it.' He beamed at me until he remembered that a serious crime had occurred. 'Course,' he added quickly, 'we're looking for his attackers.'

'You won't find them,' I said.

'Nah—no witnesses, never is, a barney like that. Still, saved us a job, didn't they? We mightn't have picked him up otherwise and the taxpayer won't have to keep him as a guest of Her Majesty. French can cross him off their list, too. You won't have to look out for him again. We can close a murder file. Suits everyone, really. It'd have been nice to be able to link it to Grice, but you can't have everything, can you? Not in this line of business, anyway. Thankful for small mercies, that's what, if you're a police officer. We can't prove Herrera was on Grice's payroll. It might've been a revenge attack. Still, don't,' finished Parry a trifle obscurely, 'look a gift horse in the mouth.'

I'd better take back what I wrote above.

Parry isn't sensitive. I'd no sympathy for Herrera, but the passing of a human being ought to be met without hand-rubbing glee. I suppose to Parry it was just another statistic. As for me, I have to say it was a relief to know Herrera wasn't out there, nursing his bitten hand and plotting a nasty revenge attack of his own.

But Parry had missed my meaning when I'd said they wouldn't catch Herrera's killers. I didn't bother to explain it. The police might choose to believe that Herrera had died as a result of a random violent attack—and his attackers had thoughtfully left his knife by his side on the pavement. It just confirmed my previous notion that Grice was a very well-organised man. Herrera had been a weak link. Picked up by the police, he'd have told them everything he knew about Grice and whether or not he'd been told to eliminate Gray Coverdale. Now he wouldn't have the opportunity. I shivered.

'I hope,' said Parry, 'that after all this, you're going to make a New Year resolution, Fran, to keep out of trouble.'

'With a little help from my friends,' I told him.

'Well, I'll be off then,' he said. 'Give us a kiss for Christmas.'

He should be so lucky. I pushed him out of the door and slammed it behind him.

I went round to the shop to tell Ganesh Parry's news about Herrera. He was just closing up. We finished off and went up the back stairs to the flat.

'Don't know what Hari wants done about the unsold Christmas cards,' he said. 'Whether I'm supposed to flog them off half-price or put them away till next year. We'll leave the decorations up until after New Year.'

'You're supposed to leave them until Twelfth Night,' I told him. We counted up on our fingers to work out exactly what calendar date they would bring us to.

'Nice to think we've got a couple of days off,' said Ganesh. 'I'll have to pop down to High Wycombe and see Mum and Dad at some point, but we could go somewhere.'

'Like where? Everywhere's closed.' I had an idea. 'We could go and see a pantomime.'

A bell rang loudly, making us jump. 'Street door,' said Ganesh. 'Hang on.' He went to lean out of the window to see who it was. 'Usha,' he told me over his shoulder. 'I'll just chuck her down the key.'

He dropped it down to his sister and went to open the door on to the staircase which led up from the street. We heard the outer door slam and footsteps running up the stair. Usha burst in.

She was dressed in a new-looking scarlet

374

wool coat, black ski-pants and nifty little boots. Obviously, being married to an accountant pays off. She was also clearly in a bit of a state and hadn't just come round to wish us a happy holiday.

Hands on hips and long black hair flying, she demanded, 'What's been going on here?' As an afterthought, she added, 'Hi, Fran. Happy Christmas.'

It was such an open question that we both stayed silent, wondering quite what or how much to tell her.

'How do you mean?' Ganesh asked cautiously.

She advanced on him, jabbing a finger at each word. 'Don't try wriggling out of it. We know! What's more, Dad's writing to Uncle Hari tonight!'

'If you mean the washroom—' Ganesh began, drawing himself up to begin his defence.

'Of course I mean the washroom! What have you been doing to it? How much has it cost? Hari didn't say anything about getting decorators in before he left. Did you get more than one estimate?'

'No, I didn't,' said Ganesh, rallying before the onslaught. 'Because I got a very good deal from Hitch. And before you go on, tell me how you all know about it.'

'Dilip saw them working here. He told his mum. She told—' Usha gave a hiss of exasperation. 'It got passed down the line. You know how it does. Dad says you must have gone barmy.'

Trying to help, though it wasn't my spat, I offered, 'It looks really good, Usha. Have you seen it?'

'No, I haven't, but I'm going to. I've got to go back and tell Dad exactly what you've done so's he can put it in his letter.'

We trailed downstairs to the new washroom. 'You wait till you see it,' said Ganesh belligerently. 'The old one was a health hazard. See!' He threw open the door.

Usha stared round it. 'Sure, it looks good. But how much did it cost?' She swung round, eyes bright with suspicion. 'And where's the old loo?'

'Hitch took all the old junk away. Did a complete job,' said Gan proudly.

Watching Usha's face, I somehow knew this wasn't the right answer.

'Took it away?' She flung both hands out dramatically to indicate the new loo, resplendent where the old one had been. 'Took away that lovely Victorian loo? He didn't, I suppose, pay you for it? You didn't knock the value of it off the bill?'

'What value?' asked Ganesh. 'It was nearly a hundred years old.'

'Too right it was!' yelled Usha, erupting in fury. 'People seek out those Victorian patterned lavatories! Collectors of Victoriana and old domestic equipment. They're what's called highly desirable. That one of Hari's was in perfect condition, glaze hadn't crazed, no chips, nothing! It was manufactured by Doulton. At auction those things fetch between five and six hundred quid!'

There was the sort of silence in which you're supposed to hear pins dropping. Ganesh was shaking his head slowly, a dazed expression on his face.

'Now,' Usha went on with the calm which makes you want to run for cover, 'I don't know what you paid Hitch for fixing up the washroom, but he must have nearly doubled it by getting the old blue and white loo, which you described as junk, thrown in. And please, don't tell me he didn't know what it was worth. Hitch knows what everything's worth. He's a fixer, a middleman. And the worst of it all,' Usha was working up the Richter scale again, 'Jay and I were going to approach Hari about selling it to us, you know, family price.'

There was a silence. 'Well,' Ganesh said at last, very faintly, 'who'd believe it?'

'I would,' I told him. 'I warned you Hitch was always on the fiddle. Honestly, Ganesh, all those magazine supplements you've been reading, didn't any of them have articles about antiques?'

Or, come to that, hadn't any of the holiday supplements featured Cuba? Even I'd been able to see the location of the photos hadn't been the Canary Islands. What's the point of being able to list the world's most eligible bachelors, in order, if you don't know anything really useful? But it wasn't the moment to get at Gan about that. He was looking utterly miserable.

'They didn't have any articles about old loos,' he was saying. 'Only silver and china and stuff.'

It was time for me to make a discreet departure. 'When you see your mum and dad, Usha,' I said, 'give them my good wishes.'

*       *       *

'Happy Christmas, Fran, dear.'

It was Christmas Day, breakfast-time. Daphne and I exchanged kisses and good wishes and produced our presents.

It was difficult to know what to buy Daphne but, inspired by the mistake over the loo, I'd ended up with the latest edition of one of those antique guides. She was interested in that sort of thing and went round the salerooms. I'd checked in it before I wrapped it up and Usha was right about that Victorian loo. Ganesh had said he was going to ask Hitch to pay for it, but we both knew he hadn't a hope. Hitch would swear he didn't know it had any value and that he'd dumped it. But Hitch knows the value of everything. Usha was also right in saying he was a middleman. He'd probably already got a buyer in mind when he'd first agreed to do the work in the old washroom.

I presented Daphne with the book. Bonnie sat by with tinsel entwined in her collar and waited hopefully, sensing goodies were being handed out. I gave her a chocolate-flavoured rubber bone. She carried it off and began to chew it happily.

Daphne handed me two small packages. I opened the one labelled 'Bonnie' first. It was a smart new lead. 'Thanks very much, Daphne,' I said. Then I opened the second, smaller, packet marked 'Fran' and said, 'Oh, Daph . . .'

'I want you to have them,' Daphne said firmly. 'Before you say anything.'

'But they belonged to your mother.' I put the amethyst earrings, lying on cottonwool in a neat little box, on the table. 'I can't accept those, Daphne.'

'Whyever not? Who else should I give them to? I've got no young female relatives. Neither Charles nor Betram is married so it'd be no good giving any of my jewellery to either of them. They couldn't wear them.'

I wasn't sure of that but tactfully kept quiet.

'I've got a sort of cousin, way up in Shropshire, who's got a daughter, and my pearls and a hideous tiara thing which no woman in her right mind would wear these days, are left to her. But I want you to have the earrings. I thought they'd match that purple 'skirt of yours,' my landlady concluded.

'Thank you, Daphne,' I said humbly. 'I'll treasure them, promise.'

'I am so sorry,' she said, 'that you'll be alone for Christmas lunch. I really don't want to go over to my nephews', but they have been apologising nonstop and really, I know I've got to make it up with them eventually, so it might as well be on Christmas Day. Bertie is a very good cook, you know.'

I didn't doubt it. 'I'll be fine,' I said. 'I've got Bonnie.'

'I had thought you might be spending the day with Mr Patel.'

'He's had to go to High Wycombe,' I said. 'He's got a family dispute to patch up as well.'

'Well, that's what Christmas is for,' said Daphne, adding on a note of doubt, 'I suppose.' She cheered up. 'I'll be back this evening. We can have a glass of wine then. Tomorrow I'll poach us that nice piece of salmon in the fridge. Oh, there are plenty of things in the freezer, meantime. There's an individual portion of chicken *à la provençale*. Why don't you pop that in the microwave?'

*     *     *

'This is it, Bonnie,' I said to her, when Daphne had left. 'This is independence. Christmas Day, just you and me, with a frozen chicken portion between us.' I brandished the foil

380

container at her. Bonnie's ears drooped. 'All right,' I said, 'you can have a tin of dog's chicken dinner. It'll probably have more chicken in it than whatever's in here. We'll eat Wayne Parry's Maltesers for pud.' The thought didn't cheer. Activity was called for. 'Want to go out for a walk?' I asked Bonnie, producing the new lead.

We set off up the road. There was a Christmas Day sort of feeling in the air, people wearing silly smiles and greeting complete strangers. Cars passed filled with people and presents, all off to lunch with family or friends. Kids cycled along the pavements on new bikes. I'd thought going out in the fresh air might have cheered me up, but it made me feel worse, isolated. All I had to look forward to was a new year which would start off with dossing in Hari's lock-up with my belongings in a couple of plastic sacks. I understood why Daphne was making it up with the gruesome twosome. In the end, they were her family, just as Ganesh had said.

When I reached the shops, things began to look up. To my surprise, I saw coming towards me Marco, blond hair flowing. He was snazzily turned out in a blue jacket in some shiny material and clean jeans without paint splashes. My heart rose.

'Hello, Fran,' Marco said. 'Happy Christmas.'

'Same to you,' I returned happily. 'I thought

you were in Amsterdam.'

'Got back last night. I'm just going down The Rose for a drink,' he said. 'It's open till lunchtime. Crowd of us meeting up there. Want to come?'

What do you know, Fran? I told myself in delight. There is a Father Christmas, after all. I asked about Bonnie.

'Don't worry about her,' he said. 'They don't mind dogs in The Rose. The landlord's got a pit bull. It's out back,' he added, by way of encouragement. 'And it's tattooed and lost its knackers and everything, all legal. The police come round and insisted. Don't seem right, somehow.'

We made our way to The Rose. It's an old pub and hasn't changed its style much in fifty years. Downmarket is where The Rose feels it should be and downmarket it resolutely stays. It was packed to the door, the air filled with nicotine and boozy Christmas cheer. I picked Bonnie up because it seemed likely she'd be trodden on, and followed Marco to a corner table surrounded by people.

'This is Fran,' he announced, propelling me forward. A chorus of voices greeted me and wished me a happy Christmas. 'This is Mike,' Marco began to make a round of the table for my benefit, 'this is Polly and this . . .' It went on until we reached a red-haired girl in an advanced state of pregnancy who was prudently on the orange juice.

'And this is Bridget,' said Marco happily. 'Meet the wife, Fran.'

You know, that Scottish poet had it right. The best laid plans of mice and men are apt to go pear-shaped. And there's not a lot any of us can do about it.

We hope you have enjoyed this Large Print book. Other Chivers Press or Thorndike Press Large Print books are available at your library or directly from the publishers.

For more information about current and forthcoming titles, please call or write, without obligation, to:

Chivers Press Limited
Windsor Bridge Road
Bath BA2 3AX
England
Tel. (01225) 335336

OR

Thorndike Press
P.O. Box 159
Thorndike, Maine 04986
USA
Tel. (800) 223-2336

All our Large Print titles are designed for easy reading, and all our books are made to last.